EYE OF THE MONKEY

EYE OF THE MONKEY

a novel

KRISZTINA TÓTH

Translated by
OTTILIE MULZET

SEVEN STORIES PRESS
New York * Oakland

The translator would like to thank the Hungarian Translators' House in Balatonfüred, Hungary, where this translation was partially completed.

Copyright © 2022 by Krisztina Tóth
English translation copyright © 2025 by Ottilie Mulzet

First published in Hungarian as *A majom szeme*, by Magvető Kiadó 2022.

All rights reserved. No part of this book may be reproduced, stored in a retrieval system, or transmitted in any form, by any means, including mechanical, electronic, photocopying, recording, or otherwise, without the prior written permission of the publisher.

Seven Stories Press
140 Watts Street
New York, NY 10013
www.sevenstories.com

Library of Congress Cataloging-in-Publication Data

Names: Tóth, Krisztina, 1967- author | Mulzet, Ottilie translator
Title: Eye of the monkey / Krisztina Tóth ; translated from the Hungarian by Ottilie Mulzet.
Other titles: Majom szeme. English
Description: New York : Seven Stories Press, 2025.
Identifiers: LCCN 2025009240 (print) | LCCN 2025009241 (ebook) | ISBN 9781644214954 hardcover | ISBN 9781644214961 ebook
Subjects: LCGFT: Dystopian fiction | Novels
Classification: LCC PH3351.T8125 M3513 2025 (print) | LCC PH3351.T8125 (ebook) | DDC [Fic]--dc23
LC record available at https://lccn.loc.gov/2025009240
LC ebook record available at https://lccn.loc.gov/2025009241

College professors and high school and middle school teachers may order free examination copies of Seven Stories Press titles. Visit https://www.sevenstories.com/pg/resources-academics or email academic@sevenstories.com.

Printed in the United States of America.

9 8 7 6 5 4 3 2 1

contents

road soaked with rain	9
rustling, living, breathing	14
someone was leaving	20
rummaging through her things	24
coming from somewhere else and going somewhere else	28
one went in, the other didn't	35
the sound of a thunderclap	40
they didn't look at each other	44
electrical current runs beneath the skin	52
one thousand deer were burned	59
repeatedly lifted up by the wind	62
delicate and elegant hands	71
little street girls	78
writhing in cold incandescence	88
no one liked it, we just got used to it	95
fraying in several places	102
they had no light whatsoever	107

faces that had lost their contours	115
no, no, my little son	117
more deeply deposited, painful	124
it was dark, completely dark	133
something trembled in her voice	143
resident of that country of stains	149
maddening, unnecessary series of movements	154
so it wouldn't crack	160
the name? our names?	167
this scent was familiar	171
those two columns of light	177
objective and restrainedly threatening	188
fist clenched in front of her heart	192
dark red finial	197
to reach the inner door	207
pine trees, squirrels, little birds	213
surging throughout his entire body	220
to play badminton in white clothes	228
carefully onto the wings	234
enshrining that moment of awakening	243
really and truly the same story	263

the invisible, thirsty dog	272
blood and rust were excluded	278
visible from up close	286
a new sheet of paper was not inserted	291
he waited, almost diffidently	296
ACKNOWLEDGMENTS	301

road soaked with rain

I rushed to a different metro car, but the man following me saw where I was going. He was right behind me. He lowered himself into the seat opposite, staring at me fixedly. I tried to avoid his gaze, not to encourage him with eye contact. I know that at times like this, the worst thing is to look directly at someone: The returned gaze will only egg him on. The one following will find evidence to support their delusions, a mirror of their own disturbed feelings. I was used to seeing strange characters roaming around the city. Loud and foulmouthed, looking for trouble. You had to avoid their gaze. I'd already been recognized a few times. The university where I work uses instructors' photographs to recruit new students: This was annoying to some of its employees. I knew all too well about the troubled kids in the closed districts. There was nothing I could do about that. But this boy wasn't from one of the segregation zones, of that I was sure.

    I didn't look up but only kept staring off to the side, into the air, toward the end of the metro car. Even so, I noticed a few details of his physical appearance: for example, his nails, bitten right down to the ends. His hands weren't ugly, but the tortured nails, chewed until bloody, looked alarming. The crackbrained gaze of his large brown eyes was frightening, the dark rings under his eyes. The matted hair falling onto his forehead. It crossed my mind that perhaps he really was insane, perhaps I should press the alarm to summon a security guard, or at least jump up and run to the other end of the car where there were a few more people. Sitting near me there was only a middle-aged woman, I noticed as I looked around, with a pink handbag too bright for her age, and an adolescent boy with earplugs, lost in his own world.

I sensed from the guy's alert body posture that there was no point in my changing seats—he would be right behind me, making this impossible chase even more unambiguous and terrifying. If he got closer, I'd panic, I'd tear into him, demanding an explanation. Absurd. Instead, I stared at the hanging straps, the ads on the metro car walls. As of late, the trains no longer stopped in the more dangerous districts where the poor lived. The metro entrances, in those areas, had all been closed. The main TV station broadcast disquieting images every single night of the homeless as they pried open the bars or tore them out using ropes. Some people even managed to drag away the steel frames with cars, forcing their way into the metro stations, howling bestially. When the cold weather came last year, the police—who ended up retreating—couldn't clear the thronging crowds from the stations as they lit fires in oil drums and put down their pieces of cardboard on the chipped marble slabs. At the former Palace of Culture stop, they pelted the passing trains. The station had to be cleared out with tear gas, counterterrorism units. Many unfortunate and drugged outcasts wandered around the city, talking and shouting to themselves, but the boy sitting across from me didn't look like he was using, and no matter how convenient an explanation it would be, he didn't seem crazy. So what did he want?

He'd been following me around for days already, turning up here and there in my neighborhood. It only became clear that this was no mere coincidence, but that he really was stalking me, or at the very least following me, when I got onto the metro that day. I'd seen him for the first time a few weeks ago, as still as a statue in front of the university. Thrice weekly I teach in this hideous cement colossus. Built two years ago, it's called the New University. Four glass elevators travel up and down the facade, completely obscuring the streets behind it. He was standing in front of the entrance, an enormous automatic door surrounded by columns. Just another student, I thought. I was still thinking that when I hurried by him for the second or third time, his gaze fixed greedily on my face. Exam time was approaching, and I thought he was a student who hadn't shown up to class, finally realizing the extent of his absences. He wanted some test sheets, or who knew—exoneration, advice, a favor.

As I was leaving the building's echoing entrance hall and glimpsed him standing by the automatic door, I got a bad feeling. Then he disappeared for a few days, and I relaxed. I went back to my usual daily routes, almost forgetting about him. Maybe two weeks went by; then he appeared again by the metro exit. I recognized him immediately. He was in front of the newsprint kiosk, where my husband usually bought his newspapers.

Only two newspapers were on sale now, but all the same, during the week my husband bought them, leaving them on his writing desk, placing the extra coins in a small dish of green glass as he'd always done. Even on Saturday mornings, he still came out here and paid for the newspapers: He read out the headlines to me in inchoate rage, then crammed the papers into the garbage can. I asked him at least not to crumple them up because I could use them when cleaning vegetables. Or not to buy them. But he was incapable of renouncing his rituals. So much had changed in our lives, and it was these rituals that kept him from falling apart. His habits, routes, movements were a handhold; without them, he might lose his sense of orientation completely. We had lived in this neighborhood for decades, and although so many things had recently closed or been torn down, whenever I stepped out from the metro underpass, I still had a feeling of coming home.

But now, here was this boy. Exactly here, on this small square. To reassure myself, I kept repeating like a mantra that maybe he too lived here and was headed home. That explained why he recognized me. I had many colleagues in this neighborhood, I tried to convince myself. Why couldn't he be living here somewhere close by as well?

Of late, it had grown increasingly difficult for me to register the faces of my students. I teach them for only one year and hardly have any personal interactions with them. I especially tend to mix up the trendy ones, they all look so much alike. With their cropped hair, tight-fitting pants, sometimes with the same eyeglasses as well. The girls are even more uniform, their haircuts and clothes identical.

But this guy was somehow different. I was struck by that from the very beginning. His hair was dark, somewhat unkempt, his skin was dark too—tanned. His gaze was penetrating, almost exalted.

Right after I stepped out of the metro car, he did as well. He was hurrying after me. I knew now for certain that I was being followed, and as I quickened my steps, my hastened tempo must have looked like an attempt at escape. At the bottom of the metro staircase, I came to a stop, abruptly changed direction, and got in line in front of a pizza stand. I stealthily glanced to the side to check if he had gone on. I didn't even want to look at him, and yet an invisible, wide-open eye in the back of my neck told me that yes, he was still there. I would have liked to turn around and ask him directly what the hell he wanted, but the anxiety swelling in my chest proved stronger than my curiosity. I knew why: The deep, tormented wrinkle cutting across the boy's forehead did not bode well. A few tiny signs, his fragmented movements, or the strange impeded facial tics surely betrayed latent madness. And that oblique, agonized crease sent a message to me that this guy did not have things under control mentally, and that I could be in real danger.

I ordered a pizza slice with arugula. I fumbled to find the small change in my wallet as the girl with a tongue piercing behind the counter looked impatiently at the people waiting behind me. The pizza was cold and tasteless, almost inedible. I chewed, feigning indifference, staring at the passersby, sometimes sneaking a look to the side to see if the boy was still there. We both knew that I saw him, and in my nervousness, I began to panic. Dropping the paper napkin, I clumsily bent down for it.

The sound of a thunderclap mixed with the echoing roar of the departing and arriving trains.

People walking down the steps into the metro shook out their sodden umbrellas; those without umbrellas wiped the rainwater from their foreheads with the sides of their hands. There must have been a downpour. The entire afternoon the air had been thick, as if portending a storm, but as I began my commute home no cloudburst seemed imminent, as if it were going to bypass the city.

I finished the pizza, folding the thick, inedible crusts into the paper plate and tossing them into a bin. I had to hurry: my pursuer might make up his mind to approach me. He was still there, I sensed it, I even glimpsed his back. This storm had come right in time for him, for he was standing outside, at the top of the stairs, beneath the metro entrance's concrete eaves, squeezed in among other passengers, as if he too were only waiting for the rain to stop. I realized I could turn around, get back on the metro, and easily shake him off. And immediately, I was enraged with myself. What an absurd situation, I thought. I've been on my feet since early morning with two thick folders of tests in my bag to be marked up, my shoulders aching with tiredness, and now my own idiotic anxieties were stopping me from getting home. Well, no. I walked around the people waiting beneath the eaves and stepped into the downpour.

The rain was falling obliquely in torrents, the stallholders on the crowded square were hurriedly pulling tarpaulins over their stands. I picked up my pace, but within seconds my clothes were soaked through, my skirt clinging to my hips, my shoes filled with water, the rain dripping down my forehead. Blinking, I waited for the light to turn green. The cars had all turned on their headlights; behind the windshield wipers of one, I saw a man's blurred face. Leaning forward, I ran, heard the thunder—I was trying to get to the medical clinic on the other side of the street where I could take shelter on the steps. My bag was also soaking; my laptop was in there, and I was worried about everything getting wet.

As I dashed across the sidewalk, I felt someone approaching, then felt someone grab my arm, as if they wanted to keep me there, in the middle of the street, bubbles welling up on the road from the pounding rain.

I knew immediately that it was him—the guy from the metro. He stood there on the crosswalk before me in the pouring rain, in his shirt, yelling at me to stop. The light changed, the cars began moving, somebody honked at us.

My strength gave out, I turned around to face him; trying to outshout the rumbling of the rain, I asked him what he wanted. He looked at me with this penetrating gaze, both of us drenched through and through, and answered:

I have to speak to you. You are my mother.

rustling, living, breathing

And so what did you say to him, the psychiatrist asked, as he filled his pipe with a bit more tobacco. He carefully pinched the stray tobacco fibers from his trousers, pressing them into the bowl of the pipe. I like the fragrance of tobacco. When I came here for the first time, he asked if the pipe smoking would disturb me, and I quickly replied that it wouldn't. Of course, I couldn't have known then that there would come a time when I wouldn't even be able to imagine this place without the sweetish scent of pipe smoke penetrating everything.

I was lying on the couch, the psychiatrist couldn't see my face. He might have thought I was just letting him smoke out of courtesy. I sat up and looked attentively at him as he was about to light up, showing him that I was present, watching him. He looked up.

What could I have said? I don't have any children, I answered.

I lay back down. The couch's kilim pillow, with its rough weave, prickled the back of my neck, emitting a strong smell of wool. It reminded me of the scent of an old sweater I used to have as a child, knitted by my mother: She always insisted on me wearing it whenever I went ice skating with my friends. The wool, damp from snowfall and cold mist, emanated the same peculiar smell as this pillow, and now, mixed into this familiar scent, the scent of the hair of other patients. I wondered how many people ended up lying on this pillow every week and if the psychiatrist ever bothered to have it cleaned. Obviously not. Here I am trying to adjust the back of my neck onto the imprint of other people's heads, and for what? Is there any point at all in me lying here babbling on about my life to a complete stranger?

The mixture of smells felt homey—rather than repugnant—just as the entire room created the impression of a cozy nook rather than a doctor's office. I spoke, fairly incoherently, about what an absurd story this whole thing was, so . . . frightening. I'd heard that sometimes people sought out a father they'd lost touch with or one they'd never known. To sit down with their father, or their mother, at least once, find out why they weren't wanted. But me? To ask this of me? Mothers know if they have given birth. Even mothers who gave up children for adoption know how many boys, or girls, they had, the year, the day they were born. But I knew one thing for sure: I have never given birth. And I had never been pregnant, not even once. What kind of craziness was this, to think that I gave birth to someone! And yet, the boy had insisted. I told him he was mixing me up with someone else, there was no way I could be his mother. Poor child. If he was an adult today, that means that I would have given birth to him while I was in college. Madness! What in the world had prompted me to start making excuses in the pouring rain to a stranger? To excuse myself, saying: Sorry, but there is no way I could be your mother, this is clearly a mistake. I just should have run away, no? I turned my head to one side, in the direction of the armchair.

The psychiatrist did not speak, as if waiting instead for me to elucidate, for me to explain why I stopped to debate this matter with a complete stranger in the rain.

Did you use the polite form with him? he asked.

My gaze wandered to the view beyond the window.

Of course I did, I answered, I don't know him. I do the same with my students. I hate informality because it erases boundaries. You hear it everywhere these days: Come on in! It's horrific. Even before the founding of the Unified Regency everyone spoke to each other on informal terms, but not me. I was glad it was no longer necessary, that this thin boundary had returned to public discourse, even if everything else was so mixed up in this world, up and down, good and bad. A student is a student and not my friend. Of course, I used the polite form with all of them. And I could not explain why I was making excuses to this boy, if only because . . . it was the most absurd of situations—much more absurd than if someone had accused me of theft or of having perpetrated some criminal act in my youth.

Someone was leaving, going along the outside walkway, causing the psychiatrist's office to grow dark momentarily. Afterward, I could once again see the sky above the roof of the building next door. The colossal clouds with their luminous edges were swept ever further apart, moving slowly like tectonic plates separating from each other in a prehuman age. If the sun appeared between the clouds, I decided, I would continue.

The psychiatrist maintained his silence, occasionally puffing on his pipe. I found the pipe smoke reassuring; it was a part of the atmosphere of the place, just like the old-fashioned samovar and the pale-hued, velvet upholsteries. I knew he wasn't supposed to be smoking, but the entire room, together with the pipe smoke, reminded me of the old world I'd grown up in—a world now completely vanished. The sun reappeared suddenly, shining directly onto the carpet, accentuating its dragon-like pattern. I tended to stare at this carpet a lot: different configurations unfolded from every corner. What seemed to me to be a dragon—looking at the carpet from the chair—appeared either as the profile of a goateed man or winding vegetative tendrils.

Why did you talk to him? the psychiatrist asked.

Maybe because I felt some pangs of conscience, I said.

Once again, he didn't reply, as if waiting for me to figure out why I had a bad conscience.

I would have been more than happy to fling some rude remark at the psychiatrist. That I do have a bad conscience, but because of the money I end up squandering every week, because of the time I lose that could be spent doing much more useful things. But I remained silent. Once again, the clouds moved closer together, as if the cracked slabs of an upper layer, having slid apart, were trying to float back into their original positions. The sky was darkening, ever more like a vaulted roof over us, the light filtering in through ever fewer cracks.

I heard the striking of a match. It seemed his pipe had gone out. I like the fragrance of a pipe, I said out loud, surprising myself as well. It makes me think of my father. And I also thought of the very first time I came here, how I sat down across from the psychiatrist by the small tea table. And how, because of my father, **this scent was familiar.**

It was almost one year ago, a warm spring day like today. The psychiatrist was probably thinking, when I made the appointment with him on the phone, that it was a typical midlife crisis. Or the sudden eruption of the hysterically guilty conscience of one of the well-off and protected of this city. That my car had been surrounded by the poor, showing me the distended stomachs of their starving babies, and now I wanted to adopt one. These private psychiatric practices are full of women in despair around the age of forty, belatedly realizing the suffocating aimlessness of their lives. But I was here for completely different reasons. I had no desire to give birth or adopt: The mere thought of having to wipe up the saliva and excrement of another foreign body filled me with aversion, as did the idea of something growing inside my body, a new living being, who—if subsequently born—I would have to tend to, day after day. And my husband had no desire for this either. We were far beyond any such plans. He had already passed his sixtieth year and had no intention of complicating our lives. Although he loved me, or I don't even know how to put it, he clung to me, he hardly yearned for us to spend whatever remaining tranquil years we might have pampering our mutual genetic facsimile, pushing it around in a baby carriage. Of course, my girlfriends saw this matter completely differently. There were those who frankly stated that childlessness was a time bomb, and my husband—no matter how fit he felt now—sooner or later would reach that life stage of being irrevocably seized by the fear of death; if I didn't stay on my toes during those dark months, he'd end up by the side of a homely and enthusiastic PhD student with a father complex who would quickly give birth to his child. No, I smiled to myself, my husband had never considered himself fit, even when he was forty, and as for the fear of death, if he ever felt it—as we all do—he always ended up sublimating it into feverish work activity, burning at a high temperature but still maintained firmly within limits. Others as well tried, with transfigured faces, to convince me to give it a try, to have faith in life, trust the unexpected and see if I could still conceive, to not be so controlling of something that pointed well beyond my own transient existence; in other words, to put my life into the strong hands of something invisible, something much more powerful than myself.

Here, in this city, in this country? Seriously? On this continent, this planet? I should give birth to a child here?

In short, I had to put up with a lot of idiocies, mainly from people who thought they cared about me. I was completely certain of one thing—I did not want a child—while I was always a little uncertain about everything else. I trusted my husband, but he bored me. My work at the university—it's not too nice to say this, but that's how it was—made me feel ashamed. We crammed our students' heads with lies, in the best case half-truths, and were horrified if they asked any questions. We could never tell if they were questioning or provoking. Almost no one was hired from the university that had existed before the Unified Regency, but when they offered me a job, I immediately said yes. What else could I have done at my age? In the sterile, prefurnished faculty room, everyone was always watching each other, for the most part no one ever uttered a single sentence about their personal lives. Instead, we preferred meaningless chatter, covering our suspicions and doubts with words. We talked about the students, exam dates, the weather. As for conversation—in the true sense of the word—we had not conversed for years. We were silent about the people who were no longer there, just as we were silent as to why we were still there. Everyone had their own justifications, obviously. My friends with children stuck more and more together. We slowly fell away from them. To them, my husband—always bored at their gatherings, his head drooping, as if dozing off—seemed an insignificant, bespectacled old man.

So why do you have a bad conscience? the psychiatrist finally asked, speaking through wreaths of fragrant pipe smoke. I could tell from the sound of his breath when he took a drag on the pipe; only in my imagination, though, could I see if he discreetly checked the time to see if our session was over. I sensed that I might only have a few minutes left—no point in starting a new train of thought because at any moment he was going to announce with his own usual warm intonation, that our discussion could be continued next time. He always sounded as if he truly regretted this, as if he had to stop watching a movie, or his own favorite TV series, at the most interesting part. To prevent this from happening, I answered with no explanation, that I had a guilty conscience because of the child.

I only realized, as I was walking down the stairs, that he could have taken this to refer to that boy as well, his tears flowing together with the rain, whom I had left standing there on the sidewalk, enraged.

someone was leaving

The psychiatrist was worried about the time: He had to drive to the other side of the city where his mother lived by 5 p.m. The boulevards were clogged, the bridges snarled with traffic jams. From his car, he observed the avenue—no pedestrians had walked along it for years now—as if it were a slowed-down film sequence: the boarded-up shops, collapsed storefronts, crumbling facades—not to mention the graffiti-covered walls, the propaganda posters pasted up everywhere, ripped off in shreds. People sat on flattened cardboard boxes, on piles of rags. For years, the police had been trying to chase away these homeless people into special districts designated for them, but the people who used to live here—or those who had simply got used to things here—kept returning. They settled in the parks, and when the cold weather came, they broke into the closed shops and restaurants to wait out the winter.

In the past, the psychiatrist visited his mother on Fridays, but after repeatedly enduring her remonstrations every time she had to wait for him when he was delayed by rush hour traffic, they finally settled on Thursdays for their weekly visit. Dr. Kreutzer would buzz the door of his mother's apartment, then rolled his eyes as he waited for the old woman to come to the door. After a few minutes of rummaging, cursing, and key jangling, she would finally open all the locks and the crossbar. He stepped into the apartment and, with a prolonged sigh, set everything his mother had ordered over the phone on the dining room table. Dr. Kreutzer had access to the best food products because, thanks to his photo ID, he could shop wherever he wanted.

His mother would check the wrapped cheese, carefully unfolding the wax paper to sniff it. She inspected the cold cuts, the sell-by date of the milk. He could only bring her one kind of milk, since she claimed that all the others were artificial, made using powders and synthetic materials to stuff the stomachs of the starving. She'd seen a short documentary on TV about the machinations of the food industry; ever since then, she was willing to consume only one kind of milk. After the civil war, a renowned local dairy had been taken over by a certain foreign company, and no one ever found out why, but his mother considered it crucial to purchase only that brand. All the other dairies produced genetically modified crap. That's why there are so many crazies here, his mother pointed to the street below.

Dr. Kreutzer often struggled to walk into his mother's apartment with the parcels. Both his arms were full: He pushed open the hallway door with his elbow, put the paper grocery bags down on the floor. There was no point in buying so much food, especially when, recently, his mother had only been eating mandarins.

And even then, she only sucked out the juice; the pulp and seeds she spat out were left drying out on small plates everywhere in the apartment. With these purchases, Dr. Kreutzer was reassuring his own conscience: He could tell himself he was indeed doing everything for his mama. At least what he could. Bringing her food from the most prestigious grocery stores.

Still, Dr. Mihály Kreutzer did not love his mother.

He now checked the time on his phone: It was two minutes to five. He rang the bell three times even though he had a key. Following their ritual, he always rang the bell three times to signal his arrival. His mama would call out in a drawn out voice, Yes. Then she would ask, Is that you, my son?

For the past twenty years, every single week, she would ask the same question, to which Dr. Kreutzer always answered: It's me, who else would it be, mama. Then he waited for the shuffling, the prolonged opening of all the locks.

His mother did not answer. She must be asleep, thought Dr. Kreutzer. She'd been taking more naps lately. Whenever she turned on the TV, she always nodded off, the remote control falling out of her hands onto the parquet floor. Dr. Kreutzer had to repair it with electrical tape because sometimes the batteries also fell out. Once, during a break between patients, he had to step outside to yell over the phone at his mother, explaining to her which side of the battery was positive and which was negative—to the shock of a patient who overheard him. After that, Dr. Kreutzer decided it would be better to wrap black insulating tape around the entire remote control.

No response came to his repeated ringing of the doorbell, so he took out his bunch of keys and opened the door. There was silence in the apartment. The TV wasn't on, he could only hear the faint rumbling of the electric massage chair. Dr. Kreutzer had purchased it one month ago at a discount on the internet. In addition to technical instructions, he found a small informational leaflet in the box proclaiming that the electric massage chair stimulated blood circulation, invigorated sluggish veins, and altogether had a positive effect on the user's mood.

Indeed, his mother's general disposition seemed to improve with this new piece of furniture. Her usual litany about insensitive shopkeepers; noisy, plebeian neighbors; and brusque, money-hungry doctors stopped. Her son was well used to these recurring grievances. Hardly even noticing them anymore, his replies suffused with boredom. Recently, however, Dr. Kreutzer's mother had become quieter, and she would complain in a little-girl voice she had never used before. She claimed there were homeless people, as well as their offspring, living in the stairwells, hiding in the cellar. These children were ragged and lice ridden, climbing up the drainpipes. They even snuck into her apartment, pilfering here and there, eating, for example, candy from the kitchen cabinet, even when she hid it in a special metal box at the back of the cupboard, behind the rice. And that wasn't all. They climbed at night onto the balcony, shouting scandalous things through the window, and she couldn't fall back asleep afterward. Dr. Kreutzer listened attentively to these new—and occasionally appalling—grievances, more or less with a professional ear, reassuring himself that these new stories of his mother's were no doubt the early signs of dementia. She always complained, when Dr. Kreutzer came by, about how her grandchildren visited infrequently. If, however, they did show up with their parents at holiday time—well-dressed and urged to practice self-restraint—then she continually tottered after them, worried they might smash the porcelain floor lamp, for which—as his mother kept reminding them—she'd had a special fringed lampshade made; or she was terrified that the children, while they played, might lean out of the living room window and plummet onto the sidewalk below. They weren't allowed out on the balcony, which during their visits was closed with a lock and chain. Dr. Kreutzer had grown up in this apartment, and despite abundant opportunities to do so, he'd never fallen out of either the living room or kitchen windows; although it was true that times had changed and children back then were less wild than children today.

Dr. Kreutzer's mother lay now in the electric massage chair, her face ashen and eyes closed.

He looked at her, immediately grasping that she was dead. The shoulder- and neck-massage program rocked her head back and forth, as if even now she were shaking her head vehemently at her son, arguing with him, **no, no, my little son**, you're wrong. You're wrong about this. But this time, Dr. Kreutzer was right, with no appeals to be made, and nothing to debate. He stepped closer, grabbed his mother's wrist: There was no pulse.

rummaging through her things

He looked for the On/Off button, then shut down the massage program as it awkwardly shook his mother's head back and forth. As he leaned in closer, his stockinged foot suddenly tread on something soft and moist. He was squashing a wedge of pulpy mandarin onto the Persian carpet; it stuck to his sock.

Fuck, he burst out loudly, like someone struck by two blows at once. Then he leaned against the arm of the massage chair. He cautiously touched his mother's face, his fingers moist from the mandarin, as if acquainting himself with some unseen, capricious landmark. His mother's face was still lukewarm.

Dr. Kreutzer sunk down onto the sofa. There were throw cushions with floral patterns on either side of him. Those embroidered, stained pillows had been there since he could remember. Shuddering, he recalled how whenever he leaned back on the sofa, even slightly, he always sensed the sweetish perfume coming from the fabric. If his mother happened to cross the room, she would always tell him with an irritated expression to stop lolling about on the sofa, it was nighttime, he should go to sleep or do something useful. However, the way in which her own characteristic scents—hair spray or her overly fragranced skin—emanated from the pillows was certainly proof that she too took naps here, even during the day. And now that she had grown so old, she clearly was doing so more often. The tassels and embroidery on the pillows were **fraying in several places**, the pillows themselves were battered. Between the two pillows, placed at a symmetrical distance, were two glaringly new pillows, tawdry with their printed poppy designs. Dr. Kreutzer thought that his mother had probably bought the new pillows in the nearby Chinese shop where he often saw items with similarly bright patterns.

It would have been good to think that now, too, his mama had just fallen asleep and everything happening here was a mere mistake, a nightmare that would be over soon. He'd be able to explain to the petulant old woman, when she awoke, that the food he'd bought for her was in the fridge, and he could continue along in his usual daily routine. He stared off into space, attempting to make his peace with another possible version of this story. Unprepared for the magnitude of this unexpected task, he stood up and caressed the length of her lower arm, speckled with liver spots. It was as if his mother's skin had grown just a shade colder.

He called an ambulance. He gave his own name, the deceased's name and address, and tried, as he waited for the doctor and the coroner's van, to say goodbye to her. Although he wasn't a believer, it occurred to him that if the soul did exist—why wouldn't it?—then this too was something that clearly lay within his professional authority, necessitating his continued presence in the room, and his attempt to address, at least internally, to himself, the substance lingering here, to connect to it one final time. Although, as he looked at the corpulent, pale body, the unpleasant feeling suddenly arose that his mother would certainly disapprove of his behavior. Once again, he was doing something wrong. He wondered what she would consider to be the appropriate step in this grotesque transition not yet designated as official mourning. He had never felt at ease in her presence, let alone right now. My family—the thought flashed through his head. He had to call and tell him his mama had died. He tasted the words in his mouth, as if preparing to speak it aloud in a moment or two. First, he should inform the children, after all, this was their grandmother—Grandma Pálma to them, Auntie Pálma to everyone else—even if they only visited rarely.

He dialed his son's number but could only leave a message on Vilmos's voicemail. After that he called Emmácska, which also went to voicemail. Then he remembered, of course, they must be at their after-school classes and couldn't pick up their phones.

He stepped closer to the massage chair again: He had time to get used to the idea that the dead body would soon be taken away. It occurred to him that his mother might end up being buried in the clothes she was wearing now, and if he wanted something different, he must dress her in it now. He shrunk back from the thought. He decided that the light blue sweater and the comfortable cotton trousers she was wearing suited the occasion perfectly; at the very least, he would put a pair of shoes on her feet.

He went into the front hallway and began examining the shoes lined up there. As he bent down, he realized that he could put on his own shoes again; nobody was going to ask him if he knew how much it cost to get the large Persian carpet cleaned. It wasn't as if old lady Pálma kept the place particularly tidy: the kitchen shelves were always filled with crumbs, the glasses sticky. But he always had to take off his shoes when he came in, because if he didn't, the old lady always sharply asked him if he was really intending to track in all the dog shit on the soles of his shoes into the flat.

Dr. Kreutzer stood on one leg, hanging onto the coatrack in the front hallway: He didn't want to put on his shoes while wearing his mandarin-pulp-covered sock, so instead he pulled off the sock, rolling and putting it into his pocket.

His mother's shoes were in a terrible state. In recent years, because the bunions on her feet had grown large, a cobbler she knew well always cut out a hole at the critical spot. This caused the leather to begin splitting, like a wound; the shoes looked old and worn. Dr. Kreutzer could not find a pair appropriate for this occasion, and so he went back into his former bedroom to look for something in the wardrobe.

He had never come in here during his weekly visits. He had an aversion to this room, even though he'd lived here for years as a child. His mother had changed almost everything. There were boxes piled up, a rusty clothes drying rack leaning against the wall. The paint was peeling off the drying rack, but old lady Pálma refused to throw it out, saying that if she washed the linens, she had nowhere else to dry them. And yet she always dried the quilt covers by hanging them over the doors, which annoyed Dr. Kreutzer. Much of the furniture had been stored away in the cellar so that there was only his older brother's old teddy bear to remind him of what the room used to look like.

Dr. Kreutzer looked at the teddy bear, which still looked perfectly new, sitting inanely on the daybed with the pilled coverlet, staring with its amber-hued glass eyes.

I came in to get a pair of shoes, Dr. Kreutzer said aloud, turning toward the teddy bear and its expressionless gaze, as if expecting a sign of accord. I need something a little less repulsive. He sighed, walking toward the wardrobe. As he opened it, a stale mixture of smells flowed out from the dark cupboard: stuffy air, mothballs, the scent of unclean clothes. The shoes were lying around on the lower shelf, and he had to get down on his hands and knees to rummage among them. One after the other, he pulled out pairs of sandals and other footwear purchased before his mother's bunion phase. He decided on a pair of ankle boots, inescapably evoking in him something his ex-wife had once said: Whenever she came home with a new, exorbitantly expensive pair of boots, she always stated that boots are also clothing, as if with this purchase, and not buying other seasonal clothes, she had saved money.

He kneeled by the corpse, taking one of the deformed stockinged feet into his hands. The toes were all crammed together; the foot stiffly resisted being shoved into the shoe. Dr. Kreutzer tried to yank it on. It occurred to him that the last time he done anything like this was when he used to put snow boots on the children, and that had been quite a long time ago. He was still struggling with the boot when his phone began ringing. It wasn't just ringing, it was also vibrating. The ring tone was Pachelbel, his wife's; he put the boot down on the rug, and picked up the phone.

coming from somewhere else and going somewhere else

Why were you trying to get in touch with Vilmos? his wife asked.

My mother died, he said.

After a pause, his wife said she was very sorry, but she had not calibrated the tone of her voice fast enough—it remained as cold and exacting as if they were negotiating the lunch check. Dr. Kreutzer called this her dispatcher's voice. Petra did not lower her intonation at the end of the sentence but left it dangling like someone waiting for a second, more important message, which she could then interrupt. Vilmos, she continued, is at the asthma surgery, he left his cell phone outside in the hallway when he went inside to use the inhalator. She had mentioned several times last week, continued Petra, that they were going to the doctor's office today. I suppose you forgot, she added in her dispatcher's voice.

There was no more discussion of his dear mama. Petra promised that she would convey the bad news to the children that evening after she brought Emma home from solfège.

Can't you tell them now? asked Dr. Kreutzer as he gazed at the one boot and how clumsily it looked twisted onto his mother's leg with its protruding bunion. This had been a stupid idea. Perhaps, he pondered, a pair of regular shoes would suffice, as he heard the clamor coming from the pediatrician's office, the ringing telephones, the closing doors, Petra's listless responses.

I don't think this is the right time, she said, ending the conversation. No time, it seemed, was ever the right time for Petra, although no one can decide when their mother is going to die. Dr. Kreutzer suggested that the children could bid farewell to the grandmother personally, but his ex-wife deemed this a perverse and morbid idea, and ended the call.

Dr. Kreutzer began to pull the left boot onto his mother's leg, but this too got stuck halfway. There was no way to get the curve of her swollen ankle inside the boot. In the meantime, the door buzzer rang.

There stood a doctor, with two white-coated mortuary assistants behind him. The two young men stood modestly and awkwardly in the hallway, as if they had come on a visit and were about to be asked to remove their shoes out of respect for his mother's spirit. Dr. Kreutzer showed the doctor in, introduced himself, then pointed at the body lying in the armchair. The doctor opened u' his bag and asked if Dr. Kreutzer was a colleague.

Not exactly, he answered. I'm a psychiatrist.

He showed the doctor his identity card, upon which the r of the two men standing in the doorway became more e doctor leaned over his mother. He accidentally rested b the control button on the armchair, which caused th interrupted massage program to start up: the corp again began vehemently shaking back and forth no, as if protesting against this final examinatir municate that the onset of death could still not be determined, this was all nothing but a mere misunderstanding.

I'm sorry, said Dr. Kreutzer, and he shut down the massage program. The doctor filled out a form and Dr. Kreutzer signed it, then the doctor filled out another form, and then finally a third certificate confirming the transfer of the previous two.

The doctor put away the phonendoscope, expressed his sympathies with a rigid expression, and asked where the bathroom was. He washed his hands, looked around, then inquired about exiting the building downstairs—was there a button to press to exit, and if so, where was it? In the meantime, the two diffident young men entered the living room, grabbed his mama by the armpits, and laid her down on the stretcher. Dr. Kreutzer retreated to the kitchen. He did not want to see what was now already unintentionally visible, his mother's mouth opening as her body was tipped forward; also, there was not enough space in the living room for the two assistants to turn the stretcher around.

The two mortuary assistants fiddled around with the plastic bag, then one of the young men called out into the kitchen:

What about these papers?

At first, Dr. Kreutzer thought that they were referring to the documents they had just filled out, that they had somehow gotten stuck beneath his mother's body, but stepping into the living room, he saw this wasn't the case. The mortuary assistants were referring to her footwear: His mother had crumpled balls of newsprint into the toes of the polished ankle boots, which had been stored carefully in the cupboard; and now the mortuary assistants were removing the pieces of newsprint, tossing them onto the sofa before carrying the body out into the hallway. And yet his mother did not set off barefoot. The crumpled pieces of newsprint remained in the apartment, and Dr. Kreutzer's mother left it vith her booted feet facing outward, like someone who had had 1ough not only of greetings but of the world's tidings altogether.

There was no more discussion of his dear mama. Petra promised that she would convey the bad news to the children that evening after she brought Emma home from solfège.

Can't you tell them now? asked Dr. Kreutzer as he gazed at the one boot and how clumsily it looked twisted onto his mother's leg with its protruding bunion. This had been a stupid idea. Perhaps, he pondered, a pair of regular shoes would suffice, as he heard the clamor coming from the pediatrician's office, the ringing telephones, the closing doors, Petra's listless responses.

I don't think this is the right time, she said, ending the conversation. No time, it seemed, was ever the right time for Petra, although no one can decide when their mother is going to die. Dr. Kreutzer suggested that the children could bid farewell to the grandmother personally, but his ex-wife deemed this a perverse and morbid idea, and ended the call.

Dr. Kreutzer began to pull the left boot onto his mother's leg, but this too got stuck halfway. There was no way to get the curve of her swollen ankle inside the boot. In the meantime, the door buzzer rang.

There stood a doctor, with two white-coated mortuary assistants behind him. The two young men stood modestly and awkwardly in the hallway, as if they had come on a visit and were about to be asked to remove their shoes out of respect for his mother's spirit. Dr. Kreutzer showed the doctor in, introduced himself, then pointed at the body lying in the armchair. The doctor opened up his bag and asked if Dr. Kreutzer was a colleague.

Not exactly, he answered. I'm a psychiatrist.

He showed the doctor his identity card, upon which the posture of the two men standing in the doorway became more erect. The doctor leaned over his mother. He accidentally rested his hand on the control button on the armchair, which caused the previously interrupted massage program to start up: the corpse's head once again began vehemently shaking back and forth, as if saying no, no, as if protesting against this final examination, trying to communicate that the onset of death could still not be determined, this was all nothing but a mere misunderstanding.

I'm sorry, said Dr. Kreutzer, and he shut down the massage program. The doctor filled out a form and Dr. Kreutzer signed it, then the doctor filled out another form, and then finally a third certificate confirming the transfer of the previous two.

The doctor put away the phonendoscope, expressed his sympathies with a rigid expression, and asked where the bathroom was. He washed his hands, looked around, then inquired about exiting the building downstairs—was there a button to press to exit, and if so, where was it? In the meantime, the two diffident young men entered the living room, grabbed his mama by the armpits, and laid her down on the stretcher. Dr. Kreutzer retreated to the kitchen. He did not want to see what was now already unintentionally visible, his mother's mouth opening as her body was tipped forward; also, there was not enough space in the living room for the two assistants to turn the stretcher around.

The two mortuary assistants fiddled around with the plastic bag, then one of the young men called out into the kitchen:

What about these papers?

At first, Dr. Kreutzer thought that they were referring to the documents they had just filled out, that they had somehow gotten stuck beneath his mother's body, but stepping into the living room, he saw this wasn't the case. The mortuary assistants were referring to her footwear: His mother had crumpled balls of newsprint into the toes of the polished ankle boots, which had been stored carefully in the cupboard; and now the mortuary assistants were removing the pieces of newsprint, tossing them onto the sofa before carrying the body out into the hallway. And yet his mother did not set off barefoot. The crumpled pieces of newsprint remained in the apartment, and Dr. Kreutzer's mother left it with her booted feet facing outward, like someone who had had enough not only of greetings but of the world's tidings altogether.

When the mortuary assistants left, Dr. Kreutzer opened the living room windows. It was a spring day with sharp sunlight. And with all the light streaming into the room, the idea of the ankle boots suddenly seemed unnecessary, an exaggeration. Dr. Kreutzer recalled a similar afternoon before his children were born. His wife Petra was showing him a pair of discounted boots that even during the spring clearances cost as much as his monthly salary; at the time, he had just started practicing psychiatry. Almost provocatively, Petra said that boots are just like clothing, placing her hands on her hips. Now, many years later, Dr. Kreutzer had to admit that she was right. Just then, the mortuary assistants emerged onto the sidewalk, lifting his mother's covered body into the orange and yellow striped van. If he leaned forward a little, he could see into the back of the vehicle. People filtered out from the grocery store across the street with their plastic bags, staring at the van. One woman, wearing eyeglasses, looked up at the building across from her, as if, by scanning the windows, she might be able to tell what apartment the corpse had emerged from. As her gaze rose up to his floor, Dr. Kreutzer pulled back from the window. He heard the slamming of car doors, the sound of the motor from below, and the van drove off.

He walked over to the sofa, smoothed out the two torn off pieces of newsprint, and looked at the date—from before the time of the Unified Regency. On one side of the newspaper, there was a report of an event on the day Emmácska was born:

Two pyramids, one in Bosnia, one in Mexico, began emitting light toward the sky almost simultaneously. For the time being, no one can provide an answer for this curious phenomenon, only that the Sun Pyramid in the vicinity of Sarajevo is the most ancient in the world, having been built 12,000 years ago. The pyramid, standing at 220 meters, is surrounded by other curiosities, namely its northern side points to the "cosmic north" with a divergence of only one degree, with its slopes comprising a forty-five degree angle. To this very day no one knows what civilization raised this building, as no one has ever been able to discover its provenance.

The photograph accompanying this article might have been on the part of the page that had been ripped off, although Dr. Kreutzer would have liked to see these **those two columns of light**. He smoothed out the newsprint, then looked at the other side, where there was only an ad for mineral water showing the face of an actress who at that time had been young but whose beauty had since faded.

This must mean that his mother had put the ankle boots away on the day her first grandchild was born. Dr. Kreutzer thought about this intensely, trying to recall the events of that long-ago day. He was certain that he arrived at the hospital in the afternoon, but he couldn't recall when his mother had arrived. Presumably she also got there later, maybe even the next day. So she would have had more than enough time to put away her winter shoes, even more so because his mother—as he'd already experienced in his childhood—had a tendency to work off her nervousness by sorting things.

But it's also possible, he pondered, that his mother had put away the shoes another time, stuffing old newspapers into the toes so the shoes wouldn't get deformed.

On one of the crumpled pieces of newsprint there was a list of campaign promises of a political party that had ceased to exist long ago (the newspaper itself had also been shut down since then) although half of the campaign promises were missing. Maybe they had ended up in the toe of another shoe.

Dr. Kreutzer's mother had not been ill. Or at least she suffered no chronic illnesses that required her to take medication and that might have caused her sudden death. Of course she had worried about her health, as all people around the age of eighty do. She had high blood pressure but took pills for it and measured her pressure regularly. She had lived through two pandemics, but she was most afraid of meningitis. Her hips often ached, and her feet hurt too, her bunions had been operated on. Perhaps that's why she had never put on these low heeled, comfortable, though tight fitting boots again, why they had rested, stuffed with newspaper, for so many years in the bottom of the cupboard. His mother, if she went to get groceries in the neighborhood, or once monthly to her family doctor, usually wore canvas shoes, and in the summer she wore slippers.

He never could tell how she really felt. She always exaggerated genuine, every day cares, while joy—not only sexual joy, no longer an issue at her age, but any kind of physical or spiritual contentment, no matter how transitory—was a source of shame for her, a kind of painful infraction; it was improper and immodest, an offense which could not remain without consequences.

During his visit last week, Dr. Kreutzer had similarly knocked and rang the doorbell in vain, his mother then too had not opened the door. On that Thursday, although it had never worried him before, it suddenly flashed across his brain that something might have happened to his mother. He had called her one hour before on the phone and they had agreed on the groceries he would buy for her, especially the seedless mandarins. At 5 p.m. he stood uncertainly in front of the door, pressing the buzzer in vain as the shopping bag handles turned his fingers white. He put the paper bag down and rang his mother from his cell phone, but she didn't answer. He then fished out his own set of keys and opened the door to the ice-cold apartment. His mother was standing in the middle of the room in her nightdress, earphones in her ears. All of the living room windows were open, and in the middle of the cold drafts of air flowing in, she was listening to Bach, her face flushed.

When Dr. Kreutzer asked her what she was doing, she yelled back at him: For heaven's sake, surely he could see that she was listening to music, *mu-sic*, she turned around, *mu-sic*, then as she removed the wireless earphones, she added that she suffered from unbearable hot flashes and this was the only way she could stand them. I stand here like this the entire day, she announced with dramatic emphasis, her head thrown back; Dr. Kreutzer found this hard to take seriously. He suspected that this operatic scene had been quickly contrived after his telephone call one hour ago, and that his mother had removed the key from her side of the door on purpose so that, letting himself into her apartment, he would be stupefied by the bizarre sight. Dr. Kreutzer, however, did not allow his tranquility to be disturbed. He closed the windows one by one in a leisurely manner while explaining to his mother that it was uncommon for women of the age of eighty to suffer from hot flashes. His mother, with a knowing look, led him over to the radiator upon which a floral-print dressing gown was spread out, drying. She insisted he touch it to feel how soaked through with sweat it was. Similarly, her entire body was sopping wet, she said. The dressing gown did really seem to be damp and clearly formed a part of the performance. Dr. Kreutzer nodded, went into the kitchen, and washed his hands in the kitchen sink, disgusted. He unpacked the groceries onto the table, and vowed to himself that the next time he wouldn't even enter the apartment. If there were no answer to the buzzer, and his mother didn't even pick up the phone, he would simply put down the groceries in front of the door and go home. Well, that's not exactly what happened.

one went in, the other didn't

Why do I have a bad conscience? I pondered in the elevator. Maybe because I never wanted to give birth. I was worried about my body, my life as I'd been living it, my marriage. And although I would not gladly admit this to others, I could not hide my own dislike of children from myself. Not only were they not endearing to me, but they also got on my nerves. One of my girlfriends, the same one who kept referring to certain higher powers, and with whom I'd been very close, before her marriage was a year younger than me. She gave birth fairly late, and she lugged her teething, drooling little boy, wrapped in a striped linen scarf, everywhere. The last time she came over to my place, she stood in the doorway swathed in cotton, like the weather-beaten emissary of a natural people, in defiance of decadent modern civilization, an aging shepherdess from the Andes. I found her ridiculous and embarrassing in her knit cap with earflaps, the unwieldy high-legged boots. The hard outdoor light emphasized her deepening wrinkles. The skin around her eyes was growing thin, drooping. As she came in and took off her coat, I saw her woven leather bracelets. It was as if she was living in an earlier phase of our lives, as if she had forgot to change her wardrobe, and as if, with this whole university student getup, she was trying to preserve her body, which had fallen apart from giving birth. When she came further inside the apartment, she asked me for a towel. I didn't know what she needed it for, so I brought her a midsized one. She spread it out on the sofa and began ceremoniously unwrapping the baby from the scarf to change its diaper. The child was decidedly ugly and puffy, its skin repulsively pale, as if it had been cast in plastic. Only its scent betrayed that it was indeed a real baby. The sudden penetrating stink filled the entire living room, and although I tried in vain, because I really did try, I really felt no tenderness toward this small, bloated, and kicking being as it lay on its back, turning its head here and there, whimpering atop the sofa cushions. I only tried to make sure that nothing would get stained. As Zsuzsa gently bent over the baby, the skin beneath her chin looked withered and creased.

Zsuzsa had really changed since the birth of this child, as if she'd become the distant, older relative of the girl I'd once known. I'd noticed this in others too, how, bit by bit, as their own personalities fell away, they clearly began to view it as their mission to yank others—away from their own lives and along with themselves—into this motherhood spiral of milk stench and poop stench. They kept planning things for the future, but I already knew they would never finish their doctorates, would never live the lives they had planned, would never go to any more conferences, never publish again, or even if they did, at most one or two articles a year, if they even had enough energy left for that. That little by little, they would give up and withdraw, manifesting every less interest in what was vanishing from their lives.

Day by day they appeared before me with their combative remarks about the right to home births and public breastfeeding, and I didn't even know how to tell them how false, despairing, and frankly stupid I felt their ill-fated, public struggle with their own private selves was. While they were preoccupied with peaceful births, inadequately equipped clinics, and obsolete gynecological procedures, they never said anything about the women in our city who gave birth crouched and starving on the street, nothing about those who, in the most impoverished segregated zones, sold their newborns to infertile, well-to-do women from the protected districts. As if none of that even existed. They used their own motherhood as a protective rampart to shield themselves from the world around them. How could I say this to anyone? Ten years ago, when she was still dying her hair and wearing pretty shoes, my girlfriend would have never put on any kind of knit cap with ear flaps for anything. Now she wore it ostentatiously, as if proving how she had conquered time, clinging to the hands of her biological clock, turning them back with her blue-veined arms.

We're not university students anymore, I said to her once when she asked me if I wanted to go with her to a concert, since her husband agreed to look after the child. It seemed they'd gotten some free tickets.

She looked at me from behind her drooping eyelids, like a cocker spaniel ordered back to its place at lunch. No doubt I looked as old and worthy of pity as she did, with my drowsy husband; my orderly, childless apartment; my pitiful and awkward job at the New University; and my dinner plates salvaged from before the time of the Unified Regency—my husband insisted on them. My girlfriend and I had become maleficent reflections of each other.

She chattered about their apartment, protected areas, connections formed with neighbors who also had ground floor gardens, as well as the sandbox the residential community had agreed to. These were all people close to the government, all well off. She showed me, on her cell phone, pictures of the ground dug out next to the trees so the sandbox would be shaded, and how they had laid the lousy, pocket handkerchief-sized piece of land all around with turf. She never could have found a better apartment, she reassured me over and over with the zeal of the unhappy. I knew all too well this overly cheerful, overly convincing tone. I could nearly feel it within myself, I heard myself talking to my friends about some theater performance, and I knew that Zsuzsa was trying, with the same activist energy, to keep going in the face of her boring marriage and the nerve-wracking tedium of child-rearing, summoning that same energy with which, in her earlier life, she had completed her exams.

She always knew to whom to turn, when to sign up for something, she always got hold of every class note and necessary information. She always had moisturizer and tissues on hand.

She would take out the latter from a small, flower-patterned container that closed with a Velcro strip. You could buy small packets containing ten tissues in the shops, but Zsuzsa refilled her own container, as if to suggest that she had her own personal way of arranging things. Order in her handbag, in her school notes, in her life, in her relationships. Whatever else might happen, nothing could sway her from this sense of order. When the institute where she had been working was shut down, she, without a word, took up a new job that many of our old classmates—as I accidentally found out—had refused. The job comprised monitoring a certain quota of social media profiles every day, writing reports on the activities of oppositional figures. She never said anything else about her work. We knew even less about the job of the man with whom she shared her life. My husband thought he might be working in a troll factory as had happened with so many former journalists—then, in the evenings, they disappeared into their gaming chairs behind their desks. You only ran into them in the shops designated for the elite. They said hello, then obliquely turned their heads away, all of them with the same movement, as if they were all the scattered members of one dance troupe moving according to a single choreography in different locales, uniformly avoiding the questions and gazes of others. If you began speaking with them, they discreetly glanced at their watches; if you gazed into their eyes, they retreated inward, disappearing behind their retinas, concealing themselves within the inner rooms of their beings.

As far as children were concerned, a long, long time ago, as I recall very clearly from our youthful years, Zsuzsa had also been irritated by the flabby, avid self-consciousness of new mothers. As they walked along with their baby carriages, struggling to get into trams and buses, then pushing their way out. She too had been bothered by how they always shoved their carriages along the middle of the sidewalk in their superior way, forcing everyone to walk around them. I too was nauseated by these bun-faced, aggressive birthing machines who simultaneously emanated determined resignation and wounded pride. And now I couldn't understand why Zsuzsa, with her oversized hippie linen scarf, would be so anxious to join this blindly propagating, brainwashed multitude. As I understood it, she had to give birth because it was expected of her: by her husband, her surroundings, the Unified Regency, and the whole damned outside world.

The baby was screaming so much that I would have been more than happy to ask her to leave, to take it home.

The yelling didn't bother her. She said, calmly, that the poor thing had colic, there was nothing wrong. She picked it up, she put it down. Things went on like this for a while until, at one point in our nearly continually interrupted conversation, she leapt up and stepped over to the sofa, barricaded with an armchair. She pushed the throw cushions out of the way. Once again she unwrapped her son, and took a small rubber tube wrapped in paper from her backpack, carefully sliding into the kid's bottom.

I didn't want to believe what I was seeing.

The baby farted for an improbably long time, like when someone treads on a woman's skirt and the material starts loudly ripping. I would not have been surprised if all the air went out of the infant suddenly. Zsuzsa would fold it up, like some prop or accessory, a small pink air mattress, and pack it away, putting an end to the tasteless, drawn out scene.

The infant smiled cherubically. Zsuzsa grabbed her phone from her backpack to take a picture, memorializing the special moment.

As they were leaving, the child was already asleep in the colorful striped scarf. Soon after, I caught up with them by the elevator, tearing the door open, and handed her the clumsy knit hat, which she had forgotten in my foyer.

the sound of a thunderclap

The two men were jolted along the winding road in the battered van bearing an official license plate as well as a decal with the official coat of arms. The younger of the two men, in the driver's seat and wearing an anorak, showed his ID, then the van turned onto the building site. The two men were supposed to be digging cables, although they were weeks behind schedule. It was a chilly, turbulent spring day with frequent rain. The walls of the dug out ditches, filled with loamy water, were collapsing. The huge cables had been placed at the edge of the mound of earth, as if giant mutant snails had crawled out of the forest nearby.

The men pulled the van door open and began unloading their tools. It was morning, but a hazy, sinister fog descended upon the bright-green land, as if twilight were already here.

They looked up at the sky and continued unloading their tools. Once they donned their work gloves, they started to dig. One of them was quiet as he worked; he took one step, then dug. The second worker, who was older, stopped from time to time, and, resting his foot on the shovel, began a lengthy diatribe. He cursed the lousy section manager who was not sending machines out here, but slaves. That bastard had taken him off the gantry crane because of one rotten thing he'd said. He was getting more and more worked up, and when he began digging again, he did so erratically, wild with rage. The younger man was quiet. They needed to dig up to where the pole was shoved into the ground by 6 p.m.

It's like shoveling shit, the older one spat out.

He felt humiliated doing this work. He had a proper trade, they couldn't boss him around like a common laborer, like this young fellow here.

The young man, on the other hand, liked digging. He also liked pouring cement. It felt good to smooth it out. When he'd been a kid, he often played with mud with the boys who lived next door. Pouring cement made him think of these old games. Always, as he completed the final smoothing, he would gaze tenderly at the moist, flawless concrete surface. It looked like a kind of darkened ice rink. This wasn't such a bad slog.

But today, while others had been sent to the construction site, they, including the crane operator, had been sent here to work on the cables. This entire cursed, slippery, windblown terrain had to be laid with cable for the containers that would house able-bodied workers from the segregated zones. It was hard to imagine what they could possibly do here on this empty and steep mountain slope. They would have no access to the neighborhoods further downhill, and even if someone tried to stroll down there, they would be arrested at one of the checkpoints.

Some people said that assembly plants were going to be built here on the mountainside to give work to the resettled families. Nobody knew what they were going to be assembling, though.

The older man took off his gloves, tapped out a cigarette from the box, and lit up. He said that he wouldn't mind living here, but only when it was still peaceful and silent, like today. As long as no one else were here. It was so much better than down in the city.

The younger man shrugged his shoulders. He would not move here for any amount of money in the world, preferring a good place in one of the already established, protected areas. Although it was true that the mountain slope was far away from the city's north and northeastern districts and their chaos. His girlfriend was expecting a baby.

He hated the smell of cigarette smoke, just as he hated having to dig so much more than the others. But he didn't stop, he just kept on digging. The older man started on his monologue again: They were nothing better than slaves, deprived of everything, taken for idiots. He himself had a proper trade. He looked down into the valley, muttering the same phrases, his grievances, over and over again. He cursed the wretched government assholes and their whores who never had to dig anything, they should be the ones dug into the earth here instead, all of them buried in a row, so that those damned quivering implants in their crappy boobs would pop out. He slandered the poor who only ran their mouths, they would devour their own children, not a one of them had any sense, they were herded here and there like sheep, then left to their own devices.

The young man suddenly grew tired. He ran out of breath, of patience. He wanted to ask the older man to stop gabbing, for a bit of quiet, but he didn't dare. He was afraid of him. Afraid the older man would yell at him, hit him in the head with a shovel. He kept on digging.

The sky grew ever darker, almost turning black. When they had been assigned the work, they'd been told that no storms were in the forecast, but here up on the mountain slope the weather was unpredictable. It was always a few degrees cooler than down in the city, and ever since they'd started working here, the young man noticed how the clouds, at times, grouped in very strange formations above the low mountains. Once, they had clustered in regular rows, as if laid down upon a gigantic glass sheet.

They heard thunder in the distance. The older man tossed away his cigarette butt, and looked up:

A storm is coming, he said.

The younger man replied that they could keep on digging until it got here. Perhaps it would pass over. He kept on working. The older man regarded him suspiciously, then pulled on his ragged work gloves and continued to dig.

For several minutes there was silence, aside from the hissing of the rising wind as it swirled around the trees. It did not rain, or at least at this altitude there was not even a drop. The clouds already hovered over the valley below. The leaves on the trees rustled and clattered.

The younger man, standing in the ditch, looked up from the clumps of earth growing moist and saw the rain beginning to fall.

At first, the crumbling debris on the ground was slickened by the rain, then tiny rivulets of mud sprang up. A cold breeze arose, swelling from one moment to another into a high wind. It began to howl, knocking over tree trunks, ripping away the green shoots from the branches, while the darkness of evening spread across the horizon. The clouds were accumulating, as if trying to grab onto the earth, to set down their roots of light onto the mountain slope. The ground was shaking from the approaching thunderclaps.

The two men in their windbreakers, hunched over, quickly tossed their tools back into the van, the muddy shovels, the surveying rod. The water streamed down the windshield; they got into the car, their heads dripping. The younger man started the ignition. The older man wiped his forehead with a vehement movement, then turned suddenly.

I have to pee, he said. I can't wait till we get down the hill.

He jumped out, standing next to the car, aiming for the front wheel. The younger man looked up and pulled over a few meters to the side. In the rain, one of the gigantic cables had toppled over. The younger man stared at the tree trunks bent in the wind, the streams of water running diagonally down the windshield, and he thought about how they would most likely be sent here again tomorrow. He would need his rubber boots. They had hardly made any progress today.

The low mountain slope was shaken by horrific thunder. The van jolted as if it'd lost its balance. In that very moment the younger man saw, off to the side, an illuminated windbreaker, whirling, and he saw the streak of lightning stringing this curled up human pearl onto its incandescent thread.

The older man collapsed in a puddle mixed with his urine. His mouth and chin had grown blue, his blackened hand spasmed into a fist.

It took a while for the younger man to reach him; it was as if he had been underwater, running in place for minutes, gasping for air and struggling against the wind, taking forever to walk around the car. The older man did not seem to be alive.

He dare not touch him at first. He shoved a tree branch into the jacket belt, poking it cautiously. Then he took the head and lifted it up. He grabbed the man's arm. In the mud, in the pouring rain, he dragged the body over to the car. The older man weighed at least ninety kilos. His heavy, high-topped boots carved two deep grooves in the mud, which then quickly closed over. His blackened hands swung back and forth as the younger man tried to somehow shove him into the passenger seat. It turned out that his entire face, his bald head was covered with mud. The younger man, his hands trembling, panting, looked for his phone, and when the EMT asked him if the wounded man was still breathing, he bent over the purplish-blue face.

Yes, he said.

they didn't look at each other

Dr. Kreutzer decided to stop at home when he knew his wife wouldn't be there. On Fridays, communication training sessions were held for the officials of the government assistance center, which meant that she usually left the apartment early, around 7:30 a.m., after taking the children to school. His wife gave presentations to groups of mostly young employees on strategic communication with those from the segregated zones: on how to appropriately talk to them when verbal contact couldn't be avoided, on how to quickly and efficiently turn down their requests for help. She gave advice—illustrating her sentences with slides—on remaining levelheaded when faced with aggression. This was not a matter of conscience, but of practicality, of verbal self-defense, necessary for the protection of these workers and their families. It was 10 a.m.; his wife's training session would have already started. The psychiatrist had not seen her car in front of the building. Petra never parked the car in the garage, except for at night, not caring if the car was caught in a rainstorm or splattered with mud. Dr. Kreutzer wanted to take a few things for himself. First and foremost, his notebook. He needed more linens as well, since he only had taken one set of bedding to his rented sublet. He had brought a sports bag and a large shopping bag, which he stuffed with old newspapers. Those would be for wrapping up some pictures he wanted to take.

They had agreed that after he had moved out—at first only temporarily—that he would always ring the bell first, not let himself in right away. But since he saw that no one was at home, he took out his key without thinking. Somehow, it wouldn't go into the lock. He tried again, but no luck. It occurred to him that Petra might have changed the titanium insert. This wouldn't have surprised him. He tried to insert the key again a little more forcefully. The key turned halfway and got stuck, the door wouldn't budge. When he was about to give up, the door was suddenly flung open, and there before him stood his wife, her hair dripping wet, a towel in her hands.

The car wasn't parked in front, he said, in lieu of a greeting.

It's in the garage, Petra said.

He didn't dare ask what had happened with the training session because after all it was a Friday morning. He was afraid of getting into an argument. Ever since he moved out, Petra viewed every question concerning her schedule or her work as an interrogation, an intervention into her personal life, and in her rage, she tried to draw boundaries, indicating that she had her own private life now that had nothing to do with him. Most recently, she had flung an old film camera from his collection onto the ground; it didn't work anyway, but it had stood for decades in his room and had become very dear to him.

I just came to pick up a few things, he said.

Petra did not reply. She went back into the bathroom, leaving blotches of water on the floor. He heard the droning sound of a hair dryer. Lately, she was always taking showers during the day because at night there was often no electricity, even here, in this privileged district of the city.

Dr. Kreutzer always hated how she tottered across the apartment like a penguin. As if that meant she were dripping less water! He looked for a rag, but there was nothing to wipe it up with. Finally he threw a T-shirt, draped over the arm of a chair, onto the floor. Petra was incapable of understanding the sensitivity of wooden materials.

Even though there was an overhead drying rack suspended above the tub in the bathroom, Petra dried the clothes on a folding drying rack in the living room. The clothes, still wet, dripped onto the lacquered floor, leaving opaque water blotches. This didn't bother Petra, but whenever Mihály walked into the living room, he saw where the lacquered floor had faded from the dripping water. He had moved out two months ago, but still, it wasn't a good feeling to think that the wooden floor, even in the foyer, could acquire these wounded, opaque blotches. He took the wet T-shirt into the kitchen, spreading it out onto the plastic cover of the garbage can where it could do no damage, and hurried into the bedroom. The blinds were lowered, the bed was made on both sides. He felt a sense of indignation. Perhaps it was only for the sake of order: Routine had always been important for Petra. In the darkness traversed by shafts of light, he bent down to the bed sheets. The left side seemed untouched. Then why was the bed made for two people? he wondered, running his hand along the cover. He found his notebook, enhanced with a leather cover and the pages nearly full, in its usual place: the Thonet table drawer, hidden beneath the receipts. Relieved, he put the notebook away in his bag. He also packed a few books, restacking the others neatly so as not to leave any gaps, then stepped over to the cupboard, surveying its contents. He decided on a more masculine looking, grey-striped set of linens, although he could not find the small pillow that belonged to it, even as he rummaged in the cupboard. Before, they'd always fought about this. Petra stacked up the small and large pillows, along with the duvet covers, in separate columns, even though he tried to make her understand that sooner or later the linen sets would get all mixed up. He wanted to store the linens as he'd been used to at home growing up. There was a logic to it. His mother always turned out the small pillow covers and stuffed the larger pillow and duvet cover from the same set inside. On these shelves though, chaos reigned, grimy bras and underwear tossed about in and among the pillowcases. Finally he pulled out a small grey pillow from one of the piled-up columns; at least the color matched, even though it was a flannel.

He took down a few photographs from the wall, wrapped them up in the newspaper. One of them was a portrait of his grandfather, the famous pulmonary doctor; the other was a photograph of Freud's study. This used to hang on a wall in his office. He wanted to restore it to its former location.

He did not find the third picture, which he also intended to wrap in newsprint and take with him. It had hung above the Thonet chair in the middle of the wall ever since they'd moved in here. That had been at the beginning of his career, when he was still working as a resident in a hospital that had since been shut down; the picture hung above his desk in that hospital as well. Now there was only a nail sticking out of the wall. Beneath it was a pale, barely visible, rectangular contour.

Where is the monkey? he turned toward Petra, who had just come in from the bathroom and was rummaging through the cupboard amongst the underwear.

Over there. I took it down. It's over there in the corner, she replied.

The picture really was there behind the armchair, turned to the wall. Petra abhorred this photograph of a rhesus monkey, its eyelids half lowered, which was taken the day after a world-famous operation of groundbreaking importance in the history of science. The photo had been captured by one of the members of Dr. Robert White's team in 1970 after the first successful head transplant, when the post-op monkey not only began to blink but could even move. Moreover, as seen in the photograph, the monkey seemed to sense its surroundings, its gaze conveying near human feeling.

Dr. Kreutzer had come upon this photograph for the first time as a small boy in the school library, browsing through the pages of a popular science magazine. After he'd gone into the library for the third time to look at the picture during recess, the librarian, unaware of the provenance of the photograph, and who had certainly not read the accompanying article, made a photocopy of the picture for him. At home, as a high school student, the picture hung above his bed, and then, placed in an ebony frame, in his workplace. Following this acquisition, he was to assemble a serious collection of pictures. Among them were images of Demikhov's dog which, in the 1950s—decades before Dr. Kreutzer was born—had been reproduced worldwide. Vladimir Demikhov had transplanted the head of a puppy onto the body of another dog, although the animal did not survive the operation, dying a few hours later. The photographs had been taken during those few hours when the dog still displayed vital functions, even turning its head. Demikhov repeated the experiment several times, although his own pictures lacked what was so clear in the portrait of the monkey: that moment when the wondering, dumbfounded soul, clashing with the impossibilities of this world, arrived, or more precisely returned to a fractured, tortured body stitched together from two parts. This is what had enthralled the doctor so much, even as a schoolboy, and what he had clung to ever since then: this image **enshrining that moment of awakening**. At that time—he remembered well—as a fifth-grade student, he had been preoccupied by the question of whether the monkey sensed itself as the monkey from which the head had originated, or if it sensed itself as the monkey of the body to which it had been attached. The dilemma was where the monkey's soul—or rather that indeterminable something that we call the soul—resided, if it resided anywhere at all. For Dr. Kreutzer, this question did not become simpler over the years, but, just as with the ongoing accumulation of his professional experiences and case studies, grew ever more complicated. The more he knew about what, for lack of a better term, we refer to as a soul or consciousness, the less he felt any possibility of identifying deeply with the functioning, motivations, and desires of his human companions. Of course this did not mean that he was unable to attain results with even the most hopeless of patients. He never mistook his ability—which he used to deftly approach those persons and their complicated, often difficult-to-interpret problems—for his own accumulated knowledge, which he increasingly felt a kind of hidden, dark instinct sprung from the depths of his own being, nourished by unknown strata. He was able to have an effect without ever feeling haunted by any identification with these people, moreover, the more purposeful he felt his interventions to be, the more clearly he felt that all of this was merely a technical matter.

Now that the monkey had turned up, and Petra stood there getting dressed, her hair freshly washed, with an attitude more inquiring than inimical, he felt that he could risk asking her what was going on with the training and why she wasn't there. His wife gazed at him in wonder. Today's a holiday, she answered, as she pulled up the blinds. It was the Day of Unity. She had this Friday off.

Dr. Kreutzer always scheduled his own office hours, needing only to account for his patients' needs, and as no one had canceled for that day, he hadn't realized what day it was.

Where are the children? he asked.

They're with one of my coworkers. She has a trampoline.

Dr. Kreutzer felt rage **surging throughout his entire body**. This was how Petra was able to make him lose his composure. He didn't bicker with her about the furniture, not even the car; everything was as she had requested, he followed her instructions accurately. He insisted only on one thing: that the children spend as much time with him as possible, and that he should be able to take them whenever he could. That day was clear and sunny, they could have gone bike riding along the protected embankment on the river, or they could have played idiotic computer games together, because he always let them do so.

Why didn't you call me? he asked.

I thought you had office hours today, she said.

Petra knew very well that he never saw any of his patients before 10 a.m. He breathed deeply, trying to buy time, so he wouldn't start yelling immediately. He took his time wrapping up the picture of the monkey in newspaper, several times, protecting the glass **so it wouldn't crack**, then he slipped it into the wheeled sports bag next to the bed linens. He walked around the French bed and stood in front of his wife, grabbing her arm decisively.

We discussed this, no? he seethed.

Petra wanted to turn away. She was not wearing a bra beneath her T-shirt, her nipples were visible through the thin material. She had always had well-formed breasts, even though she'd breast-fed both children for a relatively long time. It was particularly pleasing to Dr. Kreutzer how each pointy breast seem to gaze in a different direction.

He grabbed her and quickly turned her around onto the bed. He diverted the animal rage that had just flooded him into a different channel, although the change of direction only strengthened his impetus. He couldn't tell from the expression on Petra's face if she was really frightened or if her despairing gaze was a part of the game, and as he penetrated her from behind, he couldn't even see if she was protesting. Her vagina had always been slippery and flexible, Dr. Kreutzer noted with satisfaction. In any case, he never even stopped if he felt like Petra was dry or if she begged him to stop: It made him feel good to know that this body was under his control. He moved within her for a long time, slowly, penetrating ever more deeply, while cursing her as well: stretched-out bint, buxom cow, happy to get fucked by anyone.

When he sensed Petra's body growing stiff, no longer moving with him, but pulling inward, focusing with every nerve fiber on that critical point, then he too stopped moving, waiting for the peak of climax to penetrate his wife to her innermost core with one thrust, shooting all of his hatred inside of her. He strayed into darkness, among the walls of old apartments, feeling his way along this ecstatic daze. Cries were heard in the distance. Quickened breathing, playground commotion, faraway voices. He was a child being tossed around between the bouncy walls of an air castle, then plummeting headfirst down an infinite waterslide, sliding for a long time until the entire thing turned into a glittering ski run above which there was only the illumination of the clear, glassy sky, which was carrying him steeply, irrevocably toward an unknown abyss of infinite depths. He plunged downward, shouting.

You piece of shit, whispered Petra, wiping herself with her underwear.

The phone, which was next to the shopping bag, started to ring, vibrating on the floor.

Don't pick it up.

Dr. Kreutzer got off the bed to see who was calling. The motion sent a shooting pain through his back, not for the first time today. He changed his position, turning more cautiously, not twisting his lower back. He crouched down for his phone. It was the Regent. He picked up, going into the living room, then the foyer, then the bathroom. He closed the door so Petra wouldn't come in and sat on the closed lid of the toilet. During the phone call, he gazed at the tile patterns he'd seen so many times before. The hardly perceptible pattern was repeated on each tile, although this could only be observed from a certain angle. From the toilet, the only part of the pattern that could be made out was on the section of wall illuminated by the light above the mirror. Above the bathtub, almost in the middle of the wall, at the fourth row, the tile layer had turned one of the regularly repeating tiles around, clearly accidentally. Dr. Kreutzer was always irritated by this one tile, laid the wrong way round. It was like an error that at first seemed imperceptible, but would, later on, prove fatal. After every workout, while taking a shower, his gaze would turn to the misplaced tile, and even once he had considered knocking it off the wall and replacing it. That idiotic tile.

The Regent's voice sounded tired, slightly hoarse. They spoke for a long time, so long, that when they were saying goodbye, and he finally came out of the bathroom, Petra was already standing in the door with her keys, ready to leave.

He ended the call. I'll be there at two, he said.

electrical current runs beneath the skin

She considered buying a cake from the bakery, but it was so far away that in the end, old Auntie Pálma bought six prepackaged petit fours in the shop that required special ID and waited for her son. His birthday had been on Tuesday, but she didn't want to bother him, so she spoke to him briefly on the phone to indicate that she hadn't forgotten. She had not purchased any other gifts as it was impossible to buy presents for her son.

She picked out an outfit in a horrendously roundabout way. For the most part, she shopped in the Metmag shop because of the impeccable quality of their goods, but that was not the only reason. Old Auntie Pálma was not familiar with any of the brands mentioned by her son, and only comprehended from Mishike's train of thought that if a certain style of clothing were fashionable and sought after, that did not necessarily signify elegance. Lately, for instance, her son had bought a pair of pants with an unusual and unique button; the name of the prestigious firm was engraved on the button itself.

Old Auntie Pálma had not been so taken with this, but she kept her feelings to herself. She murmured in recognition as if Mishike himself had carved the minuscule letters onto the wooden button. For her, the button was just a button, one that could be changed at any time or sewn onto any other garment. Trousers were trousers, an item of clothing that fulfilled their function if their length and measurements were more or less adequate.

Briefly put, she had purchased no gifts apart from the petit fours. She herself never baked anything. She used the oven in her kitchen as a cupboard. There, she stored various decorative paper bags and sacks for wine bottles; they could be used later on for gift giving. As she herself used to say, she was not the baking type. She implied many things with that saying: She was neither like those mothers and grandmothers who saw their chief vocation as caring for offspring, nor like those who boasted of their kitchen accomplishments as the highest degree of self-realization. She spoke of these kitchen fairies with a kind of patronizing gentleness, which, to those who didn't know her, was nearly impossible to recognize. Her son and her other relatives, though, knew what lay behind her tone. She would pronounce someone adept in the kitchen the same way she would state that the resident on the first floor flat was a dear, simple person. Roughly translated, this meant that she considered the individual in question a backward old hen whose interest in life ended with the wooden spoon; and as for the man who had recently moved in with her, he was an ill-begotten lumpen proletariat.

There were, however, certain words and expressions which old Auntie Pálma articulated only in a subdued voice, accompanied by certain gestures and facial expressions. One of these words was *foreigner*. If, within a certain context, she uttered this word, she always lowered her voice to a barely audible pitch, cautiously, like a medieval monk articulating the name of Satan, as if she were afraid that the mere utterance could cause the conjured entity to take form right there in her neo-Baroque living room. She would cautiously glance off to the side as if to ensure that no one else had heard. Another similarly muted word of the past few years was *poor*. Mihály, smiling to himself, would remind his mother that his wife gave lectures on communicating with the poor quickly and effectively. He wondered if his mother truly comprehended the nature of Petra's training program.

He was wrong, however, if he imagined that his mother found fault with this. The truth was that she herself did not understand why it was even necessary to communicate with those people. You had to avoid the places where they were, and that was it. To his mother, the word *training* had a peculiar ring. She could hardly imagine what they did for hours on end under the direction of Mishike's skinny wife. What were they paying all that money for? She somehow imagined them jumping around in a large room, doing gymnastics, because she could only associate the word training with physical activity. Petra must be giving them instructions in that unpleasant, colorless voice of hers, like a gym teacher.

She removed the plastic packaging from the petit fours. She walked over to the oven, rummaged around a bit, then pulled out, from among the decorative bags, a golden cardboard tray with the inscription *Dablux*. She put the pastries on the tray, placing the entire thing on a nickel serving platter. Somehow it looked acceptable.

Her son was late, and, as usual, irritated because it had been hard to find a parking place. He threw off his shoes in the vesti-

bule, sat down in the kitchen, then jumped up and opened the window. Before his mother came up to him with the petit fours and her birthday greetings, he told her:
I'm getting divorced.
Old Auntie Pálma finished putting out the napkins and stared at her son. What she had been expecting for years had finally happened. For some reason, until now, she always hoped Petra would fall in love with someone else after suddenly realizing how unhappy she was with Mishike—because she was unhappy, everyone could see it. She would simply rebel, pack up, leave with the children. Of course, this had not happened. Old Auntie Pálma now felt a sense of desperation. Her first question was about the apartment, that of course he wasn't just going to leave it to that woman, was he? That three-bedroom apartment in one of the protected districts, that home, furnished with antiques, which somehow she always wove into her accounts whenever someone asked her about her son. It only occurred to her to ask about the children afterward. Those two wonderful children, my God, she sighed, folding the napkins into a triangle, those two beautiful, poor little children, she continued, as if, by this latest development, their parents had deprived them of the possibility of remaining beautiful.

Old Auntie Pálma often chided and reprimanded her son, inclined to find him at fault even when he'd done nothing wrong; now, however, there was no question of her pinning any responsibility to him. She was certain that Petra was behind everything. Old Auntie Pálma never had too great an opinion of her thin-lipped daughter-in-law. Women like that were always stirring something up.

Mishike, my dear son! I got you petit fours. From Dablux.

Dr. Kreutzer picked up a punch-flavored cake. He bit into it, the filling gushing out onto his face, and so he wiped it off with his fingers, then he cleaned his hand with a napkin and spoke as he stared out the window, about how they were going to sell the flat and buy two separate apartments with the money, but not right now. Later on. For the time being he needed to pull himself together, adapt to this new situation.

A woman stepped onto the balcony of the building across the street, glanced at a pot with oleander, then went back into the apartment. A few seconds later she came out again. She bent down to the pot, then began pushing the pot over to the balcony door. Her calves were muscular and white. As she pushed the large pot, she suddenly turned around, to the other side of the street, as if she felt someone's gaze on her back. Dr. Kreutzer spit out a mouthful of the second cake into another handkerchief and tossed it in the garbage because it had an unpleasant aftertaste. The pastries had gone stale. By the time he looked up, the woman had disappeared again; someone had helped her take the oleander pot into the apartment.

His mother wanted to know where his new sublet was, would a studio be big enough for him? and wasn't it too close to those stations on the dangerous metro lines, those stations overrun by the *poor*. When she heard that his new place was located on the other side of the city, in one of the northern districts, she shook her head in disapproval. Muggings and lootings were reported daily in the papers, and anyone who could had moved to the protected areas of the city on the lower mountain slope where the real estate prices were already sky-high. She badgered her son about how much were they asking for this one-room hole. She found the rent brazenly, almost unbelievably high. Really: highway robbery in such a bad neighborhood. She covered up the rest of the pastries, put them in the fridge, and asked her son to measure her blood pressure. She ceremoniously opened the top of the box, carefully lowering the device along with the grimy armband onto the table. The blood pressure monitor was automatic, but, as she said, she was incapable of fastening the Velcro-strip armband by herself, and that is why she always postponed this task until she had a visitor.

There was no problem with her blood pressure, her son patted her liver-spotted arm, then he went into the living room. He was hoping that the woman with the oleander plant would come out again, but the balcony door was closed. He stood in the middle of the room with its decorations. Old Auntie Pálma had, as she had done for decades, stretched a frayed banner comprising the letters HAPPY BIRTHDAY across the living room. This paper decoration had been brought back from a trip abroad by Dr. Kreutzer's father, the elder Kreutzer, for his son's twentieth birthday, which his mother, after the celebration, had carefully folded up and put away. There were rips here and there, but the yellowing string, reinforced with cellophane tape, still held together. Every year, Dr. Kreutzer wanted to ask his mother to not to hang it up, but he didn't have the heart. He felt the most awkward when his birthday was celebrated with the whole family, and his wife also asked about this battered HAPPY BIRTHDAY sign. Over time, they celebrated this occasion together with less frequency, as everyone felt uneasy, not least of all the birthday man himself. Petra herself had already wished him many happy returns on Tuesday despite everything that had been happening between them in the past few weeks. She gave him a luxurious, wood-carved corkscrew and bottle-opening set in a decorative box. Dr. Kreutzer was captivated by the steely cold impersonality of her gift: as if she had merely passed on some corporate gear to him, something given to her that she'd stored somewhere. He wouldn't have been surprised to find a discreet logo on the box. His wife had always given him gifts that were chilly and aesthetic, at times even useful, but signifying the ever-increasing distance between them. The children, for the most part, gave him drawings, which he then hung up in his office. Vilmos, this time, had drawn an enormous whale sprouting water. His young son had, for some reason, appended a Tyrannosaurus rex in one of the upper corners of the picture. Perhaps he had felt the solitary cetacean to be inadequate for the occasion. The drawing was charming, colorful, and irregular. It immediately attracted the eye. It also contradicted the basic principle that the location of therapeutic discussions should be neutral; but with so many personal objects already accumulated there, Dr. Kreutzer felt that this child's drawing was not such a coarse intervention into the aura of his office. Recently, a young, pretty patient had stared at the whale for a long time, eyes narrowed, and she asked Dr. Kreutzer why it was sprouting. Then she probed the question of what title Dr. Kreutzer would give to the picture. He did not answer but merely noted down her question in his brown leather-bound notebook.

His mother was rinsing off the plates in the kitchen, then ponderously wiped her hands, more if she were wringing them. She pulled one nail-polished hand after the other with the dish towel, scrutinizing her son's face. She wanted to know if there was some new woman lurking in the midst of this separation, but Dr. Kreutzer shook his head. He even smiled. He said that Petra simply did not inspire him anymore. They had become estranged, and this dysfunctional marriage was a hindrance to him professionally.

Old Auntie Pálma nodded as if she understood what he was saying. She trusted her son. Perhaps now he could go even further than ever before. Secretly, she wished he would buy a house somewhere, a house surrounded by walls, equipped with security cameras and its own power station, in a gated community, and settle down with a suitable woman. If one of her acquaintances asked her what kind of woman was suitable, she would not have been able to provide a precise description, but she felt certain that it would not be someone like Petra.

You're going bald, my Mishike, she said as he was leaving, in a little girl's voice, and primping—still clutching the dish towel—she kissed him on the forehead.

one thousand deer were burned

Dr. Kreutzer turned onto the road that led up to the low mountain slope. He knew this neighborhood well. It was one of the safe districts, the streets patrolled regularly by police officers the fenced parks and playgrounds could only be accessed with special entry cards. In the summer, the sidewalks were regularly cleaned, the grass was watered, which sometimes gave people the feeling that they were living in a foreign country, or in a previous era, decades ago. He recalled the spot with its row of enormous plane trees, long since cut down, the caryatids of the corner building with their bare round bottoms. One of his classmates from high school had lived around here. She'd been an unlucky girl but had attracted his interest, perhaps precisely because of her haplessness. Her breasts had begun rounding out early, already in the first year of high school, whereas the other girls were still gangly, trying to cover over their bony adolescent bodies with loose dresses. This girl, with her awkwardness, was charming, like a bandy-legged roe deer. True, she would start fading earlier than the others, only her large, hazel eyes would remain unchanged. Her mother, who raised her alone, worried about her all the time. The girl, after every pathetically overacted but joyless sexual encounter, poured sterilized water into a blue basin and sat in it. She also rinsed her hands with disinfectant after they were together. Ever since then, the penetrating scent of chlorine in hospitals always made Dr. Kreutzer think of her narrow hands, her nails painted pink. He was just now driving past the building where the girl, Tünde, and her family, had lived. Their apartment had been furnished with broad, heavy pieces of furniture; you couldn't even tell that a child lived there. Even then, the girl dressed like a middle-aged bureaucrat: garbed in brown shoes, drab brown cardigans, dark skirts. He later heard that her mother had died of heart disease and that shortly after graduation, she had married some considerably older guy. In time, the neighborhood was redeveloped, shops accessible only to the privileged opened up on the ground floor. The building where she had lived was covered with scaffolding. Dr. Kreutzer remembered the elevator, the courtyard's inner walkways on each floor, the smells of food. He remembered how much the girl cried when he stopped talking to her, even in class. Her clinginess embarrassed him. He was ashamed that this creature, her hair wreathed around her head, her birthmarks, her large eyes, kept looking at him with so much desire, and it irritated him as she lurked around his desk, rubbing her thin, sock-clad ankles together. He had only fooled around with her because she seemed approachable, in distress, alone, more developed than the others. With the other girls, he could only have gotten what he wanted through very slow, serious investments of energy, but this girl, whom nobody bothered, who, for the others, was nearly imperceptible, was easy prey. Nevertheless, it took months before he was able to get her in bed. Tünde gave herself up with the attitude of a film star, and although she clearly found no great joy in the act itself, afterward she behaved as if she were on a film set, playing the role of a marquis's young wife who suddenly perished on their wedding night. How she had trailed after him on the way to violin lessons, he now recalled. He had listened to poetry with her, and he remembered quite vividly the discussion with her mama as to whether Tünde should attend university, and if so, whether she should try for medical school.

The traffic stood still; or it hardly, imperceptibly, inched forward. To the right, he saw a wine shop; its front gate pulled down, he tried to note its location. Tünde's old apartment was now a good hundred meters behind him. A worker wearing a helmet was piling up black plastic pipes, bending underneath their own weight, onto the sidewalk. It seemed, Dr. Kreutzer thought, that these unfortunates had to work even on holidays.

A garbage truck rumbled in front of him, loudly crawling from doorway to doorway. Why do they empty the garbage bins at this hour in such an expensive neighborhood, why don't they pick up the garbage at dawn, he asked himself in vexation, drumming his fingers on the steering wheel. He knew that here, in these streets, it was nearly impossible to find a parking spot, and so he turned off at the next intersection, and drove to the nearest parking garage. His state ID card meant that he could obtain mandatory free parking there. He would not have to wait for all the garbage bins to be emptied. After another five minutes of inching forward, he got to the intersection and pulled into the garage. He was supposed to be at the meeting already, and he didn't like to be late, so he stopped the car and sent a text.

It was dark in the building, daytime disappearing as if driven out of time. It could have been evening, dawn, even nighttime. Once he had slept with a young girl, redhead, slathered in makeup, here in this very garage. He'd been with at least a thousand women. But he remembered neither the face nor the name of the one he'd been with here, only that her mouth had been soft and covered with lipstick, which then got smeared all over his shirt. The bare, rough cement—while he was now facing—made him think of that incident. He could no longer recall when it had happened. They had been somewhere in a corner, that was for sure, because on the other side of them was a car, a white Nissan. The wall across from them was swathed in darkness. He had somehow ended up here with this redheaded chick after some reception at a conference. She was ardent, elastic, moist. Clearly his official entry card had impressed her. He clearly recalled that moment when a car, driving to one of the upper stories, passed behind them. He looked up at the headlights creeping across their bodies, and he realized that there were cameras installed: on the ceiling above a revolving lens loomed close by. It was dark, but the knowledge that a third person had glimpsed into their intimacy, perhaps was deliberately staring at them, excited him even more.

It occurred to him later, at home in the shower, that the recording could turn up in the wrong hands.

It was dark, completely dark, he repeated to himself as he ran the shower head up and down his body. He tried to overcome the anxiety that kept coming over him: Someone might have recognized him, could have possibly identified him on the basis of his entry card and license plate. As much as he realized the ridiculousness and pettiness of his fear, as he soaped his chest and back, various scenarios kept playing in his mind, scenarios in which he was identified and interrogated. That evening he made inquiries as to how long the security camera recordings were kept and now, pulling on the hand brake in the parking garage, he thought with reassurance that that period had long since elapsed.

He locked the car and hurried to the elevator. He did not like the suffocating smells of petrol vapor, car tires, and dust characteristic of parking garages, whether above- or underground. He had a patient who regularly got panic attacks in such places. Now, as he crossed the gleaming, gigantic concrete shed, he empathized with the anxieties of that young man. These opaque, deserted spaces, full of darkness and exhaust, were frightening. He could hardly wait to get to the iron door. He pushed it open with his shoulder, not wanting to touch the door handle. As he reached the ground floor level, he glanced at his cell phone again. He'd received a message in return; It stated: No problem.

repeatedly lifted up by the wind

A downward sloping street led to the playground. He walked past a brick school, from which, at other times, cries could be heard from the echoing yard. The entrance gate, festooned with flags, was closed today, but the armed guard was posted at his usual place as if watching over the flags hoisted for the Day of Unity. On the other side of the street was a homemade ice-cream shop, which Dr. Kreutzer had visited quite often with his children. The metal trays containing ice cream were not displayed at this time of year since ice-cream season began at the end of May. The shop was closed, and miniature flags of the Unified Regency had been stuck into the pastries in the storefront window. Dr. Kreutzer shivered a bit, thinking of the ice cream, and pulled his jacket tighter around himself. It was coat weather, maybe even too chilly for this light jacket, but he had picked it out yesterday. The jacket was sewn from rose-colored tweed, purchased for an exorbitant price not too long ago because he liked the leather patches on the elbows. He'd always been fond of true English style, the raw colors, the soft, warm materials, the checkered woolens, the leathers. That morning, he'd picked out a light-brown scarf to go with the jacket along with a cap to cover his thinning hair. His increasing baldness worried him; yesterday, in the elevator of his mother's apartment, he'd tried unsuccessfully to get a glimpse of his head from behind. Here, in the parking garage, there were no mirrors. He was thinking that if the bald patch got bigger, he'd have to shave his head or get hair transplants. He usually tried to talk his well-off patients, all living in the protected districts, out of such procedures because in his experience it did nothing to improve their self-esteem, and they often felt ridiculous, even pitiful about themselves, afterward. Instead, he tried to help them reach an inner peace with their own selves so that they would not perceive the traces of time as decay or loss; although he believed that he was psychically well-balanced, with a nearly detached relationship to his own body, he was observing the signs of his own aging with anxiety. The mirror never showed him that slender, English-looking gentleman who, in the depths of his soul, he wished to see himself as. No, no, he knew all too well the fellow in the tweed jacket, who lived in his imagination and whose careless gestures he had emulated as an adolescent at home in front of the tall foyer mirror with its Baroque frame.

The Regent was already sitting on a bench in the playground. It made Dr. Kreutzer a little uneasy how they always met up in playgrounds, but he had no means of changing this custom, formed over many years. It was impossible to convince the Regent to use any kind of digital platform. His rationale was that his messages would be read, his conversations wiretapped; no form of virtual communication was secure. As far as Dr. Kreutzer was concerned, however, these in-person meetings were equally risky. He couldn't escape the idea that if anyone saw them sitting around in these various playgrounds, they could be taken for pedophiles. And things could get even worse—he might be identified. The psychiatrist who lectured about the poor! Or they might recognize the Regent waiting for him, collar turned up, bundled up in his scarf. That would be a disaster. Even though Dr. Kreutzer kept repeating to himself that there was nothing to worry about, that people bumped into each other accidentally all the time, so why couldn't they? Moreover two people could meet up at any given agreed-upon time. Still, he felt just how problematic these meetings were. A conversation in a restaurant, somewhere in a discreet back corner in a not too popular place, would have been a better location for these encounters, vacant as they were, and yet so important for the two of them. More than once it had occurred to him that if some journalist were to spot them together here, they might be smeared as being in a homosexual relationship. This would set off public speculation as to the nature of their connection—what the hell were they talking about? Who was he, Dr. Kreutzer? And what was he doing with the Regent? Never mind that the output of newspapers in the Unified Regency had been tailored to the authorities' taste for a long time now. Who would even dare print an expose like that? No one would have the nerve. The journalists of the Unified Regency preferred to write about the jewels of the oligarchs' wives, atrocities committed by the residents of the segregated zones, kidnappings, the enemies threatening the country's border—topics that sustained interest and whipped up passion. Most of the visual material was AI generated. The idea of someone photographing them? Come on now. No newspaper here would take the risk.

Of course, they could have also met outside of the city in some agreed-upon meeting place, as they had tried before. That had been around this time last year, or perhaps a little later, sometime around the beginning of the summer, when they met up in a nearby village; the Regent had some business at the private hospital there. They strolled back and forth along the edge of the forest, making sure to stay close to the car with the security detail. That, however, had been a onetime and exceptional occasion, as both of them were much too busy to meet up outside of the city. And the Regent feared being followed. His security staff had accompanied him here as well. For years he had never even set foot in the street without them, but his bodyguards remained in the background, not entering the playground. One of them lurked behind the fence—in Dr. Kreutzer's opinion, none too discreetly—pacing monotonously from the lamppost to the garbage can and back again while the other one sat in the car. It was an unmarked vehicle with a civil license plate so as not to arouse suspicion.

There was no other human being who strolled around with that kind of posture, the psychiatrist thought to himself with amusement after glancing at the bodyguard circling the lamppost. It was as if he were trying to mimic a robot. Dr. Kreutzer smiled to himself.

Hardly anyone was around, in, or near the chilly playground, even though they had picked this location because of the usual background noise. Dr. Kreutzer held his ID to the card reader, then closed the gate after himself. He sat down on the bench.

He apologized for his lateness.

The Regent was short, which became much more conspicuous when they were seated. He himself liked to say that he was of a plucky physique because he felt that the word had a tough, masculine ring to it. He interjected the phrase "with my plucky physique" often in casual conversation, always scrutinizing the face of his interlocutor. In general, he wore shoes with hidden elevation inserts, but while sitting, as he was now, with his stocky upper body, he seemed even shorter than usual to Dr. Kreutzer, who did not look particularly athletic himself. At the beginning of their acquaintance, a good thirty-five years ago, before the Regent had become the Regent, when he had just been yet another one of Dr. Kreutzer's desperate patients, he often complained about his height. And to this day he kept mentioning that remark of Dr. Kreutzer's which, the Regent acknowledged, had had such a liberatory affect on him that his torturous thoughts related to his physique had vanished. Dr. Kreutzer could have posed the most obvious questions, ones offered by the situation itself—for instance, why then was the Regent still wearing these shoes with the hidden inserts? Why the raised podium when he gave his speeches?—but he refrained from doing so. Their connection had not, for a long time now, been one where he could casually broach such topics. They had known each other for too long, both men knew too much about the other. For Dr. Kreutzer, this meant access to power accompanied by an ever-present sense of danger. He tended to interpret their common past as advantageous, but sitting here, next to the wheezing, ponderous Regent, he was often seized by uncomfortable, even sinister premonitions.

The Regent, resting one foot on the bench, leaned forward, his elbows on his knees. He liked to wait in this position as he believed it conveyed his readiness for action. Dr. Kreutzer usually found him in this pose. He looked at his hands: It was quite apparent the Regent was no longer young. At that time, when he had started coming to him, the psychiatrist had not been able to rid himself of the thought of how a woman might react to those thick fingers with their wide, flat nails. As for himself, even if he wasn't tall, he at least had **delicate and elegant hands**. Luckily, they were not freckled as his back and chest were. It was only now that small liver spots were visible on his skin; he treated them with lightening cream.

Dr. Kreutzer handed the pills to the Regent. This was also a part of their relationship. The Regent could have obtained this medication elsewhere, but he wanted to emphasize the confidential nature of their connection, its benefits, its drawbacks. He never downloaded anything from the cloud; he trusted no system to be unhackable. He knew more than anyone else that there was no such thing as secret data. He pictured the cloud as something like layers of medical-grade cotton pads, transparent and soft, in which rubber-gloved, expert hands rummaged through before scraping the data they needed.

Dr. Kreutzer waited, just as he used to in his office. Back then, they had both been young and at the beginning of their careers. Each in their own way had gone very far, both were somewhere at the peak of the arch that they had earlier envisioned for themselves. Or almost at the peak. Dr. Kreutzer still wanted to go further, to continue climbing that steep arch. He never put it to himself that coarsely or simply, he merely felt that some of his colleagues with similar, or even more modest capabilities to his own, had unjustly climbed higher than he did. He felt particularly embittered by his sparse media appearances; he was invited to speak on television so infrequently. He felt that he had a good sense for the language these occasions required: brief, succinct, professionally accurate and yet comprehensible to the wider public; given a few minutes, he could be much more trenchant and clever than some of his colleagues, who were oversaturated in the media. He knew a lot about the segregated zones: He liked to expound in reassuring tones on the psychological profiles of those committing crimes in these crisis-torn districts, as he implied these conflicts were merely transitional, incited by outside agitators, which the government was handling with all the sober decisiveness of a good patriarch.

The Regent was complaining about a migraine, rubbing his forehead with his stubby fingers. Dr. Kreutzer nearly retorted this was due to stress but caught himself in time. It might have almost sounded as if he were faulting the man, as if signaling that the Regent himself was the cause of his own problems, and that with his lifestyle, such psychosomatic symptoms could only be expected. Instead, Dr. Kreutzer quickly began talking about a vasodilator which should be sprayed into the nostrils at the onset of a headache as soon as the aura appeared. The Regent answered that *that* was cocaine, and throwing his head back, guffawed. He liked the expression "the *aura* of a migraine." Dr. Kreutzer could already hear him using the expression in his next conversation and smiled slightly to himself. He still had the upper hand.

Dr. Kreutzer felt that this was the moment to bring up that other, unpleasant matter. He didn't want it turning into a scandal, and there was a chance of the Regent finding out about it from someone else.

The Regent was talking about his family, about what a burden his position meant to his children. It seemed that he truly felt sorry for them for having such a great man as a father. The Regent's following remarks, however—as Dr. Kreutzer could immediately judge with an impartial professional ear—were riddled with paranoid delusions. The Regent was convinced that conjoined forces, determined to destroy him, had followed him here as well, and that even now, someone was photographing him. Here, on this playground, perhaps by drone, or from the window of a nearby apartment. The Regent muttered that he could never be sure that the barrel of the gun wasn't pointed at him from some rooftop, that a car wasn't waiting to run him over as soon as the signal was given. He always wore a bulletproof vest, which Dr. Kreutzer found both absurd and pompous: The civil war had ended long ago. But he could not say this, he could not even indicate it slightly, as the person sitting next to him was sensitive to any hint irony, even delivered in the most subtle, cheerful way, disguised in propitiation. He tried to change the subject. He mentioned the Western films of their youth, those happy times when both of them could drink a beer together publicly, aiming the empty beer cans into a garbage can. The Regent could do so now, even here, on the playground, Dr. Kreutzer mentioned. His companion's nervous system, harrowed by torturous mistrust, immediately reacted to the conditional mood. Suddenly he lowered his leg from the bench, pulled himself up, and said:

It's not as I couldn't.

For a moment, there was silence. The silence was, in part, a response to this numbing and enigmatic statement. The other reason was much more tangible, coarser. Directly behind them, a resolutely green and flowering bush grew among the stone ledges built on the playground's terrace. Its white and frothy branches reached over the back of the bench as a gentle breeze suddenly rose, inundating the playground with the smell of sperm. Yes, the bush emanated the unmistakable, unequivocally, and assertively sweet smell of sperm, and the brief pause that had arisen between them soon became the painful, eloquent and all-consuming silence of this overpowering and heavily scented breeze.

When this odd and awkward moment passed, the Regent mentioned that he had developed a fear of flying—unfortunately, he had to admit. Of course, in his position, he could not avoid getting on an airplane. Dr. Kreutzer answered that many people felt the same way. As he said these words, he realized he'd made a mistake and therefore hurriedly reassured him that the medication he'd just given the Regent would also help with this, as it calmed down all such anxieties. His voice cracked as he spoke.

Once again the wind picked up, bringing the coarse sperm smell, even stronger than before. Dr. Kreutzer began to reflect aloud on his various financial securities and called himself a sucker. He hung his head: He never should have gotten involved in something he knew nothing about. He did not mention his upcoming divorce, only that he would have to get access to his invested money soon. The Regent interrupted him, reassuring him that he himself really didn't understand these things, but he could put him in touch with someone who did. There was a solution for everything. Dr. Kreutzer wondered if he should let something drop about the fact that he would soon be moving out of his apartment, but, not knowing how much this might hurt his position, he remained silent. He knew that the Regent considered people with families to be much more trustworthy: they could always be blackmailed.

An ambulance siren howled across the silence, then in the descending quiet, a child's voice could be heard crying out, "Poppa, Poppa." Ever since the birth of Dr. Kreutzer's children, the sound of a child's voice always made his ears him prick up. He too was a father, in the end. A little boy was waving at someone in the distance from a balcony, but to whom he was waving could not be seen from here. Both of them looked up in the direction of the voice, but Dr. Kreutzer knew, or at least he guessed, the thoughts of the other.

A woman right in front of them was walking toward the sandbox, then she knelt down to her child who was cobbling together a dented sandcastle with a yellow shovel. The child had just found the shovel. It was cracked, but still, the child set to work. The mother glanced up at them for a second, straight into their faces. She quickly grabbed the shovel from the child's hand, threw it away, picked up her son, and hurried away from the playground. They were alone again.

The sperm smell spread over the playground for the third time.

I have to go, said the Regent, and he stood up.
He was cumbersome, grim, surprisingly old. He looked at least ten years older than his actual age. The bodyguard who had been strolling next to the playground sensed the Regent's motion with his peripheral vision and stepped immediately over to the wire fence. He covered them as they closed the latch on the entry gate and accompanied the Regent back to his car.

delicate and elegant hands

I was a little late, and on the way it began to rain. I had to walk around the oily puddles, the worms gliding across the sidewalk. How could there be so many worms in this asphalt-covered city? What were they crawling out of? Were they swarming beneath the sidewalk?

I walked into the office, placed my damp coat on the coat hanger, then hung the coat hanger on the nicely formed, cast-iron coat stand that had caught my eye, even on my first visit. When he saw how I was looking at it with such interest, he told me how he had saved this cast-iron coat stand from a hospital that had been liquidated in one of the poor neighborhoods; it lay among the cast-iron radiators and other scrap metal destined for disposal. He himself had scraped off the flaking white paint, of which there were many layers. I was impressed by how he had done this himself, I could imagine how it must have been a struggle for his delicate and elegant hands. At the end of each coat hook, there was a tiny human form.

Like a bunch of little Christs doing a workout, he said, pointing at it with a mischievous smile.

At other times as well, he would make similarly facetious comments. I liked his sense of humor; no one in my circle would ever make such remarks. All of the university offices had webcams installed, and if we ever joked about anything—for the sake of appearances—it was always confined to trivialities. The knowledge that we were being watched was built into our reflexes, our movements. The webcams were as much a part of our life as the performance we put on to demonstrate that we weren't taking any notice of them.

I turned around a few times, not knowing where to put my dripping umbrella. Dr. Kreutzer once again opened the office door, pointing to an old tin bucket in the foyer. I remembered that he didn't like dripping umbrellas; I had once walked into his office when it was pouring rain outside, and he had wiped up the water immediately. My husband usually never even noticed things like that.

The spacious foyer opened onto other offices in which his colleagues worked. They were also psychiatrists, whom I somehow never saw, I only heard, at times, the sound of someone pottering about, clattering sounds or the voice of someone speaking behind closed doors or in the kitchen at the end of the hallway. The entire sprawling interior space might have comprised one large apartment years ago, before being renovated.

To the right there was a kitchenette, but I saw that he preferred to prepare tea in his office, washing off the cups in a bathroom located in the back. Although, when I once tried to use that bathroom, he sent me back out to the foyer. I had never used the bathroom at the back of his office.

I apologized several times for being late, and he noted that there was no point in my doing so as the quarter hour had indeed come out of my own time. He was correct, and yet his response felt rather tactless and disheartening. My earlier enthusiasm evaporated, and it crossed my mind that he certainly didn't scrape off and paint that coatrack himself, he was only saying he did. These intellectual types often made such empty boasts about things like that. I sat down across from him in the armchair, between us there was only the small round table. I wanted to talk about my husband, how there had been nothing between us for a long time. If he asked, I would certainly reply that I was happy with my husband, but if I wanted to be completely honest with myself, then I would have to admit that this was merely an empty phrase. Because what it did it mean to say, really, that someone was happy? Never in my life had I felt happy. Not only that, but I also could not even comprehend what others meant by this word. Was it contentedness, tranquility, passionate feelings? Unruly desires that could never be quenched? I had not desired my husband for a long time, but I did not see this as a problem. I knew that it was like this for most people, they became saturated with the smell of their partner, they knew the emphases, all the movements in advance, then they began to understand each other less and less, even trying to avoid all bodily contact. They sprayed disinfectant in the bathroom if they needed to use it right after the other; they weren't pleased to take the already licked teaspoon into their mouth—but still, this wasn't enough to make them seek out the advice of a psychiatrist.

I first mentioned the boy because I had been talking about this at the end of the last session. I said that I saw him again, but he did not approach me. Dr. Kreutzer wanted to know how I felt about this. Was I still afraid of him, or had other feelings awoken in me?

How did I feel? What feelings had been awoken in me? None whatsoever, I shrugged my shoulders.

I shouldn't have mentioned this topic, clearly he would not have done so. This incident was significant only for me. He had come into my life just in time because he was the one whom I had to fear, whom I finally could fear. He somehow embodied my undefined yet permanent disquiet, ungraspable even to myself. I had actually come here to talk about this unembodied, unnamable anxiety, but during the long sessions the problem became that we never talked about it. Somehow . . . it was there, coiling perceptibly, but for the most part we avoided it, talked around it.

Dr. Kreutzer asked how my week had been and if I wanted a cup of tea. I said yes, not because I wanted tea but because I liked the sequence of movements with which he would take a match from the small basket and light up the samovar. I had never seen a real, functioning samovar before, and I somehow found his gestures beautiful as he made the preparations, placing the small tin boxes here and there. No, not beautiful, that wasn't the right word, rather I found his gestures homey. He had many different kinds of tea from different countries in his office, all of good quality, and he scooped out and measured the leaves with a ceremonial deliberateness as he made the cup of tea.

I answered that apart from the encounter with this boy, I had had a fairly good week, I had written a paper for a conference; also, my period had not come. At this he half turned around, looking at me questioningly. It hadn't come, even though it should have, and my stomach was bloated. This had happened before, I continued. He turned back to the samovar which had already began to heat up, and he sat down in his chair. He asked if I was worried, if I might not be pregnant after all. I had encountered this often enough. He could have known that I wasn't pregnant. I turned slightly away from him in my chair, and I replied that if I really was pregnant, then it would certainly create a huge stir, as the last such incident—which of course people still talked about to this very day—had occurred over two thousand years ago.

Well I thought, this was a good little reply to the coatrack. The little body-building Christs. They will certainly appreciate it.

He smiled, and he even said that he liked my sense of humor. But all the same, you're not a virgin, he said, looking into my eyes. I answered: Well no, I'm not, and instead of looking back at him, I fixedly stared at the spout of the samovar, which had begun to hiss. The tea began to drip out very slowly. He poured me a cup.

He placed the teacup in front of me. I picked it up: at last there were something in my hands. The tea was still too hot. I carefully placed it down on the saucer and then picked them up together. Lowering my face into the steam, I repeated myself: that I didn't want any children, and especially not with my husband, and we weren't in the habit of... in other words, we really didn't... I meant... we do not share a conjugal relationship. Christ, what an idiotic expression, I added.

Why is it idiotic? What does it make you think of? he asked.

It makes me think of grease. Congealed grease, I said.

He smiled again, just slightly raising one eyebrow. I liked it when his face finally reflected something, even the slightest trace of emotion, because he often looked poker-faced, like some kind of robot with a smart exterior.

He asked me if I had a connection to anyone else besides my husband. The question sounded devoid of all emotion, as if, I don't know, he were asking if I supplemented my vegan diet with any other proteins.

Besides my husband? I asked in return. But I hardly even have any connection to him!

I know, I continued, that I'm an adult woman, and I'm not even particularly prudish, I know I could have some kind of relation with one of my colleagues, but it never occurred to me that I could be a woman in their eyes. By that I mean... anything else besides another professor. That they could look at me in any other way, that it might occur to them that... I don't even know. It's not as if I don't dress prettily, I always wear nice shoes, sometimes put on makeup, always go to the hairdresser, but really, for years now, it never occurred to me that I could sleep with someone.

Dr. Kreutzer looked surprised. He asked when was the last time I experienced intimacy with my husband. Those words, *experienced intimacy*. God Almighty. I tried to think about when it even could have been: maybe sometime before the Unified Regency, when my husband and I had taken a trip to the seashore together. Yes, I think it was then. I tried to count backward, how many years ago. Maybe five or six? Or seven? It had been a brief, hurried, and uncomfortable encounter, most of which I couldn't even recall now.

He stirred his tea.

The teaspoon clinked against the teacup rhythmically.

He asked if my husband ever tried to approach me, or if I attempted at all to freshen up our intimacy. He used the expression, "freshen up," as if referring to freshening up musty bed linens in a cupboard with a nice fragrant spray. I didn't completely understand what he was thinking, but I said no, I haven't tried, nor has my husband approached me, then I added that we were doing fairly well like this too.

Doing fairly well.

Who is doing fairly well? he asked. You are? And your husband? Is he doing fairly well?

The tea was still very hot, it nearly burned my tongue. I touched my tongue and its numbed tip.

Being together with my husband never caused me any particular joy. It didn't hurt or anything like that, but I never felt that clamorous happiness that the world seemed to speak of all the time. Dr. Kreutzer asked me if I found my husband attractive. I replied with unexpected coarseness, even though I really didn't intend to. I really didn't.

His mouth stank.

I didn't want to say this. It came out of me much more strongly than I had intended.

I then tried to modulate what I had said, as if I'd uttered something impolite. As if I had to quickly change the topic of the conversation after a loud and obvious fart. I added that his mouth didn't always stink, just from time to time, and well, this was the truth. He had bad breath, unbearably bad, reeking of pestilence.

Whenever we went to the theater, I don't know why I picked that moment exactly, that horrible bad breath always hit me in the face whenever he turned to whisper something to me about the performance or some actor. I had to turn away so as not to smell it. Simply put, his tepid bad breath made me feel nauseated. I don't know why it bothered me exactly so much in the theater, but sitting there talking with a psychiatrist, I realized it was because that it was only there with my husband leaned in so close to me, never at other times. That unbearable cheese smell always emanating from his mouth.

And yet we went to the theater fairly often, every other week. We got our tickets from the New University. You needed special permission to attend these performances, as had been the case for years now. As the large, state-supported theaters were impossible to fill on a regular basis, university instructors got tickets for the empty seats. For the most part, the performances were boring propaganda, but at least we would get out of the house, I had a chance to get dressed up and meet other people besides my work colleagues. These evenings made me think of our old life, even when, standing in the entrance hall of the theater, we didn't talk to anyone, and at home we didn't even discuss what we'd seen because there was no point.

Dr. Kreutzer just listened, not answering, as if waiting for me to continue.

I didn't like these pauses in the middle of the conversation. I felt like we were going nowhere, that time, along with my money, was spinning away. My university salary was fairly modest, and it was very difficult for me to budget for these private sessions. I too fell silent, the tea was still too hot. For the love of God, it didn't want to cool down.

A few minutes passed, and then he asked me if I did not feel the lack of us being together. He put it like that, "being together." As if I wasn't spending time with my husband every evening anyway.

He did not use the word *sex*, and he did not dare ask directly if we lay down together, which I otherwise found very comical: "Lay down together." In other contexts, this phrase is used to express submission. Who had not laid down? Yes, of course, we lay down together, we turned down the blanket, we slipped into the same bed, we just didn't touch each other. But I didn't say what was on my mind, I didn't want to make ironic comments. I tried to give a considered response, or at least one that seemed so, because if I told him the truth—I felt no sense of lack, it never even occurred to me—that would mean I was a frigid cunt who couldn't even imagine making love to the man in the bed right next to me. But this also wasn't true. I had my fantasies, but I always appeared in them in some kind of a defenseless role, and the man who loomed above me was tall and strong, not nearsighted and short like my husband. Well, fine, my husband wasn't decidedly small, but rather . . . of medium build. At least this is what he would say about himself. I did not want to talk about these fantasies because there wouldn't have been any point.

Instead I asked Dr. Kreutzer what kind of tea this was. Lemon and mango, he answered. It had a very particular, fresh taste. If only it weren't burning my tongue so much.

little street girls

I watched Dr. Kreutzer sip his tea. I could hear him swallowing. This sound usually irritated me when I heard other people do it, as did any noise emerging from or produced by the body. Chewing, swallowing, shuffling or, for example, scraping, scratching sounds. The sound of my husband when he scratched his head, or my coworker who sat at the desk across from me in my office at the university munching on something from a paper sack. Why was he eating from a bag when there was a cafeteria in the building?

I was amazed that the sound of Dr. Kreutzer sipping his tea did not bother me just as the conspicuous stubble on his neck did not. The stubble was not all of the same color, there were lighter patches. I noticed for the first time the small brown spots on his hands. They were larger than freckles, more like the spots on the skin of older people. Certainly he must go hiking a lot and the sun had made his skin tanned and dry. This pleased me, somehow. The rusty-colored spots made me think of a Hungarian Pointer. Dr. Kreutzer was, as a matter of fact, a Hungarian Pointer. Well of course what I mean is that if he had to be some kind of animal, he would be a Pointer.

Once again there was silence. Someone was passing along outside along the walkway. Dr. Kreutzer asked me what I was thinking. I answered that I was thinking of a Hungarian Pointer. That I was very young, I don't even know how old, in any event, I was very small when I made friends with a Pointer. The dog lived on our street. We played together often outside, almost every day. It lived across the street, and as soon as we got to our summer bungalow, I would run up to the wire fence and call out to the dog, which always came running, sniffing my fingers. I loved that dog very much. Its nose, which tried to push through the fence, was splotched. Back then, I was so small that I could push my hand through the holes in the chicken wire fence. I fed the dog raspberries from my hand, then licked the juice from my palm.

So it seems you had a garden, he said, putting his mug down on a rattan coaster on the round table. It wasn't our garden, I corrected him, but just our summer place, or at least we used to go there in the summer. I don't recall us being there in the winter. Maybe sometimes in the fall. I seem to have a memory of my parents raking up leaves and of my older sister and myself jumping into the pile. Our parents told us not to do this. I remember the scent of burning leaves, the biting autumn cold, the stubble fields, the early twilights. I remember the curled up hedgehogs that my father found in the leaf piles. They looked as if they weren't alive anymore, but they were only hibernating. I have very few memories from those years, and for the ones I do have, I can't decide if they're genuine or like film reels, always running the same scenes, a montage of the square-format family photographs I saw so frequently, spliced together by my own brain. I can recall the garden, the musty house with its shutters. Sometimes you can still see these kinds of summer houses on the lakeshore, a few are still standing from that time: they always had two small rooms, painted green, with twisted bars on the windows. Of course, this didn't seem small to us, and today I can only judge from the photos that it was indeed very small. Later on, this house was sold. If I understood well from my mother's account, it was my father who did so as he no longer wanted to maintain it. Everything was shared equitably between my parents by way of a prenuptial agreement: My mother got the apartment, my father got the plot of land with the summer house, which he immediately sold. There was no contestation, the children were also distributed in this same fashion. My older sister ended up with my father, and I stayed with my mother. I have only thought about how difficult this might have been for me recently. At the time, it seemed natural. My parents always told Mina, my sister, and me that we needed to divide everything in two.

Dr. Kreutzer raised his eyebrows a bit, and looked at me with interest. I had never spoken about my older sister, he interjected. He didn't even know that I had a sister. To that I replied that I didn't have one.

She died, I said.

When?

A few years ago. Four. Or five?

How old was she? he asked. Thirty-nine, I answered. He looked at me for a long time, like someone who attributed enormous significance to this fact, like someone who was expecting for me to immediately strike my forehead and fall into his arms, exclaiming what a genius he was, thank you, that it never occurred to me before because here it was, eureka, the root of all of my problems. At last it had come to light—behold my dead sister. She died young and poor, and every time I thought about it I was seized with anxiety that this might be my fate as well. Abracadabra, we had conjured from its hiding place, from the bubbling, gurgling depths, the Problem itself.

He looked at me fixedly and said nothing. I felt that I had to pick up the thread, and so I added that there was not much importance to this fact. I meant, in my own life. I hardly knew my older sister. She had lived abroad with our father. There was practically no connection between us. Sometimes we exchanged letters, meaningless greetings. Merry Christmas, happy birthday. Congratulations on passing your ballet-school exam, love, your sister, Gizi. Things like that. We always sent photographs to each other. School photographs, Christmas portraits. I got her graduation class picture; two years later, my mother mailed mine to her. In her picture she was wearing a white blouse, her head leaning to one side, just like in my photo. On the back of the pictures she always wrote "with affection" and drew little hearts. I never understood anything of what she wrote to me. The only thing that made me happy in our correspondence was that sometimes she sent me 3D postcards, for example of a horse racing across a green field; when I moved the postcard the horse's mane also moved. Or she would slip some decals into the envelope, fairy-tale figures or animal stickers.

At the funeral, as I recall, on her coffin, it was written that she had lived thirty-nine years. And as I stood by the bier I remember thinking this so much better than if she had lived to forty—it was less depressing. Of course, for her to die at the age of thirty-nine was also depressing, but forty is so final. As if something had just been shut down. Forty years, I'm done, the bell tolls, enough. Thirty-nine was somehow accidental, just like her death was. On a lottery ticket, a person would be more likely to put an *X* next to thirty-nine than forty, no? Why exactly thirty-nine?

She did not die quickly. It was, let's say, bad.

Why?

I don't know, I answered. Because it wasn't she who decided. Because if she had already made up her mind, it would have been better for her to succeed. But in the end it was our father who decided, who asked for her to be taken off the ventilator. In my view, it would have been better if she had decided. If, at least, she had had control over her own death.

Are you able to decide?

I don't know.

Dr. Kreutzer wrote something down with his golden-nibbed, dainty fountain pen. He asked me to tell him more about my sister. I liked that he took notes by hand. I didn't know anyone else who used a fountain pen.

At least I was able to say goodbye, I said.

She had died by suicide. She killed herself because she didn't want to live anymore. I have few true memories of her, by which I mean ones I did not create for myself from her photographs. For example, my memory of the fence as we stood there and waited for the neighbor's dog.

In my memory I can see my sister's hand and how she reached over to the dog's mouth with a half bitten off piece of cake more quickly than I did with my raspberries. We resembled each other a great deal, but Mina was taller than me, and for as long as our parents were still together, I had to wear the clothes she had outgrown. My mother told the story they repeated probably a hundred times now, that when I was three years old, I had a temper tantrum when we bought a red sweater for her. It really hurt that Mina picked out the sweater for herself, and my mother bought it immediately. Apparently I kept pulling at the package, I ripped the paper, and I screamed that she always got new clothes and I always had to make do with a sweater that was "*wornded.*"

Dr. Kreutzer was watching me tentatively, not even smiling. And yet everyone usually laughed at this story. Everyone. I had told it many times over, and my husband always neighed, once I got to that part. As soon as I said "wornded" he laughed out loud.

I was not even four years old, I continued, when my parents got divorced. My older sister was six. My mother had wanted Hermina, my sister, to stay with us. She cried a lot at that time. Later, she kept saying that she had thrown away Mina, just thrown her way so that we could be free of my father. I didn't understand this, and she never explained it later on. What did that mean, that she had just thrown Mina away? I was happy that finally I could be alone with my mother, just the two of us. That her attention wasn't divided, and that now she would buy me a red sweater, she would only bathe me in the bathtub. At night, I could decide what fairy tale I wanted. But my mother was very worn down by what had happened. In the dark, lying in my bed, after lights out, I heard her sobbing in her room. Sometimes she made such strange sounds, as if she were about to vomit. I would get up and run to her. I didn't embrace her, nor did she pull me to herself, she just sat on the edge of the bed, bent over, weeping, as if something was really hurting her. I stood there barefoot, not knowing what to do. I said, let's go then, let's go and bring Mina home, if she really was missing her so much. There's room for her here, we can put another bed in the my room. I didn't mean this seriously, I only wanted to say something to console her, something I thought she wanted to hear. This only made her sob even more, hiccupping as she cried. She didn't answer me, only shook her head.

Dr. Kreutzer asked me what my mother told me about the divorce. What could I tell him about it?

Nothing.

That is to say... not too much. They did not get on well. They'd gotten married very young, then suddenly realized they didn't love each other. I didn't know much more about this now than I had as a child. Dr. Kreutzer looked at me with interest, slightly tilting his head to the side. Now there was really something more decisively in him that reminded me of a Hungarian Pointer.

My sister swallowed five boxes worth of sleeping pills, that's how she died. It wasn't her first attempt; she had tried before. The first attempt had been when she was very young, a first year university student. My father said her nerves were bad. That she had inherited a weak nervous system from her unfortunate mother. There was, in the way my father pronounced the word *unfortunate*, unbounded contempt, lacking even a shred of pity. My mother, in her letters to my sister, tried to persuade her to see a psychologist, but my father shook his head, he was not willing to pay for any such humbug, the charlatan massaging of souls, as he put it. He always brushed off this idea if it came up, saying that psychology was a fraud business. Useless babbling and dissecting of things that were better left forgotten—that was his viewpoint.

It was as if Dr. Kreutzer were faintly smiling for a moment, but it's possible that I was imagining it. What I was telling him about my father certainly must have been irritating to him.

Later on, though, everything seemed to even out. My parents spoke to me less about this matter. When I visited my older sister in the clinic where she ended up dying, it was no longer possible to communicate with her. She just lay there, hooked up to the ventilation machine. She had been lying like this for weeks, until finally, at my father's request, they disconnected her. I stroked her arm, but it was as if I were stroking the arm of a stranger. A poor, sick, slightly repulsive stranger. I felt nothing, only the chill of her skin. Every resemblance between us had disappeared by that point. I could hardly absorb the knowledge that this unkempt woman lying there with a tortured face was my older sister. I knew that I was supposed to look sad, or at least something, maybe angry, but I could only keep thinking about when my train was leaving and getting to the station on time. The hospital was far away, and I had to make several transfers to get to my stop.

Dr. Kreutzer asked me if I knew exactly why she had killed herself.

Hermina, that was her name?

Yes, Mina. That's what we called her at home.

I think, I continued, that it had been because of a man. She had fallen in love with a married man who had a family. I'd seen a picture of the guy, he looked fairly unremarkable. But I knew that attraction was much more complicated. The guy had dark hair and a bumpy chin. His kids were in kindergarten, he didn't want to leave them for my sister. They broke up several times, but then they always got back together, as I found out from my father, according to whom this man was a spineless, insignificant person. This guy didn't even come to my sister's funeral. He didn't have the guts, he was too chicken to show himself in front of us, to show himself to the family, who by then comprised only of us. It's good that my mother didn't live to see this, at least not this. My father applied some emphasis on the word *family*, highlighting his own irony. My sister's lover was a family man. He cheated on his wife with her for years, even going on summer vacations, even skiing in the mountains, but he never acknowledged her openly. They could not be seen together, they never went to the movies, the theater, he never met her friends. Apart from going on hikes in distant locales, where they moved together like a couple, they were never seen together in public. It was painful to my sister, as I found out from my father, to be alone during weekdays. To my father, there was no point in mentioning that he was also around. She went shopping alone, she bought clothes alone, she wore them alone. In the end, three or four years had gone by, when this man had a serious falling out with his wife; finally he made a decision. He turned up at my sister's place with a sports bag, unpacked all his things and put them in the cupboard, but after only a few days he left and moved back home. According to my father, his lawyer had helped him calculate the eventual material loss in case of divorce, and he chickened out, nice and quietly. Because he was a coward, a nobody, said my father. A gutless coward.

I don't know what the truth was, but in any event, the guy really did go back to the mother of his children, even though by that point my older sister had bought a desk for him to put his stuff in. Supposedly it was then, namely because of his moving back, that Mina decided she'd had enough. By which I mean to say that she couldn't take it anymore. I don't even know. Maybe . . . it could be understood.

Dr. Kreutzer leaned forward in his armchair like someone who was very curious about this statement, someone who was hoping and expecting a lot from it. He asked me what could be understood.

Well, the fact that she'd had enough, I answered, and put down my tea cup. She wanted something, I don't even know what—maybe stability? Maybe a child too, at least I think so. She had almost run out of time, although she still could have given birth. She wasn't like me. Because I don't want to.

Dr. Kreutzer looked at my knee and stated that our session would soon be over. He sat in his armchair, the side of which was illuminated by the light streaming in from the outside walkway. Because of the orientation of his office, the sun shone in here every afternoon, the puddles of light reaching in as far as the middle of the carpet. The edge of the spotlight trembled next to his shoe. I looked at his chestnut-colored shoes. He always wore elegant shoes, and these seemed to be a very special pair. I usually don't notice things like this in men, but as we were sitting across from each other, and as he very frequently stretched out his legs, my eyes frequently strayed either to his shoes or his trousers. I knew the session was almost over. I observed how the hand of the clock was almost at the hour. The large, antique clock hung on the wall across from me, above the small commode with the samovar. I had no idea how he knew what time it was. I didn't see a wristwatch on his arm, although he must have been wearing one, covered by his sleeve cuff. I would have liked to conclude the session on a better note. I didn't want him to interrupt me again, so I thanked him for the tea, and, smoothing down my skirt, stood up. Maybe it would have been good if he had said that I should finish what I had started. If he would detain me.

When he accompanied me to the door, for a moment I had the feeling that I was taking leave of a dear acquaintance, not leaving an office. It went through me like a flash: maybe because of the money. I had not given him the money for today's session, and he didn't say anything, although he'd never forgotten to mention it before. He only asked when I would come the next time, Tuesday or Wednesday. I decided on Tuesday, because that was one of my research days when I didn't have to go into the university, but I still felt that I had to give myself time to think over everything that our conversation had brought to the surface.

Although I tried, I could not recall the name of that Hungarian Pointer at our summer house. I was simply incapable of remembering it! Although the name of the dog was right there on the tip of my tongue.

In the elevator, I wondered where my sudden pangs of conscience were coming from. Was it because of my sister, or perhaps the mention of children had stirred up some **deeply deposited, painful** layer within me? The elevator passed the second floor.

Perhaps, I reflected, it was because I had never wanted to give birth. I worried about my easygoing little marriage. I would never claim that it was some kind of fantastic and great union, but still, it was functional. The elevator passed the first floor, then reached the ground floor with a jolt.

My stomach began throbbing forcefully. No one was waiting on the ground floor, I saw through the fluted glass, so I discreetly reached under my skirt. I was right—my underwear was already bloodied. It'd been a shame to start talking about this topic of children because the issue was already resolved. I shoved a paper handkerchief into my underwear, then opened the elevator door. I'd been mistaken because somebody was waiting, standing a little bit off to the right, but they stepped into the elevator without so much as a glance at me. I'd stuck the paper handkerchief in clumsily, though, at the wrong angle, and it scratched against my thigh.

writhing in cold incandescence

Dr. Kreutzer tried many times to think through the disintegration of his relationship with Petra. What were the most important turning points in the path that led to the collapse of their marriage? They had always fought, even from the beginning, but they made love just as frequently, and it seemed not only had his wife not been disturbed by these occasionally dangerous extremes but that they also stimulated her, kept her excitement going. She certainly had not known about his relations with other women. When she was pregnant with Vilmos, some of his more fleeting connections came to light, but he'd been able to explain the situation away, attributing his missteps to his own anxiety and confusion. Since then, he was fastidious about never arranging any meetings from any home computer. Petra had access to his email, but she could only see official messages and those sent to common friends. Once, at dinner, she had suddenly asked him why he had so many young women patients. Dr. Kreutzer generally did not know if the ratio of female patients to the others was so great, where Petra got this idea from, or on what basis had she formulated this statistic: He only replied, with great self-possession, that in his own circle of acquaintances, the men had become fathers early on, then the civil war had broken out, which had negatively impacted so many of their teenage children—he hardly knew anyone who'd escaped this fate. Most of the children of this, his generation's cohort, ended up consulting mental health professionals, and for some reason, the women always had more trust in men. Well, that was why. It was not the thoroughness of his response that dissipated Petra's doubts, but rather the tranquility he emanated as he spoke. This tranquility had, at the time, saved their marriage for another few years, serving as a frequent resource to Dr. Kreutzer during such unexpected questions and attacks. His tranquility was that of a person with nothing to hide, someone who could never be called out for any reason whatsoever. And yet, in the early years of their marriage, their major arguments had not been caused by jealousy. One of these rows, every moment of which he could recall clearly, had caused a severe breach in their relationship, of that he was convinced.

 It was wintertime, and they were driving to a recently opened shopping center in one of the protected districts. The shop sold health-conscious items, and Petra wanted to buy chemical-free bath gel, cosmetics, and organic groceries. Senseless, expensive products. They had already dropped off the children at kindergarten. They went down to the underground garage of their apartment building. Petra got in the car first. He wiped off the dirty windshield and wondered why it seemed second nature to his wife to never assist him with this chore. She got into the car as if it were a taxi, waiting for him to drive off.

 One of the other residents of the building had, at the end of November, with the beginning of the frosts, taken in a cat, its eyes clouded with cataracts, setting up a small corner for it in the corner. It was a large, unwieldy creature; Petra thought that the cat was pregnant. It loved to climb onto the car hood until the car engine had cooled off. Ever since it had turned up here there were tiny paw prints on all the cars. Dr. Kreutzer had considered, several times, locking out the cat in the garden, let it go where it wanted, but whenever he went down to the car by himself, the cat never appeared, as if sensing the antipathy surging its way. But if he came down to the garage with Petra or the children, hardly had they stepped off the stairs, the cat immediately popped up, meowing and wrapping itself around his wife's legs. The children clapped, jumping up and down, asking when the kittens would be born, to which Dr. Kreutzer always replied certainly not anytime soon because this cat was not pregnant, only bloated. If Petra was there, she immediately contradicted him: The cat was obviously going to bear a litter any moment now. Of course the children began to plead, wriggling in the back seat of the car, demanding in high, enervating voices to be able to take in one kitten, let it be theirs. Dr. Kreutzer would ask the children if they had their seat belts on, if the circus was over yet, and he shut down the discussion by stating that there would never be any animals in their home, neither now nor at any other time.

Petra, however, had yearned for this for years. She was always making references to the children, sending her husband links to various newspaper articles about the importance, in personal development, of a close relationship to pets, as well as the beneficial effects on the people they lived with. Dr. Kreutzer either did not reply to these messages or he responded tersely that she shouldn't be trying this with him, this was his profession, and that animals did not belong in apartments. He considered a more drawn-out debate risky, although to be placed under this repeated pressure in his own home enraged him. We should be glad, he sometimes replied, that we live in the neighborhood we do. Petra gave up, but only seemingly. She kept searching the internet, looking at pictures of shelter animals or animals being given away for free, she had an entire folder full of pictures of various kittens and dogs. The shelters did try to save these animals because according to the new regulations patrols were allowed to shoot down any one of the numerous strays found in the street. Because of the high tax burdens imposed many people gave away their dogs to the shelters, although certain death awaited them there, as they were only kept for one week. Well-to-do adopters could choose between various dog breeds. Everyone was proud if they could rescue an animal.

There is a breed of cat, Petra read in one of these shelter announcements, whose hair never falls out. There are hunting dogs that truly love children, and as long as their needs for movement are satisfied, they are eminently trainable.

Petra was always reading these announcements. She regularly donated to animal protection societies, and once she took Vilmos to an open day, held in an outdoor museum somewhere in the suburbs. Of course, there were arguments following this visit because he wanted to bring home a little puppy that had been injured in an a car accident, and Petra told him he couldn't because Papa wouldn't allow it. They had just gotten home as Vilmos was calming down after a long bout of crying, and with a reproachful tone in his voice, he repeated to his father that it was his fault that the three-legged little puppy had to remain all alone, an orphan, at the shelter. And no one was going to take that puppy home, he whimpered, because poor people couldn't afford to feed it and rich people didn't need it. And the poor little puppy would be put to sleep. Or would be eaten! He'd heard about it on TV. Vilmos began sniffling again as a long, green strip of mucus dripped out of his nose, all the while eyeing his father with hatred. Dr. Kreutzer had just arrived home with Emmácska from ballet school where he was supposed to sign her up for a class that met twice per week, but the pretty ballet instructor said she was too short.

That day, for the second time, he felt that his competence as a parent was being called into question. They were ganging up on him, and not only that: blaming him for something for which he wasn't responsible. First, he calmly reminded Petra that he had never wanted any pets in the apartment, that they had discussed this already, that there was no point in bringing it up again and again, and especially not when they were talking about a crippled mutt from one of the poor districts, something that concerned neither Petra, Vilmos, nor him. He breathed deeply, raising his voice even higher, and emphatically repeated that there was no place for an animal here in this bloody fucking apartment, then he added, already yelling that this was his apartment, he was the one who had pulled strings to get it, he was the one doing the bloody difficult work of keeping the family here. It was as if Petra were waiting just for this: She left the kitchen, her eyes welling up with tears. She ushered Emma, still resplendent in her tutu, into the bathroom for her bath. Vilmos was offended and silent, as always when he sensed the chasm between his parents, that dark, uncertain terrain, where, in his despair, he could end up at any time, in any one of pain's manifold disguises. Sunken into self-pity, he sat on the kitchen chair, not even touching his dinner.

Well, of course it made him short-tempered when the children kept pestering him about the cat. He cleaned off the windshield and got into the car. He asked Petra to repeat the address of the shop they were headed to. He entered it into the GPS, then they pulled out into the winter cold. He wanted to avoid the chaotic city districts. Outside, there was a sudden, enormous brilliance, the ice frozen on the tree branches. Dr. Kreutzer proceeded slowly and cautiously down the iced-over, sloping street. He turned to the right, heading toward the large intersection. Then he suddenly heard a strange sound, precisely like a tiny squeak. He listened intently. Petra wasn't paying attention because she'd immediately put on her earphones when she got in the car, as if wishing to place this music between the two of them, signaling that, even together in this confined space, she had no desire to talk to him. The car had been serviced not too long ago, so it couldn't be the fan belt. He listened with knit brows, concentrating on the concordance of the engine's thousandfold minor clatter, its creaking, buzzing, and metallic throbbing sounds, but he did not hear the strange, unhabitual squeak again. Petra glanced at him, and, seeing his face, took out one of her earphones. She asked what was going on. Dr. Kreutzer, glancing into the rearview mirror, said nothing, only that the engine was acting up, something was making a creaking noise. They slowed down at the intersection, waiting to turn. Nobody was letting them through. Dr. Kreutzer attributed this to their having too good a car. This was a recurring train of thought if they were hurrying somewhere, and they were held up by traffic. Theirs was a good car: not so expensive as to endow it with a kind of aggressive prestige, and yet expensive enough to elicit the same amount of immediate, vehement antipathy as did a government license plate. The other light turned red, the incoming traffic stopped. At last they could make their turn. For a second, it was as if he had heard the squeak again, but just enough for him to feel disquieted. He registered it, the sound passed through to some inner lane. The light turned green, the line of cars surged ahead. Suddenly he heard it again, this time with unmistakable strength, now easily identifiable. It was repeating, stubbornly and rhythmically. This was no creaking sound, but a living voice—meowing. It grew louder, with nearly mechanical rhythm, at a high frequency, transforming into an ever more desperate shrieking, multiplying like a round of cannon shots. Petra leaned forward in her seat, her back straight, her face pale. Dr. Kreutzer tried not to notice what Petra understood. He changed lanes, sped up a bit. Petra asked him in a dry voice to stop the car immediately. Dr. Kreutzer answered that surely she could see for herself, he couldn't stop here. Petra began to yell that he could stop anywhere, he should put on his hazard lights now, immediately. In the middle of her sentence she ran out of breath, her lips merely mouthing the word *immediately*. Dr. Kreutzer once again answered that he couldn't stop here, there could be a collision, a pileup, he couldn't suddenly brake on a three-lane road, he would stop as soon as he had a chance. Petra unbuckled her seat belt, and said that if he didn't stop the car right now, she would get out and throw herself in front of the vehicle. Dr. Kreutzer managed to fan the flames by telling Petra that she was being hysterical, irrational. The meowing could be heard ever more clearly. Now there could be no doubt as to the source of this sound, even the most resolute self-deception could not think it a faulty car part. But now, it was as if the meowing had quieted a bit. They kept on driving, Petra began crying soundlessly, and in a faint voice, kept repeating stop, stop, like someone who herself didn't believe it was going to happen, as if this catatonic entreaty were merely the recognition of how she could do nothing at all.

Finally, a few minutes later, they turned off the roadside exit. A woman who was brushing the snow off the cedar trees in her garden with a broomstick stepped a little farther away from the cover of a stone fence to see if they were headed to her house or if it was a government car parking outside. She walked with small, careful steps across the slushy stone pavement in her rubber slippers and thick socks. Dr. Kreutzer motioned that they were not headed toward her driveway, they only had a problem with the car; he pointed at the street and then hurried over to the engine.

Petra sunk back into her seat. She sat there in the cold without a hat, her mouth white, her arms tightly crossed together. Dr. Kreutzer leaned over the engine, evaporating steam, and he began to yell in rage:

Fuck it, fuck it. It gave birth to the kittens here.

They never got to the shopping center. Petra stood in the cold, her tears freezing white on her face. She took the bus home while

Dr. Kreutzer drove to the repair shop to get the entire damned motor cleaned out.

no one liked it, we just got used to it

We didn't stay too long in that apartment, I told Dr. Kreutzer. After the divorce, my mother got rid of all the things my father had left there and tried to rearrange the rooms for two people, so that she wouldn't always have to think about Mina.

Have I told you how my sister ended up with the name Hermina?

He shook his head, and I suddenly had a feeling that he wasn't paying attention to what I was saying but staring at my mouth. It was a little bit as if . . . I don't even know, as if he were sizing me up. His gaze made me feel discomfited, and so I asked:

I really didn't tell you the story of how we got such strange names?

At the time, my father's parents lived in a part of the city that had since greatly deteriorated and was eventually closed off completely. I remember my grandparent's apartment from my childhood. It had large, floor-to-ceiling curtains and yellowing, creaking parquet floors. My parents had been married for two years, but they had not yet had any children. My father always talked about how they were working on it, but nothing happened. Then he took my mother to his parents' apartment when my grandparents were not there. Supposedly there my parents felt, if not like a married couple, then at least something like young lovers. As if they were meeting in secret. They went to my father's old room, and . . . well, it was then that my father got my mother pregnant, or at least, that's what he said. Apparently I too was conceived in that apartment—not just my sister. It excited my father, the thought that his parents could walk in on them at any time, and so it worked out better for him there than at home. His erection was harder.

Dr. Kreutzer leaned forward slightly in his armchair.

This is what your father told you? Both of you? How he got your mother pregnant?

Yes.

When we were children he told the story frequently, not just to us, but to others, to guests in the house. But of course we heard it, and we heard how we got our names. They were the names of two wide streets right next to our apartment building. My older sister was born two years before me . . . that's how she became Mina, short for Hermina.

Is it possible to know whose idea this was? Your father's? Dr. Kreutzer asked.

The name? Our names? Meaning, who came up with these names? You don't like it either, right? I asked.

It was our father who came up with our names. In the end, it was his belief that he was the one who had made us. He always repeated that. Apparently my mother had no ideas for names, and so when she asked him, my father thought it would be funny to give us street names. He mentioned it frequently in company, that was how his girls got their names, his **little street girls**; this anecdote of his always reaped great success. He sat in his armchair, smoking his pipe, laughing shrilly at his own joke. The others liked to hear it too. Nobody ever told him that it wasn't funny, that it was denigrating. My mother was horrifically modest. She would sit there in embarrassed silence, or she used some pretext to run out of the room, to make coffee, slice pastries.

For a long time, I felt dreadfully ashamed of my name. During my entire childhood, especially in elementary school. Everyone called my sister by her nickname; the name Mina was charming. My name was Gizella, and so my nickname was Gizi. Gizi! It sounded like an old lady's name. Anyone named Gizi was automatically an old woman with swollen legs. And ugly. Anyone named Gizi could not be beautiful, could not be pretty. Perhaps if they had not named me Gizi, everything—my entire life—would have worked out differently. I don't know. In university, for a while I asked everyone to call me the French version, Giselle, instead. It was idiotic, of course, I don't even know one word of French, but still I insisted on being called Giselle. I wanted to be freed of this Gizi. From all and every Giziness. As if my being had a different side, I don't know . . . a lighter side, more alive, one my mother didn't even know about. She always called me Gizush, which was even more ghastly than Gizi, if that was even possible. I couldn't get her to stop.

My dear little Gizush, she would say. Horrifying, no?

She always spoke a great deal to me when we were alone. It was as if I wasn't even her child, but a sympathetic, grown-up female relative. I don't know if she was speaking to me or just to herself, albeit in my presence. In any event, she never expected a reply, she just said what she had to say, for hours on end, softly, obsessively. She kept rearranging the furniture, pushing the two armchairs here and there, she packed things away, hammered nails. Nothing stood in its old, customary place. Things will be good like this here, my little Gizush. Look, Gizush, I stored the plates here. Whoever came to visit us during that time had to take something that had been left by our father. All of our friends were tasked with this chore. One of my mother's coworkers brought a large jute sack and said to her, just stuff it full with everything you don't need, my dear, I'll take care of it, I'll take it away somewhere. I remember as well how I fell asleep on the sofa, then startled awake in complete darkness, the cold streaming in from somewhere. My mother, as if in some dream, stood by the open window, tossing a suitcase out. It landed on the ground with a huge thump; somewhere else a window opened, someone turned on a light. Even today, this entire, incomprehensible scene is clearly before me.

It was evening, no one was outside on the street. But still, that piece of luggage could have hit someone, no? A late-night dog walker. As a child, I didn't find this unusual or feel anything frightening about it. I accepted everything as it happened. My mother looked back at me in the darkness, but she uttered not one word, she just stepped away and got into bed. She acted as if she had simply been airing out the room. Only that there was a strange look of determination on her face.

It was always chilly in that apartment. We slept in prickly, knitted sweaters under heavy comforters. We even used a sweater left behind by my father, which reeked of pipe smoke. After the first winter like this, my mother realized that we couldn't stay there any longer. She had to sell the flat because she couldn't afford the utilities.

From there, from that old apartment building, we moved into a prefab apartment not heated by convectors but by central heating. My mother had been longing for this because she imagined that central heating would solve all of her problems. Our new apartment was on the eighth floor. The floors were indicated with Roman numerals in the stairwell, so that at the age of six, even before I could read, I knew my Roman numerals. I remember a few pieces of furniture from the old apartment that did not come with us. My mother must have sold them. They did not fit into the new, narrow rooms.

Dr. Kreutzer asked how the move had affected me and if I had stayed in touch with my father and sister.

I answered that I hadn't. We didn't really keep up any connection, as I already mentioned. We just sent and received postcards occasionally, sometimes we exchanged photographs. In those first years, my mother cried because she could not meet up with my sister. My father and sister, I don't remember exactly when, moved abroad; my father found work there. It would be difficult to visit them, he said, and anyway, Mina was going to have a new Mum.

A new Mum?

Yes, that's what he said.

Dr. Kreutzer asked me again how the move itself had affected me. How had I, as a child, experienced this period of their divorce? I replied that I hadn't experienced it at all. I had liked the old apartment, and the new, smaller one pleased me as well. I had no particular problems with either. I was only sad that we couldn't have a dog. Nothing else seemed to matter.

Of course, I missed my sister. Not very much, but a little bit. Mainly at first, and mainly in the evening.

It bothered me that I had to repeat what I'd already said. I would have liked for him to pay more attention to me. He was making very few notes during the session, but still the leather-bound notebook rested on his lap.

I would have liked to make him understand that the current reputation of that city district where I had grown up had nothing to do with my childhood, when we saw the huge housing estate completely differently. Many people wanted to move directly there because at that time it had everything. There was hot running water, there were shops and schools. Today, people puckered their lips upon hearing the name of that district. The rubber seals were coming loose from the cracks in the crumbling outer walls of the modular slab blocks, and if the wind was blowing, the long black ribbons struck the sides of the grey, gigantic buildings like whips. Once corroded by the rain, sun, and wind, they fell off in strips, laying on the concrete sidewalk, tangled together like burnt snake carcasses. Many apartments were empty now, the glass in the windows broken. The central heating no longer worked, and although in other districts, more and more people clustered under tents, sheltering beneath their own doorways after losing their homes, practically no one wanted to move to the big prefab housing estate anymore because of the broken elevators, the rat colonies, the unpredictable public transport, the closed shops. The only people who remained there were those who had been born there, who couldn't escape. Or those who had withdrawn here temporarily, into this hopelessly vacant, decrepit, ever more deserted concrete jungle. But in my childhood it was a functioning city district, full of shops and schools proudly festooned with flags. I can still see the parks, the water sprinklers, the fountains. How the sidewalks were neatly swept. We whizzed all around on our roller skates. The restaurants and the pharmacies were open for business.

I had friends there. On every floor there lived a kid who could be invited down to the playground. We would ring the bell, and their parents would either let them come with us, or not, in which case we went on, from floor to floor, trying another apartment. After a few weeks, my mother knew everyone in the building. She knew whom to ask if there was a hole in the wall, and whom to ask if she didn't have time to go to the market hall. Sometimes she sent me to a neighbor with money, to ask them to buy vegetables for us.

Really, the micro district had everything. Everything that you could only get in the government districts today. Maybe not of the same quality, but still, we had everything we needed.

Dr. Kreutzer looked at me with an unusual expression, his head slightly bent to the side, eyes narrowed. I had the feeling that he was not concentrating on what I had said, but on me, how I shifted my legs in the chair. I changed my position slightly, then I continued.

I wanted to explain to him that I had genuinely found that enormous housing estate beautiful. At night, we could see, far into the distance from our windows, as far as the low mountain range across from our neighborhood. Beneath the kitchen window, there was a folding table, and over the course of the years I often watched as the lights of the tower blocks were turned on, one after the other. The many windows were illuminated as if the entire district were garlanded in decorative lighting. I also liked, in the evenings, to look up from the sidewalk to the windows of our building because I immediately could see who was home, who I could play with for an hour. The playground was directly behind our building. You went down the concrete slide straight into the sandbox. Even today, I remember the warmth of the concrete. In the summer, it was almost baking. We had to fold our skirts underneath, using them to slide on because the concrete was already battered, you couldn't glide down properly on it.

As I said this, I suddenly felt embarrassed. I think I also turned red. It's awkward, if someone blushes at my age, it's hard to know what to do. I fell silent. I waited for him to say something, but he was holding his fountain pen, nodding attentively.

On the far wall there was a new picture in a dark frame. It had just turned up here recently. It was a portrait of a repulsive-looking monkey with a troubled gaze. At least, to me the monkey seemed troubled, as well as ill. It hadn't been there before. I certainly would have noticed it. I can't stand monkeys, they are somehow like hairy little children who are always clinging to you and making faces.

Suddenly, his sympathetic nodding came to an end. He had noticed me staring at the photograph. I said that it seemed that picture hadn't been there before, and he agreed, smiling, as he said, he had just put it up yesterday. The monkey in the photograph had been part of a famous experiment, he gestured quickly toward the back, and he'd had this photograph for a very long time. He had framed it at the beginning of his career, and it had hung above his desk in his very first workplace. I also asked about the colorful child's drawing, in which a whale was spouting water from its back. He replied that his young son had drawn it. I didn't know that he had children, I answered.

He must have noticed, as I did, how similar this statement was to what he had said about my older sister. That he hadn't known that I had a sister. It must have occurred to him, because he suddenly shifted in his chair, put down the notebook on the small table, and coughed.

I was really surprised. Not as if I had anything to do with his personal life. Only that . . . he seemed so independent and free. Of course, I couldn't really put it that way. But that's what I was thinking.

Two, he mumbled. I have two kids.

When we got to the end of the session, I mentioned that I'd seen the boy again. He was standing around in the park next to the New University, waiting for me. Dr. Kreutzer asked if I was still afraid of him, to which I replied that of course I was afraid, because he seemed deeply troubled. Who wouldn't be afraid of being followed by a lunatic on the street?

I wouldn't, he said, smiling.

fraying in several places

At the bottom of the cupboard there were dead moths and dust mice. He had already filled three sacks with clothes, but Dr. Kreutzer realized that he was not going to be able to empty his mother's apartment by himself. He placed the piles of bags of ancient bras, never-used towels, old postcards, onto the double bed. At first, he thought that he would collect any item he deemed useful in one corner, and he would take the rest to some charitable organization in one of the poor districts, but as his patience grew thin, he began cramming everything almost indiscriminately into the black garbage bags.

He came across old pastry boxes crammed with photographs. As soon as he opened the top of the box, the pictures came pouring out. There seemed to be no logic or system as to which boxes held which pictures. He dumped it all onto the floor and sat on a pillow next to the pile of photographs. He only had time until 11:30 a.m., when he had a consultation scheduled with one of the Regent's men. He had been entrusted with a sensitive and important task, and the details had to be worked out. He could not be late, and so he set his phone to remind him to leave on time.

He made a rule for himself: if he couldn't identify who was in the picture, he would toss it. He would look over the remaining photographs some other time, truly not all of them needed to be saved. Wedding ceremonies of distant relatives, various excursions, memories of tourist bus trips. His mother, who had remained alone, was accustomed to such outings. She kept going on these two- or three-day bus trips to various cities even at a relatively late age, until the civil war had broken out. After the civil war, no one could go abroad.

An unknown, bearded man—into the garbage. Plump twins in overalls, no idea who they were—into the garbage. Newspaper clippings, a six-hectare oak forest devastated by pests introduced from abroad—into the garbage. Why had his mother clipped that article? he wondered. Perhaps there was some kind of system among these boxes, after all, because in the second, dumped-out pile of photographs he found a conspicuous number of pictures of his younger brother, who had died suddenly from meningitis at the age of nine. So quickly that he'd hardly been able to grasp it. If he thought back on those weeks, even today, his strongest feeling was one of surprise. It was December, snowing, Öcsi wasn't home yet, but expected back any minute from school.

On that long ago, dark afternoon, his younger brother stepped through the door, saying he had to lie down immediately, he didn't feel well. He didn't clatter the lid of the mail slot as he always did when he got home, he just walked in and threw down his schoolbag. His hair and forehead were full of slush because on the way home he'd rubbed the snow on his throbbing head. It was Thursday. The day before, he'd made Christmas tree decorations from salt dough in the craft circle and brought them home in a paper box. He'd taken the box out of his schoolbag and placed it on the kitchen table, carefully arranging the salt-dough decorations on the radiator, putting his gloves next to them to dry. **Pine trees, squirrels, little birds**, they were childish efforts. He put them on the radiator, because their insides had not completely dried out. He had formed them the day before, but the backsides were still doughy, soft. Dr. Kreutzer remembered that he had, out of curiosity, pressed down on the lower part of a squirrel, pinched off a small piece of the salt dough and ate it. All the while smirking as he said: *mmm*, this squirrel meat isn't too bad. Normally his younger brother would have torn into him, but he just gazed at him blankly, as if he didn't care. He turned on his heels, tottered into their room with wobbling steps, and fell down onto the bed. He covered his head with the pillow, pulled up his knees, and never spoke another word again. His older brother didn't really bother with him, he was happy to be left alone. He was just then putting together a model plane, a fighter jet. He kept it for a long time after, it stood on the shelf in his room and it always made him think of his younger brother, that winter afternoon.

With his tongue sticking out, using tweezers, he assembled all the tiny pieces, checking the illustration on the back of the box to make sure that everything was in the right place. He was hunched over the table, and so he only saw, out of the corner of his eye, that Öcsi stumbled out of the bedroom. He heard him throwing up, then flushing the toilet. Öcsi went to the bathroom to vomit one more time as his older brother was placing the stickers **carefully onto the wings**. One of them got stuck on crooked.

His parents got home only late in the afternoon; it was already dark. In the building across the way the lights had already been turned on, its residents rummaging around in the lamplight of their apartments. First, his father came in. He wiped the soles of his shoes several times on the doormat in the hallway, a cold draft coming in, as he called out, Hello, it's me. Mihály knew that it was him, you could hear it from how he closed the door. His father never waited for the door to close by himself, but instead energetically pushed it back, making the entire metal frame shake. Not long after, his mother came running in with her usual string shopping bags, stuffed full. His parents packed everything into the fridge, passing the wax paper packages to each other like masons handing each other bricks. He stood in the kitchen door, and told them that Öcsi wasn't feeling well. They went into the children's room, asked Öcsi what was hurting, and took his temperature. Öcsi had a slight fever, but it didn't seem too serious, so they gave him something to bring it down. He kept complaining, though, beneath the blanket, that his head hurt, and he felt dizzy. His mother placed a cold compress on his forehead, and they all went to sleep.

He awoke to the realization that his younger brother had vomited all over the bed. The light was on, his mother was trying to remove the bed linens with cautious movements, not to smear the mess everywhere, his father was trying to reach the emergency service, futilely. They circled around nervously, phone in hand, dialing the number again and again. They handed his younger brother some clothes so he could get dressed, but they only managed to pull off his pajama top when he simply lay down in front of the bed, on the parquet floor, and, supporting his head on his elbows, knees drawn up, began to doze off. His father, irritated, grabbed him by the arm, pushing his trousers into his hands. Later, before his own death, he confessed his regret for this gesture several times, but at that time, all he cared about was getting a taxi to come as soon as possible, and Öcsi was still collapsed on the floor in his striped pajamas.

Mishike, said his mother as she leaned over his bed, you'll be a clever boy tomorrow, won't you, and get up nicely for school if I have to stay in the hospital, she said. He nodded, squinting; the light overhead was hurting his eyes. His father quickly got dressed, pulling on his signet ring, and they ran down to the front of the building.

Dr. Kreutzer never saw his younger brother again. He died in the hospital the next day at dawn. It was December 21. They still had the Christmas tree, so they put it up on Christmas Eve, but only Öcsi's salt-dough decorations hung on it, nothing else, not the usual ball ornaments, the snowman, or the glass elves with peaked caps. His mother cried all day. They did not give him his Christmas present, the remote control car, even though he knew that it was hidden in the bottom of the clothes cupboard. Although now, he didn't have to worry about his younger brother trailing after him, constantly trying to take it away. Because somehow Öcsi always had liked his presents better than his own, and this had always led to arguments and fistfights.

The funeral was at the beginning of January. It was so cold that his eyes teared up from the cold. They went to the cemetery by tram, he and his mother. His father had left earlier, carrying the enormous, preordered wreath with its blue ribbon. At the funeral, unknown relatives came over to him and kept hugging him. He felt like he was suffocating, wrapped up tightly in a large woolen winter coat. He followed his parents obediently to the morgue, where the child's coffin stood, covered in flowers. The red-nosed priest with bad teeth patted his face and told him that he would find consolation in God, upon which he nodded compliantly, then he stood between his parents shivering in his fancy shoes that left his ankles uncovered. Why had his parents insisted on him wearing those fancy black shoes in the snow when he normally wore them only for school celebrations? Why hadn't they dressed him better for the weather—why hadn't they dressed him in winter boots?

From that point on, there were no more Christmas trees in Dr. Kreutzer's family. His father lived for nine more years, but it was as if he remained with them—in the world, in the city, in their apartment—among these completely uninteresting beings out of sheer courtesy. So that he would not cause any new suffering to the people he loved. He never laughed again, at most occasionally smiling, but only a modest smile, fleetingly, as if he had realized that this was somehow improper. Within a few years, his meticulous, necktie-wearing father had aged into a corpulent old man in cardigans, who mused the entire day or listened to the radio if it wasn't raining, stuffing ragged handkerchiefs into the stretched-out pockets of his cardigan sweaters. His hair fell out, with only a few puffs of grey on either side, which he always had cut with scissors that were too large, and so he paced up and down in the apartment in this untidy state. One of Dr. Kreutzer's classmates, who often visited them, put it very succinctly when he said that Mishi's father was a koala bear.

they had no light whatsoever

After that Christmas, old Auntie Pálma always dressed in black for the holidays, weeping for days with a steady tempo. This lasted until Mishi told her that if he was going to bring the grandchildren here to give her presents, she had to dress normally, at least for a couple of hours, and put on garments that were not mourning clothes, to try to act like a normal grandmother because the little ones needed this. His mother, dumbfounded, blinked at him with her reddened, baggy eyes and stopped crying for a while. Suddenly it seemed as if she herself were relieved: After so many years she no longer needed to play the part of the broken mother, but she was not able to fill this suddenly open vacancy with any appropriate gestures. Over the years she had simply gotten used to her own Christmas rituals. Now, however, she stood there in a blue dress next to the gifting chair, and she had no idea how to act. In her house, the gifts were not placed beneath the tree because there was no tree, but placed underneath this so-called gifting chair. This particular piece of furniture was a heavy, velvet-upholstered armchair, inherited from her legendary, strapping, mustachioed great-grandfather. This chair had gained this function after they had stopped putting up Christmas trees, that is to say, after Öcsi's death. On family birthdays or name days, the receiver of gifts, most often grandma Pálma herself, sat in this chair. Mishi, Petra, and the children would stand in front of the unwieldy, throne-like chair, a ritual that, later on, Petra was not inclined to repeat. At Christmas time, the packages were slipped underneath the chair, and from there, with feigned excitement, they were pulled out one by one by the family . The same decorative gift bags had been used in rotation for years, if someone had really wanted to, they could trace their appearance in the family photographs, for example, if Petra and her husband had just given or received their yearly surprise in the striped-silver, gold-spotted bag with a pattern of pine trees. Although it was worse when grandma Pálma could not find a suitable wrapping. She would present the chocolate with meandering explanations, for example, that Vilmos was getting his present in this pretty little bag with a tiger on it so that one day he too would be as strong as a tiger.

On one occasion, when little Emma—who already knew how to walk—had, in her boredom, climbed underneath the gifting chair, she crawled out with enormous dust balls and strands of hair stuck to her clothes. Her glittery white top was filthy, her palms grey from the accumulated dust. Dr. Kreutzer and his wife exchanged glances, he could tell from his wife's gaze that she was holding herself back, but that she could have a word or two to say to her mother-in-law, all too happy to run down the other residents in the building—she called them grimy proles—even though she hardly ever cleaned herself, or only randomly and partially. Old Auntie Pálma would wipe off the windowsill because she had gotten a new potted plant. She shook the tablecloth out the window maybe once a year before Easter, constrainedly, then, tottering on a wobbly wooden ladder, took down the curtains and laundered them. Then she would have her girlfriends and her son come round so she could tell the story of how she'd almost fallen, risking her life, but now everything was fine, the curtains had been rehung. They were brilliant with fragrance, she announced. She loved this phrase, perhaps she'd heard it in an ad somewhere. Although she never scrubbed the toilet, the sink, or the bath, as if such menial tasks might implicate, unreasonably, the potential soiling of the sanitary facilities of a gentlewoman such as herself. The thought came to Dr. Kreutzer—glimpsing his little daughter's top, covered in dust mice—of hiring a cleaning lady for his mother. He had to find someone because every glass, every eating utensil was sticky with grease. The window panes were opalescent. At the very least someone would be looking in after his mother. A paid cleaner could also stop by if his mother wasn't taking his calls; he wouldn't have to come running here from the other side of the city.

In the office where he worked at the time, one of his colleagues was looking for work for one of his patients, who had been removed from care and was more or less cured. She still showed up from time to time to recount the tortures of her reentry into the world, for example, if she'd been able to top off her phone card, or if she needed help in doing so.

That's all I need, for some idiot to show up here from the poor quarter, his mother cackled.

After the winter break, Dr. Kreutzer called his former colleague to ask if his patient—the one who was supposedly cured of her nutritional issues—was still looking for work because, as it happened, he knew someone who needed a cleaning lady. His colleague was very happy, praising Dr. Kreutzer to the skies for his helpfulness, and secretly hoped that the woman would stop calling him whenever she was overcome by feelings of despair.

On the phone, her voice sounded very young at first, but the painful indirectness with which she agreed upon the time of day, the duration, and her hours suggested to Dr. Kreutzer that not all was completely well with this woman. After many calls back-and-forth and after rescheduling several times, she showed up at his workplace to discuss the details of the job and her wage. Dr. Kreutzer saw a woman in her fifties with pockmarked skin walk into his office. Not only did she seem uncured, but he found it hard to imagine her lifting a bucket filled with water. She was wearing jeans and a bomber jacket not suited for her age. She had left her bicycle outside on the sidewalk and jumped up several times from her tightly coiled position in the middle of their conversation to nervously glance outside, even though the bike was chained up.

The skin on her neck was sagging, her arms and hands were as if she had pulled on feathery, pale gloves several sizes too large. As she leaned out the window, Dr. Kreutzer looked at her loose-fitting trousers, and he saw that this woman barely had an ass. Where her buttocks should have been rounded out there seemed to be no flesh at all. Beneath her trousers, there was merely a bisected, triangular indentation. The woman claimed that she was fine, indicating how she rode her bike everywhere, and even if her problems were all not completely squared away, she still kept them "in hand." She showed him her clenched, wrinkled little fist, which somehow made it look even more shriveled. I'm in charge of my own life, she regurgitated, her gaze passing over the walls of his office.

Is the cleaning job here? she asked.

Dr. Kreutzer shook his head. He mentioned, dispassionately, his mother's name and the square meterage of the apartment. He said nothing about the moths, the dirt accumulated over decades, the greasy grime stuck to the edge of the bath, the sticky tableware. This woman, Erika, cleaned as no one else did before. In the past, other cleaning ladies had been hired to come to old Auntie Pálma's apartment, but after one or two visits they were fired, either because his mother sensed that they were **rummaging through her things**, looking for jewelry and other valuables, sniffing around and stealing, or because she could not stand their presence, but did not dare leave them alone. Supposedly one of them smelled overwhelmingly of perspiration, like meat broth gone bad, another wouldn't stop talking or singing obsessively, the third one looked up and asked why there were six lightbulbs in the six-armed chandelier when two were more than enough to light up the room.

Dr. Kreutzer had tried to prepare his mother for this new cleaning lady, who was, in contrast to the others, surprisingly scrawny, but despite her appearance, worked very hard. Yes, she was honest, she didn't steal. Old Auntie Pálma didn't care if she was fat or thin, but when she saw Erika for the first time, she was surprised, and took her bomber jacket from her as if afraid Erika might drop it.

Erika cleaned Dr. Kreutzer's mother's apartment with fastidious passion. She wiped off the tile edges and the picture frames, cleaned behind the cupboards, the vacuum hose penetrating into cavities that had been not touched by anyone for at least twenty years. She wiped off the plastic slats of the bathroom ventilation shaft. She ironed the old, stained tea towels, humming as she soaked them before washing. She descaled the iron. While she worked, she uttered not a word. She didn't tell stories, didn't croon to herself, she didn't listen to the radio, to which old Auntie Pálma was particularly allergic, and she didn't waste time puttering about. She didn't keep on making phone calls like the previous one. Later, it turned out that she couldn't anyway because for months now she'd no money to pay up her cell phone credit; her daughter had to call her if worried about her. Old Auntie Pálma observed the girlishness of her gaze and even offered her coffee, which she had never done for any other cleaner. It's true, she didn't pour the coffee into the porcelain cups from the expensive set but instead the ones decorated with little hearts, of which she had two, one for each grandchild when they came to visit. Erika downed her coffee resolutely, eyes closed, then reassured herself that one cup of coffee was only 2.7 calories, containing altogether 0.5 grams of carbohydrates. Old Auntie Pálma thought the coffee had cooled off and that's why Erika drank it up so quickly.

When it was time to clean the fridge, Erika sniffed every open jar and every bag with suspicious content, checking the sell-by dates and shaking her withered, small head, concluded that this old auntie was eating very unhealthily. She threw out, one by one, the moldy cheese ends, the withered lemons, the shriveled tomatoes, and the rancid nut substitute gumming up in the bag.

One time, on a regular cleaning day, when Erika had not shown up by 9 a.m., and then not even by 9:30 a.m., old Auntie Pálma called her son in rage. She hadn't been careful enough, she sputtered, and look, once again she'd been duped. What she had feared so much had come to pass—Erika had disappeared. She vanished into thin air, clearly taking some valuables with herself, Papa's old signet ring, maybe even a brooch. Old Auntie Pálma kept asserting, in an ever louder voice, that she had certainly stolen something, and now, when they didn't even know Erika's registered address, it would be difficult to apprehend her. She had always sensed there would be a problem, her instincts had warned her. I felt it here, inside, she pointed at her chest beneath her flower-patterned housecoat, but of course her son could not see this on the telephone.

That morning, Erika could not be reached, and she only picked up the phone when Dr. Kreutzer called her from an unknown landline number in his office at around noon. Erika only said, in a tired voice, she was very sorry, it was windy outside. Dr. Kreutzer, with a bit of an edge in his voice, replied that people usually want to work even when it was windy, and there had been no hurricanes or tornadoes. No, Erika conceded, there had been no hurricanes. And not even any tornadoes, she sighed. Dr. Kreutzer waited for her to finish the thought, as if the woman breathing heavily at the other end of the line were sitting in his office, and he calculated well, because he soon got an explanation. The woman, who always used her grown daughter's bicycle because she did not wish to spend money on tram tickets, could simply not go out onto the street in such weather with her bike.

I'll flip over in this strong wind, don't you understand? she explained.

Dr. Kreutzer thought of his mother's apartment, the armchairs, their upholstery restored to their original splendor, the newly washed throw pillow covers. He suggested to the woman that he could pick her up and drive her to his mother's house, then, in the early afternoon, before dropping off Emma at kindergarten gymnastics, he could take her home.

He was parked on the narrow side street at seven thirty on Tuesday. He had always hated these inner-city apartment blocks, sidewalks covered with dog shit, and now, that the northern districts had become so dangerous, he decidedly tried to avoid these neighborhoods. Erika lived in a smaller, disintegrating block of flats that smelled like saltpeter. She stepped out the front door in a red cap and gloves; from a distance, she looked like a teenager. As she got into his car, her wrinkles were **visible from up close**, the dark rings beneath her eyes.

When they got to his mother's house, old Auntie Pálma, avoiding Erika's gaze, loudly announced that she was going down to the market, then she asked her son to supervise the cleaner's work in the meantime. She would only be gone an hour, she said, hobbling outside. She greeted Erika superciliously as she passed her, then from the front door, she called back, saying that not only did the kitchen cupboards have to be washed out, but also the dustbin itself, if Erika could be so kind, because she always forgot to do this.

Erika nodded, then went into the bathroom to change her clothes. She returned in neon leggings and a stretched-out T-shirt. She saw the look of astonishment on Dr. Kreutzer's face and began to explain that this had been her daughter's long since outgrown running outfit.

She bent over, wiped things down, put the chairs on top of the table, and panting, rolled up the carpet. She walked over to the window to shake out the smaller carpets. As she stood with her back to him, a rag in her hand, she seemed like a little girl enthusiastically pretending to be a grown-up woman cleaning house. Dr. Kreutzer stepped behind her. Erika sensed his presence and froze in place.

Dr. Kreutzer didn't want anything particular from her, only to signal, with a minute gesture, that despite the clearly visible symptoms of her illness, he still saw her as a woman. And in any event, he had to be back in his office by ten.

The fact that things worked out as they did had nothing to do with him. They stumbled clumsily into the hallway, and when, having reached the small back room, the woman took off her clothes, Dr. Kreutzer needed all the imaginative powers of his sexual routines to maintain his erection. He penetrated her with closed eyes, turning his head to one side so as not to sense the sweetish, tepid smell coming from her mouth. After, he lay there next to this mummy-like woman who resembled a terminal cancer patient or, even more repulsively, a body exhumed from the grave. Her skin, woven through with paper-thin lilac veins creased and wrinkled in the bends of her body, in places culminating in scaly, dry folds, as if her skin were piece of clothing, an utmost layer which she would cast off only in well-deserved, celebratory moments.

As she stretched out on the sofa, one wrinkled breast hung down to one side like an empty sack. The outlines of her ribs were clearly visible, her hip bones nearly popped out of her skin. Lying down, pressed up against the wall, Dr. Kreutzer saw, above the withered breast, Öcsi's old teddy bear, sitting in its usual place, its amber glass eyes indifferently seeing the two people, ill at ease and somewhat embarrassed, resting next to each other. It was hard to think of something to say. Dr. Kreutzer felt like an idiot, just as when he had bumped into Vilmos's homeroom teacher on the nudist beach and they discussed the child's marks for effort as he stared at the conspicuously straight, pale pubic hair of the young woman standing next to Vilmos's teacher. He was reminded of this because Erika too had such straight-angled, flattened pubic hair. He caressed her thigh resignedly. Slowly, they clambered up and got dressed. Dr. Kreutzer handed the items of clothing to the woman one by one, as if he were helping a seriously ill patient get dressed.

That spring, Erika failed to show up at old Auntie Pálma's yet again. She called to say she had a fever, then she said that she couldn't come because she'd had to suddenly sell her bicycle. After a while he never even heard from her; she had completely disappeared.

faces that had lost their contours

Years passed, and the apartment of Dr. Kreutzer's mother was completely, definitively covered in dirt. Dead moths accumulated behind the glass in the picture frames, the plastic garbage lid could stick to a person's hand if touched. Dr. Kreutzer hopelessly sorted out the photographs and decided that after he had looked over the most personal objects he would call a professional clearance company, have them bring a container of six cubic meters.

On the bed, in the third pile of pictures, were yellowed photographs of his parents. In the wedding photographs his father stood next to his bride a little clumsily, with one foot placed forward in one of those unnatural poses that photographers like so much, standing in front of a floor-to-ceiling mirror.

In one very old photo, Auntie Pálma's slender great-aunt was smiling, the old dark-haired beauty queen. In the style of the time, her hair was piled up in a high chignon. Old Auntie Pálma had often told the story of how, as a schoolgirl, she had to collect toilet paper tubes for her great aunt, for which she always got some money. Her aunt used them as a support for her high piled-up hair.

Once a grown-up, she herself stopped wearing that hairstyle, but she still collected the toilet paper tubes, and later on, never threw them out. She put them aside, just as she did the plastic and paper bags. The cardboard tubes were piled up at the bottom of every closet. Dr. Kreutzer remembered his younger brother wanted to construct a sloping racetrack for his toy cars with these tubes, but it kept falling apart. A little while later, when he had gotten thoroughly bored sitting next to his mute, mourning parents, he opened up the large closet and put two of them together. With adhesive tape, he constructed a pair of binoculars, then ran around gazing through them, between his mother and father collapsed into themselves.

He longed to get away from that oppressive apartment, where hours went by without anyone speaking to him. And if anyone did, it was only to tell him to stop running around so much, he should go into his room nicely and quietly and draw.

He looked through the toilet paper cardboard tubes and into time itself. He saw his younger brother, but only in small mosaiclike fragments. A lock of hair, the pattern from his sweater. He saw him sitting on the bed, he saw him coming out of the bathroom. Then suddenly he turned the cardboard tubes around, and he looked ahead in time. He saw blond hair, he saw the edge of a carpet, an ornamental plant in a lustrous pot. He saw a standing lamp that he didn't recognize. Then he lowered the cardboard tubes, and he saw the paralyzed, silent apartment, with its own dust-covered, unchanging knickknacks; outside he saw the concrete sidewalk with the kiosk columns covered in announcements, and he saw the cars, windshields covered with frost on the road's shoulder where they were parked only infrequently.

Dr. Kreutzer put the wedding photographs aside to be scanned later on, let these memories remain for the children. The more he crouched down on the pillow, the more his lower back hurt. He stood up, stretched out his arms a bit, and went to use the bathroom. The toilet pipe was fully blackened from accumulated limestone. He looked around to see if there were any cleaning products, but he saw no bottles. There was only an ancient rolling suitcase placed on a shelf built below the ceiling. He heard his cell phone beeping through the opened toilet door. He had to be on his way.

no, no, my little son

Dr. Kreutzer was packing things up on his desk. He was not satisfied with the firm that cleaned his office every weekend. They had keys to the front door, they knew the alarm code, they came and went by themselves. He had already sent them, several times, **objective and restrainedly threatening** messages concerning their poor workmanship. The spiderwebs, the visible mold next to the caulking, the dirt adhering the curved surfaces of the toilet tank. He received courteous replies in which the firm thanked him for his comments, assuring him of their commitment to offer services of the highest quality, and of course they would mention these the deficiencies he had noted to the relevant staff members. Despite this, on Monday, as Dr. Kreutzer started his workday, he still encountered instances of disturbing uncleanliness. And now as well: long threads of spiderwebs hung from a curtain rod, swaying back and forth as he opened the door. There was still dust on the tops of the books. He checked the picture frames and as he ran his finger along them, the tip of his index finger turned dark. So it seemed that they were not wiping off the picture frames either. One of his patients had canceled their session by text that morning, so that he had a free hour, but he did not want to spend it wiping down picture frames. Instead, he organized his papers, looked over his pens, placing the ink bottles in a row. He was running out of lilac ink. He liked writing with fountain pens. He had several brand-name pens capable of drawing lines of nearly calligraphic daintiness, capable of great variation, although the ink got smeared easily before drying. He had to be careful, when writing, to not let the side of his palm touch the paper, not to turn the page too quickly. He always picked out planners with nonbleed paper for his note-taking. He liked matte paper best, but not too coarse. He preferred the paper's surface completely smooth, so that the fine fibers did not get stuck in the fountain pen nib. On the lighter-hued papers, the ink looked beautiful, but took too long to dry. He stepped into the bathroom, where, at the end of the previous year, he'd had a shower installed, and he determined that the hand towels had also not been changed, even though he had left the laundered ones out and folded up for the cleaners.

Often he spent the entire afternoon in his office: if Petra had made plans for that evening, he didn't always have time to quickly go home, shower, and change. The owner, from whom he rented this office, along with the three other practitioners, had agreed to the shower installation under the condition that the expenses would be paid by themselves. As the other three practitioners did not regard this as a necessary refurbishment, Dr. Kreutzer paid for the whole thing. He picked out simple white tiles for the shower booth, with narrow, steel-colored, decorative stripes. A malicious smile flitted across his face when the doctor who worked in the office next to his knocked on his door for the first time, timidly asking if he could quickly use the shower before he went home.

As he still had forty minutes left, he quickly got undressed, placing his clothes on the sofa armrest. He took a pair of scissors from the desk drawer and stepped into the tiny shower stall. He turned on the water, waited for it to get warm, and thoroughly looked over his own body. Red hair grew wildly all around his penis. He picked up the scissors and cut the strands of hair around his member down to the base. For years now, he had been trimming his pubic hair because he once read in a men's magazine that this procedure could visually enhance the size of one's penis. Not as if he had any worries with the dimensions of his member; even if he could, he wouldn't change anything about it. He saw the trimming of this hair as a kind of beneficial hygienic task, like a manicure or haircut. He looked at himself in the steamy, full-length mirror, and it seemed to him that despite his regular training, his shoulders were not broad enough, his stomach was rounding out too much. He pulled himself up a bit and backed up as far as he could. This small bathroom was very narrow, and the white tiles didn't help. From this distance, he could see his legs too, and once again, he found them disproportionally short compared to his powerful, freckled upper body.

The lukewarm water refreshed him. He toweled himself off one more time so as not to drip water outside of the bathroom, then, using toilet paper, he gathered up the drenched hairs from the shower basin and the drain. He lent down on one knee, it was difficult to get up again. He walked into his office, naked. He strapped his watch onto his wrist. He was about to put on his briefs, but as he bent down, a sharp pain shot through his lower back. He knew that this pain, flashing downward to his thigh, was a warning, possibly the harbinger of more torture to come. He resorted to his usual rocking procedure. He always did this when the nerve got inflamed. He had come up with this years ago, during a skiing trip, when, after pulling a muscle in a similar fashion, he could hardly get up. The others, he remembered well, were already dressed and waiting for him to step out into the blinding, snowy light while he was still crouched by the side of the bed, and although he did manage to sit up, he was incapable of putting on his clothes without help. Then he'd had the idea of this movement. Ever since then, if the usual pain signals started flaring up, he would get dressed by gently leaning forward, and with one hand, gently swaying his underwear in front of himself, manage to get one leg in one hole, then the second leg in the other. He straightened up cautiously. He observed his body, but the shooting pain did not occur again.

Suddenly, someone knocked at the door.

He glanced at the clock. It was just past the half hour with no patients expected yet. His first thought was that it could be Petra. She had come here, to see what he was up to during the day, to see if he were alone. He stood rigidly and did not answer.

The knock came again.

Before he could throw on his trousers, a young, harried-looking young man walked in. He wore no coat, but a thick, quilted vest, and beneath it a shirt that had been washed too many times. He stared in shock at Dr. Kreutzer, who stood there in his underwear, his trousers in his hands, unable to speak. The young man apologized and backed out of the office, not turning around, still looking at Dr. Kreutzer. Then, coughing slightly, he once again apologized from the other side of the door. Dr. Kreutzer said there was no problem, and asked him to wait for a few minutes.

Dickhead, he muttered to himself, and cautiously, avoiding

abrupt movements, he pulled on his trousers. How could he have left the door unlocked!

Dickhead, he repeated to himself, as he buttoned up his fly in a rage. The material was a little battered along the stitches, but he still wore these trousers because the brand name engraved into the front of the button was a pleasant reminder of the quality of this particular piece of clothing. As he buckled his belt, he decided that whoever this guy was, he would not try to treat this person—a treatment that, of course, could never begin with him making excuses for standing in his office in his underwear. He hurried to button up his shirt. He still had to put on his socks, so he lowered himself into the armchair, supporting himself with the armrest. He stepped into his shoes, looked around his entire office, to make sure that everything was in place. The scissors! Coming out of the bathroom, he had put them next to the coffee cups, on the small table. He quickly grabbed the scissors, shoved them back into the drawer, then called out:

I'm coming.

He wondered how this person had gotten into the building. He had not buzzed him in through the intercom. Maybe one of the building's residents had done so again. Even though there was a sign saying not to let in any strangers.

He cracked open the door, as narrowly as he could, to look out. He saw the shoulder and washed-out shirtsleeve of the man who'd walked into his office a moment ago. On second glance, he looked more like a boy just grown out of adolescence. In response to his question as to how he could be of assistance, the guy muttered that he would like to speak with Dr. Kreutzer. That is to say, with you, he said, looking at him through the crack in the door. Dr. Kreutzer stepped back and opened the door.

The boy looked all around the room as if he wanted to judge if he were in the right place, and if it were even worth stating what he'd come here to say. The psychiatrist picked up his planner from the small table, paging through it as if to check if he had any free time. Please do come in, he said, otherwise there'll be a draft in here. He regretted having shoved the scissors into the desk drawer. He should have left them on the small table. The cold draft flooding in reached as far as the table.

The boy didn't move, but said in a panicky, yet resolute tone, that he needed to speak with him immediately. The psychiatrist walked around him, closed the door, then circled back around to his desk. He pulled out the drawer. This, he said, unfortunately would not be possible as he had an appointment: his next patient would showing up any moment now.

The boy did not come any closer, he did not step onto the carpet. In his quilted vest, he stood rooted in place, and waited, his brow furrowed. It was impossible to decide if he was sweating because of the heat, excitement, or if he had some problem. He was of average height, with dark skin and dark hair falling into his face. Judging by the burning gaze emanating from his deep brown eyes, he could be struggling with some kind of mental illness, although there was nothing frightening in his posture. His clothing did not seem like that of someone from one of the segregated zones. Instead, he stood there like a student who had been called into the principal's office, and now here he was, but he would not take another step inside.

I want to talk about my mother, the boy said. Since this was a private psychiatric practice, Dr. Kreutzer recognized at the very least that this young man was not beating around the bush, not playing for time unnecessarily—as opposed to his other patients, who spent many years in therapy, until finally they blurted out that they wanted to talk about their mother. Dr. Kreutzer's brain was spinning as he tried to remember if anyone else, in the two offices next to his, had office hours right now. If he could call out to them, if this guy suddenly attacked. He realized that neither the other two doctors were around.

He did, though, have the scissors in the drawer.

His new visitor did not move. **He waited, almost diffidently**, as if to retract his earlier, slightly brutal entrance. He swallowed loudly.

His mother came here every Tuesday, he continued. Every Tuesday, he repeated, as his gaze restlessly darted between the window and the room interior. Dr. Kreutzer raised his eyebrows and asked who his mother was. The boy pronounced a name.

Dr. Kreutzer opened his notebook, his gaze wandering across the days. He realized who was standing here. And why he had come.

With great courtesy and reserve, he only answered that unfortunately, right now was not a good time, but he would be more than happy, insofar as he could, agree upon a different time. *Insofar as he could*—he was happy about this turn of phrase. It sounded official and reassuring, granting a sturdy frame to the blurry situation and the strangely shifting roles. In any event, he could only mention that he was unable to release any information with regard to any of his patients.

Who can I write to?

The boy looked at him with a haggard expression, then, leaning forward slightly, glanced out the window to the outside walkway, like someone who was expecting to be overcome soon by those pursuing him, to be roughly ushered out.

My name is Albert, said the boy.

He fished out a battered cell phone from his pocket and asked Dr. Kreutzer to designate any day at all, he could come at any time. He smoothed his hair with his right hand away from his face, and wiped his palm on his trouser leg, then wiped his cell phone, which he was holding in his left hand, on his trouser leg as well. As there were no free appointments that day or even that week, they agreed on the following Thursday. The boy asked if he could call him before then.

No, Albert.

Dr. Kreutzer decisively shook his head, and in the meantime tried to gently direct the boy to the door. There were only a few minutes until his next patient was supposed to arrive, and he did not want these two people bumping into each other in the waiting room or on the staircase.

more deeply deposited, painful

At Nirgends Gasse 4, the intercom rang in the chilly, echoey waiting room of the dental clinic. The assistant pressed the button, then hurried back to her office, closing the bright, white door behind her.

A few seconds later, the patient rang the doorbell again, because after crossing the inner courtyard she had to enter through the staircase door. She wasn't walking fast enough, and the door closed automatically after fifteen seconds. She had stopped to stare at the enormous glass roof covering the courtyard of this one-time apartment house through which sunlight filtered, making the reconstructed apartment block seem more like a premium hotel. She recalled that she spent her childhood, or at least her early childhood, in an apartment precisely like this, until she was six years old, until her parents got divorced. That too could have been fixed up, could have been transformed into a refashioned, elegant building.

She had never seen that building, or that country, again. She had traveled there for the last time for her mother's funeral. After that, the Unified Regency closed its borders, no one could get in. Clearly, neither could she anymore. Her younger sister, who lived there, and with whom she hardly had any connection, could still travel out of the country for the time being. She could have come here too, if she wanted. But she was always too busy. Maybe she didn't have the money for it, although she had a husband and a job.

By the time she crossed the courtyard covered in artificial stone, the door to the inner staircase had already closed. An assistant holding a bottle of disinfectant let her in again and called out to the dentist in the office next door that the three o'clock patient had arrived. The assistant had been expecting an older woman. They tended not **to reach the inner door** in time.

On a glass table, there were women's magazines and a few older copies of *National Geographic*. The middle-aged woman who walked into the room hung up her blazer, sat down, began paging through a newspaper. At random, she began reading an article illustrated with photographs about bushfires, when she heard her name being called from the office behind the glossy white door.

This woman had done her research before making an appointment. She'd browsed through all the cosmetic dentistry offerings, compared prices, and read the customer reviews of various providers on a number of forums. The dental office at Nirgends Gasse 4 had received the most positive evaluations. Some customers even provided photographs of their completed dental work, uploading before-and-after photos. Most of them were hoping for a better life, a better job, new love from the dental work, which, of course, the dentist could not guarantee; the wall in the waiting room was, in any event, filled with pictures of happy families with wide smiles who, garbed in light-hued clothes, in blindingly clean apartments, were doing all kinds of things that people usually never did together, apart from in ads or furniture department store catalogs. They were cooking together, jumping in the grass, or, with infantile smiles on their faces, playing ball games together as if participating in some kind of a surreal team-building training exercise for blood relatives.

As she glanced up from the article about bushfires in which it was mentioned that more than **one thousand deer were burned**, she saw, on the facing wall, a picture of a family playing badminton. The picture had been processed using a blue filter. She had noted previously that home-furnishing magazines also loved to use this grey-blue saturation. It suggested cool tranquility, elegance, the kind of secure life in which tragedies such as bushfires were absent, suggesting everything from which the ominous, reddish shades of **blood and rust were excluded**, along with the dull yellow of pus, the throbbing red of swelling—every hint of decay, disintegration, and destruction eliminated.

To play badminton in white clothes, barefoot, on Benetton-green grass. Perhaps that was what a functioning family looked like. A second poster, mounted in silver-framed glass, displayed a similarly blue-filtered photograph of a grey-haired man who had not only conquered the gum disease listed below his image but even time itself, treacherously attacking in the form of this gum disease. From this point on, with his barefoot body, retouched to make him look as if he were thirty, and his snow-white hair, he would sit on a minimally styled terrace, blue clouds floating on high, behind which, somewhere to the left edge of the picture, a butterfly-like sailboat floated on a glassy sea. Everything was perfectly airy and weightless: in that world behind the glass frame there were no bacteria, no lies. The woman was wondering why, in these pictures emanating unclouded happiness and timelessness, no one ever wore shoes, when suddenly the glossy-white door opened and someone called out her name. Her gaze strayed to the doctor's foot—perhaps he was the elegant, barefoot man in the picture.

It was true that the dentist, who had called her name, looked surprisingly like the old guy on the terrace, although he wore clogs. He might have been around fifty, and it seemed clear that in his free time he also went sailing, presumably bequeathing a perfect smile and a shoreside house to each one of his exes.

The dentist looked at her x-ray for a long time with a worried look on his face. The woman thought perhaps he found something that her earlier dentist had overlooked. Some kind of small deviation, or symptom. But no. The dentist was dissatisfied with the x-ray itself, finding it to be of poor quality. It seemed as if it had been prepared using an obsolete, outdated machine. He recommended, for the sake of certainty, for her to have a new set of x-rays done in the office next door.

During the procedure she was not supposed to move her jaw even by millimeter. The circling x-ray photographed her teeth like some kind of buzzing robot, clattering as it counted. She had to rest her chin on a small white support ledge, stretching out her neck. The new panoramic x-ray was in surprising contrast to the landscape panoramas on the waiting room wall. On the black-and-white image, her teeth seemed frighteningly long, their deep roots like sticks penetrating deep into her gums.

When the dentist held up the picture, fastening it with a magnet to a lightbox mounted on the wall, a hauntingly similar image flashed through the woman's brain. She realized that this black-and-white pattern reminded her of her father's manual typewriter: black, sturdy, and ancient. The letters were the teeth, and the long teeth roots penetrating into her jawbone were the typewriter's fine metal arms that sunk down and rose up again while typing.

As a child, she had not been permitted to touch the Remington that her father had inherited from his own grandfather. The cleaning lady wiped it off only cautiously, with a damp cloth, and although the typewriter still worked flawlessly, no one was allowed to use it. Only her father could wind a piece of paper into the roller, only he was permitted to pound the keys. One day though, sitting in his lap, when he finally allowed her to type, she was astonished at how much strength was required to strike the black keys, to get the machine to obey. If she simply pressed down on a key with her child's hands, you couldn't even see it on the paper, apart from *d*, because if one did not strike that key carefully enough, the lever pressed the letter all the way through the sheet of paper. Her father bought a computer only years later, when she was in middle school. But he never learned how to use it, never got used to it. Even afterward, he always wrote his official correspondence using this museal, antiquated typewriter.

Later, when she came across similar typewriters as an adult, she always felt the cold, repulsive rigidity of the keys of her father's old typewriter at the tips of her fingers.

The doctor was still explaining something to her, pointing at the x-ray. He said that her teeth were basically in good condition, despite certain irregularities and the two molars with fillings; he was reluctant to chisel down healthy teeth. The woman, at her age, so young—he continued in different, persuasive tones—still had plenty of time for carefully planned braces, worn only for a period of approximately two years. One of his colleagues would be more than happy to be of assistance.

The woman sat up very formally from the dental chair tilted far backward, and answered that she did not have two years. Maybe two weeks, but it was possible that she didn't even have that much time. She needed to have perfect teeth, the kind of teeth she'd always longed for. She could not wait.

The dentist sighed in resignation, and told the woman that if it were really so urgent, then he would have to chisel down the incisors as that was the only way to correct the overall outline. He checked the two offending teeth once again, looking with a mirror to make sure there were no cavities or other damage. From behind his medical mask he asked again if she truly wanted this, if she really wished for him to chisel down these healthy teeth and place crowns on them.

Ye-eees.

In that case, the dentist continued, as he placed his tools on the tray, and, pressing a button, once again raised the chair into a vertical position, you first need to pick out the material you want for the crown. He himself recommended either zirconium or ceramic, both looked natural, and apart from an expert eye, nobody would ever notice that work had been done. But it could be, he smiled, that she had her own strong opinions about this.

No, I don't, answered the woman, as she spit into the cup.

They made an appointment for the following day for a mold of her teeth to be made and sent to the dental technician as soon as possible.

On Thursday afternoon, she once again rang the bell at the office at Nirgends Gasse 4 and was able to cross the inner courtyard before the buzzing sound—which indicated that the door was open—stopped.

The dentist himself opened the door, and as she took off her trench coat, because it was windy outside, much cooler than the day before, he asked her if she had thought over their previous conversation.

Yes, she had.

They took several bite patterns, then the dentist created an impression of her teeth. She was injected with anesthesia. She had wanted to read more about the bushfires in the *National Geographic* article, but the magazine had disappeared. Who could have taken it?

While her teeth were being shaped, she tried not to pay any attention to the sounds, to the trembling that penetrated her entire skull. To think of something else—of the next few days, of her father's typewriter. Those two eyeteeth, what letters would they be? She decided to look into it later. Just to get this procedure over with now. After the contouring, the doctor coated the teeth cementum with some kind of liquid and handed a mirror to her.

She shuddered at the sight. The two incisors were stiffly pointed, as if, in some kind of primitive rite, someone were trying to conjure a resemblance to a totem animal, perhaps a tiger. The chiseled-down teeth made her face frightening, just as the powerful, blue-white light emanating from above turned it ashen.

That's what I look like, she thought. That's what my face is like.

After few minutes, the dentist, with powerful movements, affixed the temporary crowns, and once again handed the mirror to her.

Suddenly, as if through some kind of cinematic trick, she had been conjured back to her old self, she looked civilized once more. Once again this was her face, the usual outlines of her mouth, her eye teeth jutting out slightly.

After four days, on the following Monday, she could come back for the permanent crowns. Until then, she shouldn't bite into anything hard.

As she hurried along the wide street, she ran into early-afternoon traffic. A woman was trying to drag her screaming child away from a storefront. The girl did not want to leave and was ripping her hand out of her mother's, laying down on the sidewalk in her pink coat. Her face was full of mucus and spit, her mouth was purple. When her mother tried to gather her in her arms, the child began pounding at her shoulders with her tiny fists.

It was hard to walk around them on the narrow sidewalk. The mass of people, who all seemed to be wearing trench coats, took no notice of the painful scene, as if they didn't even hear the hysterical screaming. The sound, however, followed the woman as she moved through the crowd. She had no idea what she would do in that situation.

The man whom she'd loved had two young children of a similar age. She had never met them, but she had often imagined what it would be like to be their stepmother. When later on, she would be living with the man, and the children would come every weekend to stay at their place. In her mind, she'd already rearranged the spare room. She figured out where to put a pullout sofa big enough for two children. But there was no need to think about that anymore.

She had to walk around the sidewalk in front of a produce store, packed with fruit and vegetables. As she passed, she pinched off a grape. Then she realized that perhaps she wasn't allowed to eat it, so she threw it away. Walking toward her were well-groomed men and women with unreadable faces. All well-dressed locals. Even though she had lived here since her childhood, she did not consider herself one of them. She was a stranger.

Just like that grape a moment ago. She had thrown it away, littering, as these, the ones who had always lived here, who were born here, would never do. Not even if no one was looking.

They were all headed home to their families, headed to their well-tempered lives, their orderly homes. She glanced into their faces, finding them nondescript, nearly uniform. She imagined that each one of them had someone who loved them, even the most boring, unattractive man would have the love of his life waiting for him; similarly, that thin-haired woman crossing the street over there, whose pink scalp shone brightly beneath her blond hair, even this unknown woman slept every night in a double bed in the proximity of the warmth of another human body, and at dawn, when she kicked her scrawny, pale feet from underneath the blanket to get up, a sleepy man's voice would ask her in the dark what the problem was. Even this bloodless body knew occasional human touch, was found beautiful, lovable, by someone. These were the kinds of thoughts she mused over as she walked along the twilight streets.

A car honked at her, even though she'd already stepped onto the crosswalk and had right of way. She saw a man wearing sunglasses behind the windshield, but it was just a flash, like in a movie. She hurried across the street. She still had a few important things to take care of. She had to pick up the blue dress that she'd ordered from the shop. She had to write a letter to both her father and to her lover. She considered a third letter as well, but then she realized that there was no point.

She had to decide what to write the letters with. She found handwriting to be too dramatic. Ridiculous and theatrical. If she herself had used handwriting more often, then perhaps using paper and pen would not have been so alienating to her, perhaps she wouldn't have found this idea so contrived. But she did. And she had an aversion to any kind of melodrama. She thought of her own mother. Drama queen, that's what her father always said about her. Whereas she herself was no drama queen, no.

A farewell letter, written on a computer and carefully printed out, would be too official. Too impassive. It would seem like a deed, a decree of some kind.

Once again she thought of her father's ancient typewriter with its key levers. Her father had kept it. It was standing in his tiny apartment on the middle of the commode, with a couple of photographs to either side. She felt galvanized by the idea that she could write a farewell letter using that. Yes, with that bloody heavy, ancient Remington. Or at least something similar. That would be the most elegant solution.

As she hurried home, her tongue kept probing, involuntarily, the two strange eye teeth. She was unaccustomed to their smoothness: she felt as if they were merely visitors in her mouth. Her thoughts wandered back to the old typewriter, and how, in the dentist's office, a memory had floated back to her from that afternoon, when her father had unexpectedly allowed her to roll a piece of paper into the Remington, and she was permitted to type something out. She already knew the alphabet, although her handwriting was illegible. And it ended up staying that way, she never did take to writing with a pen. Most likely her father was ashamed that even though she was in the second grade, she couldn't manage to write even a brief message, so instead he dictated some kind of courteous missive to her. He spelled out the words slowly. It was a message to her younger sister because now she too was going to school. A message about how she'd become such a big girl.

But she kept ruining it, hitting the wrong keys. Her father ripped out the paper, put in a new piece. They finally got to the end of the second line, but then she pressed down too hard on the letter *d*, pushing a hole through the paper at the end of the words *class period*. They stopped typing the letter.

Once again she probed, with the tip of her tongue, the two strangely slippery artificial crowns, and she smiled.

She would certainly be able to find an old typewriter. She didn't need her father's, just something similar. She would look into it. She would take care of that as soon as she got home. Then she thought about that the meaning of that sentence that her father kept repeating to her when she was a little girl.

Why do you always need to chew everything over, why?

it was dark, completely dark

The woman adjusted the pillow behind her back. Dr. Kreutzer took this as a good sign. Ever since she arrived, and he'd asked her to sit down, her posture had been overly stiff, suggesting suspicion. In response to his query on what she knew about the assignment, she said that she had been acquainted with the essentials. That she would be working in a team, under the direction of an engineer. That it was dangerous work, but if everyone followed the instructions, there would be no risks to their health. Dr. Kreutzer asked if she understood and accepted being bound by complete confidentiality.

The woman nodded.

The psychiatrist continued: You are bound by this confidentiality, even if you withdraw from the assignment for some reason. But this clearly won't happen at this stage. He looked deeply into the woman's eyes.

Why have you taken this on?

Because I want to do something useful, answered the woman. **Something trembled in her voice**, something in the back, behind the pronounced words, the sentences, which made her statement sound less than fully convincing.

Useful? Dr. Kreutzer asked.

The woman looked back at him so penetratingly, as if their roles had suddenly been exchanged, and she were the questioner.

Useful.

Tell me about your son, Dr. Kreutzer asked in a voice that was just a bit more animated than usual to regain control over the discussion.

What is there for me to tell?

The woman stared into space as if focusing on some invisible, faraway point. Memories were emerging within her, moments, seasons of the year, photographs. She began telling her story measuredly, not speaking robotically, not with ready-made sentences constructed from phrases she had pronounced many times before. She looked inside, as if weighing what was important, and for a long time, she did not raise her gaze to that of the psychiatrist's.

My son had been seventeen years old, she said, when everything began. We'd had a hellish year. Our apartment was leaking, and it turned out that my husband was ill. We had no more money left.

And . . . there were ants crawling everywhere. I know this isn't the most important thing, but when I think of that year, I think of those ants. Marching next to my husband's bed as if they sensed that he was about to die. She fell silent.

The silence lasted for a few seconds, but Dr. Kreutzer felt he had to nudge the conversation forward.

Are you afraid of ants?

No. I exterminated them. But then they also disappeared by themselves.

In March of that year, our child dropped out of school, unable to complete his final exams. Then somehow his father, who was in very bad shape at that time, convinced him to enter a detox clinic, but the day he turned eighteen, he left on his own accord. There was no sense to those two months, none. On his birthday we waited for him in vain: he didn't come home. I had gotten him a cake and a pair of jeans. I was a little unsure of his measurements because he lost a lot of weight at that time, so I couldn't use his old trousers as a guide. I could only guess his size. He turned up four days later. He was filthy, his nose was bleeding, he'd lost his backpack. He couldn't let himself in because he'd lost his house key with the backpack; he rang the bell at four in the morning, leaning on the button. He collapsed onto the staircase, the stone step was covered in blood.

At that point I thought things couldn't get any worse.

Dr. Kreutzer was quiet, he waited. He knew that the entire conversation was being recorded, that he would be held responsible for every sentence uttered because if this woman suspected anything it would mean a risk for the entire team given the work they were undertaking. It was his job now to filter out all the hidden obstacles. Tests can lie. Tests can be cheated on. He had to use his instincts. He tried to concentrate, but for years now, he had been haunted by the feeling that it was **really and truly the same story** that he was hearing over and over again, only in different performances, that he already knew what was going to happen, he recognized the assembled choreography of destitution as well as the awkward, error-ridden routes of attempted escape. The falls occurring in succession, then the remaining on the ground.

The woman still wasn't looking at him, but now she raised her head, glancing out the window as if she were trying to pick out, from images visible only to her, images slowly dispersing into the air, which ones were the most important.

I don't even know, she continued, what I can say about all of this. The whole thing lasted three-and-a-half years. In the meantime, the boy's father died. My husband and son couldn't even say goodbye to each other. Sometimes he disappeared for weeks, then he turned up again. I noticed several times that he was taking money from the drawer, so that from that point on I didn't keep too much cash at home, only enough for that day's shopping, and always putting it in different locations. One time he rifled through the entire cupboard, everything was on the floor when I got home. Even his children's teeth were lying on the parquet floor, his milk teeth which I kept in a small metal box. Everything. I knew that I shouldn't be giving him money, but I couldn't help him in any other way because he wouldn't let me. He wouldn't let me hug or caress him. I hadn't touched him in years. One time I wanted to hug him and he just said: You're sweating. Your skin feels sticky, mother.

When he was nineteen, he moved in with a friend. He yelled at me that I was suffocating him, that the entire apartment smelled like cadavers, and that I wanted to kill him, just as I'd killed his father. I just looked at him, his eyes were red, he had a bald patch on his head, the size of a half a hand, as if someone had ripped out his hair.

She raised her hand and showed where the bald patch had been.

He screamed that I was poisoning him, ruining him. He didn't take anything with himself, only his clothes. He left behind his Rubik's Cube, his earphones, his childhood toy cars, everything. I didn't know the name of his friend whose place he was moving into. I had no idea where to look for him. He didn't even tell me if he was staying in the city or not. Then, in that same year, maybe sometime before Easter, he suddenly reappeared. It was cold, but I'd been able to get a hold of some catkins, I remember well. He was banging on the door.

I was happy to see him again. He pushed me aside, leaned on the wall, and immediately started telling me how he needed forty thousand forints right away. He kept coughing as he spoke, his fists were red. He stood in the foyer and kept repeating that he needed the money as he stared at the large framed tapestry on the wall. It was next to the coatrack. Afterward, whenever I passed by it, I always saw him clearly standing there, coughing, looking at it. I don't even know why we hung it up there, I had inherited it from my mother, afterward I didn't even bother taking it to the new flat. As a matter of fact, **no one liked it, we just got used to it.** I asked him what he needed the money for, I asked him to come in and sit down for a little bit, we could talk about how I could help him. He looked at me as if I'd gone mad. He said that there was nothing I could help him with, it would have been better if I had never given birth to him, but if I'd already fucked his father and shat him out into this wretched, fucking world, then at least I should pay for it. He stepped closer and muttered that if I didn't give him the money, he would kill me. Then suddenly he turned around and punched his fist through the glass door to the living room. Then, with the same movement, he pulled everything down from the coatrack, and tramping on the shards of glass, he threatened to smash my flabby face to pieces, because the time had come for me to croak. I didn't dare move. I simply . . . froze, as if I were watching a film. As if this weren't even happening in my own apartment. I was incapable of answering him. I saw that he was out of his mind, and I tried to measure the distance to the door. He noticed what I was getting ready to do. He sensed I wanted to escape, and he took one step forward, blocking the door. Then . . . gathering all my strength, I stepped toward him to try to flee into the stairwell. He grabbed my arm, pushed me to the ground, and began kicking me, almost as if in a trance.

Two of my ribs were broken, my collarbone was cracked.

The woman fell silent. She kept moving things around on the

small table. She placed the cup in the saucer, fiddling with fitting it together. Then, she drew soft circles around the edge of the cup with her finger as if she were walking in circles in her head. Soon she began speaking again in a soft monotone voice.

I lay on the ground for a long time. I didn't dare to get up, then he left. I didn't know what to do. I didn't know to whom I could turn—to get up, to be able to open the door. I was ashamed of the entire incident, as if it were my failure. Not his father's, who by then was nowhere at all, not our collective failure, by which I mean all of us, but explicitly, only my failure. What kind of mother raises such a child? I asked myself. A drug-addicted piece of shit. A deadbeat monster. A criminal. What kind of mother raises someone like that, really?

Did you not consider reporting him to the police?

No. I felt . . . I couldn't, with him.

Even the year before, my girlfriend had told me, when he took money from me, that I should file a report. But somehow I didn't have the heart. A person can't call the police on their own son, can they?

Did he assault you again after that?

No, the woman answered, not then.

After that, he only broke into the summer house. You know, we have a small cottage, I bought it with my husband. It isn't large, altogether thirty square meters. I go there only rarely, but still every spring I cleaned it up. I would air it out, put out the musty bed linens to air. When I got there in April to turn on the water, I found the door open. The room was ransacked, somebody had thrown all the plates onto the floor, and by the entrance, in the middle of the rag carpet, someone had . . . taken a crap. I don't know why, but I immediately thought that it was him. Him and his drug-addicted friends. When he was a child, he'd spent a lot of time there. The badminton rackets and the frisbee were smashed to pieces.

I got out a large black garbage bag, I threw everything in, then called a locksmith to put in a new lock. The locksmith could only get there by six in the evening because he was working in another village. I also ordered a crossbar for the door, then I sat outside in the freezing cold, in the wicker chair. The trees were flowering, but it was still chilly outside, and I recall how I crouched on the terrace motionlessly until it grew dark. I was thinking of what my son had been like as a little boy. I remembered his clothes, everything. His rompers. He had a striped romper as well as a colorful one with spaceships. I remembered his red T-shirt, the size 7 plastic sandals he wore when he went swimming so as not to injure his foot on anything.

The locksmith came that evening. He called across the fence twice until I realized that someone was there. I didn't even hear him parking his car next to the fence. I just sat there as if turned to stone, and I believe now I really had turned to stone. Something... I don't even know... became frozen, here inside, yes, something happened with me then.

She raised her arm, **fist clenched in front of her heart**.

Then, the next year, when that... horrible thing happened, I wasn't even really surprised. It was as if that feeling... how should I put it... that feeling within me had become so calcified, that eternal pain, that it was as if the things happening around me no longer even touched me. I felt reality was like some kind of oppressive movie playing night and day. By then, I had lost him. I could no longer scrape together even the tiniest remnant of love. And if I tried, I only felt emptiness, endless fatigue, indifference.

My girlfriend, to whom I told this whole story, because I dared tell only her, had a different opinion about this. She has deep faith, very deep faith, and I've never heard her shout at anyone. I don't know if this is good or not, but I've never heard her shout.

You are not a believer?

In what? No, I'm not.

My girlfriend said that she was still praying for Norbi, my son.

Then she came up with this bizarre idea. I know that what she advised sounds strange, and believe me, I was astounded at first too, but then it really worked. At least for a while. I was able to find my way back to my son, I was able to believe that one day I could touch him again, and that there was a chance of him becoming who he'd once been. In retrospect, looking back on these years a little more soberly, it would have taken a miracle, of course, but still I hoped.

And what was her idea?

She suggested that I watch remembrance videos, mainly memorial videos of young men who were no longer around. Who . . . had died. And that I should give thanks to the Lord, take consolation in the fact that Norbi still lived. My girlfriend sat down next to me, turned on the computer, and she kept murmuring that this would help, would help me to realize that this was merely a temporary state, a kind of trial that both of us had to pass through so as to find each other again, so that our relation could . . . how did she put it? . . . begin again on new footing.

I believed her, of course, because I had to grasp at something so I didn't completely fall apart. I took care of what I had to, I taught my classes, I wiped the aphids off the plants, I cleaned the apartment, then every night, before showering, I looked at one of these memorial videos. Sometimes I watched several. Videos of children with their birthday pictures, videos of young men. One died in an accident, another had leukemia. They were all edited with horrendous music and there was always something idiotic and false about the whole thing, but after a while it didn't bother me. After every single video, I said to myself that Norbi was alive, he's still here in the world, and at some point he would get better. He would come back, he would walk through the door, and he would be just like he used to be. That is . . . before his illness. There was nothing else I could do. He was a grown man, and he had to decide that he wanted help.

As I watched these strangers' faces on YouTube, I once again became capable of loving him, I could once again recall his face as a small child, then as a teenager. I remembered his cello lessons, the long train trips when we sat across from each other and both got bored. He loved playing cards. And I could love him once again as I always had, even though I had no idea of where he was and what he was doing.

I hadn't heard from him for four months when he reappeared. He was sitting on the staircase; I was coming back from shopping. Someone had let him in, they recognized him from when he'd been a little boy. I put down my bag, and I only said that I would make him deep-fried batter with apricot jam. That had been his favorite dish when he was little.

He laughed harshly, took the key from my hand, and went into the apartment before me. He had a large black sports bag; he began packing everything into it. I put the milk and the kefir into the fridge, and I asked him what he was doing, where was he taking these things. He grabbed a nickel silver candleholder, put it in the bag, then he wrapped a parsley leaf-patterned ashtray in a tablecloth and put it next to the candlestick holder.

What are you doing, my little son, I asked him, to which he answered that obviously I didn't want to take all of this crap with me into the grave, and he needed it. That was all.

He zipped up the bag.

I didn't dare approach him, in case he was on drugs again, although he seemed fairly calm. He looked up once, and told me that I was a fat toad, it was time for me to fuck off already.

I asked him why he hated me so much.

I don't hate you, he answered in a lackluster voice, then he looked around and took the porcelain lamp, which had been my mother's, from the commode. He turned it around in his hands, he took off the lampshade. Precisely and carefully, he unscrewed the bulb, then screwed it back into its place. From this I saw that it was completely clean. He wrapped the lamp base in a tea towel and put the lampshade on his head as if it were a hat. For a moment I thought that he'd really gone mad. With the lampshade on his head he looked at me, deeply into my eyes, and he said that if I croaked, he would finally have his own apartment. Could I please do this favor for him? he smiled. All of his friends had an apartment, only he didn't. The flower-patterned lampshade tilted back and forth. He grabbed it with one hand, and we stared at each other.

I answered that he already had his own apartment because this was his home too, he could come back at any time. I had never told him to leave, he was the one who wanted to move out. To which he, still with the lampshade on his head, began mimicking what I'd said, then guffawed. He said I was seeing him for the last time, I should forget about him forever. And he would see me next, he added, if there was an open casket.

I said nothing. I had not been able to cry for a very long time. He was wearing a short-sleeved T-shirt and cheap rubber slippers. I looked at his arm which I knew so well. I suddenly felt as if this person were the evil double of his old self, as if it were not him speaking but some kind of demon who had taken over Norbi's body. His teeth were bad, his face fallen in, and this demon was using the form of my son to destroy his being, while my own true small boy was pounding on the door, locked up someplace abandoned at the end of the world; he wanted to come back, only that he no longer had a body to come back to, no longer had a voice of his own to talk to the people who'd once known him.

What more can I say. He left. He threw the lampshade onto the ground. He put the handle of his sports bag over his shoulder, and went out the door.

Then I saw him one last time. That was at the beginning of September. It was still warm. The following January, someone called from the police station in the seventh district to tell me he had died. At first I couldn't even grasp what they were saying. Then

I understood, but only with my mind. With my brain. Not with my heart, because my heart was still waiting for the real Norbi, who had left when he was eighteen years old.

They turned the sheet down, like in the movies. It was a car accident, he hadn't been driving. He never even had a driver's license. It was interesting, as I saw no injuries on him. His body was perfectly intact, only skinny. Much skinnier than I had ever remembered seeing him, and nearly blue-white. I caressed him, and even now I could feel his cold skin on my fingertips.

I looked at that tortured, fallen-in, unshaven face, and once again I saw the small child he'd once been. His face looked peaceful and very tired. Go to sleep now, my little son, I said to him as if he were lying down in his little room for an hour. As if he'd just come home. And then, I felt a little bit, that perhaps we were reconciled, perhaps he had found his way home.

And as for me? What is left for me? Only to do something useful.

something trembled in her voice

The tall man with dark hair sat in the hospital corridor, in front of the maternity ward, his gaze fixed on the door. He was waiting for someone to come out, to finally hear some news. A heavy-set nurse walked by with hurried, rustling steps. She didn't even slow down in front of the row of chairs and avoided his glance as if out of hostility. Her calves were bulky and thick, she wore ribbed terrycloth socks, like a schoolgirl. There was a pattern running all the way along the linoleum, which from here, from one of these plywood chairs, looked something like a pointy, stretched-out dog's head. These heads zigzagged all along the ground, all the way up to the frosted glass of the swinging doors. Half of the chops of the last dog head disappeared beneath the door. Above them ticked the minute hand of a metal-framed, severe-looking clock.

It was exactly 7 a.m. Outside, the sky was beginning to loom grey; here inside, the fluorescent lights strained, making faint crackling noises.

A young man arrived, overheated and panting, his shoes squeaking. He walked down the hall from the elevator. He dug his hands into his hair, then collapsed into a chair. He blew his nose loudly, then looked up. Some sentence, or question, was beginning to form in him, but as he looked around, his gaze met up with that the man already sitting there, and he remained silent.

They sat this way, in silence, for perhaps fifteen minutes, when the young man began to shake his outwardly extended right leg, garbed in cloth trousers. He wore ungainly dark brown shoes, his foot stretched as far as the middle of the hallway; it hung down over two zigzagging dog's heads. The plywood chairs were all connected by one metal frame, and his shaking caused all the other chairs to start shaking as well. The noise irritated the older, dark-haired man. He looked at the younger one emphatically, but the other took no notice. He kept shaking his leg and stared in front of him with an empty gaze, into nothingness.

The older man suddenly realized why this rhythmic shaking was irritating him so much. If he didn't look at the younger man, and only listened to the creaking sounds, it seemed as if, over there, three seats away from where he sat, the man were pleasuring himself. As if, in a darkened movie theater, a nearby viewer was masturbating. Once again he looked up, but the younger man stared, with a rigid expression, at the white wall with its slashes of door openings, and continued to shake his leg relentlessly.

The situation was unbearable. This indifferent, blue-white neon light. The sight of the dead, dried out insects caught in the grating of the fluorescent lights above. Outside, the empty **road soaked with rain**, the bare trees, the decaying white window frames, the peeling paint, the treacherous smell of chloride disinfectant permeating everywhere. The uncomfortable plywood chairs. Not a single nurse came along, as if they'd all gone home, as if by morning, they'd cleared out the entire hospital. Then all the same, a distant rumbling began sneaking along the corridor. Somewhere, there was a huge clatter, somewhere, people were shouting, a telephone rang, but no one appeared.

The older man thought that perhaps it would be best if the baby were to die suddenly. Things like this were known to have happened. Everyone concerned would be better off.

He looked up the clock: it was seventeen minutes after 8 a.m.

He stood up and began to pace nervously back and forth, cautiously trying to peek through the frosted glass door. Inside, he saw no one, only another corridor with newer linoleum, from which the distant, hungry cries of infants filtered out.

If only he could light up somewhere.

Later, another slick-white, unglazed door opened, and a nurse looked out, but as he stepped forward, she immediately smiled and went over to the young man. She placed her red hand gently on his back. They knew each other. The nurse leaned down to him and whispered excitedly in the man's ear for a long time, then she led him away somewhere.

At least that leg shaking had stopped.

Once again there was silence, broken only by the crackling sounds of the fluorescent light tubes. Altogether, there were forty-three dog's heads leading up to the swinging doors. He also counted the dog's heads that were cut in half by the plastic edging strips along the wall.

Hermina was lying there inside somewhere. They had to leave by 10 a.m. if they wanted to reach the border by noon and get home. And the papers still had to be taken care of. Hermina had been informed that she could think things over for a week. The nurse he'd seen earlier appeared and finally looked at him:

Are you the father?

The older, dark-haired man jumped up from his seat: it was, after all, his daughter lying there inside. As he walked along the hallway, it occurred to him that the nurse was thinking of him in relation to the newborn, not to his daughter; this young creature thought he was the father of the baby. That's why she was staring at him so cuttingly, coldly, as if he were a man who was not taking responsibility for his own child.

Whatever. This was a foreign place. And she a foreign woman.

Creaking, strange chairs, white walls.

This was foreign country to him now.

He followed her, in the chlorine smell, to that other, inner corridor. They passed by two closed doors, also painted glossy white, then stopped at a third. He had to repeat, several times over, that he did not wish to see the baby.

This woman is so aggressive, he thought.

Don't bring it out.

No, he said, he didn't even want to see it through the glass.

So then do you really not wish to have a look at this healthy baby boy, fifty-two centimeters long, with a head circumference of thirty-four centimeters?

He weighs 3,520 grams, his reflexes are good, the nurse reeled off more measurements, now with the chart in her hands, occasionally looking up.

Finally, Mina was there. She shuffled out from behind, from the darkened six-bed hospital ward. She was pale, the whites of her eyes bloody. She pulled the hospital gown around herself, her stomach rounded, as if the baby were still inside. As she approached, the two flaps of her terry cloth robe opened, the dreadful compression bandage on her stomach flashing white. Her mouth was bloated, her lips cracked. She was only nineteen years old, but in that moment she looked much older, like a used up woman of forty. A bone-weary, liver-diseased, jaundiced woman. As if she were her own mother. Here too, there were plywood chairs next to the white wall.

They sat down, they were silent.

They didn't look at each other, only down at the ground.

From close-up, it was clearer that the yellow smears on Mina's skin were from iodine. Her hands were also covered in it as well as many visible needle pricks. Another nurse wearing slippers and white socks appeared, and repeated loudly above their heads that at ten o'clock there would be breastfeeding instructions in room seven. They would show the mothers how to place the baby correctly on the breast.

Mina didn't even move.

She wasn't going to breastfeed because there wasn't going to be anyone to breastfeed, correctly or not.

The nurse repeated her statement of a moment ago, with a loud and slightly threatening tone, as if she were an impatient gym teacher instructing the pupils to get into line.

Did you bring it? Mina asked her father.

The man nodded. He turned away for a moment, fished out a dossier.

Did you type it?

I typed it.

The statement?

Her father became irritated by how his daughter kept questioning him.

Why do you always need to chew everything over, why? he asked.

It was hard for Mina to keep sitting, she stood up again. She looked at the familiar letters, produced by her father's typewriter, the letter *d* punching a hole through the paper at the end of the word *child*, then she signed her name on the first page as well as on the duplicate. As she did this, a sleeping baby in swaddling clothes passed by them, pushed down the hallway in a metal carriage, but neither of them looked up.

Before they put the statement into the envelope, Mina said that she had written a letter as well. She shuffled back toward the back, to the ward. Her father didn't understand why, overnight, her gait had become that of a much older woman, why she wasn't picking up her feet properly. Why was she so hunched forward, nearly bent over?

Mina came back with a sheet torn out from a notebook, carefully putting it down on the chair, then folded it and put that into the envelope as well, and before she sealed it, she turned to her father:

And the photograph?

The man once again opened up the folder on his lap. He rummaged around uncertainly, not sure what photograph his daughter had been thinking of, there were so many in the drawer at home.

I think this is the one. It looks like a school picture.

The young woman took the photograph. She looked at it for a long time, holding it with her two fingers at the lower edge, almost beneath her stomach. She stiffened; suddenly a flood of tears came down, like someone who had unexpectedly given up, was done, exhausted, someone who had dragged this burden, much heavier than three kilos and fifty-two decagrams up to this point, but who now suddenly collapsed, who had perceived that this was too much, too difficult, who perhaps even now had not been capable of bearing this burden but for a secretive, hidden strength working in her soul and her muscles, almost instead of her, but now it ebbed away, leaving this empty, iodine-spotted body, this pale paper shell grown thin and collapsing, on its own.

She turned to the man, and in a drawn out, lachrymose voice, not even looking at him, said:

For the love of God, Dad. This isn't me. It's Gizi.

She wiped her tears and the snot spurting out of her nose with the sleeves of her bathrobe, then carefully, so as not to smear it, slipped the photograph into the envelope next to the letter. She stood up, shuffled after the nurse, while her father, with a reproachful movement, tossed a clean handkerchief on the chair, tapping his passport in his pocket.

It seemed they could still set off for their journey home by ten.

resident of that country of stains

Petra wanted to redecorate the apartment. At least to the extent that it would remind her less of her husband and the time they'd spent together. Whenever she glanced at the oakwood nightstands, she always thought about that afternoon when Mishi came home with two glass panes cut to a size of one meter. He entered the apartment, sidling in through the front door. He set down the sheets of glass, which were wrapped in paper and secured with adhesive tape, in the foyer, and as he untied his shoes, he kept saying how this would be the end of the eternal pigsty. No more watermarks, no more ring stains. Petra watched, uncomprehending as he tore off the paper from the package while mumbling to himself, then clumsily began scratching the wide brown adhesive tape off the glass surface. At first she thought he'd finally purchased some glass for the cheap gilded frames they'd bought in one of the poor districts. The frames still stood there in the corner, propped up against the wall, waiting for pictures to be placed in them.

She only comprehended what these glass panes were for when her husband placed the panes, their edges polished, atop the night tables, and, stepping back, examined the result with satisfaction. Only then did it become clear to her what pigsty he was referring to, how much he'd been bothered by the tea mugs that she placed on the night table next to the bed, how the bottle of mineral water brought in from the kitchen while watching TV irritated him to no end, the rinsed-off grapes on the small saucer, the grape seeds and water droplets still trembling upon it. The sight of these stain rings had been vexing him for years.

And yet these new, cut-to-measure glass panes still didn't cover up everything. The earlier condensation stains left by the cups and saucers were still visible through the glass. Mishi removed the glass panes again, looked through them, carefully set them down, and left the room. He came back in, applied furniture polish to both nightstands, and then replaced the panes of glass. It didn't help at all.

He stood there with a rag in his hand, looking worried, and he stared at the stains, visible now only to him.

The next day, he tried using walnuts.

This is what his family had always done if a wooden surface was scratched, or to repair smaller flaws in the family furniture. When he was a child, his father, in the dining room, would rub the cracks in the large oak table with walnuts wrapped in gauze. The walnut oil, along with the tiny scraps of walnut, would fill up the fissure, settling in the crack little by little, filling out the unevenness of the surface. From close-up, bending over the table, you could sense the walnut fragrance. Pale, hair-thin veins showed where the table had been damaged. In Mishi's memory, he still saw his father from that time, when he'd definitively let himself go, and yet he also recalled how he bent over the table, scrubbing the wooden surface with his empty gaze, as if so much depended on whether he could make what was evident to the three of them every time they sat down at the table disappear with that catatonic scrubbing. He couldn't.

Mishi had taken advantage of these occasions. He vexed his father deliberately, pointing out where the scratches and cracks were still visible. Here, and here, he drew his child's finger all along them. Then his father would pick himself up again, wordlessly taking out the jar with the walnuts, and once again he would start the entire **maddening, unnecessary series of movements**. Later, his mother sold the table with its scratched surface, and Mihály purchased a similar one for the dining room. How the walnuts were wrapped in muslin squares was indelibly imprinted on his memory.

Mishi's father, who had aged quickly, would fold the walnut into the small muslin squares with the same ceremoniousness as he placed the powder for his wife's headaches into the thin flour wafer. His mother suffered from terrible migraines in those years.

As he rubbed the small muslin bundle, the fragrance of walnuts seeped out; the moist walnut oil filled the hardly visible scratches.

Although this too was futile: The surface damage was not repaired. A few days later, Mihály removed the panes of glass and slipped old family photographs beneath them. To completely cover the wooden surface, he used many photographs, arranged in no particular order. Petra knew that if her husband finally moved away from here, she would have the furniture repainted, including these ugly, squat night tables. Not because she wanted to get rid of the ring marks, but because she wanted to transform them—if possible, to the point of unrecognizability. Mihály couldn't stand painted wooden furniture, a trend he considered idiotic and barbaric. It was disrespectful, made a mockery of the original material. Senseless antiquation, he would burst out when he saw such a piece of distressed furniture. He always said that the sight of housewives smearing paint on distinguished, carefully crafted pieces of furniture—pieces that should only be touched by professional carpenters—gave him the shudders. Housewives dabbling in art, he would mutter scornfully.

And yet, Petra was planning to do exactly this: home dabbling, making a mockery of the original material. With no preparation at all, just like that, in an amateur fashion. Until then, every night, she planned to gleefully place her cup exactly on top of a photograph of the young Auntie Pálma. She put the cup just where she used to, before the night table had been covered in glass, so that she could easily find it in the night if she woke up thirsty.

She could not, for the time being, buy any new furniture because the pieces she saw for sale on the internet were far too pricey. Not only that, it was nearly impossible to get a decent piece of furniture, there was no wood left in the country, the Unified Regency had shut down all imports as well as domestic factories. She and Mihály had also not been able to agree on what would stay in the apartment, what he would take. Although she wouldn't have minded for him to pack everything into a truck and cart it away. Amidst these old family pieces, preserved during the civil war and subsequently through various moves, she felt as if she were in a stuffy, airless museum.

For years she had fantasized about moving away from here, to anywhere. To leave this apartment, this city, perhaps even to escape from this country. She would pack up her most essential items, take the children, start a new life, only leaving a message on the family computer. A short letter. This new life shone in her imagination, carved out of time, detached from her childhood, from all of their shared, stifling stories, from the ruins of the civil war; it would be separated from everything like a floating, immaculate glass cage. Perhaps that's why in that other apartment, where she imagined this other life taking place, everything was airy, spacious, functional, perfectly lacking anything from the past. Every night, when another detail popped up in her imagination—a chilly, polished metal armrest, a mirror-smooth, light-colored kitchen counter—she would get up from bed, turn on her laptop, and start browsing real estate sites until the point of exhaustion. Before falling asleep again, she erased all traces of her online search. She only lay down again, for the most part early at dawn, when her husband was already sleeping deeply.

She did, though, collect her favorite real estate ads in a folder. Spacious light-filled homes, with huge, plateglass windows. The strange backdrops of strangers' lives, where, later on, among these new backdrops, the clean walls limewashed white, she would begin her own new, strange life.

She knew, of course, that all of this was a mere dream, an escape, procrastination. Mihály would never let her take the children. She wouldn't even be able to move somewhere else in the city, she would have to stay here. Even though they lived in a desirable and protected neighborhood, the apartment was in her husband's name. The amount left to her after divorce would never allow her to acquire one of those advertised properties she yearned for. Any such apartment would cost magnitudes more than what she would ever get from her husband. She had to wait until Mihály made a move—to wait for that which had wanted to fall apart for years now, to fall apart by itself.

Until that point, she got new curtains, at least. She made smaller changes where she could. One by one, she took down the pictures that her husband left behind. That horrific snowy landscape with the gold frame her mother-in-law gave them because it always made her think of that long-ago afternoon, when Ösci died at Christmastime. That hideous monkey with the frightened eyes that hung above her husband's desk and which scared little Vilmos so much, and rightly so. It was truly a frightening photograph.

There were lighter stains on the wall where the pictures had been taken down. It was only visible now how much the wall had yellowed in the past three years.

She bought new blankets, brightly colored pillowcases, and table cloths, in the middle of which she placed cinnamon-scented candles. At night, if there was a power cut, the room was still filled with the fragrance of pastries. She carried plants, even large ones, home. She pushed heavy flowerpots into the now-empty corners. She knew how much these voluminous planters irritated her husband. Every time he came here, he walked over to them, pushing them farther away with his foot to check if they had left water stains on the parquet floor. When they still lived together, he had never allowed any planters in the apartment as the dripping water might damage the lacquered floor. The sight of the white mold covering the earth in the planters disgusted him, and he did not believe that these green, living, breathing, at times parasite-infested decorative plants, hauled here from the department store, cleansed the air in the apartment any better than a good cross draught. He hated to see any kind of lush, burgeoning, leaf-shedding, photosynthesizing bush in this immaculate living space. He didn't even let her get a Christmas tree. When the children were very small, they tied together some pine tree branches. Once, later on, Petra had asked sharply if they too were going to have a "gifting chair," and if he was planning to ruin every subsequent Christmas for the children if only because a living pine tree would shed unruly small needles all over the floor, as if precisely to annoy him. Mihály, then, brought home an extremely expensive artificial pine tree, one-hundred-and-eighty centimeters tall. He dragged the coffin-length box into the foyer and rested it on the floor.

Here you go.

There was going to be Christmas, there was going to be a tree. An artificial tree of human height. It was so bloody heavy that after the first year they didn't even carry it back into the garage, they just shoved it into clothes closet, so that in the following year, in those hours when Mihály's mother was already donning her customary mourning clothes, they took it out again, unfolding its clattering, lifeless branches in the living room.

maddening, unnecessary series of movements

Petra moved much more freely around the apartment once her husband left. She kept it tidy, but she no longer paid so much painful attention to the details, she didn't clean the kitchen table with a damp dish towel, lest Mihály find any blotches on the table, and she didn't change the children's bedsheets every single week.

Now they too could, without fear, stick the decals they'd gotten in the Metmag store onto their bed frames without their father scratching them off in rage. In the cupboard, the T-shirts and the sweaters got all mixed up, the winter and the summer clothes.

Even though she had changed the old, beige curtains for new, flower-patterned drapes, in the falling light of the afternoon, the air, turning into the color of tea with its granulated light, reminded her of those old oppressive afternoons—lasting many years—when she sat home with the children, and she just waited. She loaded the washing, took out the clothes after the spin cycle, hung them on the drying rack, and she waited. She would tidy up the carpet in the children's room, and she waited. She'd push the baking pan into the oven, take it out, then she waited. She got the children dressed, got them undressed, and she waited. She gave them their baths, helped them into their pajamas, and she waited. She told them fairy tales, she sang to them, and she waited. She was bored out of her mind.

The she'd call her husband: Where are you? she'd ask.

Mihály always had some answer, for the most part designating a specific location: He was either here or here, in neurology, at the clinic, in the stairwell, in a therapy seminar, in a meeting, then he'd quickly get off the phone, arriving home only hours later, throwing his brown-leather messenger bag onto the chair next to the front door.

She often woke up, frequently after midnight, or even at dawn, to the clicking sound of the bag's metal clasp. He always left it in the same place, stiffly thrown onto the chair's wooden seat.

He'd come home.

He was here, she heard the rustling sounds as he took off his coat. He placed it on a hanger. He set down his shoes next to each other.

How much she hated these damn chairs with the curved backrests! In the last few months before he moved out, every time Petra turned the key in the front door to let herself in, she felt as if she were suffocating. She recoiled as she stepped into their common space. As soon as she sensed their apartment's characteristic smell—a mixture of the fabric softener she used for the children's clothes, eternally drying, and the pipe smoke penetrating her husband's clothes—she felt an inexplicable weight pressing down on her chest. The pressure of years condensed into cubic metres, firedamp which the spark of one single sentence could ignite.

This scent was no longer her own; this was not the air of her own home. In her own soul, she wasn't even living here anymore.

Now she was getting ready for Emma's birthday, and she wanted to clean this space. She packed whatever she considered unnecessary into cardboard boxes, everything belonging to the scenery of their former life. She took the boxes down to the garage so that she could decide later what to keep. She crammed Mihály's ski sweaters into a box along with the lavender-scented sachets placed among them, because her husband had a terrible loathing of moths. She also crammed in the dried out sauna glove and the sauna brush with the wooden handle that he used to use but had not taken when he left, probably because the lacquer paint was peeling off the handle; he'd always had an aversion to damaged objects.

The coasters, the chess set, the repulsive little card box with the inlaid cover, the gilded rococo frames, unnecessarily piled up at the bottom of the wardrobe, the old faded, chipped photographs which Mihály had never enlarged and had never organized.

As she leaned over the boxes, the scent of pipe smoke from the sweaters struck her nose, and suddenly she was overcome with a feeling of suffocation again. This smell was nauseating. She flung the windows open, breathed deeply, and stared down at the steep, chestnut tree-lined side street. Even after so many years, this place was alien to her. She had never wanted to live here, she just somehow ended up here, unprotected in this protected city district, in this apartment, in this fate, among these heavy antique pieces of furniture. As if the past ten years had been a mere mistake, a mere accident. Before getting married, she hadn't even known of this district, she never had any reason to come here. Here there were only elegant, unadorned apartment houses, reticent people with suspicious gazes who had lived here forever, then further up the mountain slope, shadowy gardens with high stone fences, embassies with security guards standing in sentry boxes, and state-owned plots of land. It took a long time until she learned how to navigate this city district inhabited by the coolly inscrutable and privileged, a long time until she realized what routes to push the baby carriage along, the easiest path to the grocery store, and when to go to the post office so as not to have to stand in line with the children.

How she had struggled with the shopping, good heavens. She was always out of breath by the time she hauled the stuffed shopping bags to the front door. Mihály tried to convince her to get a cleaning lady.

At least the apartment would be cleaned properly, he had said.

But she protested against it. She couldn't bear the idea of her husband enlisting an observer, disguised as a cleaning lady, into their home, a cleaning lady who would be keeping her under watch, reporting on her days, digging into her things.

She began to enjoy cooking only once Mihály moved out. She used spices generously, not measuring, not being overly careful. She didn't immediately wipe off the splashed grease from the induction stove, didn't immediately start the dishwasher as soon as the table was cleared, to prevent the bacteria from multiplying.

How does this fork look? her husband once asked her, holding the utensil up to the light. Squinting, his head tilted to one side, he examined the smears between its prongs.

It's as if I'm still at my mother's, he muttered.

Except that the food here is edible, Petra answered.

She stood up, took his fork, holding out a new one to him which first she wiped vigorously with a tea towel. There was no emotion whatsoever on her face.

The suffocating feeling that came over her from time to time was caused by the condensed essence of these old moments, by the silence, ready to explode, still filling the rooms with floating questions. Silence, which broke out from the living room in the form of too-loud Baroque music instead of words.

Those speakers. They were like two high tech skyscrapers, erected by accident in an ancient city made of Biedermeier furniture. They cost as much money as Petra, who now led her own training group, earned in half a year. Those loathsome speakers.

Interestingly, it only occurred to her later, as she was vacuuming, that Vilmos's asthma developed right around that time when she began looking at real estate ads every night, and she felt suffocated having to get underneath the blanket next to that other evaporating body. As she herself could not move out of the apartment, from this space of their common life, little by little, she moved out of her own self, her own body.

She would get under the comforter, lie down, eyes open, and listen to the child coughing on the other side of the wall.

Back then, if her husband woke up at night, he would get out from underneath the blanket; and by the sharp light of the small lamp, he would look at Petra's body. He insisted that they both sleep completely naked, even in the winter. He inspected her like a suspicious owner ensuring that no damage had been done to his property by unauthorized persons in his absence, that it had not been groped or scratched up if it was in the same state as it had been the last time he penetrated it.

Turn over, he told her.

Petra hated these occasions, and yet somehow expected them. At times Mihály asked her to get up and stand at the end of the bed. Sometimes he had her open the window, and he watched

with intrigue as his wife stood shivering, as the cold draft flowed in, her nipples shriveling.
Don't cross your arms, stand properly!
Petra hung her head.
You are not normal.
Now that Mihály was no longer living there, she wanted to get a new bed. If she couldn't buy new furniture, at the very least she could get a new bed. The rosewood bed frame was heavy and unmovable, but with effort and determination, she could tip over the wide mattress by herself. Whenever she moved it while making the bed, the stale air beneath the lower slats billowed up as if this mattress, which they had slept on for years, had not just absorbed their sweat but their thoughts, their words, their common story with all of its vapors and their bodies' moisture. It was a map of stains that could never be cleaned, left by accumulated sperm, menstrual blood, coffee, children's poo, diapers bursting open and waters spilling out onto the yellowed spring mattress, delineating, all around, the realm of their shared existence with its faded, yellow contours. As long as this bed stood here in this room, there would be no liberation because until that point she would, in a certain sense of the word, continue to feel like her husband's sexual plaything. She would continue to be the **resident of that country of stains**—there, where she slept, where she got up, where she dreamed.

Every time Mihály lay down beside her, the mattress shifted, and as if on some trampoline, his body pushed her much lighter body up from the darkened, evaporating depths of her dreams and up into the partial darkness of the seemingly immutable present.

You're too heavy, she said to her husband, whenever he pressed down on her with all of his strength. He held down her arms, nearly pressing the air out of her chest.

Too heavy? Mihály smiled in the dark.

I'm a heavy person?

The thought seemed to please him.

so it wouldn't crack

What were you doing when he died? Dr. Kreutzer asked. He wanted to be sure that this woman didn't know anything more than what she was showing. That she really wanted to live, and that she wasn't just toying with them to ease her own departure. The team was already formed, the concluding tests were being performed, and out of the eight team members, only this woman was giving the right answers to everything. He found it interesting that it was precisely two women who had attained the best results: the little nurse and this one. Of course, it helped that she had been a chemistry teacher, whereas the other was young and obviously clever.

Everything seemed to indicate that they had chosen well, and yet he had felt this second conversation necessary, because he wanted to be sure that the older volunteers also planned to see their work through properly.

The woman, surprised, gripped the armrest of the chair, slightly leaning forward. She had just hung up her coat, now she was sitting.

Right then and there? You mean, that very day?

She had been waiting for some introduction. A courteous inquiry as to whether she still felt ready, or if she'd possibly thought things over. She had spoken about Norbi, her son, she had told the story to this person, not of her own accord but only because he'd asked her. She never would have said so much on her own. And she'd revealed so much more than to anyone else. It confused her that this doctor was now immediately starting the conversation by mentioning her dead son, with no small talk or pleasantries. He wasn't asking for her health records, or for her dossier, not yet complete. It's true that her son had died, but that wasn't why she was here. She was here to work, not ask for help. She wanted to be employed.

Dr. Kreutzer had calculated from his notes that the car accident must have happened at least two years ago. He wanted to know where this woman stood in the grieving process, how stable she was mentally. Could she really bear the burden of this assignment, as she had claimed? Would she lose her equanimity, if provoked? There was a gentle half smile on Dr. Kreutzer' face as he caressed the pages of his leather-bound notebook.

Yes, on that day. What were you doing?

The woman didn't respond right away. She was pondering, like someone who wanted to collect her thoughts before answering. She was observing herself inside, as if preparing for an exam: not with unpleasant excitement, but prudently, coolly. The skin on her neck was slightly slackened, loosening the outline of her jaw, but the former harmonic, roundish outlines of her face could still be imagined. She was wearing a silver-chained necklace with an enamel blue heart pendant, which echoed the color of her eyes. She had beautiful blue eyes. Broken, but still beautiful.

Dr. Kreutzer waited. He knew that their conversation would be heard and analyzed by many people. He had to make sure that it would not seem as if this woman was having a therapeutic session with him. He did not want her to become dependent on him, only for her to provide the answers they all wanted without having to pose any concrete questions. As she sat there silently, he somewhat regretted that he'd broached this topic immediately, asking about her son so quickly, almost greedily.

I was cleaning, the woman answered sluggishly, not looking up; she was still observing something inside herself.

Little by little, nicely, I was cleaning up everything in the flat.

As a matter of fact, for weeks I had been packing things up, walking around the apartment. Separating the summer and the winter clothes. Everything. The shoes, the old gloves. By that I mean the winter gloves. Later, he didn't wear them anymore, but I still had them somehow.

There were still so many things.

Suddenly, the image of his mother's wardrobe flashed across Dr. Kreutzer's mind—the lower shelf and the ugly, worn out shoes with the sides cut out. And that teddy bear: his younger brother's old shabby teddy bear. How strange it was that his mother never threw it out. And now when it was possible to do so, he hadn't done either. He too kept it for some reason.

You packed everything of his away? he asked sharply, as if calling her to account.

No, the woman answered contemplatively. Not everything. There wasn't time enough for that. First, I just put away the clothes.

That's natural, thought Dr. Kreutzer, but he didn't say so, lest he interrupt this monologue which was gaining strength, becoming filled with life. Instead, he watched attentively, head cocked to one side. That always worked.

Clothes—he continued to think—stand within the closest proximity to the body. They are something like skin. A slipcover, a textile slipcover for the living. They absorb sweat and smells. Maybe they absorb thoughts as well. They form the ones who wear them, they hold them together. In a shoe that has been taken off there is the invisible foot. In a glove negligently tossed to one side there is still the movement of the hand that wore it. Clothes remind us painfully of the ones who wore them, the contours of the bodies that have left forever, the bodies that the clothes are lacking, bodies no longer present. When he had to liquidate the apartment, the first thing he got rid of was his mother's clothes. Oh, that smell!

He remembered how, his movements hurried, his head turned to one side, he stuffed the knitted cardigans into the garbage bags, the mothball-stinking overcoats, the crimped Persian lamb jacket, which he'd hated so much in his childhood, especially after it rained and a raw, animal smell emanated from the black fur. He crammed the disfigured, slashed shoes into the bag as well. The clothes, still on the hangers, were quickly tossed into the black plastic bag, which made it burst. One hanger sharply protruded from the inside of the bag like the elbow of an embryo pressing against a bulging abdominal wall before birth.

The woman suddenly fell silent, then took a deep breath.

I wanted someone else to keep wearing his clothes, she said. It was a bit like I was donating his organs to someone. That's how I thought about it. His sweaters, his coats. Obviously I couldn't donate his organs.

His organs? Why couldn't you?

Well, because . . . he was an adult, the woman raised her eyebrows.

What I mean is that I could not decide about this, that is . . . I could not decide about such a thing. To tell the truth . . . at the time, it didn't even occur to me that I could do such a thing. Only afterward—when it was no longer possible. I thought about it weeks later, that perhaps I could have done it, and he wouldn't have been able to say anything. It never occurred to me that he might die. That is, before me. No one thought about this.

But his clothes . . . at least I could give his clothes to someone. At the end of the street, near the shop, I knew a woman who lived in a ground floor apartment, whose son had attended school with him—with Norbi—a long time ago.

I knew their lives were very difficult. For years now, the woman had been sewing curtains and altering clothes. I mean retailoring, turning up hems, and so on. After the founding of the Unified Regency, they became even worse off. There was a sign in their window, clearly homemade, written with large letters on a piece of cardboard. I took a few pieces of clothing to them. At first, I rang the doorbell, as if I were coming with an item of clothing to be repaired. Just then she was hemming a large green curtain, and she didn't ask me what was going on with Norbi. In our street, everyone knew about him, and tactfully, no one brought him up. Nevertheless, she had no idea he died. When I told her Norbi had passed away, she stopped hemming the curtain. She came out from behind the sewing table and just stood there. I know she wanted to embrace me, but somehow she didn't dare. Somehow... she felt uncertain. We didn't have that kind of connection.

Dr. Kreutzer wondered if he should ask about this woman. Did you stay in touch with her?

No.

Suddenly he had a bad feeling, as if the woman were reading his thoughts. As if she knew that a moment ago his attention had wandered, and although he was looking at her attentively, for a few minutes now, he'd been thinking about his mother's wardrobe. The dusty shelves that were still waiting to be cleared. He should have been strictly leading this conversation. He decided to take control.

And? Did you give her the clothes?

The woman nodded wearily while staring out the window, somewhere in the distance, with a faraway look on her face. Dr. Kreutzer got up and opened the window, but instantly regretted it because from the building's inner courtyard they could clearly hear the commotion of jostling plastic scooters and children's shouting. The woman was sitting with her back to the window; behind her the curtain, like a veil, was lifted by a light breeze. It was as if a stage designer had arranged the entire scene into a powerful image, the grieving mother sitting across from him. Mater dolorosa.

Once, quite a while after his death, I was going home in the evening, she continued. It was already cold outside. I got off the bus and headed up the sloping street. Suddenly I saw, from a distance, Norbi standing in an entranceway. It was him standing there! He was leaning against the wall and ringing the doorbell. My God. He was there, it was really him. I came to a stop, and it flashed across me that he'd shot himself up again, even though he was dead. He was here, trying to find our building. He was waiting there in a black jacket, pressing the buzzer at a stranger's door, the streetlight illuminating the red inscription on his jacket, beneath his hood. My heart was pounding, and I was telling myself that he's not there, not there, he's dead, he's dead. I could hardly move, but still I walked ahead as if in a bad dream. I stepped across the crack in the sidewalk that had been there for at least ten years, the root of some tree had pushed up the asphalt diagonally, and then, from closer, walking up almost right next to the entrance of the building, I saw who it was. It was the son of that woman, the woman who did tailoring from her apartment, who was pressing the button on the intercom. He must not have a key, I thought, that's why he was ringing the doorbell. I almost collapsed, my ears were buzzing.

I said hello, but he didn't recognize me, or I don't even know.

By the time he looked up, I had walked on farther.

The woman fell silent here and made a hesitant, rounded motion with her hand, like someone who wanted to light up a cigarette. There had been nothing in her file about her smoking or giving up smoking. Dr. Kreutzer observed her with narrowed eyes, then he realized that maybe she wanted a paper handkerchief. He kept a box underneath the small table, which he now put in the middle of the table. He was looking to see if she was crying. He pushed the box of paper tissues closer. The woman did not take any, it was as if she hadn't even noticed it, she kept staring off into space. Perhaps she was ashamed of her earlier weakness, in any event she didn't wipe her eyes, nor did she blow her nose. Everything was fine. She sat there, back straight.

The next week, she said, looking soberly into the psychiatrist's eyes, I gathered up his old Legos, all of them. I sat in his room on the carpet, and I separated out all the different sets. I spilled out the contents of the boxes onto the floor.

It was a great deal of work.

I remembered every single set, even when each one had been purchased, because they were all fairly expensive. I never told him, but life was difficult for us. Every Christmas, he always wanted me to get him some kind of Lego vehicle.

I sifted through all the parts of the *Star Wars* set. I simply couldn't understand what he liked about that film. Ever since the civil war, I can't bear to look at weapons. But he never got tired of it. Although . . . the whole thing is so idiotic, isn't it?

I don't know.

He was ten when he got a Naboo Star Chaser. This was very popular with children at that time, and they were always being manufactured. Later that same year, I got him a Star Destroyer for Christmas. He was so happy! He stayed up till midnight looking at the little assembly instructional manual on his bed.

That Star Destroyer, well, that was incredibly difficult to put together. Guests came over and they also helped us. My older sister and her husband. Here, the woman's face suddenly clouded over.

Do you yourself have a child?

Dr. Kreutzer hesitated for a fraction of a second. He wondered if he should say that his son also collected Star Wars figures, but he said nothing. The people who would be analyzing the recording of this conversation did not need to know if he had a son or daughter. It was none of their business. But still, he nodded.

Then you will understand what I'm about to say.

The last set I put together was the large Imperial Walker. You know, that strange creature whose legs are like . . . I don't even know. Like a hen's.

Dr. Kreutzer had no idea what the legs of an Imperial Walker were like. He watched as the woman leaned her two hands on the top of the table and demonstrated how it walked. He found the sight of her splayed, elderly fingers awkward. There was something obscene in the thinning membrane stretched between her fingers.

The woman kept on talking.

She placed her index finger on her nose. Here—she jabbed the tip of her own nose—you have to attach some kind of long . . . I don't know . . . maybe a gun barrel. On the picture it showed that the Walker should have one, but I couldn't find it. I looked everywhere. Under the bed, I looked in all of the Lego boxes, but it didn't turn up. And it's not good without this piece. It has to be attached to the Walker.

It couldn't have just disappeared like that.

And yet I was always so careful, always pulling stockings onto the head of the vacuum, when I cleaned up in his room.

An image appeared to Dr. Kreutzer: of the woman standing in her son's room, maneuvering the transparent stocking onto the head of the vacuum.

The woman once again put her index finger on her nose, like someone who was trying to examine if she had spoken the truth, then she lowered her hand.

When she left, Dr. Kreutzer wrote down only one word in his leather-covered notebook with his thin-nibbed, fountain pen, held at an angle.

the name? our names?

She didn't call him back. Dr. Kreutzer thought he would get into the car, drive over to Giselle's apartment, and park in front of her building. He knew where she lived, they had driven there several times already; she had pointed out her two apartment windows trimmed with dark green curtains to him.

He would have liked to go upstairs, to step into that space where the woman went home every day, but Giselle just shook her head with the zeal of someone who was not at all certain that she didn't want the same thing. He wanted to penetrate her in one of these slowly opening, enclosed spaces. He liked the strange smells emanating from unknown apartments. The coats that hung on the coatracks. The men's shoes left in darkened foyers. The stale body smells diffused by towels hanging in the bathroom. The panic on the women's faces when the door creaked in the apartment next door, or when the elevator jolted in the hallway outside. The unrestrained intoxication, the closed eyes, the pleasure when they did something in the marital bed that they would never do with their husbands, or hadn't done for years. The embittered self-revelations, the birthmarks, the sweat, the moisture of bodies, the absurd promises, the repeated vows, the excited moans, the secret wishes, never revealed to anyone, whispered softly into a pillow, the wandering from the clothes cupboards, in cramped apartments, along narrow hallways, along windowless entranceways packed with chairs, in bedrooms, across the airless and untidy rooms of teenagers, the fingerprints left on mirrors, the pubic hair gathered in the drain, the mugs left in the kitchen from that morning's breakfast, the two wounded slices left on the white plate, the hopeful, misty gazes on the **faces that had lost their contours**, faces that were careworn, torn, dried out, that were beginning to gain weight, that expressed desire. He liked the reflections, the light falling from outside, the last sparks flaring up during penetration.

The fear that somebody might walk in at any moment, the whole thing could be over within moments, that it not last for too much longer now, this pulsing hope, condensed into one protracted moment.

Once, Giselle showed him her husband from a distance. They were sitting in the car in the drizzling rain, behind the misty windshield, silent. Giselle placed her hand on his fly. He immediately got hard, and he began unbuttoning his tautening trousers in case the lady might feel inclined to jerk him off before she got out. Right here, in front of her own apartment building.

This had happened before, but in other places, not the street where she lived. Giselle hadn't complained, moreover, she seemed to explicitly enjoy it in broad daylight in the Metmag store parking lot. She'd never dared before, but also, she hadn't really wanted to. Even now, it wasn't she who desired this, but some alien, invincible strength awakening within her. Like a hurricane or a vacuum, it pulled her with compulsive yearning toward the dark depths of the man, and through him, toward her own dark depths, toward another Giselle who had never existed, into a dark unconsciousness.

People were coming and going, pushing their large shopping carts; later, a car pulled up next to them, but Giselle did not stop what she had started. She worked with a serious expression on her face, concentrating on her own motions just as when she was cooking, with a slight frown on her face. Dr. Kreutzer, with a practiced movement, pulled out a tissue from the glove compartment before he came; even so, a bit of sperm dripped onto the seat.

At first, it sat on the grey slipcover, then slowly, as it was absorbed, it left a tiny dark spot in the fabric.

Giselle. Giselle. Giselle.

Dr. Kreutzer was now staring at the damp windshield and wishing for the woman to repeat this sexual act. He wanted her to cross this boundary—in front of her own building, on this section of the street so well known to her—but in that moment when he was about pull on his belt with his left hand, so that he could yank down his zipper with his right, Giselle said in a hoarse voice:

He's there.

Dr. Kreutzer looked up, trying to return to the external world from the throbbing, extruding fantasies.

Giselle indicated, with her chin, through the misty windshield, a man in a cloth coat walking on the other side of the street. The coat was grey, out of fashion, and looked stained and worn out. The insignificant-looking man of average build stared at the asphalt as he walked along, lost in his own thoughts. His age seemed difficult to guess, because he was like the type of person who was already going bald by the time he graduated from university, and who only wore one kind of dark-colored socks and conservatively styled underwear, which were always white. The kind of fellow who always knew what the temperature would be that day. As he grew closer, it was ever clearer from his posture that he was a good deal older than his wife.

It seemed fairly unbelievable that this was Giselle's husband. That she bore the name of this insignificant geezer wearing a cloth coat.

He stepped along rather formally, gripping the wooden handle of his black umbrella. He walked by the car. As he reached the corner, he suddenly stopped and looked up, as if he were weighing the worthiness of opening the umbrella for the twenty or so meters that still lay between him and the entrance to his building. He squinted as he looked up, but it seemed that he did not find the quantity of precipitation sufficient as it was only drizzling.

Dr. Kreutzer found it impossible to imagine that this person had ever slept with Giselle. He seemed like the embodiment of a bookworm, a deskbound scholar, someone, who, even if he had sex, would sublimate it into long-term research, and, instead of wasting his strength on meaningless gymnastics, would lean with his entire libido into the keyboard, spurting the productive drops of his intellect into the darkened, distant cavities of cyberspace.

He glanced at Giselle, across whose reddened face there suddenly crept the refined, erotic excitement of betrayal, as well as confusion caused by that excitement. Dr. Kreutzer's cock had already gone limp, but this made him get hard again, and he carefully guided Giselle's hand. The man in the cloth coat, seriously walking along, stopped—he'd made up his mind.

He stood on the edge of the sidewalk, and, with a powerful movement, yanked open his old-fashioned umbrella.

this scent was familiar

Giselle was not responding to his calls. Dr. Kreutzer had the idea to get into the car and drive over to her apartment. He knew her husband was always sitting somewhere in a university room during the day. He's researching, Giselle would say in cynical tones, puckering her lips derisively.

He would go over there, press her buzzer on the intercom, and if she didn't let him in, then he would wait until someone came out. He'd show his ID card, shove his way in through the door, run up to the second floor, and ring the bell at that damned apartment. He'd close those repulsive green curtains. No, he won't. He'd take possession of her right there in the foyer, forcing her onto her knees behind the front door. He scrolled through the contacts on his phone, pondering who else he could see at this time of day, but in reality, he did not want the body of another woman, he wanted Giselle to finally show up at his office, to sit in the armchair, to adjust the ornamental, poppy-patterned pillow behind her back, and let him pull down her stockings.

She had promised she would come and help him. She promised she wouldn't leave him alone with his dead mother's things.

Alternating within him were rage and self-pity. The box that he intended to give her sat on the table in the kitchen of his mother's apartment. It was a small pewter casket that had darkened over the years; in it, he had placed within it a few pieces of antiquated jewelry with rattling clasps. His mother had never worn the necklace of tiny amber beads. According to family legend, his father had bought it for her in Gdańsk because his mother had yearned since girlhood for a piece of genuine amber jewelry. Until then, she'd only possessed a fake amber pendent made of yellow plastic.

The thing about the genuine amber beads was that **they had no light whatsoever**, but it was not time that had done that to them: Even originally, the necklace resembled raisins strung together much more than any piece of jewelry. Old Auntie Pálma had worn it once, if at all, then put it nicely back into the box. When she put on the necklace, it looked as if there were warts growing in a circle around her neck, that was the impression it created. Afterward, she wore the fake amber-plastic necklace until she died. These were not the kind of amber beads she had dreamed about as a teenage girl, but this is what she got: one fake yet attractive necklace made of honey-colored, glittering plastic; and one real necklace, insignificant and ugly. So she put the true necklace in among the linens, in that little pewter box, where it was joined later on by a copper buckle, purchased in a museum shop, and then by a silver ring with a garnet stone.

These were cheap and battered items, unsellable, but still, Dr. Kreutzer would have regretted throwing them out.

He had it all planned out: He would stand behind his chair and fasten the amber necklace onto Giselle's neck, her eyes closed, while he whispered that this was one of his mother's most cherished pieces of jewelry. It was his father's love-gift from the time even before his little brother and he were born.

The Gdańsk part of the story didn't please him too much, so he decided to leave it out, substitute it with something else. Let's say, Kraków. Kraków was more romantic, there was the dragon legend and the atmospheric main square with its enormous market buildings, the scent of roasted chestnuts in the frosty air, the vendors wrapped up in their parkas, stamping their feet in the cold. There was the enormous, brightly lit market hall, where, yes, this amber necklace could easily have come from. Why not? His father had taken his mother there, before he and his brother were even in the world. Ever since the founding of the Unified Regency, and travel was no longer possible—only the political elite had permission to leave the country—almost every foreign locale had come to be seen as romantic and distant; still, though, Kraków seemed the better choice.

He imagined Giselle sitting in the armchair, her legs stretched out expectantly. He could sense the faint smell of nail polish on her toes through the nylon stockings.

He saw himself standing behind her.

For some reason women always loved that move—when a man stepped behind her and, gently fumbling at the nape of her neck, adjusted a necklace and closed the clasp.

It was as if a proud goldsmith were placing a piece of finished jewelry onto his creation. As if the woman stood at a wedding, and, as a last-minute caress, the diamond pendant—fulfilling its bridal splendor, glittering, cold to the touch—were placed upon the bride's chest. As if a coronation were about to be held, and, in advance of the procession, hearing the expectant roar of the exulting crowd, the lady's maid carefully placed the ancient jewels salvaged through grievous, bloody wars and national borders.

Women always adored necklaces, for some reason. They got goose bumps if you touched the napes of their neck, it made them think of something that was going on behind their backs. Giselle still did not return any one of his calls.

Dr. Kreutzer stared at his argyle socks, then kneeled and reluctantly continued to pack. The children's room had been emptied, for the most part, and there were more black garbage bags lined up next to each other in the hallway. The porcelain from the living room had been carefully wrapped in newspaper, one by one, and then placed in boxes. These were ghastly pieces. No one was going to need these saccharine figures of children, these candy dishes, these branched candlesticks decorated with tendrils where the grey candle wax had hardened, no one was going to need the pale glass vases with their soiled bases, or the gaudy decorative plates with their hem-work trim. No one in the entire world.

He washed his hands as if he still sensed the several decades of dust adhered to these objects, now sticking to his fingers.

One side of the clothes closet was filled with rough towels that had been laundered almost to fraying, amongst which his mother had placed crumbling bars of soap. On the other side of the closet, which did not have shelves, shoulder bags were hanging. Although his mama had deeply despised artificial leather—it was for the proles, in her view—there still hung a few useless artificial leather bags which she clearly had never gotten rid of. Lurking in their compartments were tattered ironed handkerchiefs and old theater tickets. The worn surfaces of the bags were peeling off; the cupboard door was covered with these ash-like laminated fragments. Dr. Kreutzer pulled his hand back in revulsion.

In the back, beneath the handbags, he felt a plastic shopping bag, embellished with the logo of a famous department store from before the founding of the Unified Regency. Perhaps a collector would have been happy to find this plastic bag from prewar times, but he threw it suspiciously onto the floor. Something was twisted up inside. He took it out.

It was a rag, a grey rag that had lost its color, but not moth ridden. Why would his mother have held onto a worthless dustrag?

As he brought it closer to his face to examine it, he recognized the smell. It was his *blankie*! It was not a mere rag, but a genuine piece of his childhood, greatly worn out by overuse.

The blankie had started its career as an ironing blanket back in those days before Dr. Kreutzer's younger brother had been born. His mother, whenever she was about to start ironing, would lay unfold the blankie—back then, it was still bright blue—onto the dining room table. As his mother ironed, he would totter about, clutching at the splintery, battered table legs. He heard as his mother kept repeating in even tones, Careful, hot, careful, hot, as she sprinkled water onto the fabric to be ironed.

He waited for the characteristic smell of the steam rising out of the iron.

He would rub the corner of the blanket, hanging down from the table, against his nose, and after the ironing was finished he would pull the entire blanket down onto himself, making a lair for himself underneath the table. The untreated underside of the table had a different color, with strange notches along the perimeter. Dr. Kreutzer imagined it as an expressway. He often fell asleep there and was woken up hours later by the clatter of dishes and the shuffling sound of his mother's slippers. After this had occurred more than a few times, his mother took out her big scissors and cut him a piece out of the blanket so that he could take everywhere with himself. He dragged this piece of blanket everywhere, he clutched it in his stroller, he rubbed it between his hands while his mother did the shopping, he even brought it to nursery school. Without his blankie, he couldn't fall asleep: He only lay awake on the little unfolding bed, pulling the nursery coverlet, which smelled like disinfectant, up to his chin.

It was as if his blankie still bore that faraway, faint fragrance, even now. His mother never washed it because he wouldn't let her. He remembered well how his mother tried to sneak it away from him, pilfer it at night from his bed, but he held onto it even while asleep. He dragged it with himself even when it had grown grey, dirty, and frayed. Later, to wash it, his mother tried cutting out strips. She would excise a newer piece from the edge of the original, blue ironing blanket, and she would cram that into his child's hands so that the blankie could be washed. But this new strip of blankie was nothing like the real one. It had neither the same fragrance nor touch. The trim of the corner of the original blanket was a little frayed, and he always rubbed this corner against his nose: that was how he rocked himself to sleep. That worn out corner had absorbed the scent of his child's skin and his spit, the vapors of his dreams and the familiar warmth of the family apartment. It waited for him every day in his little locker at the nursery, and if it was nap time, or if he started crying, the nursery school teachers would bring it out.

Here you are, Mishuka, don't cry.

Dr. Kreutzer's symbol at nursery school was a cherry. What a stupid symbol! Of course, his brother's was a little car. He decided that he would ask Giselle—once she came over—if she remembered what her symbol was in nursery school.

She wasn't picking up the phone.

He called her five times in a row, sent her a text.

I love you, I miss you.

Then he sent another text.

Giselle, you damned whore, I want to fuck you. I'll die if you don't come over right now.

The phone rang, then went to voicemail. He repeated the message, his voice hoarse, filled with longing. Then he put the phone on a shelf with the ring volume turned up all the way. So the time wouldn't pass by emptily, he dragged out the full garbage bags and lined them up in a row next to the wall in the foyer. The simplest method would be simply to empty out the clothes cupboard without organizing anything and to carry the contents out to the container, but still he started sorting through things. He pulled out a large, yellowed bath towel. He thought he could keep it in the car to place atop the seat, if needed. He went into the living room. In the sharp light, the stains on the towel were all too visible. He stuffed the towel into a garbage back, then tightened the bag's mouth.

He didn't have the heart to throw out his old blankie. He lifted it to his nose, searching for that one-time soft corner in the material that was now thin like mesh. He was filled with a strange, old feeling, as if molecules that had been asleep for decades were being awakened through the material's frayed threads.

He went back to the shelf, and muted his phone.

One afternoon, no one came to pick him up in the nursery. He sat on the blue storage chest where the pillows were kept. Through the enormous nursery windows, he saw the garden under falling twilight. He saw the climbing frames in the playground glittering from the rain, the slide's concrete roof. All the other children had gone home already, inside the lights had been turned on, the cleaning lady was ringing out the washing rags in a regular rhythm, then the wooden head of the mop knocked against the edges of the linoleum floor, over and over. Mishi listened; in this monotone repetition there were a kind of lulling permanence. Auntie Hajni, the nursery teacher, went into the office from time to time to call his parents; he lay down on the top of the chest, pulling his knees underneath him. It was already dark outside, and next to the nursery school fence the streetlight was burning white, and from afar the rumble of the bus could be heard as it turned and braked.

He called Giselle one more time, then picked up his blankie, went into the small room, and pulled down the blinds. An enormous amount of lint had collected on his socks, so he slipped out of them, throwing them on the floor next to the bed. He closed the door. Above the bed were vibrating points of light, as if someone were projecting illegible writing onto the wall, blurry, waiting to be deciphered.

He got up and pulled the blinds down farther. The vibrating message disappeared, the room was plunged into nighttime darkness.

He lay down, turned off his mobile phone, placing it on top of his socks on the floor. He pulled the glass-eyed teddy bear to himself, and clutching his blankie, he fell asleep.

those two columns of light

Albert crossed the courtyard and stepped through the door of the ground floor apartment next to the entrance gate. He set down a shopping bag full of wood chips, which were wet and needed to dry out. They were comprised of children's building blocks, furniture legs, drawers, as well as pieces of pale green chipboard, perhaps previously used as backboards, but now emanating a rotting smell. Albert stepped out of his shoes so as not to spread the mud around and hung his drenched coat on the edge of a plastic chair.

The apartment was precisely one room, with a small kitchen located along the facing wall. Because it was raining, Bianka had brought in the plastic table, but when the weather was good, they often placed it next to the front door and ate dinner there. If they both were going somewhere, they dragged the table and chairs back into the apartment so they wouldn't be stolen. If Albert were alone during the day, he didn't sit out too much, even though the light in front of the door was better. In windy, cold weather such as today, he lounged inside or slept crouched on the sofa. He didn't have his cell phone with him. Bianka had taken it to the hospital to charge it. On lonely days like these, he sometimes would go out, walk around the neighborhood, but the twigs had already been gathered from the park, and the small trees had already been broken up for fuel. There were only the old plane trees standing. So he made no move to go outside, only waited defenselessly, like a small child at home alone.

Since Bianka had three weekly night shifts, he usually wouldn't even go to sleep when she worked. Not that he would have been able to. He puttered around or made sandwiches for her. He wrapped them up in cling wrap so they wouldn't dry out and placed them by the back window. He opened up the bed, pushed the pillows sewn from old T-shirts to the back, and lay down in the dark. The next morning at dawn, when the neighbor left, slamming the door, he knew that it was 6 a.m., time to go and meet Bianka. He did not want her to have to wander through the dark, unlit streets by herself. As they walked home, Bianka enumerated the supplies lacking in the hospital: butterfly needles, bandages, iodine. She couldn't leave the stomach tube in the disinfectant overnight as she should have since there was only one. But she had to sign off that it had been disinfected because that was mandatory.

Here's your phone.

They walked around the potholes. They crossed tracks where no tram ran anymore. They were silent. Albert noted that Bianka always grew quiet when they reached the tracks, overgrown with weeds. She looked around to the right and the left as if something might be coming, and crossed.

The stomach tube must soak in the disinfectant overnight, Bianka continued, once they were past the tracks, but how can they do so when they need it? She placed the tube in the disinfectant and took it out immediately, carrying it back to the surgery even though it was not fully sterilized. But if they don't take it out of the disinfectant, what will they use to examine the next patient?

They stumbled along the unlit streets. There were hardly any cars, but there was a smell of tar and cooling smoke floating in the air from the oil drums filled with rags, cut up tires and garbage, to keep the fire going. Torn posters hung down from the walls, people wrapped in blankets crouched in doorways. The shoulders of the road were covered in garbage.

When they got home after Bianka's night shift, she usually wouldn't even wash. She was exhausted, and it would have been too complicated to heat up the water, to keep lifting up the pot. She only splashed water onto her face, pulled off her sweater, her trousers, and fell into bed in her T-shirt and underwear. Albert crawled into bed next to her; he looked at her. It was hard for him to fall asleep. And even if he did, it was only later, at around 10 a.m., when the other residents of the apartment block were already clattering and yelling outside. The doors kept slamming as if in unison.

Carefully, he pulled out his numbed arm from beneath the

woman's head. If he couldn't sleep, then he lay awake, rearranging their room in his head.

Painting the walls had been a success considering that it was the first time they had ever done anything like that. If, in daytime, they folded up the bed, their space was fairly large. He would have liked a proper wooden table where guests could sit as well as a picture on the wall. He did not like the posters that Bianka had pasted up, not understanding why she'd hung the picture of a puppy with a beribboned gift package. It made their apartment look like a children's room. He himself would like to see a real painting, in a gilded frame, on the wall. If he could ever find the right frame, he would even paint himself, so much did he see it in his mind's eye, the kind of landscape that would fit this room—an autumn landscape.

And it wouldn't hurt for them to get some more pots and pans because they only had one large pot, one small one, and a scratched-up skillet. Nothing more. He'd acquired the enamel colander with its battered edge from a street vendor. He hadn't paid money for it but had bartered plastic bags. At first he'd offered the street seller a pair of thick socks, but the guy looked at him with such revulsion, as if he had just pulled them off his feet. They were in perfect condition, socks with writing on them. Albert would have thought that everyone always needed a pair of socks, but if not, well, then so be it. He took out the plastic bags, thirty of them. They were all new. At the bottom of his backpack there was also a bunch of wax candles held together by a rubber band, but these were of much higher value, and he didn't want to squander them on a battered colander. Little by little, Albert and Bianka collected the things they needed for housekeeping, and already they had something to cook with, a bed to sleep on, chairs to sit on. And they got the stove to work as well: They certainly weren't going to freeze anymore.

He was proud of this apartment. He didn't mind the neighborhood. There was a roof over their heads. At the institute, six of them had slept in one room, so the sounds didn't bother him, only the sound of slamming doors. He wasn't afraid of being attacked or robbed. Let them try! He loved coming home to this place.

Now there were few people in the street. The afternoon storm had cooled off the air, the black rainwater gathered in oily puddles. He walked around the potholes, cut across the dark, muddy parks where the leaves of last year had disintegrated into mud, becoming mixed with the eroding, sodden garbage. The bag of drenched wooden chips was heavy. He thought with relief of his own home, just around the corner on the other side of the square.

He stepped into the warmth of the room, music was playing loudly from the cell phone. Bianka, her behind swaying, was cutting up vegetables at the counter. A bell pepper! Where could she have gotten it? She only left off cutting when he embraced her from behind.

Did you get soaked?

Albert laid out his coat, then pressed his cold face into the back of the woman's neck.

Yes. But I spoke to her.

Bianka turned around, gently caressing him. She stealthily sniffed her own fingers, which smelled of garlic, put down the knife, and washed her hands at the kitchen tap. She knew what an important step this had been, that Albert had been trying to trace this woman for months: The woman who, he was convinced, was his mother.

What did she say?

That it was a mistake.

Bianka nodded. She had been with Albert when this entirely incomprehensible, absurd story had started, one month ago. They had been riding the metro late at night, on the way home, when Albert suddenly jumped up and began reading a poster on the metro car wall, leaning over to it very closely. The city was full of colorful announcements promoting the New University, which everyone had heard about these days. Many students were signing up, albeit reluctantly, because, despite the promise of tuition-free education and a well-located, guarded dormitory for the out-of-towners, they had to sign a paper obligating them to work for a state-affiliated institution after graduation, regardless of other job offers. Additionally, every student had to pledge to volunteer thirty hours of their time each month while enrolled. Everyone knew this meant working in a government troll factory: Glittering advancement and a secure future awaited those industrious students who posted the wittiest and most hateful comments, who mobilized a maximum of people online to verbal attack—just as everyone also knew that employees of state institutions had virtually no private life, no free will of their own. The preliminary security clearances, which investigated all of the prospective employee's relatives and friends, were necessary for the security and protection of all citizens, conducted in their interest and for their benefit. In this way, no enemy organization would be able to infiltrate state institutions, would never gain access to confidential information, and would not be able to further their destructive aims as they had been secretly organizing to do for years now.

This was all in the interest of safeguarding the young. So that the coming generation would not have to study in this poisoned atmosphere, festering for generations. Educational study should begin with complete forgetting; this was the university's motto.

But this time, Albert jumped up in the metro car and began scrutinizing the photographs on the poster. More precisely, he was scrutinizing one single face: a woman who, in the third square of the fourth row, was smiling emptily into the artificial light, into the midst of the few, exhausted passengers traveling at that late hour. Next to her, in slightly larger dimensions, was her graduation photograph, half covering up the smaller one. Despite the difference in age, it was clear that this was the same face, the same woman with brown hair and big eyes. The ad was designed cleverly, showing how the one-time student had become a university professor.

Do you want to apply for university?

Bianka did not understand the young man's sudden excitement nor what the hell he was looking at. And she definitely did not understand why he wanted to remove the poster from its metal frame. Two men, sitting a bit farther on, were staring at them, leaning forward, their gazes unfriendly and suspicious. Their upper bodies were turned toward them, their hands on their knees. All metro cars were equipped with surveillance cameras. Bianka was afraid they seemed too conspicuous, they could end up being greeted by police officers at the ground level. She tried to pull Albert toward the door, but he wouldn't let her: he was trying to pry open the screwed-down metal frame. He couldn't shift the plexiglass out of its place, so he took out his phone and photographed the poster.

What are you doing? Have you gone mad?

They stepped out of the metro car, and Albert showed her the photograph. He didn't answer her question, but frowning, was staring at his phone. He dragged his finger across the touch screen, and he showed her the same photograph as before, only smaller this time.

I see it, said the girl. You just took this photograph.

That's not it.

With a reproachful glance, he looked at Bianka, who had no idea of what he was talking about. She realized that Albert had already photographed this poster. She just didn't know why. The city was plastered with these advertisements for the New University, for the most part they passed by them without even noticing. Both the radio and TV stations were filled with clips encouraging students to apply, the voice of a young woman repeated, at least ten times every day, that the New University embraced the nation's talents—all talent.

It doesn't matter if you don't have clean clothes, it only matters if you have a clear picture of the future.

There was a cold draught, and they should have hurried out of the station, but Albert just stood there on the platform, mesmerized by his cell phone. Bianka wanted to nudge him in the direction of the escalator, but he stood, planted to the spot.

He was searching for the name he'd seen on the poster.

He kept gliding his finger across the touch screen until an announcement came over the loudspeakers warning them to leave the underpass because the station was closing for the night.

On the escalator, Albert read, among the 12,400 results for the woman's name, that she was a docent in the Department of Modern History. On the university website, only her name was listed, with no photograph. They made their way up to the ground floor level where two armed guards waited by the exit for them to leave so they could lower the barred gate. Albert searched for images to go with the name until he found the same brown-haired woman from the poster. She was either younger or older, her hair pulled back, but it was still her.

He kept scrolling on his phone the entire way home, Bianka steering him as if he were blind, then at home, he threw himself onto the bed and continued scrolling, kicking his shoes off from the bed.

He lay on his stomach, leaning on his elbows.

Bianka caressed his shirt, up and down, mechanically. Beneath his shirt, she felt his back, the two jutting shoulder blades stiffened from leaning on his elbows, the contours of his vertebrae sticking out. Albert was fully absorbed in his telephone.

Don't bite your nails!

You're not even watching me. You never pay attention.

Bianka should have recalled that Albert had once shown her this picture, not long after they'd gotten to know each other. Perhaps she had forgotten because she hadn't taken it seriously back then, not finding his hypothesis to be credible. Now, too, she kept asserting that the woman in this photograph was not who he thought it was. It was fake. She was certain that the photograph he'd found in the envelope given to him by the institute was not his mother, how could it be . . .

That woman said herself it was a mistake, didn't she?

Bianka had a theory as to how this could have happened. She imagined that a packet of phantom memories was created for every resident of the children's home once they'd grown up and had to leave. So that they wouldn't have to start their adult life with empty hands, so that they would still feel they'd been given something. Bianka was convinced that they used old graduation photographs from before the time of the Unified Regency. Clearly, they thought that someone leaving the institute would never bump into these people, or even if they did, they would, by then, be elderly and unrecognizable. The carers at the institute fabricated a small bundle of memories for every resident, a kind of spiritual survival kit, telling themselves that any human face was still better than nothing. It will give them hope and strength, they probably thought, something to clutch onto, just as, in the old days, during the wars, in the trenches, the smiling faces of women concealed in the pockets of the soldiers' fatigues.

Albi! Think about it a little bit!

And what about the letter? he asked.

There had also been a short message from Albert's mother, written on a lined piece of notepaper. It was just a few lines, asking him to forgive her, explaining that she had no other choice. They'd given it to Albert in the institute, along with the photograph, at his Celebration of Rebirth. A large-scale celebration of group rebirth had been organized for the people leaving state care and entering their adult lives; during the celebration, the names of the residents' mothers and fathers were officially replaced with that of the state. The residents stepped through a large, red gate; they stepped into their adult lives. With these new birth certificates, having left the system of state care, they could now start looking for work, and while the newly designated state parent granted them all kinds of advantages, they could no longer make any inquiries about their own past. After completing this ritual of rebirth, they lost all access to their own documents.

Albert had told Bianka a lot about the years in the institute: his roommates who had been taken away, who had ended up with a family, a mother. That was all she needed now, for him to get wrapped up in this story all over again, Bianka thought. She didn't want him getting upset again, embracing her at night as he wept, pressing his face between her breasts, making her solemnly vow that she would never leave him. She knew that during all his years in the institute, no one had looked for him even once, no one ever came to make any inquiries. From his room with five other children, four were taken away, four new children took their place, but not one family or any single mother ever came forward to collect him. Even that belligerent boy with the harelip was taken away. But nobody was interested in Albert, not even the ones who otherwise would have taken in a dark-haired, dark-skinned child. Because he was not only skinny and dark-skinned, but his temperament was difficult, and he was unmanageable. Even though it was written on his information sheet that he was intelligent and creative, and that his relinquishing mother had been a university student, the abbreviations noted down in the columns, abbreviations such as G12 and F93 frightened everyone off during the initial inquiries.

Albert turned over onto his side, frowning in rage. He had finally gotten to where he'd wanted to get, even if by accident, and now Bianka was trying to talk him out of it. She wanted to deprive him of this chance to get to know his mother.

That woman is frightened of you, don't you understand?

He had to convince her, Albert explained, that there was nothing to be afraid of. Not from him. If she would talk to him at all, he would show her the letter.

If Albert had reached adulthood three years earlier, then he might have gotten the chance to learn where he came from and the identities of his parents. But he was too late. A government decree had come into effect, which prohibited all nongovernmental family tree research and DNA testing; all procedures were now under the control of the state. All human reproductive activity and other genetic testing could only be carried out, under strict surveillance, at designated state institutions of the Unified Regency. Only selected authorized researchers with official permission had access to archival resources and civil registries. Individuals leaving institutions of state care could receive psychological help and assistance in finding jobs, but not any information regarding their own origins or possible relatives. This was justified for reasons of protecting the interests of young citizens who had been, as it was termed, "reborn." Opportunities were being created for them, the authorities emphasized, just as a newly born person could turn toward the future with a blank slate, leaving behind their own past, their mistakes, their sins, as if having shed their skin. If certain conditions were fulfilled, individuals discharged from prison or one of the penal colonies could also qualify for a certificate of rebirth. With their new name and identity, they were granted new opportunities, namely those who passed through the red gate virtually had no possibility any more of any renewing connections with their former families—in the latter case, either because they had killed them, or because the relatives in question had fled, leaving no traces behind.

The Unified Regency had been founded, and so it must be protected, reasoned the authorities. *The sins of the parents may not despoil the children.* This had been their motto early on in the civil war, along with the slogan, *Struggle is the future of the future.* The future of the future: so abstract and incomprehensible. But that future had to exist somewhere, albeit in the far distance, because it shone everywhere on the posters like a artificial sun disk comprised of LED lights.

Bianka insisted that neither the letter nor the photograph could be real. There was no way the people at the institute were telling him the truth. Why would this be true if everything else was a lie? She was suspicious of everything and everyone ever since she started working shifts as a nurse in the hospital, where, every day, she observed the statements that seriously ill patients were forced to sign; the stories, crimes, and nonexistent relatives they were conned into acknowledging before their deaths. Her job was to relieve bodily suffering, and yet she was convinced that only truth, the full truth could grant liberation from spiritual suffering. This photograph had nothing, absolutely nothing, to do with the truth, she was convinced.

Albi got it into his head that he would show the woman the letter.

objective and restrainedly threatening

The driver, who was sitting in the background, scanned the valley with a posture that he'd picked up from war films; he looked ready to jump, as if, from somewhere in the distance, from the direction of the small town, an uncomprehending, enraged crowd might emerge, and, gesticulating with their signboards, loudly demand the truth from him.

Of course, nothing like that happened. The languid autumn sun, low in the sky, seemed about ready to break through the thick, slowly dispersing layers of a cloud. Down below, everything that normally happened during this hour was happening. The oil drums were burning on the side of the road. The poisonous columns of smoke, arising from the nearby poor district, could be seen from here. Ragged crowds of people were clustered around the fires, talking loudly, bartering with each other. The entire city had not yet become gangrenous: In the functioning districts, the grey veins of the streets still ran, cold-blooded life circulated yet. Two pizzas were being pushed into the oven in a pizzeria. A dreadlocked man on a bicycle patiently waited, fiddling with a leather bracelet on his wrist, and you could see through the wide openings in his earlobes. As he stood in front of the pizzeria's red poster, the hole in his ear also turned red, as if pierced by a bullet.

A mother with short blond hair, who seemed irritated, was directing a child on a balance bike onto the asphalt, while making calls on her phone.

The cars drove around the potholes on the broken down roadway, people milled about, dragging their parcels, as if in some kind of genre painting. The light glittered on the chassis of a red car rolling by, which was not far away but located at a higher altitude, where the Regent was sitting with his people, and where the edges of the spread out pieces of paper were **repeatedly lifted up by the wind**.

Everything was happening all at once along the banks of the great river, in cities lying distant from each other, on farmsteads with collapsed fences, in muddy, quiet villages—everywhere. In harmonized, glittering synchronization, neither too quickly, as if clutching, nor with sluggish swarming, but at a walking pace that could be followed by an intact mind, in dreamlike intervals wedged in among the walls about to founder, already foundering.

Once, decades ago, there had been an accident: The fuel rods, cleaned of deposits, were damaged during transfer—which was what occurred just now. Radioactive material leaked out, though not as much as what leaked now. Monitoring at that time had not indicated truly dangerous levels, as opposed to the current incident, where they were a good deal higher—and rising. The remaining tree foliage was turning incandescent red and yellow, the high-voltage cables above the ground whispered beneath the clouds. This newer release of radioactive material was measurable not only in the direct vicinity but in settlements all across the country.

When the bespectacled man mentioned the broken fuel rods, the Regent involuntarily imagined a package of giant spaghetti split in two.

Fuel rods. If he said the phrase aloud to himself, it sounded metallic and empty, eliciting no kind of feeling the way, for example, the word *sarcophagus* did—a word the Regent hated. He didn't understand the meaning of "fuel rods," but *sarcophagus*, on the other hand, grated on his ears, he almost felt it obscene. Now that this expression "fuel rods" had been repeated so many times within a few sentences, he looked away as if someone had insisted on repeating a dirty joke several times over. He looked at the city below, the glinting roofs, the greenish waters of the winding river, and he wondered how dangerous it would be to get on an airplane and flee. Did it make any sense to leave the country by plane, or perhaps it didn't matter anyway because he would have to complete his work wherever he happened to find himself? After the previous accident, the broken heating rod, which weighed ten tons and was still located in the operational area, had been covered with a concrete lid. It had been sunk into a casing, then poured over with concrete. This hermetic seal had been in compliance with international standards—until now.

No one, really no one, could have suspected what was happening beneath that gigantic concrete cover over the course of so many decades. A newer concrete lid would not stop the contamination from spreading. The radioactive leak could not be stopped.

He thought of his children, his grandchildren. Everything seemed so distant in this moment, as if it were taking place in another life where, one day, he might be able to return. As if here, his consciousness—of which he was now relieved—was dictating the words that needed to be said, one after the other. This mechanical consciousness prescribed everything, he merely had to obey it, to obey this rational, steadily functioning intellect—to concentrate on the next word, the next sentence, the next command, always on the next one, so he would make his way forward little by little, not panicking, his breath and energy in perfect alignment.

Down in the valley, a large group of people proceeded forward in two orderly rows. From here, judging from their movements, they looked like soldiers. The Regent asked, musingly, who they were.

Those ones, down there?

The question diverged from the topic of their conversation. The man with the eyeglasses suspected a clever trap. He answered that the people in the valley were part of the civil defense. The ones who knew their job, he added.

He took a deep breath.

Our goal is the maintenance of tranquility, the avoidance of panic, to prepare the populace for some amount of damage and its eventual reduction. Perhaps later we can discuss providing the public with protective equipment, or arrangements for resettlement, he said.

Later? he exclaimed. When?

Suddenly, the Regent became intensely concentrated. His gaze, until then, was unfocused, wavering between the power plant and the gentle slopes; he now looked at the bespectacled man, settling his eyes on his forehead like a precision missile.

How many people do you need? he asked, turning to him.

Not too many.

Still, how many? One hundred, fifty?

Not even that much. A smaller unit.

The Regent was thinking about the convicts—they could be sent in. Or anyone, for that matter. Thick clouds were forming above them, the sky slowly becoming overcast. The sun, now at twilight, had been shining across from them, gleaming across the thickening swirls of mist like darkening seeds on the opalescent flesh of frozen grapes, forgotten on the vine.

fist clenched in front of her heart

The driver held the door open but didn't dare help the Regent get out, as he couldn't stand when someone extended their hand to him as if he were a woman. He wasn't elderly, but he looked older than his age, and even though he had spoken many times in public about how strong and flexible he was, journalists often caught him massaging his lower back or leaning against something. All of this would have been perfectly natural, if he himself saw it that way, if he were not overwhelmed by waves of anger and despair every time he was forced to confront one of these moments, captured and preserved for posterity. Every picture had to be disappeared from the printed press, from all digital platforms—immediately—not to mention the photographer. The Regent was irritated by his own impotence, how anyone might be able to view one of these images. He felt near aversion for any manifestation of physical weakness. He was deeply convinced that pain was merely the projection of spiritual inertia, and that only soft, weak-willed people were crushed by these fleeting symptoms. As a young man, he had worked his own body into a state of enduring ruggedness. Now that he'd started to grow old, his stance toward his own body was as if he was responding to some strange mechanism, occasionally in need of repair, that he was compelled to obey, compelled to execute all of its yelping commands. He struggled to get out of the car. He looked around, rubbing his aching back.

When they left to come here, and the driver closed the door, pain had shot through his spine, zigzagging all the way down to his thigh. Now, out of the car and straightening up, he acknowledged with satisfaction that he had not sensed the slamming of the car door just now. The medicine really had taken effect within one hour. This Kreutzer knew something. It's true he said it would kick in after a half hour, but even so it was good. And it hadn't made him sleepy, something he'd feared: He could not permit himself that right now. The psychiatrist had been struggling to treat his herniated disc for years and had tried many different methods. He claimed that an anti-inflammatory would be best; there would be no side effects, no slowing down. Kreutzer said that now he'd even be able to play tennis, and his back wouldn't bother him during any other activity. Here, he'd winked at him. The psychiatrist's confidential tone of voice pleased the Regent. He realized he hadn't been with a woman for months.

He pulled himself up, trying to concentrate on the details of the upcoming conversation. The gravel-covered lookout, which had a good view of the valley, might have been a roadside rest stop at some point but now that it had been placed under military supervision, every civilian structure had been shut down or removed. The public toilet no longer worked, the two flat-roofed kiosks were boarded up.

The tallest element of the enormous power plant complex, comprised of three sections unfolding before them, was the anthracite-grey localization tower; the shortest element was the turbine hall.

Behind this concrete complex, the river glittered. On the left river bank, the roofs and windows of the nearby town blinked in the low, cold sunlight. Narrow columns of smoke meandered among the houses. Here, rags, car tires, and garbage were being burned, despite the prohibition.

From the right-side of the valley, two cars approached along the meandering road. They were still too far away to be heard, especially here, at the top of the low mountain, with its rumbling wind. Vineyards ran parallel down the slope, below the three blocks of buildings. The Regent wondered if the vineyards had been here before the plant was built, or if they had been laid down afterward. The cars arrived. The Regent straightened his shoulders, assuming a wide stance. His posture conveyed a mixture of cool self-confidence and severe disapproval, even though the two cars were not late; he and his driver had arrived early.

The cars pulled up, parking next to each other. Three men got out, approaching him one by one, shaking his hand. The Regent had never met the bespectacled man with the dark-blue coat, he'd only spoken with him yesterday by phone. He'd issued instructions to Dr. Kreutzer on the basis of this man's report and his plan, and now he awaited a more accurate description of the tasks to be completed. There was not much time; they should have begun their work already.

The shorter man of the two, wearing a cap, was inquiring about protective clothing. It's been delivered, said the third man, a horse-faced officer, it's in compliance with international regulations, and we have the necessary quantities.

No one raised the question as to why so much protective clothing was necessary, or if larger quantities, as well as protective gear for children, would be required. The army was securing respirators, which could be attached to the hazmat suits. These were available in any quantities needed. Ever since the civil war, every county seat in the Unified Regency maintained a supply, stored on military bases.

The man in the dark-blue coat began pointing at the route map of the area surrounding the power plant. There was a gentle breeze, but it was strong enough to keep lifting the edges of the map. The Regent almost reprimanded him for not displaying the map on a tablet.

He could not waste his time on such details.

The man in the dark-blue coat showed where, in a designated zone, the insulated container houses for accommodating volunteers would be set up; they could be assembled in a day and took even less time to disassemble—just a couple of hours. There were more than enough as they'd been mass-produced with a view to the liquidation of the segregated zones. Each city had its own supply. Putting them together required no special expertise.

The short man with the cap nodded.

Unfortunately, the man in the dark-blue coat continued, robots cannot be used for moving the old casings and the concrete cover; the completion of these tasks must fall to the team of selected and trained volunteers. The operation of the machines was simple, requiring only brief periods of instruction. The volunteers would begin their work under the direction of skilled technicians, who would supervise their every step on location, observing them via webcams.

At this point, the man wiped his forehead.

Everything is functioning perfectly in the active zone, the horse-faced officer said, leaning over the map, the edges of which were fluttering up again. The problem is with the hermetically sealed container covered with cement during the previous incident.

The Regent was incapable of following this verbal deluge. Rods, cooling pools, he didn't understand a single word. Or rather he did, but only the most key expressions. He didn't want to ask any questions, fearing even more detailed explanations crammed with expert terminology. His head was aching, his back was throbbing again. With an attentive, and slightly demanding expression on his face, he followed the finger of the man in the dark-blue coat—at times it was joined by the bony index finger of the short man wearing the cap—as they jumped around on the map.

Already two and a half days had passed, almost three. Three precious days had been wasted because of these impotent, idiotic people, incapable of making a decision, and they still hadn't taken any steps. With an impatient gesture, he interrupted the two men in the middle of their explanations. He turned toward the man in the dark-blue coat and asked:

How much time do we have?

Suddenly there was deafening silence. One could almost hear the sound of the wind blowing down below in the valley. The man with the eyeglasses felt a sudden chill. He had not been able to sleep for the past two days. If he closed his burning eyes, he saw flashing diagrams, ground plans, severed red lines. He only had time for aggravated phone calls, cold meals eaten out of a box. His armpits were pungent, his breath had turned sour. His family had been moved to an unknown location, and when he got permission to talk to them on the phone, the voice of his wife, meant to reassure him, sounded dull and strange: Little Lili's fine, she said. The wee one too. She spoke in the rhythm of the international distress signal.

As he prepared for today's conversation, he had also tried to prepare, in his own head, for all possible eventualities. But somehow, he had not been prepared for this crushingly simple, almost blatantly obvious question.

How much time do we have?

He took off his glasses and wiped them: his mind was fogging over in horror. Seconds went by, and he felt that his rapid heart rate was perceivable even beyond the fabric of his coat.

What do you mean, how much time? No time at all!

The Regent should have realized the extent of the problem from the reports and today's measurements. Critical levels were being emitted in the capital city just a few hours away. The Regent should have known that down below—on the slopes densely planted with vineyards, in the nearby small town shriveled to terrain model size—it was not safe for a single civilian, and that the evacuation of the population not only should have begun, but should have been completed a long time ago.

The horse-faced officer listened with a blank expression.

Even he knew that the wind—which they had just heard picking up a moment ago, and which stubbornly kept making the edges of the map flutter up—was already scattering waves of contamination among the grapevines situated below, across the plowed fields farther on, onto the river's lead-colored, chilly surface.

The Regent should not have asked this question. And yet, since he had asked it, the man in the dark-blue coat should have replied, without hesitation, that there was no time. They were late.

But it seemed that he could not formulate the words. His mouth had dried out. His eyes were stinging.

Such a response would imply the Unified Regency had committed an error. That something had been carried out inappropriately, deviated from the correct sequence. Because the man in the dark-blue coat could not say this, he answered in a hoarse voice: *the smallest amount of time possible.*

Possible? the Regent asked, raising his eyebrows.

dark red finial

I woke up in the small room, it was already past 8 a.m. I was awake, but couldn't bear to open my eyes. I lay trapped in my own body, as if in a solarium comprised of human flesh, radiating darkness. I listened to the sounds coming from outside the room. I heard my husband making coffee, walking up and down, clearing his throat. He always cleared his throat in the morning, although he'd never smoked in his life. I heard him hawking up phlegm, spitting into the sink, then running the water. Every morning had begun like this for decades. The apartment, the beings moving and breathing within it, and the noises of the building's pipework dissolved into one harmony, as if a ruthless perpetual machine, eternally creaking, clattering, and buzzing, were not only keeping me alive, but readying to push my insensible and yet obedient body through the hours of the day to come.

I heard my husband getting dressed, as he opened the cupboard door, then closed it again. I knew exactly where he was reaching, I could practically see his hand picking up his shirt. I heard him closing the lid of the washing machine, because it irritated him when I left it open. I could almost sense the vaporous stink that would hit my nose when I opened the lid again to air it out.

He did not knock on the door, nor did he say goodbye, obviously thinking I was still asleep. It happened often that I would withdraw to this room with my blanket at bedtime because I was reading or making notes, and the lamplight bothered him. I was always the one who had to relocate, carrying the bundled bed linens, because he insisted on staying in the large bed. He couldn't fall asleep anywhere else, he said: The mattress in the small room was too soft for him, the air too dry.

As I woke up, my first thought was of the notebook. Yesterday, at the university, I copied the whole thing, and as I copied it, I kept rereading it. It's interesting that I did not feel any kind of pain. As if the discovery of this object—my investigations into it, I would almost say—had worked as a kind of anesthetic. Now, however, as I woke up that morning, and the noises of the apartment reached me, pain suddenly cleaved through me so fiercely, with such unexpected, overwhelming strength, that for some time I was incapable of moving.

Once again, I had to realize that of everything I had felt during the past few months, none of it was true. How ridiculous I must have seemed as I wove my plans. As I tried to arrange the pieces of furniture on the grid paper! Good Lord. The drawings, made with colored ink, appeared before me over and over again, the sentences written so tidily. I got up and went out into the kitchen. In my nightgown, drenched with sweat, I looked for a clean cup.

I was alone in the apartment, alone in my life; neither seemed familiar anymore. Neither seemed inhabitable.

I was in love with a man who had covered the pages of that notebook with his handwriting.

What could I do now with this knowledge? That this creature of blood and flesh whom I had been clutching with desperate resolve, like a dried out plant clutching at the earth in the flowerpot, that acidic earth that could be removed in one dried clump—the knowledge that this creature of flesh and blood in no way resembled the person of my imagination. It was nothing but an avatar—dangerously unknown—that that I had garbed with my own desires.

I sat in the kitchen with my coffee, and I tried to understand that that person, with whom, four days prior, I had been planning my future, was the exact same person who had written the notebook which I'd made a copy of yesterday. That it was not a different man—an unknown, a mysterious and pathological monster—but the very same person who'd laid next to me, who had unbuttoned my dress, who had caressed my breasts.

I thought of the green dress with the leaf pattern, and I started sobbing at the kitchen table, crying into my lousy, lukewarm coffee. What a pitiful and idiotic woman, ordering herself a low-cut dress. Some of the coffee went down the wrong way, and I coughed up a bit of it on myself; I had to change my nightgown. I threw it on the tile floor. I looked at myself, my breasts drooping down. My own body was alien to me, as was my own apartment and the thought that I was meant to live the rest of my life here, amongst these pieces of furniture, next to a person with whom I had absolutely nothing in common, completing the same routes day after day, and now with the irrevocable knowledge that it all could have been different, that there were different kinds of lives—lives interlaced with passion, throbbing, luminous, breathing passion—but that I had no entry point to this kind of life, because I had definitively excluded myself from the living, the lock had rattled shut, I had exiled myself from the garden because I had wanted to know, to see, to read what I never should have known, seen, or read.

The coffee was practically undrinkable. I added a good amount of sugar, stirring it in. I had no more reason to try to lose weight. I sat naked at the kitchen table, my skin sticky from the coffee I'd coughed out, my consciousness just as sticky from self-pity.

How could this have happened?

I wiped myself off with the stinking kitchen sponge, then went back into the bedroom. Slowly, painfully, I got dressed like someone who was seriously ill, who could hardly lift their own limbs. My stockings were all twisted up, the overextended heel kept bunching at the instep. Every garment that I'd purchased recently seemed like another painful reminder—they all were unmasking that hope, the possibility that there might be even some temporary divergence in how I had perceived myself over the years. Earlier, I never would have worn such transparent stockings. They were expensive, and ever since the civil war it'd been hard to get such items. I had never even gone to the Metmag store before purchasing them. Everything there was so exorbitant.

I had to leave.

I got some of my things together and took the umbrella too. My husband had left it next to the door. He always knew the weather forecast for that day. He even measured the humidity in the apartment. He placed water-filled pots in the corners, in front of the curtains, if the humidity dropped below the ideal level, and according to the hygrometer, the air was too dry.

There was always, on the floor in our apartment, one or two aluminum pots, their insides yellowed with lime scale, as if we were always putting out water for an invisible, thirsty dog. Every once in a while, I collected these worn out pots and put them into the dishwasher. Then my husband filled them with water again and placed them on the ground. This is how we lived, especially during the winter, when the humidity content of the air was apt to fluctuate.

The invisible, thirsty dog silently paced around in our midst, but we never noticed it.

I got into the car, and as I started off, I recalled that until last Friday, I had been driving to his office twice a week during the weekdays. Since June, I'd been going to the small apartment that Mishi rented. How, after all this, could I ever move along these routes? How would I be able to move around in the city without thinking that I might bump into him one day, just as in those days when we were planning our life together, before I found the notebook?

It began to drizzle, I turned on the windshield wipers, then dried my eyeglasses. It was impossible to bear. In my imagination, there exists a house where I live with him. This was insane, but the image was still there: a beautiful house, not too small but not cramped either, in a good neighborhood, in a protected district, a good distance from any neighbors. There was, in my head, a life that had never existed, a prearranged life, the backdrop of a ridiculous, middlebrow film. We were the main characters, and life was incomparably more livable; even with its lies and squalor, it was more real than the one I lead now: a seemingly dead existence.

I wished that I could have at least gotten back the anger I felt yesterday, something from that liberating, delirious rage that had allowed me to breathe. Or at least some desire for revenge to blunt this insidious, dull pain seeping into every organ, saturating every cell. As I drove along, I felt the ache in my guts, a real sense of emptiness and destitution. Like a lung disease patient whose oxygen bottle had been removed, I gasped for air in the morning traffic. I rolled the window down and the noise of the street flooded in.

I should not have moved, gotten up, gotten into the car, driven to the university, I should not have entered the parking lot with my bar-coded ID and parked the car, I shouldn't have gotten into the glass elevator, I shouldn't have walked along the long corridor, shouldn't have taken out the key to our department room, I should not have taken out the photocopies and started looking at them again, I should not have lingered over those drawings, longer than anyone with an intact mind could bear without their consciousness rupturing, longer than the time it would take for every detail, every minute flaw in the paper's surface and every microscopic jolt of the pen nib to be burned into memory, even longer than it would take for electroshock treatment to scorch everything, definitively and irrevocably, from writhing memory, longer than a sustained, absurdly extended and slow orgasm imperceptibly turning into spasms, longer than the agony of death by suffocation, longer than five boxes of sleeping pills measured in dreams, no, I never should have looked at these pictures again, and not one by one. While I was doing so, someone came in: a student, wearing high heels, holding some paper. I had to gather up these photocopies and look up at this person as I was obliged to make an effort at answering her questions, then I needed to go to my class, and, with some composure, stand in front of my students.

It felt shameful to walk down the hallway. The lovestruck teacher. Ridiculous and humiliating. I decided to get rid of the green dress with the low neckline, the uncomfortable high-heeled ankle boots. The pain did not abate, in vain I straightened my shoulders, in vain I tried to walk briskly with my head held high.

I taught my classes while aching inside, repeating the same sentences I had repeated the year before and the year before that as if I were a robot, not thinking of anything, with no energy and no soul, not even understanding what the hell I was doing here in this oversized, echoing lecture hall with its artificial lights, in which, even with a microphone, a human voice was dispersed into scattering echoes.

Who were these people all around me? All of these young people, their faces all the same. What were they looking for here, what did they believe, what were they hoping for?

At the end of my class I repeated to them that before the time of the Unified Regency, most of them would not have been able to attend this university. I rattled off the sentences which I had delivered so many times, now worn and battered from so much repetition. I raised my left hand theatrically, as if I was at once warning and blessing them, as if it mattered that they were here.

They were sitting far enough away from me that I didn't have to look into their eyes.

There was no one in the faculty office. I closed the door behind myself, slid onto the floor, and I had an epiphany: I would never see the body, or the face, of that person ever again. Never. There could be no more contact.

And with that—with that simple observation in my head—I threw down my notes, I lay down on the floor, I pulled up my knees, waiting for the pain to lessen.

It would have been good for me to find my way back to my anger and that inner, darkened labyrinth. To be able to find my way to any emotion in which there was strength to help me to get up again.

It would have been good to find my way back to my rage, that for months, he had used me, strung me along, manipulated me, that the future did not exist, even the present did not exist, there was only that wretched notebook, there had only been two empty bodies conversing with each other, and that even if they said something, here, in this dimension it did not mean anything, it was only a kind of unintelligible ambient music, a game of nerves and feelings, a series of reflections along the infinite glass surfaces of corridors. I could not stand up.

I huddled on the floor with my knees drawn up.

In my childhood, my mother always closed the door to my room while she decorated the Christmas tree. I could not come out until she rang the bell. After a while she didn't even need to ask me to close myself in my room, by the time I was in fourth grade, I was the one who insisted on the game. I was eleven years old, in the fifth grade, when Christmas came around again, and I withdrew after lunch so that my mother, in her usual way, could set the tree in its stand. She kept it on the balcony as she had done every year before, and we both acted as though the tree was not there all tied up. We simply pretended not to notice it. My mother stored the potatoes, the onions, and the eggs on the balcony, and she also put the cooked dishes out there to cool. Whenever I stepped onto our chilly balcony with its artificial-stone tiling, when she sent me to get something, I always saw the tree. One Christmas morning, I heard the clunking of the wrought iron stand, the clattering of the thumbscrews, my mother panting and coughing slightly as she struggled to set up the tree. The rustling tree tipped to the right, then to the left, and my mother kept adjusting it. Peering through the crack in the door, I watched how she began hanging up the decorations. Then suddenly she turned on her heel and walked to my room, where she opened my door, looked me straight in the eye, and said:

Come help me.

I didn't understand what she was doing. She had upset the rules of the game. I remember my shock and disappointment, my belief that she shouldn't have been doing this. It was as if I truly believed with my entire soul that the angels and baby Jesus, in December, came flying, holding the Christmas tree and its shedding leaves, into our living room, and that now my mother had definitively chased them away with this insensitive and aggressive command. With my mouth wide open, ready to sob, I threw myself onto my bed, and I let my mother's consoling hand rub my back. Even that much gentleness was enough for my tears to start flowing, for the sobbing to burst out of me. My snot came down onto the plaid blanket and the legs of my doll Kati, whose toenails I had colored with a felt pen in nursery school.

But now there was no one who came to place their warm palm on my back, to help me get up. I was alone in my life, alone on the floor, alone in this room with its high walls, as if in a glass box. If at least I could have kept my sense of shame. Perhaps that could have masked this unbearable throbbing anguish. This absurd pain, however, as if breaking out from the depths of my body, pulled me down with an almost paralyzing force. I did not understand how I could be aware of what was happening to me, and yet incapable of controlling myself. It was as if a strange, wakeful consciousness sat in my head, as if my brain no longer communicated with my body, as if it were incapable of connecting these two pieces of information, to slide the contours of the two ghost images on top of each other and to say, yes, that was him. And that other one, that was also him, the one who wrote down those words.

My gut had declared independence. In the most unexpected moments, my stomach shrank, or my heart began to pound. If a similar-looking person with red hair, wearing a tweed jacket, crossed the street while I was driving, my breath quickened. Lying on the floor, the legs of the furniture in the faculty room made me think of the strange-smelling tubular furniture in his small apartment, and I began to yearn to be there again. There, in that oblique, curtained, faraway room with its shabby furniture, its creaking parquet floor.

To know nothing again, for once and for all to know absolutely nothing, for just one more time in my life to lie there naked, let it be the day before yesterday, let us be together somewhere else in time, but not here in this bleak, sharp light, in this barren present, enlarging every speck of dust, every abrasion, every scratch.

This was like mourning, when a person somehow wishes to wind back time, to arrange every single detail into a constellation in which that last unsuspecting moment can still be seen.

I turned onto my other side, pressing my hand against my stomach, as if the pain were insidiously radiating outward in all directions from there—from my womb, my ovaries.

In the end, we were also lying to our students. We lied about what had happened. Certainly, there had been fatalities in all of their families. There had been people who had been attacked and humiliated, who, during the civil war, were forced to flee the country. People whose dossiers had been sequestered, who were blackmailed, wiretapped. And the ones who stayed here, did they ever speak about this to their children? Did they say anything at all? Or was that also part of the bargain—that no one would ever tell them anything about their parents or their grandparents? In the university, we kept forcing these contradictory stories on the students, stories that they willingly repeated back to us while—in my opinion—never believing a word. They didn't even think about it twice. It had nothing to do with their own lives.

Nor did it have anything to do with my life. Here I was, lying in this wretched office, then soon I would pull myself together again, and go home to that person whom I hadn't seen naked for many years.

Suddenly another image of the small apartment flashed across my mind along with an image of his chest. I didn't want to think about it, but it appeared in my mind, completely magnified, and I saw myself with him, looking improbably more beautiful in this fantasy than the woman whose face I glimpsed every morning in the bathroom mirror.

Somebody was impatiently fiddling with the doorknob. They were pushing and pulling on it. They couldn't come in, because I'd left the key in the lock from inside.

They knocked. They kept pressing on the doorknob.

I had to get up, breathe evenly, somehow rearrange my face and open the door.

Please come in.

A woman, a spiky-haired coworker, was standing outside, a docent. I knew that she had no classes today; I'd never seen her here before on a Friday. Well, of course, it was the camera. They'd sent her here for me. The woman pushed the door open forcefully, and as she stepped in with her right foot, she stared into my face, scrutinizing me. She cast a quick glance around the space, at my desk. Clearly, she'd already seen the photocopies I'd made, now locked away in my desk drawer. Perhaps she'd already made her own copies of them—most certainly she had.

Everything okay?

Everything's fine. I just finished teaching.

I would not have been surprised if she suddenly announced that baby Jesus did not exist, and that I should go help her out immediately.

to reach the inner door

Dr. Kreutzer had just arrived at his office. He aired it out, then ran his index finger over a few pieces of furniture to check if everything had been thoroughly dusted: it had not been. He washed his hands and then started brewing tea. When the water began to boil, it was 10 a.m., but his patients were often late for the first appointment.

He heard the valve of the samovar gurgling. As of now, he wasn't afraid, and he didn't take the stories he'd heard very seriously. It was something like a fire drill, or a theatrical dress rehearsal, a scene in which what would be done in a genuinely dangerous situation was being acted out in real time. He concentrated exclusively on the tasks entrusted to him, and wove his plans for the future, once he got through this series of tasks. He focused on the designated team members, their abilities, their personalities, any possible vulnerabilities. He was curious about the guy who would be showing up now. Judging from the photographs the hospital provided, he looked like a wild beast, but his coworkers—the ones who had forwarded his file—had focused on his qualifications, which, for this first round, were promising. This hulking guy could be given the most important task of all: Among all the individuals selected so far, he was the only one who knew how to operate a crane.

That morning, he had tried to reach Petra, but her phone must have been turned off. He wanted to know what was going on with the children and possibly convince them to go on a trip with him. On paper they were still husband and wife. Petra could leave the country, and she could also take the children abroad, although only with his permission. He called again, but she didn't pick up. The tea was ready; the intercom buzzed.

The man was on time. In a deep voice, he wished Dr. Kreutzer a good day through the intercom. Well of course, thought the psychiatrist, for people like him morning means 6 a.m. at dawn.

He placed his cup onto the small table, and his telephone beside it. If Petra called him back he would take the call during this session.

The man had been sent to him from the Second Clinic of the United Regency. The day before, he had received instructions to contact Dr. Kreutzer, who himself received instructions to meet this person as soon as possible, as his papers contained the numerical code 009. They had made an appointment for this morning. Dr. Kreutzer had another appointment scheduled for 11 a.m. with another person coded 009; and this second individual had been sent to him from the Human Distribution Center. There was no time to lose; he had to move quickly.

The bald man stood rigidly by the outside entrance and did not step in farther. Dr. Kreutzer went out to get him and introduced himself. He was much taller than he had appeared in his photographs. His bodily measurements were indicated in his dossier, but Dr. Kreutzer hadn't read those, only casting a passing glance at the man's medical history.

Once again, the man came to a dead halt at the door of Dr. Kreutzer's office, looking around. Dr. Kreutzer offered him a seat, and noticing his scrutinizing gaze, asked him if there were any problems.

This doesn't look like a doctor's office.

A psychiatrist must always take pains to create—as much as possible—a secure, homelike environment for his patients, Dr. Kreutzer explained to the man as he ushered him inside. In any event, he had wished to avoid a sterile hospital atmosphere, he explained. The man hesitated to sit down in the chair pushed out in front of him, as if ready to leave, repeating that he had already explained everything to the head physician. He had also received a release form from the Second Clinic. Here it is, he said producing the document. He was ready to work. He had been prescribed no medicine, and his wish to be active again had remained unfulfilled, despite his insistence. That was why he was here now. He had been sent here for some reason, he said, blinking, looking up.

This man had suffered a workplace accident six months ago. He'd been struck by lightning, which had not killed him but caused serious burns, causing some damage to his nervous system. He could not sleep properly—only for two or three hours at a time. But he experienced no physical pain and could miraculously use his injured left arm. His medical history indicated that after the accident, he had been afflicted with muscle inflammation for weeks, but this condition had since subsided. His increasingly manic state, however, gave his physician pause. The man kept repeating to everyone that he had a mission. But apart from that, his mind seemed clear.

The man showed Dr. Kreutzer his upper arm. There's always a pulsating feeling in it, he said.

As the man calmed down, his body posture loosened up. He began the customary narrative, one recited to the previous doctor so many times, that he felt himself to be one of the elect. Ever since the accident, he felt like someone who had been designated.

Who designated you?

Dr. Kreutzer did not mean to sound ironic, but his head tilted slightly to one side, accompanied by his serene, interested facial expression, which aroused the man's suspicion. The man's posture once again became tense. He considered his response for a relatively long period, straightened his shoulders a bit, his eyes narrowing.

What do you mean, who?

Dr. Kreutzer tried to help him.

Was it God who designated you? he asked. Or was it . . . Mother Nature?

In the evaluation of this interview—that is to say, the evaluation of its recording—it was important to note if the man avoided answering certain questions, or if other questions made him nervous. His former colleagues said he had a choleric temperament. He was still thinking about his answer, then shrugged awkwardly. Dimly, he recalled a fantasy novel which he had read a long time ago with his girlfriend. It happened to be the only book he'd ever picked up as an adult, all for the sake of a girl. Something came back to him now from those long-ago paragraphs, from the depths of his memory. He threw back his head and answered:

It was the lord of all that exists. He designated me.

I see.

The man explained that this was why he had survived the lightning strike—because he had something to do in this world. Not only that, but it was something very special—his mission!

Not, he continued, what he'd been doing up till now, but something much more important. Something much more sublime, he pointed upward with his unwieldy hand.

Look here, he turned toward the psychiatrist, as he began unbuttoning his flannel shirt, look at this here! If I had this inked on me, I would die. No one would ever take on a job like that, not for any money. And yet it happened to me. Here it is—what the bolt of lightning did.

From the man's shoulder, all the way down his thick, muscled arm, there coiled a Lichtenberg figure—the mark that arises on the skin of lightning strike survivors—sixty or seventy centimeters in length. Where **the electrical current runs beneath the skin**, the discharge creates a complex formation reminiscent of the tendrils of window frost in the tissues. Later, the branching patterns gradually disappear, although the burn mark remains forever. The Lichtenberg figure wound all the way down to the man's hand where it came to an end in pointy leaf formations. Dr. Kreutzer had heard about this phenomenon before, and he had seen photographs of the man's arm in the materials forwarded by his colleague, but it was very different to observe this richly detailed, incandescent purple tracery in real life.

Dr. Kreutzer was surprised by the man's robust back, his enormous, hairy upper body, in which there was something animallike, something uncanny. He asked if the wounds were sensitive. Slightly so, the patient answered, mainly when he showered.

In the end it's still a burn, or whatever, the man said, caressing the wound.

Dr. Kreutzer inquired as to whether there had been any repercussions of this accident that disrupted his daily lifestyle. He knew about his sleep problems, but he was curious to know if the man would mention them himself. As a doctor, he was also interested in the man's sexuality. The man answered that it was fairly difficult for him to fall asleep.

I don't even sleep, he said.

He began buttoning up his shirt.

The man said that he sometimes woke up in the middle of the night, his heart pounding; he showed the doctor how as his hand, marked with crimson burns, jumped up and down in front of his shirt. Thank God there are no problems with screwing, he laughed. Nevertheless, he'd only been with a woman once since the accident.

Do you have a wife?

No. Why would I?

He usually went to brothels. Although now he didn't even miss it that much. He went to make sure that everything was still in working order. It reassured him see that everything was still functioning.

In response to why he was using the services of prostitutes instead of forming genuine connections, he asked what the point of genuine connections was. Those too were genuine chicks, he smiled, miming two large breasts with his cupped hands.

He'd always gone to whores, he added, as he continued doing up the buttons, because he didn't trust women. Long ago, he'd had a proper girlfriend, but she left him for another guy, some scrawny little nobody, and he did not want to compromise himself anymore. Never again, he muttered.

Not even for a slut.

It was hard for him to do up all the buttons on his shirt, not because of his wound or a lack of fine motor skills, but because of his thick fingers, which fumbled with the tiny plastic buttons.

It seemed that this man's colleagues had sized him up correctly: He had no long-term partner, no children born from previous relationships. His parents were no longer alive, and no one in his district had any knowledge of any close friends. He lived in a rented studio apartment. He paid his bills on time, consumed alcohol in moderation, did not take any medications on a regular basis, and had no chronic illnesses.

When Dr. Kreutzer asked him if he would like a cup of tea, this hefty man was almost offended. He refused a cup of tea as if somebody had asked him if he were interested in men. He snorted. Tea? Maybe on the moon.

He was planning—once his skin calmed down, once it finally healed—to have the entire pattern inked in black and yellow, so it would look like a real lightning bolt. No matter the cost. Because now it looked like some kind of fern.

I'm no gardener. And I've done enough digging, he said.

The fern is a very beautiful plant, Dr. Kreutzer said, smiling. It's so . . . mysterious. The pattern on his arm did not make him seem at all like a gardener, he reassured the man. Instead, it made him think of shadows.

Shadows?

Yes, shadows, and concealment.

And something else too, Dr. Kreutzer added, as he poured himself another cup of tea. He stirred it to let it cool off while glancing furtively at his phone. The hulking man raised his eyebrows, it was a childishly curious expression.

Ferns multiply through spores. They have neither flower nor fruit. Did you know that?

pine trees, squirrels, little birds

It was past one o'clock, and she had to go get the children: first Vilmos at 4 p.m., and then Emma at four fifteen.

Petra came home from her training session, took off her coat, and sat still in the kitchen. She could have started some work at home, but she didn't have the energy.

She stared off into space, exhausted, nearly shivering from weariness. She should have been getting her warmer coat out of the closet, but she just sat there with the coffee as it slowly cooled, staring out the window. The kitchen window looked out onto the firewall of the building next door, where there was only one window, which had been added later, one story above hers. It opened onto a bathroom—the windowpane was frosted glass, so that no one could see in if the lights were on inside.

Right now, the light was shining yellow, so perhaps somebody was having a bath. Or another, unknown woman, with her eyebrows raised, was applying makeup before a mirror. Petra, too, would have been happy to take a bath, but she was afraid of getting even more drowsy, leaving her even more enervated throughout the rest of the long afternoon before she had to pick up the children. Instead, she decided to make a mug of warm coffee.

Once they got home, she mused, she would give the children their baths, then she too would wash. The apartment was well situated, equipped with generators, located in the protected district, but still sometimes the power went out in the evening, and there was no warm water. She had gotten the children used to bathing between 5 and 6 p.m., so that they were already in their pajamas before it became completely dark. Still, there should be something she could do to fill this narrow, weary strip of time before picking up the children. Something useful.

The gloves and scarves were kept in the clothes cupboard in the foyer, on the upper right-hand shelf, above the coat hangers. She could take them out and pick out the ones that the children weren't using anymore. She set her mug down, got up, turned on the light in the hallway, and stepped over to the cupboard, opening the door.

Something tumbled out of the closet. A heavy, tall, dark object keeled out from inside, something like a rigid body. She could hardly catch it, almost reeling in her fright.

It was the Christmas tree. That goddamned artificial tree.

It rested in her arms as if it were a drunken partner and she a dancer holding it up. She grabbed the tree, bloody heavy, and now she recalled that of course, they had crammed it in here, not taking it down to the basement storage last winter, where it should have been, so that they wouldn't have to bother hauling it up from the basement at Christmas.

She propped the tree against the wall and looked at it. It was tied up badly, with branches here and there slipping out of the string's grasp and somehow dislocated on one side, which gave the unhappy tree the appearance of a fraying mummy trying to untangle itself from its own gauze bandages. It was shedding too, covering the entire floor with artificial pine needles.

Mihály had already taken his own scarves and gloves out of the basket on the cupboard shelf. It seemed that he was the one who had stuffed the wretched tree back into the closet so stupidly that it came tumbling out as soon as the door was opened.

Petra stood on her tiptoes, grabbed the basket, and dumped everything onto the floor. There were now only her own scarves, as well as Emma's little squirrel hat. Emma didn't wear it anymore, her squirrel phase had come to an end. I should give the hat away to someone, Petra thought.

The artificial tree was propped up against the wall, as frightening to look at as a skeleton. There was really something so oppressive about it. Petra couldn't decide if it was because this lifeless tree somehow embodied her husband's antipathy to all plants and animals, his attachment to sterile things, or if it was just plain ugly because it was dead, formed as it was out of green, shit-colored plastic. As if, with its little plastic leaves falling down, it was sending a message that even though there had never been a real Christmas at her mother-in-law's, there would never be a real Christmas celebration here in this apartment too—because it was forbidden to celebrate, because no one should forget for a moment that this day was not, first and foremost, the glorious day of the birth of our

Lord, but the death day of someone else. Christmas was the anniversary of the day, eternal and immutable, that Öcsi left the family.

Petra had seen many pictures at her mother-in-law's of Mihály's younger brother who had died so young. Always at the end of any family gathering, old Auntie Pálma would take out the wooden box. Petra knew the nondescript child's face by heart. And when she looked at his photograph, she never felt anything beyond indifference and unease, which was also what she felt in relation to that strange word that came to mind while turning over the pictures—she almost smiled to herself—it flashed through her that this freckled, dull-looking little boy with light eyelashes was indeed her brother-in-law.

She needed to stuff the artificial tree back into its place. She stared at it. Then she had another idea—a better one.

She quickly grabbed the scarves and the squirrel hat up from the floor, pushed the basket back into its place, and, as if it were another person waiting for her in the foyer, she spoke to the tree:

Well, let's go!

She put on her boots, stuffed a pair of gloves in her pocket, then glanced at the clock. She had plenty of time until 4 p.m.

If she set off for the school at three thirty, she could get there in time even with traffic—the school was located just uphill in a guarded quarter surrounded by trees.

She pulled the tree out of the apartment, dragging it down the stairs. The plastic needles kept shedding, which made rustling sounds, littering the entire staircase. In the garage, she propped the artificial tree against the wall to open the back door of the car. She took out the child car seat and the raiser, set them by the wall, and then shoved the tree into the car.

The artificial tree lay in the back seat, tied up, silent, dark. She drove up to the garage entrance, opened it with the remote control. She was counting on there being light traffic, and getting out of the city within a quarter of an hour.

She thought of the statement she had heard from her husband's mouth so many times, and it made her smile. She saw Mihály's face in front of her, head tilted to one side, and she heard his voice repeating the sentence she'd heard a thousand times before: *You do realize, don't you, that you're behaving completely irrationally?*

No, no she wasn't behaving irrationally; on the contrary, she had made an extremely rational decision.

On the road, she passed other drivers swiftly, passing the gas station, headed uphill. At the old monument—where the children used to go on school trips—she turned farther up the steep incline. She passed by the old Outlook restaurant, now in ruins, its roof collapsed, the tree nursery, the ever-sparser villas—their cold windows staring down at the city beneath them, guarded by uniformed and armed men—as she drove along the winding road toward the forest.

At one point she stopped and looked around. The dirt road was empty.

They did not come here very often for walks as they feared encountering people hiding in the woods, or drifters, their senses warped by hunger. Fanatic joggers, escaping from the outer world into perfecting their bodies, dissuaded by neither cold nor danger, ran their circular forest routes at dawn into the morning hours. At this time of day, there would be at the most some well-to-do dog walkers, armed with pepper spray, but even they would have nothing to say to a woman dragging an artificial pine tree. At the very least, they would think that she was worrying too much and had decided to get her Christmas tree early.

For safety's sake, she looked around once again, opened the car trunk, and pulled out the tree. It was heavy, long, and difficult to grab onto. She lowered it onto the ground, then started rummaging around in the trunk. Somewhere here there was a collapsible box containing a first aid kit, an ice scraper, and bungee cords of various lengths. She pulled out two sturdier bungee cords, attaching the hooks to the string wound around the tree. She could pull the artificial tree using these cords as if it were some kind of oversize, disheveled sleigh.

She looked around again to make sure that no one was around. She fished out a pocketknife, shoved it into her pocket, then closed the trunk, locked the car, and headed into the forest.

She wanted to get to the densest part of the forest where nothing from the town or road could be heard.

Here, at the top of the low mountain, it was a few degrees colder than in the city. She struggled to pull the tied-up tree along the bumpy ground.

She proceeded cautiously along the forest path, slowed down by branches or tree roots jutting up from the ground. A small bird shot up from the dead leaves suddenly. Among the trees there was silence, a cold fog. She saw a few garbage bags, as well as other debris left alongside the path. Tile pieces tumbled out onto the loamy ground from a ripped garbage bag.

She felt that what she was doing was not littering, but instead putting things in order. The partial purification of one of the locations of her life. She pricked up her ears for the sound of anyone else in the thicket. She'd heard that sometimes unhappy people sought refuge here, and so there were regular armed patrols along the winding paths.

She passed by a few trees that had fallen over, their trunks covered with fungus, and after about twenty minutes of hauling the tree, she finally arrived at a clearing.

There was a stand of a few pine trees.

This is good, she thought.

She dragged the artificial tree over to the pine trees and untied the string. She opened up the metal tree stand unfolding in four directions and set the tree on the stand. It was a little wobbly, so she pulled it a bit to one side. She unfolded the branches and arranged them. The plastic needles were shedding heavily, their dark green color in striking contrast to the decomposing shades of the loamy ground.

With the heels of her boots, she pushed the tawny earth onto the metal stand. She collected some stones, pine cones, and twigs, spreading them on top of the tree stand. She prepared it just as carefully as she did at home during the holidays, and she was just as pressed for time, because she had to pick up the children at 4 p.m. She had to get the tree ready quickly.

She bent down, panting as she worked, then took deep breaths of the bitingly clear air. Soon she was done. She had concealed the metal stand.

When she stepped back, the difference was not so conspicuous: The tree nearly blended in with its forest companions. As she walked farther back along the path, she could hardly see any diversions in color, only sensing lighter and darker green hues. She started heading back, and already, having walked twenty meters, the artificial tree was no longer distinctly visible as something that was artificial: She could no longer discern its specific contours. She only knew that it stood there among the other pine trees.

She was still panting, still walking animatedly along the forest path, although she felt all the weariness leaving her muscles. As she walked back to the car through the **rustling, living, breathing** forest, an inexplicable feeling of tranquility came over her. It was a kind of certainty: She had done this, moreover, she had done it well. This one matter, at least, had been taken care of; she had done the right thing. For she had had no other choice. Trees must be planted, the dead must be buried. But what to do with the past? Where to put all those years? Could they be enclosed somewhere, or at least placed under tight lock and key, so that the door of time could never be opened again, so that nothing could ever come tumbling out from the depths in the most unexpected moments?

For nothing ever to come tumbling out.

She got back to her car. She was drenched in sweat, her hands red from the cold, even though her gloves were in her pocket. There were four missed calls on her phone, and she had thirty minutes to get home and possibly shower before picking up the children from school.

surging throughout his entire body

Dr. Kreutzer slammed the car door shut, glanced at the back seat, and drove out of the parking lot. He hoped the surprise had not wilted after all these hours. It was very hard to get cut flowers. The shopkeepers often froze the more expensive and beautiful blooms; then, once at room temperature, the newly purchased bouquet would start wilting, the leaves falling off.

He could hardly wait to see her again. Somehow, Giselle had to be propitiated. He wanted to show her where he had spent his childhood. And he had promised her that they would celebrate his birthday together, to clear up the situation by then. There was only one week left.

He looked at himself in the rearview mirror. His stubble had grown in somewhat again since his morning shave, but he didn't mind. He found this reddish-brown hue manly, it always made him think of that imaginary guy who looked much more like a Camel cigarette ad than his own reflection with its thin, ever sparser, smoothed back hair.

He wondered if he should quickly stop off by his office for the electric razor to shave again before driving to the other side of the city. One time, his stubble had caused Giselle's nylon stockings to rip. She was not too happy about it. Giselle kept looking at the tear; she stood up and saw that the ripped section was lower than the hem of her skirt. She would have to go teach her class like that, in ripped stockings.

Sometimes she could be so petty.

Fuck her, said the man from the Camel ad to the rearview mirror in a deep, insouciant voice. Fuck her and her fucking stockings.

He wondered if meeting at his mother's apartment, crammed as it was with boxes, was such a good idea; perhaps it would be better to meet up in their usual place: his office. At least everything there was clean and orderly, and you didn't have to keep washing your hands every time you touched something. His own small flat was out of the question. He had neglected to look around earlier, to make sure that there were no earrings or any other items left behind by other women. He had dashed out, not even making the bed. And it takes women less than a nanosecond to detect another woman's perfume: He would have had to change the bed linens. All the same, his mother's apartment seemed the ideal location for that day's meeting. He wanted Giselle to trust him again, to feel that she could draw him into her life, to start planning their own shared future during their meetings. He wanted to show her his childhood photos, his old room and his kid brother's old teddy bear. Good thing he hadn't thrown it out when he was sorting through his mother's things.

He was frightened by how she had run away from him last week. And then by her dull indifference, lasting for days, his messages left unanswered. He imagined, yes, he believed that he would be helping their relationship by seeking out Giselle, by asking her to start furnishing, at least in her imagination, the roomy apartment they'd be sharing together in the future. They could at least plan it out together on paper! And of course, later, in reality too. He had sent her floor plans—his tried and tested method. This always worked when a woman began to doubt their relationship. It made them enthusiastic, awakened their nesting instincts. At first, Giselle had not reacted, then asked him to send normal photographs, because to imagine the space she needed to see the placement of the walls, windows and doors, not just empty floor plans. And she would also need to see the exact dimensions, she wrote in another text.

It was hard to argue with that. And yet, he did not send anything else. He had been certain the damned floor plan would be enough—it had always been before. Where the hell was he supposed to get photographs of an apartment? Where could he even find some empty apartment with four rooms that he could take pictures of? He texted Giselle back, saying the apartment still had another renter. He could not walk in and start photographing a stranger's furniture and personal items. But he would send another set of floor plans which showed where the doors were. Sod it!

Fucking cunt.

The voice of the man from the Camel ad deepened, and in an operatic voice, he sang to a red car that cut in front of him.

Fu-u-ck-i-ng cu-u-nt.

He had taken pictures of his own furniture—he murmured to Giselle as he palmed her left breast, exposing it from the leaf-patterned dress that she had clearly just purchased, freeing her breast above the underwire bra—so that they could plan, together, where the pieces would go in their new, shared apartment. All of his old family furniture: the large dining room table, the Thonet chairs, at least one of the large wardrobes, and everything that she herself would be bringing. Certainly, she must have one or two antique pieces she'd inherited.

No, I don't, Giselle muttered, looking down.

Dr. Kreutzer looked at her breast. It was spread out and pale, like large white cheese. A slightly moist, crumbling piece of mozzarella. It was sweating beneath Giselle's new, polyester-fiber dress. Giselle, like so many other women, wore a padded bra, which rendered both breasts completely uniform. This also made impossible the amusing activity of guessing the location of the nipples or the true form of the breasts, which could be glimpsed only at the very last moment of undressing.

The red car from a moment ago was forcing its way across, trying aggressively to pass into the other lane. Dr. Kreutzer looked at the license plate, it was not a state car. He wanted to grind this peasant down.

That's the bus line, you scumbag.

Prole. Stop honking!

The last time they'd been together, they looked at photographs on his phone, and Giselle had suddenly grown somber. She hadn't reacted even though he caressed her back and rubbed her breasts. Later, he took her right nipple into his mouth, to try to shake her out of her lethargy. He sucked on her nipple, eyes closed, and found that it was a bit salty. Suddenly he remembered the inflatable water wings he had as a child, and the hard little rubber spout that always sunk back into the swollen plastic. You had to grab it with your teeth if you wanted to blow more air into the water wings.

The mozzarella breast was not reacting to his fondling, as if it wasn't even a part of her body. Giselle put her hands on Dr. Kreutzer's head and moved it slightly to one side so she could see the phone's touch screen clearly. She scrolled back with her finger, her gaze settling on the two carved, dark wood wardrobes. She was silent, anxious.

After a short while, when she gave herself to him pleasantly and dryly, she only said that it seemed that Petra's things didn't count. The renter's things did count, the privacy of those things had to be respected, but not Petra's personal objects. She was, in the end, only a wife.

She looked up at the ceiling while Dr. Kreutzer fumbled around in her vagina, lying there apathetically as if she herself were Petra. A woman she'd never seen, but whose hairbrush was there on the commode in one of the photographs, whose shoes were lined up in the foyer next to the children's shoes.

This had not occurred to Dr. Kreutzer when he was taking the photographs of the furniture in the family apartment. He had not even noticed the folding drying rack hung with the children's clothes, the toys scattered around the kitchen, the half-opened curtain in the bedroom, the woman's red purse hanging on the coat hook.

I want you to help me create a dream for our shared future, he murmured.

He pronounced the word *dream* soft and low, in deep tones, as deeply as any human creature could dream. It was as if the name of an exorbitantly priced brand of chocolate, with 90 percent cocoa, was being cooed in an ad for sweets. Melting on the palate, tepid on the tongue, a shared future. Carved, chocolate-brown antique furniture.

Giselle pulled her knees to her chest and didn't answer. She got dressed as if she were leaving a gynecological appointment. She had a class to teach at two o'clock, and it was already half past. She said goodbye, then only muttered in the doorway, as if to herself, that those were her best stockings.

Dr. Kreutzer realized he should have gotten a new dammed pair of pantyhose in addition to the flowers. Some nice thigh-high stockings.

The line of cars became ever more congested.

To get to the southernmost part of the city, where his mother's apartment was located, he had to drive across two districts overrun with the poor. At the red lights, grimy children and impoverished people with caved-in faces clung to his car. They kept knocking, trying to wipe the windshield with rags, and if he didn't hand them some change through the window, they spat on the glass. He had to step on the gas to make them scatter. He didn't have enough time to drive by another route. The studio apartment that he was renting was far from here, in the northern section of the city, and he had forgotten about peak afternoon traffic in this area. That was obviously why the rent was so low, he grumbled, because you had to fight your way across half the city to get there, had to drive through these chaotic neighborhoods. It was a miracle that the traffic lights were still working, that they hadn't been smashed into pieces or that this riffraff hadn't ripped out all the cables.

He would have to get the car washed again, he said to himself, annoyed.

On the right-hand side of the road, tents were surrounded by debris and sheets of tar paper hung from stakes lined up along the battered grass. Long ago, in his childhood, a gravel-paved park with logs and a sweet shop had been right there. Now, rags were burning in the oil drums on the sidewalk and people crouched along the edge of this sidewalk, as if sitting on an endless low, flat gym bench. With expressionless faces, they gaped at the traffic that passed by them, the cars **coming from somewhere else and going somewhere else**, heading from and to parts of the city that were eternally closed off to them, inaccessible, located at distances which they would likely not even be able to cover with their festering legs shod in overworn, deteriorating shoes.

People were gathered atop the empty plinth where the Freedom Monument had once stood; the Unified Regency had been planning a new Statue of National Unity for that spot. The Statue of Unity, however, which would have measured 120 meters tall and weighed 600 tons, was never erected in this square—formerly comprising the city center and today inhabited by vagrants—nor was it erected anywhere else. Every six months, new visualizations were created for the statue's location, with the local papers leaking seemingly confidential details concerning this undertaking: the foundry operations, the solidity of the material, methods of delivery and assembly, the mandatory installation scaffolding, and finally, the metals used in creating the alloy, symbolizing the components of the national body. Dr. Kreutzer had garnered a surprisingly large amount of information about the planned statue, as last year, Vilmos had chosen this topic for a homework assignment on the environment, and Dr. Kreutzer had downloaded all the plans.

The giant plinth—two years after it had been constructed—had started to erode, however, and in windy weather, rough, grey debris covered the entire square. If it wasn't raining, hordes of poor people settled on the top of the Anvil, as it was called, watching the traffic, or the streets leading up to the square. At that time, there was a good deal of reporting about the company—belonging to one of the country's oligarch circles—that had supervised the landscaping, the preparation of the locale, as well as the building of the reinforced concrete plinth. This firm had never assumed responsibility for the deficiencies in construction. Above, on the crumbling plinth, just as on the square below, fire was burning in an oil drum, surrounded by silhouettes moving uncertainly. Among them was the woman with no nose, known throughout the city, who somehow was able to get through every checkpoint, drunk as she was, frightening everyone in the protected districts. Everyone recognized her from afar as she leaped around and scythed the air around herself with her thin arms like an emaciated animal. She jumped up and down with her crackbrained squawking and her unmistakable movements.

Dr. Kreutzer was relieved that the party was not being held right next to the roadway with its traffic but up in the smoky heights, on the Anvil. It had happened to him many times before that the scrawny woman with sparse hair would run between the cars, dancing in the rain with twisting movements, at times flinging herself onto the windshield of a car, horrifying the driver inside, so that grimacing, she could point to the two dark holes where her nose, putrefied from syphilis, used to be.

Now there were only grimy children running in between the cars; it was easy to shake them off. As soon as the light turned green, Dr. Kreutzer stepped on the gas, and they dispersed as if they'd never even been there. There was a tiny child among them, even younger than Emma, but who'd never been in an accident: The older children always pulled the clumsier, slower ones out of the way just in time. These unfortunate kids had been born here in this district and raised on the street. They observed the accelerating cars so indifferently, as if they were the gnarled-legged, mangy pigeons occasionally caught by their parents and roasted above the iron drum's blue flames.

Dr. Kreutzer thought about the stockings. He should still try to get a pair from somewhere. There really weren't any shops around here. To purchase something, he would have to drive to one of the protected districts. There were vendors standing alongside the main road, but they were haggling locals, bartering used and broken pieces of junk among themselves. Items such as canisters, shoes, and lighters. Only sporadically did someone park here to buy something, because the car could be broken into within a few minutes, someone well-dressed would be surrounded and robbed, though sometimes only their coat was yanked off.

Petra always bought her stockings at the Metmag shop. You could only get in there with a special ID card, and it was far away. He would not have time to drive back into the city even if he decided to try to lure Giselle to his office with some pretext.

The sun was beginning to set, and in another part of the sky, the moon was already shining high in the sky. Dusk illuminated the long boulevard with its low orange light. For a fleeting moment, everything suddenly looked as it had so long ago, in his childhood, when, with his parents, he used to walk back home along this route. Back then, there had still been shops here, people strolling in the falling twilight, and in the enormous, gravel-covered park in front of the Freedom Monument, the park with its shade-giving trees and benches, you could get roasted chestnuts in the winter and ice cream in the summer.

The traffic came to a standstill again, and the setting sun, squeezed between two residential buildings, was **writhing in cold incandescence**, as if it were wedged in between the buildings and could sink no further. The windshield, in this light, suddenly seemed horrifically grimy and stained. The noise and screeching of the frenzied people atop the Anvil broke through the car engine's drone, thickening into a roar that seemed completely close, almost threatening.

to play badminton in white clothes

My name is Wille, Giselle thought to herself. *Wille*—she pronounced it aloud. It didn't sound too bad. At first, when she had the idea of sending the photographed copy of the notebook to Petra, she thought she would write no return address on the envelope. She would merely toss the horrific package into the post box, then the addressee could do with it whatever she wished. To try to process this information, or collapse, whatever, according to her own taste and endurance level. In any event she, Giselle, would be liberated, she would be putting down this burden, namely, she'd be giving it to someone else. She got the idea of using a pseudonym afterward.

The name that she'd come up with pleased her greatly because it sounded like an unusual anagram.

She never believed she would be thinking about things like this. That she would be pondering how to gain entrance to the stairway of another building. Or what she would say if somebody asked her what she was doing there. She had come up with the name—behind which she could conceal herself as she plotted—

nearly accidentally. This was a name she could hide behind, hide away from her own desperation. At one point those five letters stood before her eyes on a letter, the farewell letter written by her sister—she had taken it out after the first few weeks of therapy with the psychiatrist. She had looked for it at the bottom of the cupboard among all the papers she kept there because she recalled that she was the one who held on to this letter, because it might help her understand what was happening to her.

"I didn't even know that you had an older sister"—she recalled the psychiatrist's words.

When she had, for the first time, glanced at the message Mina had left behind after so many years, her relationship with the psychiatrist had not yet begun, there was only troubled desire whirling inside her along with many questions. What did she want from this person? Was it really from him that she wanted what she wanted? And as for the psychiatrist himself—what could he himself want from a middle-aged woman who wasn't even beautiful, and not even that interesting? Who was, in reality, perfectly nondescript?

By the time she read her sister's letter for the umpteenth time—after finding it, she read it many times over—the entire absurd, erotic madness had already come to an end. The letter though, that short missive, helped her to find a name for that new, desperate woman, the woman she had become during these few turbulent weeks. The woman who wanted to deliver the envelope to its recipient.

She kept her sister's farewell letter in a green paper folder, with the few remaining photographs of her and many of their crumpled childhood letters. After one of her sessions with Dr. Kreutzer, she'd gone home with the suggestion to retrieve the letter. In her stockings, she crouched in the living room in front of the low commode, rummaging around, her heart pounding. She dumped everything onto the carpet. There were all kinds of folders, old x-rays, marriage certificates in velvet slipcases. She needed to find the green folder. She had never taken it out before, she only knew that it was there somewhere in the bottom of the commode, lying somewhere between the diplomas, official documents, and all sorts of other papers.

After Mina's death, her father, both embittered and flustered, wanted to get rid of everything; he was like someone intent on revenge for this betrayal, this scandalous thing that had happened to him. Mina never acted like this, he conveyed to the world with his enraged, inarticulate mourning. He had not given her permission to do this. He was furious at his daughter. He despised and blamed her, called her irresponsible, as if this entire playacting at death were aimed explicitly against him. He threw her notebooks, filled with scribblings, into the garbage, her university notes. He sold her car as quickly as he could. He kept nearly nothing of hers, not even the drawings she'd made for him as a present in childhood, or her letters.

Giselle, however—her younger sister—felt that this farewell letter could not be thrown out so easily, that would be a crime. Because to do so would be to deny her sister's death—the ultimate betrayal.

Someone in the family had to keep that letter. And that person was she. She brought home the green folder.

There were many typos in the letter as well as words mistakenly typed together or missing a space. Mina seemed to have rolled one piece of paper into the typewriter, then pummeled out a couple of brief sentences, the inky sediment of which had since hardened. Some words were missing a letter; in other places two words were written as one. Mina hadn't corrected anything, **a new sheet of paper was not inserted**. And so this part of the text remained as well, where she wrote: *And otherwise, if I die, from all of this, what wille v enabide.* The words, broken into pieces, suddenly looked like a name: Wille V. Enabide. She reread the letter once more.

That's who I am, Giselle thought.
I am that Wille.

In those days, she glanced over the letter again and again compulsively. She nearly knew it by heart. It was an impatient, flustered message to the living. It was still hard to believe that her sister had typed the letter, taken the pills, and died. And yet that is what had happened. When she didn't show up for work on Monday, she was found in her apartment, wearing a blue dress. She had paid all her bills in advance, the plants had been watered, the kitchen immaculate. She left copies of her bank transfers on the white writing desk she'd recently bought; her letter was lying next to these receipts. She could have easily written the letter on a computer and printed it out, but for some reason she had typed it, moreover on an old typewriter, the kind that their father used to have. The quarterly car-insurance payments, a language school, a dentist, cosmetic dentistry, the receipts for the bills were lined up next to each other. Why had she enrolled in a Spanish class? And why had she gone to the dentist before she died? What the hell was she fixing her teeth for? Why did she need a beautiful new smile when she was planning to kill herself? She must have been saving up the pills for months, she couldn't have gotten a prescription for so many at once. Or perhaps she did not really mean to die, she just wanted to scare them? To teach the two men who dominated her life a lesson? She wanted to blackmail them, and then died accidentally? No one understood. No one.

She read the letter again, then took it to the university department. Where her sister had written, *I have now decided*, Giselle began to feel something. Was it pain, sadness? Or was it merely an obscure, inexplicable envy? In any event, it was something. It was pallid, only slightly looming, hardly graspable in words, but still.

Her ultimate decision not to assemble and send the photographed and printed-out pages from Dr. Kreutzer's notebook pages as an anonymous package had something to do with her sister's farewell letter, even if indirectly. Something to do with how Mina had fallen in love with a married man, had collapsed, and then taken her own life.

I'm next, she said to herself aloud.

She sat in the department office with its huge glass panels, talking to herself; she was alone, apart from the cameras installed in the ceiling corners, their lenses moving back and forth. The letter lay before her.

What she had just said to herself was a frightening thought, but she was not Mina. She knew exactly what she didn't want. No, she was not her sister. And from now on, she was not Giselle either.

She was Wille.

Wille did not want to crouch on all fours naked on the carpet. She did not want to pose before the opened window, her skin covered in goose bumps. She did not want to keep checking her phone all night, she did not want to moisten her nipples with a licked finger, she did not want to make love in the car with the seats pushed down, her skirt hiked up and crumpled, and she did not want to keep sniffing the tissue damp with sperm, keep taking it out of her coat pocket in the university elevator.

It was the photographs on his phone that made her want to meet up with Petra and not send her the envelope anonymously. The photographs in which she had seen the objects of that unknown woman lying around the apartment, the children's clothes. From these details, this Petra—who, until then had merely been a name, an unpleasant, grey shadow from the not so distant past, a shadow following her in the present, even at times covering the future, who was merely a loud ring tone on Mihály's phone—this Petra now stepped out of these photographs as a living person, defenseless, suspecting nothing, and with whom she could have so much in common without even knowing her, so much more in common than with this other, ever more alien individual who had showed her the photographs while lying in bed.

And who was that person anyway? And who was she, when she sought to decipher his desires, when, ending her class early so that she could sit in her car to drive across the segregated zones, honking and passing other drivers to spend one hour in that curtained off, bleak lair in the northern district of the city? Who the hell was that man? If she happened to glance at him while they were making love, she saw the coupling of a debauched, balding old man and an enthusiastic, overeager ugly little puppy. She was repulsed by his red freckles, his clothes as he folded them and put them down.

These were troubled feelings, surging up from dark depths. Leaning over them, she saw clearly that they had nothing to do with love or intimacy. She saw neither her own face, nor that of the other. Although she did see Petra's face.

This relationship was like some kind of a drug. The more she was liberated from it, the more she wished to keep it going. Her sister might have fallen captive to a similarly vertiginous passion. She had inhaled it; she could drown in it, could too easily drown in this looming, powerless, sorrowful yearning that could never be satisfied. That someone had grabbed her ass, and she had lost her own free will. He had undone the buttons on her dress, taken her breast in his hands, lifted it from the bra; and her mouth went dry. She grew dizzy, and was incapable of completing a sentence that began: *Look, what I wanted to say is* . . .

The photographs she had seen on his phone had at last yanked her back to where that sentence began and where she could finally complete it. That hairbrush. That red purse hanging from the coat hook. She wanted to give Mihály's wife the copies of his notebook, to give her the strength to regain her own self, to pack up, to go far away from here. To disappear without a trace, together with the children.

If, at that time, Giselle's mother had taken a more forceful stand, if she had not collapsed, if she had not let Mina move away with their father, if she had fought for her, then perhaps her sister would be alive today.

Perhaps.

It was not true that their mother was neurotic, as their father always said. She was not a drama queen. What an insidious, loathsome phrase that was! She recalled another aspect of her mother: the mum who would sing, who, crouching behind the backboard of child's bed, played marionettes with them, creating a different voice for each role. No, their mother had not been mentally ill. Over the years she had gradually been destroyed by the medications and her own despair. She had wilted, lost her voice, her features, her friends, her work, and that small place in the world where she could squeeze in her own body of fifty kilos.

But I'm not my mother, she said to herself.

I am Wille.

carefully onto the wings

Albert got the ornaments from a street vendor. It was the last thing they needed. Bianka would certainly not be happy to see him coming home with Christmas tree decorations, and yet he still stepped over to the counter, cobbled together from boxes, to look at them. These were the real, old-fashioned kind of ornaments! There was an angel, a little house, and two silver spindles. Not only that, there was a **dark red finial** wrapped in paper. As Albert picked up the decoration to look at it, the toothless vendor growled that he wasn't selling the ornaments separately, only together.

It was still only the end of October, the holidays were a while away, and they needed six proper plates for their household. Even more than that, they needed tableware, as they only had a few old, battered pieces.

Albert felt hesitant, so he decided that if the guy was still standing here on his way back, he'd ask how much he wanted. They had always celebrated Christmas in the institute, but there were never shiny ornaments hanging on the tree put up in the dining room, only colored paper chains and Hungarocell-foam balls decorated using decoupage techniques, the kind of thing the children made during craft hour. Even during the civil war, there had always been a Christmas tree in the institute. In his last year there, one of the teachers brought them straw decorations which her mother had made. They all stood around the tree, and they hung up the decorations, but they weren't particularly beautiful. They weren't even shiny. Albert certainly wouldn't have put any decorations like that on his own tree.

He asked the vendor if he happened to have any plates or any kind of tableware, then he moved on. The cold wind nipped at his skin.

When he got home with the Christmas tree decorations, it was nearly midnight; he was completely frozen. Bianka wasn't angry. She didn't even try to find out how much he'd paid for them. She climbed out of bed and took them in her hands one by one. She lifted up the angel, placing her palm carefully on its wings, then she lowered it into the paper box. She took out the little house, holding it before her eyes. Then, dangling it from her index finger, she went into the room, trying to figure out where they would put the Christmas tree, where it would fit so they wouldn't keep bumping into it. Because they would have a tree this year, that much was certain. She stood in front of the window.

Here would be good.

If they wouldn't be able to get hold of a real Christmas tree, they would at least bring home some branches. Albi could get some from another district, or, if necessary, he could have a look around in the low mountains.

She put the little house back among the other decorations and placed the box on top of the cupboard. Her legs were ice cold when she slipped back under the cover. The stretched-out man's T-shirt she wore suited her, although it hardly covered her long thighs covered with fair down.

Albert only admitted two weeks later that he had traded an entire bunch of wax candles for the box of decorations, in addition to a pair of gloves.

You've lost your mind, Bianka said, looking at him gently.

She never mentioned the candles or the gloves again. Other times she would go on for weeks about half a tin of spoiled canned beans, or a dried out piece of bread, but this time she didn't grouse. They already had a real table, and now they would have a Christmas tree too, that was all that mattered. That was why they had invited some guests over too, to inaugurate the round plywood table. It had not been easy to haul it home. They'd found the table in an entranceway: perhaps it had been put out to be made into firewood. They had carried the table, wobbling, from the intersection to their apartment, walking sideways across the weed-overgrown tracks. Onlookers probably thought that they were taking the table for fuel. As the weather grew cooler, it became ever more difficult to find anything to burn in the stove. Even the more slender-trunk trees had disappeared from the parks; people gathered up rags, even paper refuse. Sometimes fights broke out. The round table gave off a strange, acidic odor until the wood fully dried out, and even then, when they sat down at the table, they sometimes caught whiffs of rotting forest leaves on an autumn morning.

They spread out a large, colored shawl atop their new find. The red-and-blue pattern was vibrant, and the four corners of the shawl covered the entire table. Albert arranged their four plates, each one different, on the table. Bianka then moved them over a bit. You put the plates near the table legs, she said, pointing downward, where you can't sit properly at the table.

They had invited over a girl who worked in the same hospital as Bianka, only one floor below, in the second medical ward. They had invited her over for lunch, as well as the orderly she'd been seeing for a while.

They arrived precisely on time with a box of tea bags. They looked around, then took off their muddy shoes. They praised the poster with the picture of a dog, the pullout sofa, which, for this festive occasion was exceptionally folded up.

That morning, Bianka had stored the bed linens on top of the cupboard. Albi wasn't satisfied with how the large, white bundle looked. He would have preferred to put them somewhere else, but they were too big to fit inside the cupboard. The other solution would have been to fold the bundle in two and ram it behind the cupboard, but Bianka would not permit this: Firstly, there wasn't enough room, even if they pushed the cupboard forward, and secondly, the clean bed linens would get all grimy. It was very difficult to deal with the laundry in chilly weather like this with no washing machine. The smaller pieces of clothing could be washed, wrung out and hung in the apartment, but Bianka had to sneak the larger items into the hospital laundry in her backpack where they would get washed along with the hospital linens. This carried certain risks. She had to stand there as the laundered items on the long aluminum tables in the basement were being sorted, checking the ink-printed marks, grouping the disinfected, perfectly steamed pieces by hospital ward. If she could not rush downstairs and pull out her own laundry in time, then one or two of her own pieces might get mixed up. She couldn't bring her colored bed linens as the laundry room personnel would immediately notice. Even so, during folding, they grudgingly tossed the smuggled laundry to one side and said nothing: In exchange for keeping their mouths shut, they could expect to receive a little "sweetener," which was what they called the tranquilizers administered during the evening rounds. The nurses on the night shift could always pilfer a few, as so many of their patients, permanently drowsing off, or already in a vegetative state, had no need of them. It would be an unnecessary waste; some of the patients even slept soundly without medication. They dozed off during breakfast and lunch; a couple of doses were easily pinched. When the nurses collected one full vial of the "sweetener," they handed them over to the launderers. Bianka was not the only one who brought her washing from home; still, she feared being reported. In warmer weather, she preferred to wash the bigger items at home. She would light the stove and boil the laundry, stirring them in the pot, then both she and Albert would wring them out in the courtyard. Still, the damp sheets pulled down the clothesline, their edges brushing against the ground. Or they would spread the larger pieces of laundry out on the awning above their doorway. During heat waves, the sheets dried smelling of sun; in the winter they smelled like glass. Sometimes the fabric froze solid; after they took it down from the clothesline, it stood in the room on the parquet floor like a plaster folding screen. It brought in a biting, strange smell from outside, then made cracking sounds as they tried to fold it up. Smaller items of clothing tended to disappear from the slackened plastic clothes line—the building's residents had put it up in the courtyard in front of the tar paper–covered, collapsing garages—and so everyone preferred to dry items such as socks, underwear, and sweaters in their own apartments. At night, when the lights were on in the crumbling building, the shadow trousers and shadow sweaters dangled from the curtain rods from behind the draped windows like human-looking silhouettes looming after a mass suicide.

    Albert walked around the room. He was satisfied with how their arrangement had worked out. Only the rolled up bed linens seemed amiss. He wanted to take them down from the top of the cupboard because it was the first thing you saw when you walked in.

Nobody will be looking over there, Bianka said, narrowing her eyes.

Then, at that moment, the two guests arrived.

The blond orderly stood in the doorway, greeted them, then strolled in. He lowered his head, as if entering a low-ceilinged room, then collapsed into the closest plastic chair in the kitchen and from that point on was mostly silent. He hardly looked up. If he was asked a question, his girlfriend answered for him. Bianka could not understand what she saw in him, but she knew that not only was this girl enamored by him but that he was also adored by the patients. Bucktoothed, flaxen-haired, and lumbering, he was everyone's favorite at the hospital. If he walked down the hall, the older patients began making smacking sounds with their lips, and as Bianka herself had seen as, gesticulating with their bony arms, they tried to give him some napkin-wrapped hospital pastry or shriveled-looking apple that they had gone out of their way to set aside for his sake. She had watched as the guy, with great gentleness, lifted up these tiny bodies, withered like raisins, from their beds, as he beat and adjusted the pillows, which smelled of disinfectant, or when he occasionally took the patients in a wheelchair for a stroll as they awaited this or that visitor. And he grinned all the while. Every time Bianka came across him in the hospital, wearing his white, rubber-soled shoes, he was smiling like a Cheshire cat. Now, however, he wasn't smiling, he just sat hunched over, his head hanging down.

He just came off a forty-eight-hour shift, his girlfriend explained.

Bianka met up with the orderly several times per day as he steered terminal inpatients, almost completely incapacitated, into the elevator. One sat nodding in a wheelchair, pointing backward at his own thinning, cotton, woollike hair in the elevator mirror, as well as the deep bedsore on his skull, indented as if hit by a bullet. The old man was so medicated that he clearly sensed nothing of either this hospital joyride or the clattering elevator.

His lilac-veined bare feet dangled out lifelessly from beneath the plaid blanket. I'm taking him to a book signing, the boy smiled at Bianka, as he steered the wheelchair down the long basement hallway, then, with creaking steps, turned off to the right.

Sometimes this meant that consent to stop treatment was being sought out, although that happened rather infrequently. For the most part, it meant that the patients were being taken down to the basement office to sign all sorts of papers. This had to be done while they were still physically capable, meaning that for the duration of one photograph, a pen could be placed in their hands as evidence that they were signing with a clear mind and of their own free will. For the most part, these "book signers" were appending their signatures to long, detailed confessions of crimes they had committed during the civil war, voluntarily undertaking reparations as well: all their movable and unmovable property would be transferred to the state. The signing of these documents took place in a proper manner, there was a military lawyer present as well as a psychologist whose official stamp authenticated that the signer was of perfectly sound mind, could orient themselves correctly in space and in time, understood the documents read out to them and fully agreed to its terms.

Once, the blond orderly steered a hospital bed into the elevator, pushing the rolling infusion stand with his foot. He ensured that the pole stayed within one-half meter of the bed. He had to maneuver it carefully so as not to inadvertently pull on the transparent tube. When they were in the elevator, he pushed the stand closer to the gurney with his foot, and looked up. He smiled at Bianka with one of his broad smiles and pressed the button for the first basement level. The woman lying on the bed seemed naked, hardly covered by the blanket beneath which she was shivering. They had gotten on at the third floor, the Gynecological Unit.

Are you taking her for a book signing? Bianka asked.

She looked at the woman with her trembling, veined skin; the blond orderly merely shrugged his shoulders, indicating that he had no idea, it was only his job to take her downstairs.

This orderly now sat next to the laid table, spooning his soup silently. Every once in a while, he coughed or blew his nose. He only looked up at Bianka once, as she was collecting the plates.

Why do you have two tables? he asked.

Albert answered that one of the tables was meant for outside, but they had to bring it inside so it wouldn't get stolen. Bianka carried everything over to the sink as the orderly's girlfriend stood next to her, ready to help. She handed Bianka the plates until they had all been washed. She turned around to see if there was anything left on the table. She saw, next to the cupboard, the paper box placed on top of the stacked woodpile.

Where did you get those from? she asked.

Bianka wiped off her hands and was about to start telling them about how they'd gotten the Christmas decorations, how these street vendors really had everything, but Albert spoke first.

They're from my grandmother. An inheritance.

As is this table, he said running his hand along it.

My grandmother, he continued, always had a tree that reached as far as the ceiling, that's how big it was, and she always played the piano at Christmas time. Because she was a piano teacher.

Bianka froze. She watched, standing by the sink, her back straight, motionless. She held the damp rag in her hands, waiting for the moment she could interrupt. She wanted to change the topic of conversation. To talk about the cold, the hospital, or the teacups.

Shall I make some tea?

All three of them nodded, so she put the kettle on the stove. As she lit the flame, her back to the other three, she listened intently.

Albi didn't stop, even though she had tried to change the topic of conversation. He continued where he left off, saying that his grandmother always roasted stuffed chicken for Christmas, even baked sweet rolls. On Christmas Eve, the animals were allowed to come inside from the courtyard, because on that night, but only on that night, they were allowed inside the house. They made an enormous clamor in the living room. And each one of them got a present. The dog, the cat, even the chickens. And his grandmother made a whole bunch of money by selling her homemade pastries because her poppy seed rolls were so delicious that everybody wanted some. The entire neighborhood. She wrote down the orders on a piece of grid paper.

Didn't you just say she was a piano teacher? the orderly suddenly perked up.

She was, said Bianka.

Yes, she was, answered Albert, only that she was also very good at baking. And she kept animals too. All kinds of animals. Albi began showing them photographs of animals. She had an enormous garden, he continued, with all kinds of bushes, a duck pond, and many fruit trees.

Where was this? asked the girl.

In the countryside. Far away, Bianka said, trying to end the conversation.

Finally, Bianka moved, collecting the teacups, turning her back to the company again. She placed three cups without saucers onto a platter, then a fourth mug with a broken off handle and a drawing of Little Mole. She turned to them.

His grandmother lived in the countryside, she repeated. She always played the piano, the window wide open, to the hens, so they would lay eggs better. And they did.

Balancing the tray in her hands, she set it down on the table, went back for the teapot, and poured out the tea. They sat silently, drowsy in the candlelight. Albert put more wood in the fire and watched the flames. The thick pipe leading from the stove through the kitchen wall released the smoke outside. The orderly suddenly asked if they had installed the pipe themselves. Bianka shook her head.

No. We paid someone to do it, she said.

They were both thinking the same thing. Every day, ambulances transported deathly pale, blue-mouthed, unconscious people to the hospital; with the onset of cold weather, they had been heating their homes with stoves that they'd set up themselves. They ventilated the smoke using cobbled-together piping, the holes patched up with polyurethane foam or improvised plastering. Entire families died from carbon monoxide poisoning in the segregated zones. Bianka looked at the orderly.

Should I open the door? she asked.

That wasn't why I asked, he answered.

After 10 p.m., they left. Albi, who stuffed a bottle of pepper spray in his pocket, accompanied them. It wasn't as if they were afraid to go out by themselves, but still, he knew the neighborhood better, he knew where it wasn't pitch dark and where, cutting across the blocks of silent buildings, they could quickly reach the wider, more-trafficked road, where there would be people walking around at night, and where the vendors, stamping their feet, hands numbed with cold, offered their wares. He accompanied them as far as the Anvil: from there they could safely walk along the boulevard to the next stop; they could also catch the metro there.

He hurried back, hands sunk into his pockets, his breath flickering whitely in the cold air. He pulled his sweater up to his nose. It was good to think that at home there was still warm tea, and that by now the folding bed would be opened too.

enshrining that moment of awakening

I had imagined Petra as completely different. Perhaps because of the red purse that I'd glimpsed in the photograph. I was expecting a tall, striking woman. Mihály always described her as a determined, almost aggressive woman, and every story he told about her depicted a tough, shrill character. I associated her name with sharp colors: high-heeled boots, a penetrating gaze, dramatic eye shadow and long lashes. I also associated her name with the loud Pachelbel ring tone I'd heard so many times. I tried to rearrange my features to radiate strength, keeping my back straight, approaching the place of our meeting with a measured gait. I felt anxious, planning my first remarks, trying to find some kind of convincing opening, while having no idea what to expect. I had arranged to meet near the university, partly because I knew this area, partly because my teacher's card got me a discount here. I'd been spending too much money recently, especially on clothes, but it occurred to me that perhaps I should have chosen a more distant and discreet location because what if she ended up making a scene here, jumping up and shouting accusations. Or maybe she wouldn't even show up. That seemed the more likely. That she wasn't curious about me, that she hadn't even bothered to read my message. I knew nothing about her.

As I left the university for our meeting, I was already regretting the entire thing. My anger had evaporated, my initial vehemence had petered out with only a kind of suffocating, bad mood remaining in its place, a mixture of shame and pangs of conscience. In hindsight, it wasn't at all clear what I had to do with any of this: with them, with the brown leather-covered notebook, with their entire pathological, pitiful existence, with this idiotic boy who was stalking me. But I ended up having something to do with them because the thick, waterproof envelope was here in my bag.

It had not been easy to gain access to the notebook. I'd been trying for weeks. I kept peeking into Mihály's bag, folding back the flap softly so the metal clasp wouldn't make a sound and I could take the notebook. I planned how I would open the creaking oak drawer in his office, but even if he went to the back, to that tiny bathroom, he would be gone briefly. He peed, brushed his teeth, or took rushed showers, always within a few minutes, then he was already in his office again. Even though I heard the water running, his foolish shouts as he flailed under the cold water, I still feared him hearing the sound of the drawer through the closed bathroom door and the noise of the running water. I wasn't afraid of pulling out the drawer, though that too made a sound, but rather the clatter of the wooden surfaces knocking against each other as it was pushed back in.

   It happened only one time that a colleague called him out to the entrance hall, and I was alone by myself for quite a while as they spoke. I immediately got up, and I picked up a cup, as if about to make myself some tea, and cautiously, moving sideways, always watching the door, slowly, very slowly, I pulled open the tight-fitting, creaky drawer. I wasn't even wearing underwear: stark naked, my heart pounding, I rummaged in his desk. The notebook with the brown-leather cover was not in its usual place. Centimeter by centimeter, I pushed the drawer closed. It made the usual knocking sound. I stepped toward the door, opening his bag, which he left on the chair, with lightning speed. The door was half open and he was telling someone that he could not take care of that situation right now but would look into it. A deep man's voice that I didn't recognize was explaining something about hospital referrals. I looked into his bag: the notebook wasn't there either. I dug around the bag. I only came across a wallet and a long wooden sheath for his fountain pen. In the meantime, he was repeating to someone in the entryway that he would look into the matter as soon as he could, while I carefully folded back the flap on his bag and collapsed into the armchair with the high armrests next to the tea table. My heart was pounding in my ears. I grabbed the armrests as if on a roller-coaster ride.

   This is where he usually sat.

I should have put on a pair of underwear, so as not to leave any marks on the velvet. On my side, I glimpsed that framed picture, that repulsive monkey. The wall clock was reflected in its glass. It was exactly half past seven, that is to say half past three. I could not stay much longer—at four by the latest, I had to leave for the university.

Once again, he was repeating that he would unconditionally look into it. He used the word *unconditionally* very often. I imagined him nodding as he pronounced that word with his affable smile.

Where the hell could he have put the notebook?

I had decided that, if I found his notebook, I would steal it. I had no intention of taking it for good, I merely wanted to read it, to look and see what he had written. I generally had no idea of what I could expect from this brown leather-covered notebook, what kind of reassurances I might have been seeking because if I am being completely honest, by that time I knew, or at least suspected, everything—in my body, in my guts. It was only my brain that needed confirmation. I wanted to see what he had scribbled down. Because, I kept repeating to myself: What we cannot confirm is merely hypothesis, feelings, empty speculation. With all of my strength, I wanted to keep alive that old, thinking, rational being and not give way to that other one who kept insisting that it was all the same, that it didn't matter, that nothing mattered, except those few hours I spent with him; I hardly wanted to upset my own life, so how could I expect him to do the same at his age, and in the midst of such circumstances, and really, what would I do if I were suddenly to step into Petra's place. Did I want to be her? In general, did I want to be anyone else, if I had never even succeeded in becoming who I really was?

I even tried to look at his phone.

I had never done anything like this in my entire life.

When he returned, he quickly clicked the lock screen of his phone and placed it face down. When he charged it, he always put it face down. We spent long hours together, but he never touched it, I never saw the screen, only sitting in the car as he was leaving, I heard the device repeatedly beeping. He would scroll through his missed calls with a concerned look on his face. Sometimes he called people back in the car. I knew Petra's ringtone well, just as I knew that reassuring, almost kind tone of voice, as he said into the phone:

There's no problem, is there?

No, he would tell her. I'm headed home now.

I could not get used to his small, rented apartment. He had brought a lot of things from home. His clothes were hanging in the cupboard, and he'd put down a carpet as well, but everything seemed so provisional. The standing lamp with the lathed column and wooden base didn't fit in here, the pictures were leaned up against the wall, the boxes of books shoved in the corner. I missed the scent of pipe smoke from his cozy office, the small lamps with their orange-yellow light, the pictures, the textiles. The rented studio with its shoddy furniture was bleak and merely functional, like some kind of language school. The stained fabric curtains, the tubular smaller pieces of furniture with their cold surfaces. We got undressed, flustered. We were always in a hurry, one of us always late. If he asked me to keep my glasses on, I felt ugly sitting on the animal-patterned fake fur blanket, as if I were in a casting call for a low-budget porn video being shot in the outskirts of the city.

The door buzzer wasn't connected, the intercom didn't work. Nobody could bother us here, only the two of us knew about this place. Or at least, that's what I thought because that's what he told me. On one occasion, however, shortly after we'd gotten there, someone knocked on the door. It was cool and dark in the studio, the lowered curtains letting in only a small strip of light, and the sound came from so close that at first we thought that somebody was nailing something into the wall in the upstairs apartment. Then the knock came again. Mishi scrambled to his feet, his cock still erect, his face tense, he listened in the direction of the hallway. I too was afraid, it would have been horrible to get mixed up in some kind of family scandal, but after the third knock, a man's voice, that of a stranger, was heard outside, reciting Mishi's license plate number. Lying on my stomach, I began feeling around for my eyeglasses on the floor, next to the bed. I was always afraid of stepping on and crushing them, and thus being unable to teach my class afterward.

If this is your vehicle, the person in the hallway said, then please come out because someone has broken the windshield of your car.

Fuck, he muttered.

He got dressed quickly, clearly irritated, then yanked open the curtain. I put on my glasses. I did not like to see my own slackened, pale body in this sudden bleak light.

I called out to him while he was downstairs, telling him that I would take a shower. And as soon as he closed the door, I stepped over to his bag. I was certain that he wouldn't come back right away; dealing with the broken windshield would take a while. My ears were ringing, I was so nervous. I opened his bag.

The notebook was there.

I took it out, leafing through it quickly. There were hardly any blank pages left, almost all the pages were completely covered in regular lines written in colored ink. I tried not to start reading, only to keep taking photos with my phone, but even so I could see that these were not simply notes. There were monograms in green, lilac, and blue ink. The colors changed, and beneath them there were drawings. Vaginas, breasts, legs spread apart. My vagina, my breasts, my legs spread apart. My ass. Hatched in black, with a hole and a date. Orgasm, monogram. Brown ink, vagina, date. Orgasm, monogram. Lilac ink again, a sketch of a penis in a woman's mouth, date. Green ink, a penis squirting out sperm, next to it a strangely shaped breast. Date, monogram. Half a page of notes, words, question marks, in one place, the word *stockings* underlined twice.

I kept turning the pages, kept taking pictures. The sketch of a house, a tree next to it, the crown of the tree was a heart, illegible words. There was my name again: two breasts and a date. Orgasm. Green ink, date, a detailed drawing, ass, vagina, a skinny woman on her hands and knees. A monogram. Blue ink, lilac ink, a bizarre drawing of a woman's hand, the middle and index fingers were two legs shoved into two stiletto heels with underwear stretched between them. Clouds which accumulated to the form of breasts pointing down. A tank with a penis-shaped cannon.

This person was not normal.

I photographed every single page. Monogram, date, orgasm. This person was raving mad! Mad, mad, mad, the word clattered inside me, as I worked ever more quickly, turning the page, snapping a picture, turning the page. I quickly understood that the lilac-tinted ink was associated with me.

I managed to get through all the pages, and he still hadn't come back. I slipped the notebook planner back into his bag, closed the flap again, then draped his mohair sweater on top, as it had been before. I ran into the bathroom, turned on the water, and began drenching my hair. I was standing under the shower, on the smooth floor, then turned so the water would beat on my back when I recalled in a flash that I had left my telephone in the room. It was sitting there, unlocked. The photo gallery, the pictures! I ran out for it, dripping wet, and just in that very second as I reached for my phone, my hair dripping, pressing the wine-colored bath towel to myself, in that fraction of a second, the front door opened. He stepped in, agitated, a draught of air blowing in.

What are you doing?

Somebody called me, I answered, as I turned off my phone, my hands shaking.

You're getting water everywhere.

I ran back into the bathroom, terrified, my skin covered with goose bumps. He came in after me, and in the bathroom doorway, began telling me that someone had broken his windshield.

On the left side, he yelled out.

I turned off the water so I could hear what he was saying.

They didn't take anything.

I'm lucky I brought my bag up here, he added. He handed me a larger bath towel through the door as well as a rag for wiping up the water. I was deathly pale, my wet hair clinging to my forehead.

The next day, on Wednesday, I printed out all the photographs in my university office. Luckily, I was alone, so I didn't need to try to conceal the individual sheets of paper as they were printed out, nor did I have to wait to look through them thoroughly. I sat down next to the window, and for two hours, I looked through his notes. It was all legible, with the exception of one or two words scribbled hastily. His handwriting was tidy, right leaning, with longish letters. I deciphered every syllable greedily, with determination, like someone wishing for nothing else than to sink deeper and deeper into this stifling darkness. I was fumbling around then, little by little, taking deep breaths. But I felt nothing. Neither a sense of loss nor pain, not even shame. Instead, I felt a kind of reassurance—my instincts had not deceived me after all, what I had always suspected was here before me now, and there would be no more uncertainty, no more self-accusation, no more doubt. I was seized with a kind of impersonal curiosity, like someone working in an archive. It was as if I were trying to decipher a faraway story, as if I were rummaging for the end of the piece of twine, to see what kind of secret was tied to it down below in the sludgy depths. I wanted to understand what had happened, what was happening now, to understand who he truly was, and what I was looking for in this notebook, me among all these other unfortunate women. I considered them victims, but not myself, for some reason. I was different from them because I had gotten a hold of this notebook. I tried to find some kind of repetition, some kind of system in the drawings. One color of ink was always used for a given name. It turned out from his notes, that the names in this notebook—all of them—were those of his patients. The sketches of Tuesday and Thursday, in lilac and green ink, were repeated in regular rhythms, but I did not find a similar system with the other colors. Or, this too was possible, that he did not make notes at every single session, only for certain ones. I did not find any men's names or drawings of male patients, which of course did not mean that there were none in his practice. At the back of the notebook, he had indicated, in careful columns of numbers, who had paid him, when, and how much. I had paid him for the last session in October, and next to my monogram there were four question marks and a circle drawn within a square. What could that have meant? I did not find a similar symbol next to the other sketches.

I felt like an idiot as I walked into the nearly empty, chilly café. I was moving nervously, as if walking on a film set, made uneasy by cameras recording my every movement. I should have been playing the role of a self-assured, middle-aged woman, hurrying to an important appointment, but inside, I was not adequately prepared for this role.

I looked around for a woman who could possibly be Petra, I only knew her hair was dirty blond. I couldn't find any photographs of her on the internet. When I searched for her, I only found company logos, Buddhism-themed pictures of brooks dotted with grey stones or bamboo groves. Petra was a grey stone, Petra was a stock photo, a bright-green bamboo grove. Petra was the first few beats of Johann Pachelbel's *Magnificat*. A well-groomed woman from one of the protected districts, always keeping a chilly distance, her face stoic. She almost certainly did yoga, used organic hair dyes, and regularly gave donations to benefit poor children. I seriously felt like I was going to throw up. I tripped over the rail holding down the mudguard mat as I walked in, almost falling on my stomach, waving my arms around wildly to keep my balance.

There was no woman in the café who looked like the Petra in my head. A young couple was sitting in the corner mutely, an expression that suggested they were about to break up on both of their faces. And by the front, next to the window, there was a drunk charging his phone, slumped over the table in a way that made me think he was the one in need of energy to get up from that table. In front of him was a half-filled pint glass. He stared into it, neck stretched forward stiffly, as if he were no longer capable either of raising the glass or leaving it here.

She didn't come, I thought. At least she hadn't witnessed my dramatic entrance. I sat down, far away from the couple and the delirious bearded man, facing the doorway, so I could see her if she walked in. I felt the coldness of the chair through my coat. The woman behind the counter didn't even look at me, she was making a loud clatter with the clean cups and wiping off the drip tray on the espresso machine. I sat on the cold artificial leather chair, my bag in my lap, the envelope inside it.

What was I doing here?

What was I doing anywhere?

The woman with baggy eyes cleaning off the espresso machine suddenly looked toward the entrance. A woman with dirty blond hair, in a beige coat, opened the door. I could not picture her at all with that red purse. Everything about her was drab and beige: her coat, her boots, her checkered scarf, her hair.

She looked around, then walked decisively toward me. I had imagined Petra as a more beautiful woman, and much more exciting.

I stood up and as I introduced myself, the shoulder strap of my bag got caught on the arm of the chair. This was not the opening I had planned, I had no intention of making excuses, but she radiated a kind of disconcerting focus, which made me feel uncertain.

She pulled up a chair, put down her car keys, sat down, and looked straight into my eyes. She moved precisely and sparely, like a yoga teacher. Each of her movements signaled that she was present, that she had done me this kindness, although she really didn't have the time.

What did I wish to tell her? she asked me.

I was surprised by the dullness of her voice. There wasn't even the slightest trace of an edge, of any interest at all. It was a restrained voice, tempered pale, just like her clothes, her unpainted nails, her longish, serious face. She waited for me to start talking. What was it I had to tell her? she asked again.

I took out the envelope, at which point she smiled slightly, her mouth pulled to one side.

So you have found something.

I was stupefied, as she sighed loudly, and pushed her chair just slightly back. She said that she presumed that there was a notebook in the envelope. If that was the reason I'd called her here, then there was no need. Her husband had always kept such notebooks. If I was really curious, and if I were to reach into her bag slung over her chair, if I were really interested, she had a pen drive containing all of his other notebooks, which she would be happy to lend to me. I could read all of his notes going back sixteen years. If I could stand it. She did not recommend this, as it would not cheer me up, but if I really wanted to, I could read them. Her thin fingers were still red from the cold outside. An icy recognition came over me.

They're sick, I thought to myself. Both of them.

She clearly saw how dumbfounded I was because now it was she who suddenly began encouraging me. She said I should try to pull myself together, I wasn't the first one this had happened to. She advised me not to take any rash steps: it would be pointless. I should never think for a moment that I would be able to gain anything. All the while, she kept looking straight at me. Not decisively, but instead as if she were deeply fatigued.

Then she fell silent. I was also silent. I was not prepared for this. The bearded drunk in the corner stumbled into our silence; leaving his pint glass behind, he set off toward the bathroom. He walked very close by, carefully placing one foot before the other, mistrustfully surveying any furniture that might get in his way or considering if they were firm enough for him to lean on in this expedition of his. Petra didn't look up at him, the half smile was fixed on her face.

Why are you protecting him? I asked her.

She answered wearily, like an exhausted teacher about to retire, who had to repeat the same thing for the thousandth time, and although she would do it—as she loved her pupils—it was horrifically tedious. Petra crossed her legs, slowly looked toward the glass in the doorway, from where the sparse, cold light filtered into the café, and she said she wasn't protecting him, of course she wasn't protecting him, only that she was aware of what was possible.

I'm not protecting him, she repeated. I know how you're feeling.

Finally, the waitress came over to us and asked us for our orders, as if hoping that we would order nothing. Her eyes were round, and as she looked at Petra, it was painfully clear that her eye shadow had thickened into dark rheum in the corner of her eyes. During the civil war, it had been difficult to get a hold of good-quality cosmetics, and obviously, this waitress was also using the cheap stuff. Petra asked for cappuccino, I ordered an espresso. An espresso would not go with the color of her clothes, I thought to myself scornfully. I placed the envelope, which had been holding in my hands until then, on the table, pushing it toward her a little bit. In my imagination, this theatrical moment was meant to be brief, nearly resigned. But suddenly, the whole thing had lost its meaning: Instead it seemed ridiculous, despairingly officious. She opened the envelope, took out the copies, flipped through them with a bored expression, as if a complete stranger had asked her to look through their lab results.

These are the latest ones, yes?

Again she looked toward the window, into the distance, holding one of the printed pages in her hand.

She had been four months pregnant with her son, she began saying, still looking outside into the distance, when she had read her husband's notebook for the first time. She had taken it out of the desk drawer, thinking she'd find all kinds of professional secrets. Mihály was at home, he'd brought up an old crib from the cellar, it had been his younger brother's. He dragged it out onto the terrace to wipe it off with a rag. The wood was stained with blotches, the bottom of the crib was damaged. While Mihály was on the terrace with the crib, she went over to his desk and simply took out the notebook. He used a different kind back then: it was large, with spiral binding. It was only later that he started using smaller notebooks with soft-leather covers. She wanted to know what her husband was doing when he wasn't with her, what happened during those hours of which he spoke so little. She thought she would find case studies, hard-to-decipher sentences, perhaps even strange abbreviations. Instead, she found something completely different. She read the notebook, then she grew dizzy and began to throw up. On the terrace, Mihály was applying clear varnish to the crib, which he'd just cleaned and dusted, with a brush. He thought that Petra had become ill from the chemical odor filtering into the living room. He closed the terrace door, but Petra just kept on vomiting, leaning over, clutching at her stomach. She couldn't stop: She kept vomiting for weeks. They went from one doctor to the next, they placed a basin next to the bed, Petra carried plastic bags in her coat pocket, but still sometimes they had to clean the vomit from the carpet. Everyone attributed her continual nausea to the pregnancy. If her husband opened the fridge door, and she sensed the raw smell of packaged meats, even from the bedroom, she would immediately begin to retch. She sometimes didn't even have time to run to the bathroom. She could not bear any smells, including that of wood stain, her stomach immediately began turning. In reality, it was the notebook that was making her throw up, but nobody would have understood. And whom could she have explained it to? Her parents were alive, but they lived far away, in the countryside. She hardly ever met up with them, only if Mihály somehow had the time, and they went down to see them for part of the day. And when they spoke, they didn't really talk about anything important, only everyday things. Her father showed her what he had repaired around the house, all by himself, with little money. She could not go back to them, and in the capital city, namely here—Petra looked back again—she knew no one. She had no idea how she could get on by herself, with a newborn, without money, without any friends. And even though she'd read everything her husband had written, she was still in love with him. Don't ask how this is possible, she said. She simply loved him. The more distant and incomprehensible he seemed, the more she loved him.

And later? I asked.

Later?

When the child was born, she told him. She confessed that on that afternoon, when he had dragged up the wooden crib from the cellar and was cleaning it on the terrace, she had read his notebook. And that there had been moments when she had wished that the child had died in her stomach, that this marital obligation would cease, and she would be free to leave. But then the child arrived, so she didn't give a fuck about the diary, she didn't give a fuck about anything, the child was healthy, and they somehow had to keep on living. They became parents, they were the parents of this child now. Back then, her husband told her that this whole thing had only been a troubled and transitory time, and that he'd only slept with other women because of her pregnancy. He had not dared approach his wife, he explained, because her large, taut belly, crisscrossed with brown stretch marks, disturbed him, and he had been full of all kinds of anxieties. He was afraid of the child crying, he was afraid of the nights, he worried about his wife. This was how he had tried to solve the unbearable tension. It had been a mistake, he explained gently, and he regretted it. He claimed those women were not his patients. He would never sleep with his patients. He said nothing about the drawings.

I really wanted to believe him, Petra asserted to the coaster and the tabletop, I really wanted to believe him, from willpower alone, so that I would not have to go back to my parents, so I wouldn't have to give everything up. Mihály tried, at that time, she said, to spend a little bit more time with his family. She, for her part, tried to win his attention, tried to show herself as an exciting, independent woman, who wasn't dependent on him.

Why, were you dependent on him? I asked.

Yes. I don't know.

The waitress brought the coffee.

I myself never went to cafés. They were too expensive. Petra pulled her cappuccino closer to herself, stirred it, stared into space, and once again, with the same tone, repeated that she didn't know.

But you have two children, no?

That was unkind of me, I know, a low blow, but somehow I had to understand how she was able to give birth to a second child with this person, to remain in this absurd bond. She'd seen these drawings, if she had really read his notes, then she should have fled, no? What was she counting on? What could she expect from this person? She lowered her head, as if she were trying not to get me to understand her feelings, but the inscription on her sturdy cappuccino cup.

Then there came the civil war, she explained. They had to move away. Petra's parents died. Not in the war, she anticipated my question, no. They were simply old. At first her mother became ill, then a year and a half later, her father. In the meantime, she found another notebook, hidden among the documents kept in their apartment, folded in between newspapers, and she realized that everything that had gone on before was still going on. That perhaps there had never been a break, that her husband was sleeping with someone every single day, sometimes with more than one woman. She got ill twice, Petra looked at me, twice, she ended up getting a sexually transmitted disease from him. He never used condoms.

He probably didn't use them with you either, she said.

I looked at her, paralyzed. My coffee had grown cold.

He hasn't blackmailed you? she asked.

I shook my head.

He's blackmailed others, she said, taking a sip of her coffee.

You should know, she said.

Petra looked up at me, and continued.

He has threatened several women.

She took another sip of her coffee.

And he got one of them sectioned. Can you imagine that?

I shook my head.

He had her sectioned in the closed ward. The woman's adult son trusted my husband without question and was somehow helping him. He thought a doctor would only want the best for his mother, that he was going to cure her. That woman—the boy's mother—was a lawyer. When she finally realized, as you have, what was going on, she began collecting evidence. She sought out other patients, she wrote to them one by one, she made phone calls, she wanted Mihály to be held accountable, no matter the cost. She somehow thought that she was going to make the entire sordid affair public. Poor woman.

You weren't jealous of her? I asked.

No, Petra answered.

I felt sorry for her, she continued. She'd first made an appointment with Mihály because of her husband. The guy had been defamed during the civil war, accused of spying. It was the usual story, he wasn't the only one. There must have been people accused by the government in your own family as well. Later, when the borders were closed, just as he was about to be thrown into prison, her husband fled. This unfortunate woman was left here by herself, and of course she lost her work, precisely because of her husband. She had no more cases, no more clients. She couldn't hang on to her apartment, she had to move out. She was in distress, so she asked my husband for help. Then Mihály, fairly quickly, became her lover. At that point she was still an attractive woman. Tall, with a high forehead, wavy hair. The Amazon type. She herself stated how safe she felt, how much she believed in my husband. She thought that Mihály would help her get back on her feet again, help her start a new life. My goodness—him!

When she realized what was going on—because she wasn't stupid—she stole the notebook. She photographed it, just like you. Mihály's response was, within half a year, bypassing all customary procedures, to have her put away in a psychiatric institution. She's still there, in the closed ward. Her son visits her regularly, apparently she can't even chew her own food now from all the tranquilizers. And she's gained weight. You really have no idea, Petra said, staring at me fixedly, how much reach he has. You have no idea. He can ruin anyone at any time, I know. And this includes you.

You teach at the university, isn't that so? Petra asked. The New University? He can get you fired.

I couldn't tell if she was thinking aloud, if she was really trying to protect me, or if she was surreptitiously threatening me.

During the civil war, Petra continued, Mihály helped the Regent a great deal. His wife is extremely ill. Truly. Mihály told me all about it. For years now, she's been taking medicines. She's bipolar—the worse kind of bipolar—and depressive. When the Unified Regency was established, her children were still young.

After every birth, she collapsed, was hospitalized, sometimes for months on end. She tried killing herself twice: both times it was Mihály who brought her back from the brink. When she wanted to kill herself for the second time, she wasn't doing it to frighten anyone, she meant it seriously. She took an entire handful of sleeping pills. For this second attempt, she planned everything, made sure it would work out. She took the children to their grandmother's, then went up the mountain so she wouldn't be found. She took a taxi, ordered the car from an address that wasn't their home.

It was Mihály who realized where to look for her, she continued. He suggested searching in the area where she usually took the children on picnics. Supposedly she fought frequently with her husband when they went on these excursions. Her husband hit her. Mihály said that the Regent has serious problems with anger management. They positioned half the army there, and they found her. She had been lying in the forest for two days, in the dead leaves, unconscious. Mihály told me how slugs were crawling over her. He seemed to enjoy telling me these details. He wanted to frighten me: this is what happens to anyone who tries to get out.

The Regent's wife lost her hearing, one of her eyes was damaged. She can't sense anything with it, only light or shadow, this too, I know from my husband. He kept on treating her, and even today they call him if she seems to be losing her mind. The poor thing got used to it now. And she never became fully cured, her eyes are always retouched in photographs.

You've never noticed? Petra asked.

I didn't look, I answered.

Now that you know, it's a much bigger problem than that stupid notebook, she said.

Mihály had a lover—Petra started telling me a new anecdote—whom he diagnosed with borderline personality disorder.

He determined that she was incapable of raising children and, thus, a danger to her own young kids. The woman was already divorced; her children were taken away. She struggled for months to get them back—asked for diagnoses from other doctors, lodged appeals, ran from pillar to post.

And then?

Nothing. She died.

What you mean, she died? I exclaimed.

She died, jumped out of a window.

She didn't want to—Petra once again spoke to the tabletop—maim her children or lose them. She didn't want to end up on the street, or behind a chicken wire window in a psychiatric unit, being fed little colored pills every fifteen minutes. She knew no one, she had no one to turn to. Her friends were her husband's friends, her acquaintances were all his colleagues. She had never built up her own connections, she didn't even have her own money or her own bank account. She lived from what her husband gave her. And even that was strict, only enough to buy the groceries. The only person she could have spoken to was her husband's mother. But her mother-in-law would never have understood anything; she was so enamored by her son. And then she died. So this woman truly had no one to turn to. If she had not been so afraid of Mihály—Petra's voice suddenly became very soft—then she might have looked for somebody to talk to in the neighborhood, a confidante. Anyone. A stranger. But she didn't trust anyone, though perhaps she could have confided in a complete stranger. Sometimes she dreamed of such a thing. That she would get into a car stopping just for her on the street with a stranger, and her husband would start chasing them. That she would bring home a dog, drenched in water with muddied fur, from the shelter, a dog whose gaze was unusual, somehow human. Then, as she was bathing it, she would suddenly realize that this scruffy dog was, in reality, her husband. The dog would turn its head, like this, to the side, and she would see the white of its eyes, and suddenly she would recognize him. These were the things she would dream.

As Petra was telling me this, she cocked her head to one side, and looked at me like that. There was something exalted and horror-stricken in her gaze.

She was always picking out strange people, she muttered, fiddling with her napkin. She would single out complete strangers, trusting them to help her. Sometimes she even fell in love with them, temporarily. Just to have someone to think about. You could say that they became something like stand-ins in her head.

I was surprised and troubled by Petra's sincerity. This was not what I had been expecting.

She even fell in love for a while with her son's pediatrician. Petra laughed nervously. A bearded old guy who examined her children in the asthma clinic. He helped Vilmos put his blue-striped, long-sleeve T-shirt back on, then he tied up his shoes too. One bunny ear, two bunny ears, and Petra had fallen in love with him.

Ridiculous, isn't it?

No, I answered.

Often, she imagined that she would take the bull by the horns and ask for help from someone, but she could work up the courage. She didn't dare. Really, who would believe her? Her husband was a serious, known figure; she was a nobody. Suddenly she looked into my eyes, as if, during her long monologue, her initial, chilly self-discipline had completely evaporated. Her face looked like that of a little girl, vulnerable.

Forget about that notebook!

In the meantime, it seemed as if the drunkard had succeeded in reaching the toilet, because he was now stumbling back to his seat, relieved, swaying, grabbing onto the chairs along his path. As he passed by, he stared at the two women for a long time and muttered in contempt:

Coffee—a coffee klatch!

really and truly the same story

Dr. Kreutzer carried the folding bed into the stairwell in three parts. To load it into the car, he had to remove the polyester packing material, which he now spread out in the doorway, so as not to leave the separate pieces on the grimy tile floor. The folding bed had been sitting in his mother's attic for years. After emptying out the apartment and putting it up for sale, he went up to the attic to look around and see what his mother had been storing up there and came across the convertible sleeper chair.

Getting it out had not been simple. He had looked for a long time for the key to the iron attic door; his mother had dumped it into an empty ice-cream container along with other keys that she used infrequently or never at all. He'd already found the key to the gate of their old summer house, labeled as such, as well as the door key, a key that no longer opened the door of any building, as the house had been sold before the civil war and subsequently demolished by its new owner.

Here, in this ice-cream container, were all kinds of screwdrivers, an ancient lock cylinder, smaller padlock keys, or keys for old and unused postal boxes. The attic key should have been here somewhere in this chaos, although it seemed nearly hopeless. In the end, he took all the keys upstairs and dumped them onto the floor in front of the iron door. He put down the ones he'd already tried next to the ice-cream container. He would have bet on a long, dark-colored key, but it didn't fit into the lock in the grey metal door. His mother hadn't come up here for years, and now he feared the lock might have been changed since her last visit. As he was thinking about this, he rummaged through the container of keys, suddenly coming upon a completely insignificant-looking, round-headed key that not only fit in the lock, but turned as well. The door opened. Cold air flooded into the stairwell.

Nobody in the building used the attic. In the past, a resident on the third floor, an older female teacher, would always bring up her plants here in November, for storage over the winter. Dr. Kreutzer recalled that a few years ago, as he was walking into the building with groceries, she'd asked him for help in moving a large pot out of the elevator. Together, they dragged the pot the few steps up to the attic entranceway because the woman wouldn't let him lift it by himself. He left the shopping bags next to the door of his mother's apartment, then tottered up to the iron door with the pot, which was bloody heavy. After the death of this teacher, only chimney sweeps went up to the attic. The beams were, in places, interspersed with patches of grey mold, leading him to conclude that the rain was at least partially leaking through the insulation. That was no surprise, as the last installation of the new roof tiles took place during his childhood. This was after Öcsi passed away; still, he came up here with his father to jump around the glittering streaks of light and flit among the dust particles drifting down from the disassembled roof. The old tiles were removed in sealed packages, hauled away in rumbling tracks. The roofing had been manufactured using old technologies involving asbestos, and so had to be completely replaced. At the time, no one really took this seriously, moreover, while the roof was being disassembled, the children made drawings on the street asphalt with the fallen debris. It was only decades later that he read about the microscopic threads contained in asbestos roof tiles, the damage to human organs when they were inhaled. In the ensuing decades, the replacement roof had also started to age, just as the people whose organs these invisible threads had settled into, in whose pleura and lungs there lurked, clutching at the tissue, these tiny particles that could not be traced or be removed, so that at one point they would awaken, and commencing their murderous wanderings, set off among the membranes, digging ever deeper. It was chilly in the attic. He stepped carefully over to the corner so as not to stir up the cold dust that covered everything. The sleeper chair, which was wrapped in plastic, was still there in its old place.

Fortunately, there had been no leaks, the dampness had not penetrated here along its secret paths; the chair seemed completely dry. They had bought this piece of furniture before the civil war. More precisely, Mihály had bought it, during that time when he had to spend nights in his first office so that he could sleep a bit while on duty. When he took naps on the office sofa, he would wake up early the next morning at dawn with a throbbing neck, his limbs numbed beneath his coat that he'd thrown on top of himself. This sleeper chair had already been ordered when he was unexpectedly appointed to a new institution, and he no longer needed it. He never even took it out of its packaging, but merely stored the sleeper chair up here, and, despite his mother's worries, had pushed it into the corner.

Who would even take this, mommy?

Then the civil war broke out, and the troubled residents of the building hauled up boxes sealed with brown wrapping tape up to the attic, then hauled them back down, not even deigning to glance at the plastic-wrapped, upholstered sleeper chair waiting in the corner. Later, after his children were born, old Auntie Pálma often said that once they grow older and became a little more mature, her dear little ones could stay over at her apartment for the weekends but of course, God forbid, not in Öcsi's old bed, but in that nice new sleeper chair. She glanced up at the ceiling, in the direction of the attic. The years went by, and Öcsi's bed, in the corner with the old teddy bear, remained in the former children's room, while the grandchildren never stayed over their grandmother's once, not even for a few hours, which might have been a relaxing afternoon for their parents.

The multinational corporation that manufactured these inexpensive items of furniture had left the country a long time ago and so any intact pieces preserved in households or somehow discovered had greatly rose in value, as did all items that were no longer obtainable after the founding of the Unified Regency.

Dr. Kreutzer had thought of this convertible sleeper chair the third time it proved impossible to meet up with either Emma or Vilmos because their mother had taken them to stay with one of her female coworkers for the night. He had suggested to his wife that the children could sleep at his place. Petra hemmed and hawed, then left him standing there in the living room to pick out the books he wanted to take with himself.

He had taken this to mean she agreed. That week, he rearranged the single room of his rented apartment. He pushed the round coffee table to the base of the double bed. He freed up a corner facing the window, separating it from the rest of the room with a tubular shelf. The space was tight, and he would have to make a detour around the shelf when headed to the bathroom, so as not to bump into it, but for the time being the small corner seemed more than suitable for the children to occasionally spend the night here. He brought the desktop computer from his office along with a games console from the apartment he had purchased for the children last year. Petra didn't allow any screen time, even though the homework for their Little Patriot class had to be completed as an online group assignment. He had explained to her many times why the children could not risk any absences, why they could not lose any points, and why they, as their parents, must never create the impression of keeping their children out of one of their most ideologically important classes—the teachers often showed up online as well—but Petra just shrugged her shoulders. She listened to him with an indifferent expression, then the next time, both children, Vilmos and Emma, missed the class again.

I completely forgot about it, she said in a wan voice.

Dr. Kreutzer reckoned that he would help the children catch up with the missed online sessions, not only for the points but so that they would be registered as having logged in. He was therefore happy to think of them sleeping over at his studio, his busy plans filled him with a kind of contentment just as when he used to pick up after Petra, restoring the organization of the kitchen drawers.

His new neighborhood was not too safe, so he could not leave the components of the sleeper chair in the doorway. Instead, he carried them into the stairwell landing and from there one by one into his apartment.

At home, they had never purchased ready-to-assemble furniture, not even for the children's room. He had learned from his parents that furniture was something crafted from hardwood by carpenters. He had deep contempt for this department store trash, but now, that he had to temporarily furnish the studio apartment, it seemed like a good idea. It was too wide for one person, too narrow for two grown-ups, but perfect for two children.

He cut off the plastic with scissors and pulled out the assembly instructions. The upholstery was dry, although the small booklet had yellowed, the paper warping over the years. He spread it open and started gathering up all the components. Four large screws, two strong coil springs, four smaller screws ,and an Allen wrench to attach the armrests.

The job did not seem too complicated, so he set to work immediately. He attached the boxy seating base to the longer perpendicular backrest, propping up the two armrests on either side. So far, it was not taking up more space than a larger reading chair. He stood up to estimate how much space the sleeper chair would need, when suddenly the two armrests fell onto the parquet floor with a large clatter. He turned over the boxy seat construction, found the pre-drilled thread holes, and began inserting the screws. **One went in, the other didn't**: it was as if the opening had been blocked up with something, perhaps sawdust was jammed in the hole.

He wondered if there was a hammer here in the studio. There wasn't. However, in the kitchen, he did find among the unfamiliar, battered plates a wooden meat tenderizer. He energetically began screwing in the stubborn screw, which obediently sunk into the hole but wouldn't catch on the threading. When he finally tightened both of the screws—at last they were catching on to the threads—he sensed that the backrest was still wobbly. He pushed the piece of paper with the instructions in front of himself with his stockinged foot. He realized that before fully tightening the screws, he should have attached both springs to the small hooks on either side of the seating-base surface.

Dammit.

He loosened the screws and pulled them out, then tried to figure out how to attach both coiled springs at once. The multinational company that had manufactured this sleeper chair traditionally conceived its furniture in the spirit of teamwork: a large, noisy, and clever family that stuck together, that assembled and disassembled things together. Now, retroactively, it seemed clear that this was no mere empty marketing concept. Because even the assembly of a simple piece of seating furniture required at the very least a couple, which is to say four hands. Still, Dr. Kreutzer did not back down. He told himself that a wretched, preassembled chair was not going to get the better of him: he himself would hook those two springs into place. He needed to pull out the metal arms on either side that held and elevated the backrest while attaching the two coil springs. He lay down on his back on the seating surface, bracing a stockinged foot against the parquet floor as he stretched out his arms and tried to locate the hooks for both springs. He slithered from side to side like Christ writhing on the cross, his back itching, but he could not hook on both springs at once.

Then he had an idea. He jumped up. He released the right spring, it jumped out of place. The metal arms closed shut, the backrest raised up.

He decided that he would hook one spring while pushing down the other side with some kind of weight to keep it in place while he attached the second spring. After he hooked the coil on the right-hand side, he placed the sack full of books he had brought from the family apartment on the left-hand side and pulled down the arm. He stood up carefully, about to attach the second spring, when the sleeper chair suddenly contracted and cast off the sack full of books.

Dr. Kreutzer now stared at the sleeper chair as if it was an enemy, who, with one final blow, must be eliminated.

Bloody hell.

The sleeper chair waited with sly motionlessness.

Wait a second!

He went into the kitchen and returned with a rolling laminated storage cabinet. He deliberately did not remove the drawers. As he placed it on its side and lifted it up, the rattling junk in the drawers all rolled to one side. He placed the cabinet on the seat of the sleeper chair, then, walking around it, attached one of the springs as he pushed down on the metal arm. There was a brief moment of silence, as if the sleeper chair were concentrating, gathering all its strength. Then it shuddered and threw down the storage cabinet.

The front panel of the second cabinet drawer fell out. A pile of cheap utility knife blades spilled onto the floor. As he bent down to pick them up, the cabinet, fallen onto its stomach, puked out a measuring tape and an electric bulb.

Dr. Kreutzer sunk to the parquet floor, looking at the junk rolling around. He pondered a change of strategy. But to ring a neighbor's doorbell was tantamount to admitting defeat. No, he wanted to struggle, he wanted to emerge victorious on his own. He could not be bested by a wretched metal arm and a coiled spring.

He imagined how, after the bed was assembled, he would lie down carefully with Giselle on this squat little sleeper chair. Not only that, but if he could adjust the angle of the backrest in a certain way, he could make her kneel on it, the height was just right for her. The thought excited him, gave him new strength, setting in motion a series of fervid fantasies.

He picked up the utility knife blades, kicked the measuring tape and the drawer's front panel farther away, then returned to assembling the sleeper chair. He attached the spring on the right-hand side and pushed down on the cabinet with his full weight while lying down on his back on the chair in such a way that when he released the support, he could put his right leg onto the cabinet. The chair did not contract as he lay on it with the weight of his entire body. It was, temporarily, disarmed. The metal arms were extended. He slithered to the left side millimeter by millimeter, just enough to try to reach, groping, behind the cabinet's cold corner, the hook onto which he had to attach the spring.

Scabby, rubbish coil spring.

It was a strong spring, very hard to pull on, whereas the little cabinet was slowly headed downward. He sensed the metal arm giving way through the fabric of his trousers, he sensed the storage cabinet slipping down on the upholstered fabric. Dr. Kreutzer, sweating, pulled forcefully on the end of the coiled spring. Only two millimeters separated him from his goal. Then one millimeter, then half a millimeter.

With a huge clamor, the cabinet tumbled onto the floor.

The sleeper bed palpably wanted to contract again, but the body lying upon it would not permit this. Dr. Kreutzer, panting, was still stretching out the coiled spring on the left-hand side but now his hand groped in the air in vain. To find the hook, he needed to sit up.

The struggle lasted for one or two seconds, then he gave up. He sat up. There was a longish moist stain on his shirt from his sweat, and the backrest jumped up lopsidedly, ejecting the two smaller wood screws. One of the metal arms remained extended, the other was bent at an angle.

Dr. Kreutzer clambered off the sofa and moved away. His left foot accidentally trod on the light bulb that had rolled away. He jumped back on his other leg, sat down on the bed. As he picked out the shards of glass from his sock, he examined the yellow, chilled sole of his foot. It was not bleeding: there was only a tiny scratch at the base of his big toe. Avoiding the mess, he carefully made his way back to the chair and slowly raised the meat tenderizer. It occurred to him that now he could smash the entire bloody sleeper chair into small pieces, but then he lowered his arm and only spoke to the piece of furniture in contempt.

Your stinking mother's cunt.

The sleeper chair endured this offence motionlessly, not contracting in the least. Moreover, it seemed that in this calm position it would be easier to attach the two coiled springs, even both at once. Dr. Kreutzer took a deep breath and tossed the meat tenderizer onto the parquet floor. He headed toward the bathroom, then stopped in his tracks. He picked up and raised the round coffee table which had been pushed next to the bed. It was not too heavy, but with the drawers, somewhat heavier. He laid it, surface facing down, on the obstinate, half-assembled piece of furniture. The coiled springs dangled flirtatiously, obviously waiting for someone to start fumbling with them again, for someone to play with them again as if with some impish, overly varnished lock of hair. The tabletop sat firmly on the chair, not sliding around, so that, with a leisurely movement, he hooked one spring into place, pushing down the metal arm. He went over to the other side to attach the second spring, although the hook it needed to be attached to was no longer in place. It had somehow loosened and rolled away.

It was already half past three, and Dr. Kreutzer had no more time for messing around with the sleeper chair. Walking on his heels, he waddled into the kitchen for a broom to sweep up the utility knife blades and the glass shards. He shook out his sock forcefully above the garbage can, then pulled it back onto his foot. He hoped that while cleaning he would find the hook that had fallen out as well. The sleeper chair peacefully tolerated his sweeping all around it. It stood on the yellowed herringbone-patterned parquet floor, with the large round coffee table at its head, the dangling coiled springs on either side, like a sad and offended rabbi who, having lost his prestige, was asked for counsel by no one.

the invisible, thirsty dog

Petra woke up late. She had pulled down the blinds the previous night so that no light filtered into the bedroom. In the dark, she groped for her phone to check the time, but it was dead. She rolled over to the other side of the bed, looking for her charger. She had slept well for the first time in months. Mihály had taken the children, and he'd promised they'd be back today at around noon. She would have liked to see some photographs of his studio apartment, to at least be able to imagine where the children would be going, but Mihály ended the discussion by telling her not to worry, it was at least as good as at her colleague's place with that sofa covered in dog hair.

She found the charger, plugged in the phone, then went to take a pee. She kept thinking of the woman who'd gotten touch in with her yesterday about the notebook. She had seemed fairly determined to get mixed up in some kind of idiocy. She felt neither pity our curiosity toward her. Earlier, it had been painful to imagine her husband with these other women, but now, this pain had almost completely passed. It had grown dull, she hardly felt anything, neither regret nor joy: She merely completed her tasks, one after the other. This bespectacled woman, who had such a wan face, meant nothing to her. She had saved her phone number, but she felt no impulse to try to help her. She had little energy and she wanted to concentrate on her own life. She went into the kitchen to boil water. The apartment building across the way seemed quiet, no movement anywhere. It was as if everyone had gone to work, even though it was Saturday. She looked for the Nescafé, and she saw that there only was a bit left at the bottom of the glass jar. She poured boiling water onto the grains stuck on the bottom, screwed the lid back on, and shook the jar. Mihály called Nescafé dormitory coffee; he only drank it reluctantly if there was nothing else at home, and only if he was really exhausted. He was always annoyed if the vacuum storage container with the inscription COFFEE was empty, if Petra had not refilled it with proper, genuine coffee in time. Or, if she had bought the coffee, but had not stored it into the airtight container. This quality coffee was expensive for them too, but her husband insisted on a certain brand which he always drank, and which was once again available, although at unbelievably high prices. One packet of coffee cost as much as a pair of shoes and could only be purchased in designated shops—if it was even in stock.

She took a sip from the jar. The bits of foil stuck to the edge of the jar scratched her lips, the coffee was still too hot. She left it there to cool on the table.

She went back into the bedroom, stretched out on the bed. Her telephone was charged at 21 percent, she turned it on. A brief message appeared on the touch screen: SMOG ALERT. She read the news item. The levels of concentration of airborne dust and nitrogen dioxide had exceeded safe levels, therefore all residents were requested to remain indoors. Petra recalled that Mihály had planned to go for a walk with the children. She called him, but it didn't go through.

She went back into the kitchen and drank the rest of the tasteless coffee from the jar. She was about to step into the bathroom to take a shower when her phone beeped, notifying her of four missed calls.

Her stomach suddenly dropped as she wondered if that woman who'd sought her out with the notebook was calling her impatiently to ask for advice; but no, all the calls were from unknown numbers. Two from the same number, ending in a six, then two other calls. She found this level of activity fairly unusual for Saturday morning, but she merely shrugged her shoulders and went into the bathroom. She didn't want to call anyone back until she was fully awake. First she checked to see if there was hot water, and when she saw that it was running, she crouched in the bath for a long time under the showerhead. She wanted, though, to reach her husband before he set out with the children because it wouldn't be good for Vilmos to go out to the park in the smog, especially with his asthma that tended to flare up.

She rubbed herself off cursorily with the towel, then, wrapping it around herself, ran into the children's room to look in Vilmos's drawer to see if he had taken the inhaler. It wasn't there, so it must be in his jacket pocket. She went out into the hallway, then into the kitchen, where she turned on the radio. It was strange how the music was being interrupted every five minutes, how this smog alert was on continual repeat as if war had broken out. The government was requesting everyone not to go outside, and if possible, not even to open any windows. Petra glanced out from the kitchen window. From here, the air outside looked chilly, transparent, and pristine. It was as if the sun were shining a bit, throwing an oblique shadowy triangle onto the wall of the building across the way. She looked through the windows on the far side and saw no movement coming from the inside.

She went into the bedroom, opened the double-leaved windows, and sniffed into the silent morning. Nothing seemed amiss. She sent a message to her husband.

Don't go outside, there's a smog alert.

From behind a curtain in the building across the way, a woman was watching her suspiciously, then quickly closed the window, pulling the curtain. Petra sent another message to her husband.

Do you have the inhaler?

A biting chill flooded in through the windows, the room became cold within seconds. The outline of the street was fairly crisp, as if an early spring illumination were inundating the steep side street. Perhaps the level of air pollution was quite high, but here, from this higher-story window, it was not apparent. An older environmental expert, with a nasal voice, continually coughing and clearing his throat, was now on the radio explaining how the rags and car tires burned in the segregated zones in wintertime had overburdened the air in the larger cities; fines levied for such polluting activities had not yet brought the desired result. A certain section of the population, ahem, was still not capable of cooperating with the authorities, ahem, despite the many informational posters and campaigns, ahem. It sounded as if this expert were trying to illustrate the data concerning the deteriorating air quality with his own voice. After more discourse, it emerged that the residents of the larger segregated zones were fully responsible for the current state of affairs, and if, in these districts, the regulations were followed, if the use of harmful combustible products were phased out, then the level of contamination would demonstrably lessen. But now, ahem, that was not the case, ahem, unfortunately, because on the basis of data measured this morning, ahem, ahem, it could not be excluded that the populations of these districts might have to be temporarily evacuated.

Petra sat tensely, smoothing out the edges of the blanket. She straightened up and adjusted the two pillows as well. She hated herself for always making the bed as her husband did. If she didn't know that he was bringing the children back at noon and might come into the bedroom to take more books from the bookshelf, packing them into yet another carrier bag, she probably wouldn't even have made the bed. This realization vexed her. The perfectly smooth-out bedspread demonstrated all too well how Mihály still dominated her life and her movements. On the radio, the discussion concerning the poisonous smoke released by burned tires continued. The man on the radio, who kept clearing his throat, seemed to be exaggerating. The air in the city was bad, undoubtedly, but she found it hard to imagine that it necessitated removing people from their homes; it was even more difficult to imagine that those masses of unhoused people, who for years had been moving in hordes along the cold, muddy streets, would tolerate resettlement to these designated locations.

As she adjusted the pillows, a horrific thought flashed through her.

For a long time now, the starving, derelict residents of those city districts, fallen into ruin, had posed a serious problem for the government. The residents of those districts were designated as hazards to public security and public hygiene, spoken of not as human beings but as parasites. Suddenly, it did not seem fully inconceivable to Petra that the Regency was planning to annihilate the residents of these troubled zones. They were announcing an evacuation, but the real plan was to get rid of them quickly.

She sat on the made bed, her back straight, she stared into the air, she pulled her palm along the bedspread, her heart frozen in terror. She suddenly had no idea what to do. Run away from here? But where, and how? The civil war was still too recent, sirens still wailed every night, acquaintances still thrown into jail, the state of emergency continued. What had just occurred to her did not at all seem impossible. She went out to the kitchen for her phone, she called her husband, but his phone was still turned off. She searched for her own boss's number, and called him as well, to at least talk to someone, to hear a sobering human voice. The call didn't go through.

From the bedroom window, she looked down at the sidewalk across the street: still no movement outside. Mihály's apartment was in the northern part of the city; she didn't know the address. It was considered one of the worst districts, the price of apartments there was continually plunging. In the news, there were frequent accounts of robberies and looting. Sometimes cars were surrounded, other times warehouses were set on fire. She wished Mihály would call her back, bring the children home as quickly as possible.

It occurred to her that she could call that desperate woman from yesterday. She had her phone number. As an employee of the New University, she might have access to some kind of official, government information. Then she realized that she could not call this woman while the children were still with Mihály. If this woman flew off the handle and started threatening her, somehow alerting her husband to the fact that they both had met, then Mihály could easily blackmail her by threatening to remove the children.

She should not have let them stay with him for the night.

She paced up and down the apartment, packing up things at random. She gathered up the strewn toys, as well as Vilmos's toy cars, scattered everywhere, and shoved them into the linen chest: Vilmos called this his "underground garage." She paired up the socks and put a load of laundry into the washing machine. The rubber edge of the drum seemed to be smudged, so she wiped the groove in the ring with a damp cloth, the tip of which became blackened with grime. Once again, she thought of her husband and how he ran his fingers along the shelves.

Mihály was still not picking up his phone.

She was angry at herself for not having asked about his address. She had a right to know where her husband was taking the children. His lovers certainly knew where this apartment was, but she didn't know who the current ones were—apart from this harried, bespectacled woman.

She dialed the numbers of the missed calls from earlier that morning. She heard the voicemail greeting of a strange man and left a message. She called one of the other numbers, which was answered by a different man. She didn't get his name. He wanted to know if her husband was home. He also wanted to know when he had left. She answered that he was not at home but was afraid to reveal that he had also moved out a while ago. The unknown voice asked her to call back immediately if she heard from her husband. Without delay, Petra in turn asked a question, repeating his words, namely that she would also like to hear from her husband as he had taken the children somewhere, and she had not been able to warn him that the air quality outside was bad.

There's a smog alert, she said to the man, as if he'd arrived from outer space.

Yes, madame, there is a smog alert, the man said, repeating her words, as if he too were an automated message, and he quickly hung up the phone.

blood and rust were excluded

He massaged his forehead, then rubbed his eyes with the palms of his hands. He was completely exhausted, and it was difficult to focus on the screen. His eyes were tearing up from this forced labor. He had looked at the recordings more than twenty times. At first the uncut versions, then the edited versions as well.

He really did not understand the rush. It was not clear to him why these short videos had to be prepared during one single night if, in the most optimal case, they would never even be shown. These short clips would only be broadcast if the operation did not, for some reason, succeed as planned—if they were unable to stop the leak. If that happened, the government would be obliged to announce a minor operational malfunction while also informing the public that volunteers had already signed up from all over the country to repair the damage. If panic broke out, the people must be made enthusiastic. It would be necessary to demonstrate to the surrounding hostile powers, as well as to the international press, just how much strength and solidarity there was in this small, isolated country, left to itself, pushed into a corner—even in such a critical situation. This, of course, was the contingency plan. It did seem as if the malfunction could be fixed. Detailed plans were being drawn up for the temporary enclosure of the hermetic seal, to reopen it beneath this enclosure, then to reload the damaged fuel rods. It was estimated that the more modern storage container, created for this purpose, would solve the problem for at least a few hundred years. The team—comprised of expert engineers from a protected indoor location—was getting ready to instruct civilian volunteers on the ground the precise sequence of emendations, using outdoor cameras. The members of the crisis team were, for the most part, convinced that broadcasting the film would not be necessary. Everyone was hoping that the individuals entering the terrain now, directed by team leaders, would successfully execute the necessary tasks; in that case, the footage would be shelved and classified. The mission participants would then imperceptibly and quietly disappear, as far as the outer world was concerned. The treated and untreatable comorbidities listed in their files had already been transferred, in the central registry, to the older data sheets.

Enthusiastic music, growing ever louder, was edited into the beginning of the five-minute video; during the monologues it grew gradually softer, although it was still audible in the background, providing a rhythm to the series of portraits. The faces were shown one after the other, interspersed with images of the country's rolling-green hills, starry-night skies, happy children frolicking in water, wavy-wheat fields, galloping horses, their manes fluttering in the wind, and, at the end, the flag of the Unified Regency. The girls conducting the interviews had been slightly made up before the takes. They waited for their interviewees next to a table packed with savory buns and soft drinks.

Right before the interviews, the makeup artist applied eyedrops containing atropine, making the interviewee's gaze more intense, more glittering. The light makeup almost caused wrinkles to disappear, and though everyone's true age was visible—it was also listed on the chyron—even the most elderly team member, a retired chemistry teacher, appeared ready for action, like a cheerful grandmother in an ad about to pick up one of her sturdy grandchildren. A thin layer of powder was applied to everyone's face. The crane operator grimaced: the elderly engineer completing a prison sentence experienced a strong erection from the youthful breath of the makeup girl leaning above him. The retired chemistry teacher was thinking, while the bridge of her nose and her chin was being gently brushed with powder by the squirrel-hairbrush, that nobody had touched her face in years. She closed her eyes as the brush gently circled her face.

When her son had been very little, sitting in her arms, he had touched all around her face with his tiny hand, as if getting to know his mother.

We're done, thank you, said the makeup artist.

She opened her eyes.

The younger engineer and the bearded man who seemed to be about the same age were reluctant to have makeup applied, but its necessity was patiently explained: in the heat of the lights, human skin begins to shine, which looks poorly on film. Gazing straight into the camera, every team member had to deliver a short message as to why they were undertaking this risky, albeit uplifting assignment, and discuss their motivations.

Dr. Kreutzer was taking notes.

There was nothing in the uncut version that the international press could find fault with, and the final, edited version clearly conveyed that the people speaking here were all part of a select group, worthy of envy, their hitherto insignificant lives now redeemed. Anyone could be a hero.

A couple of troubling details still remained, and so Dr. Kreutzer kept rewinding the video to the frames he had already noted down.

At 01:25, a man who looked like a manual worker said that he had been sentenced to prison for four years for financial crimes, but he did not want this one bad decision to ruin the rest of his life. He wanted to contribute to the success of this mission with his own expertise, he said. He had undertaken this task voluntarily and had experienced no coercion whatsoever. The second half of this sentence had been cut from the final, edited version: The statement now ended at 01:34, with the man saying that he had undertaken this task voluntarily. Dr. Kreutzer pressed the stop button and looked at the man's face. He was forty years old, a pallid-looking guy who'd been promised clemency. His features showed no feeling whatsoever, and despite the preliminary instructions, he did not create the impression of someone who wished to contribute to anything at all. Instead, what he said sounded as if he wanted to get this performance over with as quickly as possible. Insert cutaway shot here, Dr. Kreutzer noted to himself. Clearly a great deal of thought had gone into the initial editing of the film, because right after this man, the crane operator with the burnt arm spoke, beginning at 02:02. His eyes shone with the flame of the truly crackbrained, as if the makeup artist had dripped too much atropine into his eyes. The hulking man said that he had been born into this world precisely for this task. He stared into the camera for a long time without blinking, a hirsute messiah wearing a checkered shirt. His shirtsleeves were pushed up his arm to make his wound visible, although the frame only showed his face. The chemistry teacher, fifty years old, who followed this man, only stated that she had not been able to save her son and so she wanted to help others. It was a severe, credible sentence, and she gave a slight nod at the end, but still it left Dr. Kreutzer with a bad feeling every time he viewed it. Her nod came at 02:21. At first, he wanted to cut this frame because it looked as if somebody was instructing the interview girl behind the camera, and the woman was nodding in consent. This contradicted the conception of the film, which was to show the volunteers as enthusiastic, resolute, and above all, independent. In the end, the woman's nod remained, as if approving the previous interviewees' statements. The sixty-year-old engineer, also serving a life sentence for financial crimes—he had first been jailed shortly after the founding of the Regency—loudly rattled off, with theatrical vehemence, and through a number of different takes, just how much this opportunity meant to him, how much he believed in the success of the mission. He was asked to repeat the same words a little more naturally.

Not so loud!

Try to speak as you usually do, he was told. The man acknowledged the request, then, with the same contrived, recitation-like intonation, repeated his excited message into the camera. He was simply incapable of employing an everyday voice. He was like an amateur actor, although he only had to convey who he was and what his task would be in the team. Insert cutaway shot here, Dr. Kreutzer noted at 02:48. He could only imagine that, before the brief preparations for the video, this man had not spoken to anyone for years, and in this new, surprising situation, he was incapable of behaving naturally. He clearly seemed afraid.

Dr. Kreutzer wound back to 02:48. It's still not good, he sighed to himself.

The uncut version was even worse. There, the engineer repeated the same simple sentence twice with an awestruck expression on his face, like a schoolchild about to rattle off a poem at a recitation contest.

Dr. Kreutzer lowered the sound, watched the section again, then made a note that this sentence would have to be filmed again. There wasn't too much time, the man would have to be taken to the studio to record a new message today.

Clearly the editor had also felt that the older engineer's message was the film's weak point, because right after him, at 03:01, he had edited in the young guy with the dark eyes, who only said, his face transfixed:
I know that my mother will be proud of me.
This message was perhaps the strongest of them all. Dr. Kreutzer leaned back contentedly in his chair, he stared at the boy's face, frozen in the frame. He considered this sentence to be his own personal success. The guy had walked into his office a few weeks ago: it emerged from their conversation that he thought Giselle was his mother. That she had given birth to him, then abandoned him. The entire crazy theory rested on the basis of one photograph. Dr. Kreutzer never shared his doubts because he immediately saw the possibilities. This child was sent to me by fate, he thought, right at the beginning of this rescue operation. It was clear that the boy was extremely determined, had no family whatsoever, and could be persuaded to do anything if he thought it would lead to meeting his mother. In the frozen frame he was blinking, his long dark eyelashes covering his pupils. Only the silhouettes of a few house plants could be seen in the light background. The plants suggested homeliness and security, as if the interviewees were in the hallway of a wellness hotel. Right after this guy, a young laborer, at 03:15, said that he had a daughter on the way and after this special operation, they'd be getting a roomy apartment in one of the protected districts. This is the future, he raised his diluted, luminous pupils to the viewers at 3:25. The last interviewee was a young, blond-haired woman. Before the recording, she had been asked to wear her nurse's uniform, but she arrived in a T-shirt and jeans. She explained that she was not allowed to take her uniform home and that she liked to keep to the rules. She ignored the second request, which was to use, if possible, the word *family*. Dr. Kreutzer had repeated to her several times that certainly she and her sweetheart were hoping to start

a family one day, and their future progeny would be so proud of them. But he hammered this word into her head in vain, the girl nodded briskly, but then avoided the word during her statement.

Now that the video was edited, Dr. Kreutzer looked over her dossier: her verbal maneuvering made him anxious. The girl did not appear to be stupid, clearly something else lay behind her phlegmatic nature and seeming lack of comprehension. He was annoyed by her jeans and her T-shirt, as if she were trying to send a message that this whole thing didn't matter. The reports she made on her hospital colleagues were considered completely trustworthy. In the column under "Personal Motivation," she had written that she had applied for the mission because of her love; that she wanted to accompany him. She used those exact words: on the official form she had written "my love," which, coming from an adult woman, was childishly romantic and slightly ridiculous. With a ballpoint pen, she had crossed out the designations "life partner" and "spouse," and instead had written "my love" in rounded letters. When asked by the team trainer as to whether she wished to get married and, after the completion of the operation, claim an apartment in a protected district of their choice, she merely shrugged her shoulders. On her datasheet, in response to this question, she had written that she didn't know, just as he had; although he designated her as "life partner." The boy had a certificate of rebirth—potentially simplifying the entire procedure—but the girl said that they already had someplace to live. She signed the application in the end but without any particular enthusiasm. The desk officer, assigned to the evaluation with Dr. Kreutzer, noted that that the presence of the girl in the team could be decidedly useful, as she was described by her colleagues as a balanced personality and someone who worked hard in addition to being a nurse. That an attractive woman of childbearing age was being placed in a closed environment with six men, did not, however, look overly promising from the viewpoint of group dynamics. It seemed, instead, a disadvantage, as it could lead to rivalry between the male members of the rescue mission.

Her pupils enormous from the atropine, this girl looked like a pale-blond manga figure, her long hair tied back with a rubber band, her simple light-blue T-shirt faded from repeated washings. Her posture was slack, her shoulders rounded. As she sat in front of the camera, she conveyed no excitement whatsoever. The word *family* did not cross her lips in either the edited or unedited versions. In each of the two shots, she repeated the same thing, leaning forward slightly, in a calm clear voice: *I can't do anything myself, I only make my judgements as I hear from him.*

Is there anything you'd like to add to that statement?

Me? No, nothing.

It was hard to know what to do with this message. She was asked again if she was enthused by the mission, to which she only uttered, impartially, yes. To leave this *yes* in the film would be absurd. In the uncut version, she uttered an entire sentence, answering at 00:47: "Yes, I am enthused by the mission." This longer version of her bored reply was in no way better, so the briefer, somewhat obscure statement remained. The director had written that despite her beauty, the close-up, and her ashy skin, this was not a good ending for the film. Instead, the director suggested that the sequence with the dark-skinned boy close it out. Dr. Kreutzer agreed. The recording had also been sent to the Regent, who watched it twice, and he only said that it was fine to leave in the girl's message, just as it was. Later, he confirmed this by telephone as no one could necessarily know what she meant by the words *from him*. It sounded good like this, from the mouth of a young person of such natural beauty. The girl's statement ended up at 03:28, around two-thirds into the film, although the young brown-eyed man did end up comprising the final sequence following the director's recommendation. The final moments of the film, as the young man smiled, shaking away the hair falling onto his forehead, and he stated:

I know that my mother will be proud of me.

visible from up close

The children were fast asleep in the back seat. Vilmos's head drooped to one side as he drooled, his pirate comic strip book fallen onto the floor. They had gone to bed late, on the computer until 11 p.m., but even so it was unusual for them to nap so deeply in the morning. Mihály had been glad that the electricity—unusually—had been on the entire evening, so he let them play on the computer. Afterward, they were all able to take their showers, and they even made up the missed homework assignments from their Little Patriot class. His neck was aching. He hadn't slept well because the children had, in the end, slept in his bed, tossing and turning the entire night. Emma woke up in the morning with her face turned toward the window, her pillow fallen onto the parquet floor.

He drove carefully, as he always did, so that they would not be woken up by the car suddenly braking. Petra never let them take naps during the day, not even for a brief period because it then would be impossible to get them into bed and she wouldn't be able to work. Recently, the children became especially excited if the electricity was on at night: Petra could hardly sit down at the computer, or only very late, because Vilmos kept coming out in his pajamas asking for water, or to be allowed to stay in the bedroom. Emma fell asleep more easily, and she never had to be nudged from the hallway back into the children's room, whereas Vilmos frequently stood lurking behind the bedroom door or stealthily climbing into his mother's bed, crawling under the comforter. This always woke Petra up, and she would lead him back to his own bed, its frame covered in decals. She never let the children sleep with her—she had her own rules.

There was hardly any traffic in the city. Usually, during the day, there were always vendors standing around in front of the boarded-up storefronts on the wide boulevard, but today, the street was practically deserted. The cardboard boxes, the empty oil drums, the garbage swept along the street—all of this indicated they were driving by one of the poverty-stricken districts, but only one or two shabby, unfortunate people wandered around after waking in their dens assembled from rags and climbing out from some cellar. Dreamy and dull eyed, they loitered, at least the ones who had not yet been instructed to go down to the metro underpasses or hadn't yet heard that it was forbidden to remain outside. Dr. Kreutzer recalled that the children had gone out into the street, their heads uncovered, but this had only been for a few seconds, just as it would only be a few seconds for him to send them up to their mother. If the situation were really that serious, he would have been informed. Of course, he knew that this entire smog alert was fake so as not to inform the public of the radiation leaking out from the power plant, twenty-five kilometers in all directions—a leak which, at least for now, did not present any serious danger. No point in giving rise to useless panic when there was so much societal tension already. Dr. Kreutzer considered it likely that the government would, under the guise of the smog alert, begin the hasty evacuation of the segregated zones: They had been planning the relocation of these unmanageable populations to container houses for a long time, to isolate them from the settled districts, far away from the city center.

Up ahead, the wide boulevard was barricaded by military convoys. He saw the orange, gold, and green shield of the Unified Regency festooned on the military vehicles. Dr. Kreutzer hit the car brakes, got out of the car, then carefully closed the door.

Get back in the car!

He suspected that Vilmos might wake up as he always did when the car stopped and the fine rocking motion ceased. Dr. Kreutzer showed his ID through the glass of the car door to the soldier inside. He was asked where he was going, to which he replied that he was going home. Then hurry, they urged him on, adding to get the children out of the open air as soon as possible. The soldiers in the convoy were all wearing plexi masks, army raincoats, and plastic-lined caps that also covered their necks; they looked like legionnaires.

Vilmos asked sleepily what the men wanted.

Nothing. Go back to sleep.

They were stopped in more places, but they didn't have to get out, Dr. Kreutzer only had to show his picture ID. At the second check, they asked him if he was headed to the airport. He was surprised because even though the airport lay in that direction, they had no suitcases and no other indication that they planned to travel.

It was 11:45 a.m. He had to try to get back by noon as he had promised, otherwise Petra would use this as an excuse the next time he wanted to take the children. Even so, he could count on her raising a fuss. When he'd gotten his wife's message, he'd asked his son to take the inhaler out of his bag. It had remained in the apartment on the coffee table, and by the time Vilmos noticed, in the car, that they didn't have it, there was no time to turn around. Petra would be upset that he'd forgotten it exactly during an emergency. Vilmos didn't appear to be having any difficulties, but that was not really an argument he could use. Mihály decided that he would bring everything that the children had left at his place, including the canister with the fox on it, on Monday.

The city was strange like this, nearly empty. He tried not to think about what he'd been working on yesterday, that video reworked frame by frame, parsed to bits. By his reckoning, the repair work would be starting this morning. The volunteers would have already received their instructions and protective gear. The image of the blond girl with the ponytail kept coming back to him. Her open and yet inscrutable gaze, her light-blue, worn-out T-shirt. She had not worn a bra for the recording, certainly she never wore one.

He signaled, made a turn. Emma woke up suddenly, and asked when they would be having lunch already.

In a moment.

He turned onto the sloping street and parked in front of their building. Across from the entranceway, there was a dark-blue civilian vehicle. Two men got out, even before he himself could clamber out of the car, telling him to go with them.

He found it strange that he had been previously notified. His cell phone was on, he had gotten Petra's messages. He suspected that some problem had cropped up with the video, which they had not wanted to communicate in writing. Obviously, this is what had happened.

I'll send in the children, okay?

He honked the car horn briefly, and Petra's head appeared in the window above.

Close the window, the taller man called up.

Both of them were wearing legionnaires' hats that covered their necks and, despite the good weather, khaki rain cloaks. The children ran inside, and Dr. Kreutzer got into the dark-blue car. When he asked where they were going, the shorter man replied:

To make a recording.

Dr. Kreutzer presumed that the statement of the blond girl had to be filmed again, or possibly that of the engineer. He was annoyed that they were dealing with this now, so late in the game, when already yesterday morning, they had, along with the director, indicated the problematic sections in the edited material that needed to be covered with cutaway shots. They drove around and around for a long time in the empty streets, Dr. Kreutzer was beginning to lose his sense of orientation, until he finally realized that they were not headed to the city center, where the studio was located, but beyond the city limits.

The closed-down factories of the Rust Belt of the Northeastern district had never been pulled down, the buildings stood empty in the feral lots. The homeless no longer came here from the segregated zones to squat in the blackened, crumbling buildings; the rats, though, had taken up residence everywhere. Weeds of human height thrashed at the road shoulder, the corrugated siding on the abandoned factories shone dully in the sparse sunlight. Along the ring road, there was a series of uncultivated arable fields. They drove under a concrete overpass, on top of which a military convoy scanned the road below. Emaciated dogs ran alongside the road, crows soared up and alighted farther on, the rusted scaffolding of former advertisements framed the lime-white, cold, empty sky.

Dr. Kreutzer stared out through the tinted window. He had to think over the next few months. He counted on there being more than enough from the sale of his mother's apartment along with his current consulting fees to buy a new piece of real estate in one of the protected districts. He didn't want to be too far away from Petra, but he didn't want to stay in the same neighborhood either. Giselle worried him. The woman played no role in his long-term plans whatsoever, but he wanted to keep her around until he completed the move and finalized the divorce. He had never shown her the photographs of the four-room apartment that he had described in such detail, but he reasoned that if he could draw her into apartment hunting and planning, he would gain a bit of time, even if not too much. Sooner or later the woman would want to move in with him, start arranging things, after which, on the basis of some fabricated pretext, she would break up with him and start acting hysterical.

The fact that she worked at the New University reassured him. Every time he conjured up that monstrous concrete building in his mind, he felt relieved. This woman would not want to lose her job. She had made too many compromises already to sacrifice her research career for such a trifling matter. In fact, she could be happy that anything was happening with her at all. Perhaps he was the last adventure in her life, he thought smiling to himself. He thought of Giselle's cool skin and her large, pale breasts, indifferently spreading out. He didn't want to think about this now, sitting in the back seat.

The two men in front of him were quiet for the entire route. They spoke neither to each other nor to him. For his part, he did not attempt any inquiries. He knew that they had probably received instructions, no point in bombarding them with questions. Even in the car, they were wearing their khaki cloaks, which made a rustling sound against the back of the seats. The one sitting on the left suddenly started bending down, reaching for something, then handed him a similar outfit in a vacuum seal. This made Dr. Kreutzer suspect that they were getting closer to the studio, they would be getting out soon. His phone pinged, he glanced at it. Petra had sent him a message.

Where is the inhaler?

Before he had time to reply, another text immediately followed.

And the pirate comic book?!

a new sheet of paper was not inserted

I didn't have to teach on Wednesday. I didn't mind, my meeting with Petra had consumed what was left of my energy. I tidied up at home. I pulled out the drawers, picking out socks and stockings. I wanted to chase the pictures from the notebook out of my head, and I tried not to think of what Petra had told me.

My husband was also at home. He suffered from not being

able to go to the library. He sat in front of the computer, sometimes getting up, annoyed, wandering around the apartment. By Saturday morning he could hardly contain himself. He clattered together his small change as if he were about to go out to buy a newspaper, but there was still a smog warning, a prohibition for going outside. It seemed that the air quality had not improved, even though military cars had been circling in the city for days, surveying the critical zones.

What a shame that there's no wind, he said, staring out the window.

The rooms were filled with a stale smell, the stink of food kept insidiously filtering into our apartment from the stairwell. Some people in the building were airing out their apartments clandestinely at night. Others fled the city to family members elsewhere, or to bring their children back home. More and more, people were trying to guess what the government intended with these strict measures. There had been no official announcements since the radio discussion on Tuesday. Many were presuming that the government was trying to evacuate poor neighborhoods, that another civil war was about to break out, that the Regent had already left the country. That morning, the radio had announced that starting from Thursday, rations of longlife milk and bread were being made available. The food packages would be delivered by the military; the designated deputy for each apartment block would be responsible for their further distribution. Allocation of these packages must only take place indoors. In zones with single-family houses, the packages would be placed within the fence, sirens indicating the arrival of the delivery trucks. The residents of the garden suburbs were instructed not to wait outside on the street under any circumstances, not to leave any rations outside, and when picking up rations, to step out onto the street only with their bodies fully covered. All residents must minimize any time spent outdoors. Rations would be distributed to the residents of the segregated zones in the metro underpasses. According to the reporter, these unfortunate residents, forced to reside underground, were instead pleased by this unusual situation, as normally they were never the recipients of allocated foodstuffs.

I brought home the copies of the notebook from the department. It was here, in my cupboard. As much as I tried not to think about it, from time to time I felt an irresistible impulse to tell my husband. To show him the drawings and for us to try to figure out what this whole thing meant together.

At moments like these, I had to look at him for a long time to sober up. As he sat in his frayed cloth trousers, staring at the screen, with the TV on in the background too. As he nodded when I spoke to him, but never looked up, never answered.

I went into the bedroom and closed the door. I lay down on the bed and looked at my stomach, my breasts. Wille, I said to myself. If I had given birth to that kid, the stomach would look completely different today. It would be covered with fissures and striations.

Although perhaps it's just a cliché and not every pregnant woman gets these mother-of-pearl-like stripes on her stomach. What would it be like to grow a baby in there? We didn't even have any space to put an infant in this tiny apartment. My husband wouldn't be able to tolerate the screaming at night, everything being turned upside down, someone touching his things, the sticky doorknobs.

I had no idea what I would do if this smog alert ever came to an end. Move away from here? But where? Give up my job? Escape abroad? How? Did I have anyone to turn to? I thought of Zsuzsa, then just as quickly dismissed the idea.

I kept thinking of the small studio, the dark curtains. The creaking parquet floor. Our nakedness. No matter how it had happened, even with this dreadful knowledge, even with those hours, I still felt all of it was real.

Outside, the late autumn sun was beaming. From here, lying on the fully made bed, I could see the bare trees where just a few trembling, nervous leaves still clutched onto the branch. For years I had been staring at that same piece of roof, that same section of wall, the crowns of the trees reaching into the picture, growing slowly taking up ever more space. In the beginning, the sparse foliage did not reach our floor, the branches, growing ever stronger, did not yet hang in the twilight, its hues changing, framed by the window.

Even through the glass pane you could feel that although the sun was shining, this was the last, strained and desperate, flaring up of autumn. The birds' chirping filtered in from outside as did the sound of the television from my neighbor's apartment. I had listened a moment ago, and they were still talking about rations, methods of calculation and outgoing deliveries. They were saying nothing new. From time to time they repeated archival recordings about the rabble gathered around the Anvil, the broken storefront windows.

If only we had a dog. But then suddenly it shot through me, what about the dog owners now? If no one could go out onto the street for two days, how could they walk them? Because of the tax code, dogs were mainly kept by the well-to-do living in the protected districts. But if even they couldn't take out their pets, where would they pee and poo? There were many stray animals in the city, so much so that from time to time they were gathered up and shot; only the privileged could afford to keep such darling pets at home.

Clearly, they would be able to go out, I thought. There must be other regulations in place in the protected districts.

Once again, I looked at my stomach, then I pulled up my bra toward my throat. I was neither skinny nor fat. Instead, I was just too pale.

My husband opened the door. Just at that moment, I was

holding my breast with my right hand. He looked at my pulled up bra in shock.

It's lunchtime, he said.

He pronounced this in such a reproachful voice, as if asking what I was up to. I rolled my bra back down, yanked my clothes into place, then I sat up, straightening the blanket. It was half past noon.

I went into the kitchen to heat up the potato dumplings left over from yesterday. My husband had dumped them onto a plastic platter, covering it with aluminum foil. I couldn't find the pot I'd used for making the dumplings. I wanted to use it again. I began to suspect that he had taken it to humidify the apartment, and I was right. There it was in the inner room, beneath the desk, on the floor. I took it out, asking him if it the air needed even more humidification. He looked, with a satisfied expression on his face, at the barometer on his table.

No, it's ideal now.

I heated up the dumplings and put them out with the silverware and napkins. Soon we would have to go shopping as we were running out of bread. It would be good if they hurried up already with those food packages.

You're not eating?

Not now.

After 1 p.m. he lay down, as he'd been doing every afternoon for twenty-five years, bunching up the pillow beneath his head. I carefully closed the bedroom door. I didn't wash so as not to make any noise. I quietly put on my shoes, quietly slipped out into the stairwell. I was taking the invisible, thirsty dog for a walk.

I peeked out the doorway, but I saw no one on the street: no passersby, no patrols. In the sudden sunlight the cellar entrances emitted a musty smell. There was an echoing silence, I had to be careful of my steps calling attention to my presence. I knew that my husband would sleep until at least 2 p.m., and so he wouldn't be looking for me. I had to make sure that no one could see me from any of the apartment windows. I walked around the house, stopped by the base of the three-story building on the other side. The low sun shone brightly, as if on fire. I threw down my coat, and there, next to our building, on the concrete strip, I lay down. The late autumn light traversed my wan, tired skin, warming it, and for the first time in months, behind my closed eyelids, I no longer saw images zigzagging one after the other but only the sunlight's changing patterns in front of the dark-purple curtain woven through with veins.

he waited, almost diffidently

The two men accompanied him as far as the entrance hall, then handed him over to another man, who led him down a long, planked, echoing corridor. It was very narrow, as if they were about to board an aircraft. Most likely they were in a light temporary building, with one room set up as the recording location. The sliding door in the background made him think of the location of the earlier interviews, but there were no plants here in the ceramic pots, only trees that had lost their foliage, looming outside through the floor-to-ceiling plate glass, as well as one or two rusty-colored cypresses swaying in the light wind.

Dr. Kreutzer looked for the girl with the blond ponytail. He presumed that he would have to talk to her, that he would have to convince her to record a more useful message than the previous one—or the engineer, that was his second guess. The camera was there, and pots of makeup and soft drinks had been placed on a camping table off to the right. One of the men offered him a seat, then asked him if he had succeeded in thinking up a succinct and effective message that would now be recorded. Dr. Kreutzer was outraged by this request. He answered that to the best of his knowledge, the professionals, such as himself, working in the background, especially those who had formed a personal connection with the selected team members, were not required to record messages; the mission did not involve them. The glory belonged to those who would be carrying out the work. The two technicians—Dr. Kreutzer assumed they were technicians—stepped a bit closer to him. They both wore black sweaters and black trousers.

The glory belongs to you as well, one of them said.

The psychiatrist smiled, more out of courtesy than anything else. This guy was starting to make him feel nervous. He was disturbed by the lack of order, the chaos. He had no business being here, he had completed the work entrusted to him, even more thoroughly than could have been expected. He had finalized the editing, wrapped up the final version, and had given his opinion on the intermediate versions as well. He was so enraged that he decided to call the direct number he had in his contacts. He had used it only once, years ago, when they were looking for the Regent's wife. Ever since then he had never dialed this number. And he wouldn't have done so if this idiot here wasn't overdoing things, and trying to get him, an outside expert, to record a message.

I have to make a phone call.

I'm afraid that won't be possible.

The two men in the black sweaters stepped over to him; one of them took his phone. Not violently, merely decisively, like a schoolteacher who had announced that cell phones were not allowed during class.

What's going on here?

We are asking you to be so kind as to transmit a brief, informative, and preferably enthusiastic message to the people as to why you have chosen to take part in preparing the team and supporting its members.

Why is that necessary?

Everyone going in has recorded a message, came the reply.

Dr. Kreutzer was confused for a moment. He stared at the man who returned his gaze. He was tall, almost good-looking, but a little overweight. And he was going bald. Dr. Kreutzer noticed a liver spot on his right temple. That could be burned off with a laser, he thought; his brain suddenly switched to emergency mode and struggled to transmit the entirely useless information. He looked at the spot, not into the man's eyes, and he said:

But I'm not going in.

The man, who had been standing, suddenly sat down facing him. He crossed his arms.

He told Dr. Kreutzer that as far as he knew, this was not a matter of choice. That the team of volunteers was in need of continuous psychological support. Unexpected situations, conflicts could arise. These could only be solved by the presence of a mental health expert. The Regent himself had decided that he, Dr. Kreutzer, would be the most suitable, and therefore he had entrusted him with this task, which demanded extraordinary preparedness, knowledge of human character, and situational awareness. No one else was as capable of guaranteeing discipline and tranquility among the team members in such a critical situation, qualities that were indispensable to the success of the mission.

But I'm not going in.

The man looked at him, disappointed. He pulled his folding chair just a few centimeters forward, and he said, that of course that was his right, although he believed that would be an ill-advised decision. He spoke to him softly. He suggested that Dr. Kreutzer reconsider, in light of the charges brought against him, if it would not be better for his public image to crown his distinguished career with the supervision of this glorious mission.

What charges?

Three counts of sexual harassment, twelve charges of sexual abuse committed in the course of employment, public indecency, lewd acts, inducing persons struggling with mental illness, incapable of self defense, to sexual acts, forcing minors below the age of eighteen to perform sexual acts.

I never forced anyone.

The man became absorbed in his phone for a moment, scrolling, then held up the touch screen to the psychiatrist. It showed the picture of a thin woman, her face like a withered lemon, her hair pale.

That's not what she claims.

And as if this weren't enough, he pulled up another picture. The man said that the woman in the photograph was sixteen years old. He showed him the picture of a red-haired, boyish-looking student. Dr. Kreutzer did not recall ever having seen her.

Beginning with the founding of the Unified Regency, sexual crimes were treated with particular severity. Drug use had grown in the segregated zones, therefore the government, maintaining a stance of zero tolerance, had, three years ago, through public referendum, reintroduced the death penalty.

We also have your notebooks, I'm afraid.

Think of your children, the man added.

Yes, Dr. Kreutzer was thinking exactly about them. As the man in the black sweater was taking away his phone, he heard the ping of a new message. Maybe it was from his wife, maybe it was Giselle. Suddenly he felt unsure: perhaps the teacher from the New University had been sent to him by these men; she hadn't really had any serious problems. She merely lived as others did, as did everyone here—unhappily.

While they were applying the face powder, he was thinking that Giselle must have tipped them off. He was certain it was her. That is why she hadn't picked up her phone for days—she knew what was going to happen. He couldn't remember the red-haired girl though, no matter how much he tried to scroll through the faces in his brain.

A few moments later, he couldn't even figure out what to say for the recording. He tried to look into the camera openly, in a way that would inspire trust. He babbled some shameful cliché about the future, that they were the pledge of the future, he and this little courageous group. They would help each other, he muttered without any conviction, while the cypress trees mutely rocked themselves in the background like some kind of lip-synching girl choir instructed by the director to gently undulate during the playback. As they took off the wireless microphone, they handed him a set of protective gear as well as a kit containing underwear, hygienic items, and some basic medicines.

You can get changed over there, the man said, pointing to some kind of changing booth.

There was a chair and a mirror. From here he could not take the items of clothing back into the studio nor could he leave on his own, and say, thank you very much, these will do just fine. He got undressed and stood there stark naked, holding the items, sterile to the touch, in his hand. First, he put on the strange, long-legged underwear, then the white-cotton T-shirt, the stocking-like cotton trousers with an opening at the fly, and finally the over-size, zippered, hooded anorak closing tightly at his throat. Before leaving he stepped closer to the black-framed mirror and glanced once more at his reflection. Suddenly, for a fraction of a second, he felt a sense of recognition. And a mere one-tenth of a second later, he understood why.

In his own pale, powdered face, seemingly irrevocably aged and devastated in the bluish-neon light, he had glimpsed the eye of the monkey.

acknowledgments

During the writing of this book, the author was awarded an Erzsébetváros Literary Scholarship (January–March 2021). From May–July 2021, she enjoyed the support of the Centre National du Livre in France as well as the hospitality of the city of Lyon, the Villa Gillet, and the École Normale Supérieure.